Waiting for Time

Bernice Morgan

BREAKWATER

BREAKWATER
100 Water St.
P.O. Box 2188
St. John's, NF
A1E 6E6

*The Publisher gratefully acknowledges the financial assistance of
The Canada Council.*

*The Publisher acknowledges the financial assistance of the
Cultural Affairs Division, Department of Municipal and
Provincial Affairs, Government of Newfoundland and Labrador
which has helped make this publication possible.*

*Front cover drawing, "Northern Window" and back cover
drawing "On Avalon" by Janice Udell, courtesy of Christina
Parker Gallery, St. John's, NF.*

Canadian Cataloguing in Publication Data

Morgan, Bernice

Waiting for time

ISBN 1-55081-080-4

I. Title.

PS8576.O644W35 1994   C813'.54   C94-950212-X
PR9199.3.M67W35 1994

This book is dedicated to young Newfoundlanders
who must go away—especially to my own children
Greg, Jackie and Jennifer. May you all find that a
going away can be a homecoming.

"*Random Passage* is a great Canadian story. It is a wonderful mixture of love, power, forgotten pasts and missed opportunities. It paints a picture of outport Newfoundland as a unique place, while at the same time illustrating experiences typical of frontier life everywhere. *Random Passage* is an unforgettable and thoroughly entertaining book."

Annmarie Adams, *The Montreal Gazette*.

"*Random Passage* is a rich and exciting novel. The writing is passionate but understated, never slipping—as it easily could with such subject matter—into sentimentality, romanticism, or melodrama. In contrast to the starkness of the setting and the lives of the people, there is a restrained sensuousness in the description: textures, colours, shapes and smells are powerfully evoked.... Besides all that, it is a great read."

Gordon Inglis, *The Evening Telegram*.

"This chronicle of an isolated family's struggle to carve out a life along the rugged shores of Newfoundland's Bonavista Peninsula in the early 1800s is impressive: it unfolds its powerful scenes of human privation and elemental violence with a sure sense of time and place."

Douglas Hill, *Books in Canada*.

"In *Random Passage* we are greeted with the work of an accomplished novelist. This is a story of human frailty and human courage. It is the story of the people who look out at us from the dusty photographs and the glass plates of the archives."

Wade Kearley, *CBC Radio*.

"*Random Passage*, the first novel from Newfoundland writer Bernice Morgan, is a fascinating—and frequently horrifying—glimpse into the lives of some of the bravest of Canada's early settlers....Morgan writes with convincing authority about the period, and the dialogue in particular, in evocative and colourful dialect, is wonderfully realized. *Random Passage* is no pastoral idyll, but it has the ring of truth to it. Given that, it's a miracle this country got settled at all."

Susan Sutton, *The Globe and Mail*.

"*Random Passage* is one of those small-press gems that do not get much notice outside their own regions, but which tell fascinating stories about this country. This is a life-affirming story in spite of the hardships it portrays. A compelling novel...a hard book to put down."

Verne Clemence, *The Saskatoon Star-Phoenix*.

"Home soon. Tied up in St. John's. Cargo on board.
Waiting for time."

—message on *The Doyle News* circa 1930.

"We'um just waitin' for time, maid. Just waitin' 'til
our ship comes in."

—Ned Andrews to Mary.

LAV ANDREWS' INCOMPLETE CHART OF THE ANDREWS FAMILY

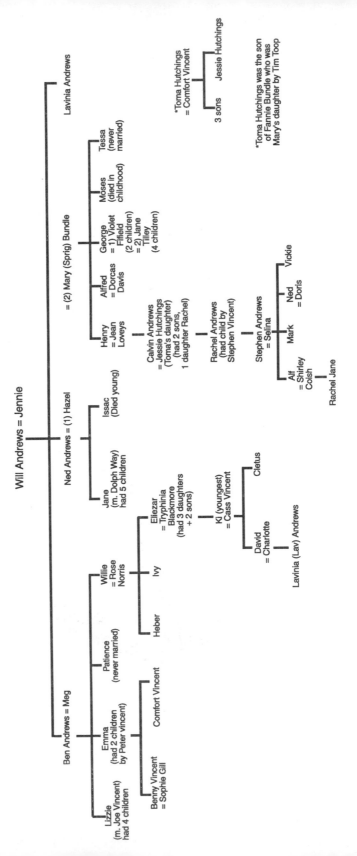

Will Andrews = Jennie

= (2) Mary (Sprig) Bundle

Lavinia Andrews

Ned Andrews = (1) Hazel

Ben Andrews = Meg

Henry = Jean Loveys

Alfred = Dorcas Davis

George = 1) Violet Fifield (2 children) = 2) Jane Tilley (4 children)

Moses (died in childhood)

Tessa (never married)

Calvin Andrews = Jessie Hutchings (Toma's daughter) (had 2 sons, 1 daughter Rachel)

Rachel Andrews (had child by Stephen Vincent)

Stephen Andrews = Selina

Alf = Shirley Coish

Mark

Ned = Doris

Vickie

Rachel Jane

Issac (Died young)

Jane (m. Dolph Way) had 5 children

Emma (had 2 children by Peter Vincent)

Patience (never married)

Willie = Rose Norris

Heber

Ivy

Eliezar = Tryphinia Blackmore (had 3 daughters + 2 sons)

Ki (youngest) = Cass Vincent

David = Charlotte

Cletus

Lavinia (Lav) Andrews

Lizzie (m. Joe Vincent) had 4 children

Benny Vincent = Sophie Gill

Comfort Vincent

*Toma Hutchings = Comfort Vincent

3 sons

Jessie Hutchings

*Toma Hutchings was the son of Fannie Bundle who was Mary's daughter by Tim Toop

part one
Lav Andrews

one

"I'm getting married today," my mother says. She smiles into the heart-shaped mirror above the bureau.

I am behind her, sitting on the bed we share in the big upstairs room of the Petrassi house. My mother has dressed me in the eyelet blouse and cord jumper I wore on my first day of school. It is springtime, but still cool in Ottawa—probably the Easter holidays. Hoping my mother will keep talking, I smile and nod. She does not notice. She is studying her own reflection, coldly, appraisingly. She makes a little sighing shrug, lifts her face to the mirror and begins to dab at her lips with a tube of colour. Her movements, usually so quick and sure, are hesitant. She does not like makeup and seldom wears it. People should be themselves, my mother says.

I grow tired of watching her and lean forward to admire my dazzling white socks and shiny t-straps, the first strapped shoes I've ever had. I am very proud of them.

I know what married is. Randy Petrassi got married last summer. Audrey and I threw rice into Randy's and Donna's faces as they ran down the steps of St. Kevin's. Afterwards there was a party in the front room which Mrs. Petrassi and my mother had decorated. They had covered the table with a pink cloth, tied pink and white balloons to the light fixture above the table and draped pink ribbon out to the corners of the room.

The bride's parents and grandparents, along with all the Petrassi relatives, aunts and uncles, a baby cousin, two grandfathers and one grandmother, came to the wedding. There was only room at the table for Randy and Donna and the seven grandparents. The rest of us stood around. Mrs. Petrassi gave everyone cake on her good plates and Donna's mother passed the grown-ups drinks in glasses with stems.

Mr. Petrassi played his accordian and we all sang

> Lavender's blue dilly-dilly
> Lavender's green
> When you are king dilly-dilly,
> I'll be your queen.

Even my mother sang, looking so foolishly young that I felt uneasy and edged my way between dark suits and flower splashed dresses until I could touch her. After the singing there were more drinks for the grownups, ice-cream sodas for us children and presents for Randy and Donna.

Then Donna went upstairs and took off her lacy bride's dress and put on a pale blue suit—lavender blue, I thought—because she and Randy were taking a train to Timmins where he had a job. When the taxi came all of us went outside to see them off, everyone milling around on the sidewalk, close together, smiling and getting kissed. Audrey and I squealing and throwing more rice we'd found in the kitchen. The boys trying to hang tin cans onto the bumper of the taxi until the driver made them stop. The uncles shaking hands and patting Randy on the back and the aunts hugging everyone—even me. It had been wonderful there surrounded by Audrey's family, all of us waving and happy as the taxi pulled away.

Dangling my feet from the edge of the bed, I watch reflections dance across the toes of my shoes and wonder if my mother is going to have a wedding party. I'd like that. Will Audrey and I be given rice to throw? Will there be cake and ice-cream afterwards? My mother and I don't have relatives—who will come? Most of all I want to know who my mother is going to marry. Will she go away? If she goes will I go too? I like school, like living in the Petrassi house with Audrey as my best friend. I really don't want to go away.

I was born in a different place—in the Maritimes, I think. But my mother and I have lived on Dugan Street in Ottawa for as long as I can remember. I don't have any brothers or sisters. Audrey has lots of brothers but no sisters, so we pretend we are sisters. Audrey says brothers are not much good. Her brothers are big and rowdy. Mrs. Petrassi calls them hooligans, she makes them stay outdoors most of the time. Mrs. Petrassi takes care of me when my mother is at work. On nice days she sends Audrey and me outdoors too. She says we must learn to amuse ourselves.

But on rainy days, if we promise not to touch anything, Mrs. Petrassi lets Audrey and me play house in my mother's room. My mother's room is called a bed-sitter because it has a big chair by the window. Audrey's Aunt Celie used to have our room but now she works in Eaton's downtown. The bed-sitter is sunny and looks out on the street. It is the nicest room in the Petrassi house. At night my mother and I sleep there together.

I want very much to ask my mother if we will have to leave the bed-sitter when she gets married. But it is best not to ask. Grown-ups never tell you anything they think you want to know—at least my mother doesn't. If I stay still she sometimes tells me things accidentally. I press my hands together, clamp them between my knees, I stop swinging my feet and wait.

"The child's father was a sea captain—from the Maritimes," I once heard her tell Mrs. Petrassi.

I hate the way my mother says "the child"—as if I belong to someone else. I do not know where the Maritimes are, but like the way they sound—marratimes, merrytimes, marrytimes—maybe my mother is marrying in the Maritimes. Will I see the sea captain who is my father? Will we go to live with him in the Maritimes? Will she let Audrey come to visit during the holidays?

My mother is intent on fastening a clasp beneath the collar of her good dress. She is not going to say anything. "Are you going to marry my father?" the question pops out.

"Your father died in the war—you know that, Scrap!" My mother turns away from the mirror, lifts me down from the high, old-fashioned bed and sets me on my feet. "Come on now, we have to go to Milady's."

Had I known that my father died in the war? Perhaps. I cannot remember feeling sorrow, or even surprise—just disappointed that we are only going next door to Milady's.

Milady's is a tiny dress shop squat between the Petrassi house and Saul Rosenberg's book and stationery store where my mother works. Audrey and I call the woman who owns the dress shop Milady—which we think is her name. Milady is grand, tall, with pale, pale skin, purple lips and purple fingernails. She wears dark velvet turbans pinned at the side with huge, glittering pins. Audrey's mother has told us that a great tragedy in Milady's life caused all her hair to fall out.

"She's bald as an egg!" was what Mrs. Petrassi said. Because of this, Audrey and I never pass the dress shop without stopping to rest our chins on the window ledge and stare in. We hope one day to catch Milady without her turban, to see her gleaming egg-like head.

"It's your big day, Charlotte," Milady says when we come into the store. She smiles her juicy purple smile and takes a round box from beneath the counter. She reaches into the box with both hands, as if lifting a baby from a carriage. When her hands come up they are holding a hat.

"Dusty rose—just the shade to go with that dress," Milady passes my mother the hat and holds up a hand mirror for her to look into.

Tilting her head this way and that my mother smiles at her reflection. Her dark hair curls against the rose coloured brim and the brim reflects a pink glow onto her face. She is very pretty.

"Do you have anything suitable for Scrap?" she asks. Then, seeing my scowl, she corrects herself, "Lav—she wants to be called Lav," she tells Milady.

Something hot and unpleasant stabs at me—resentment mixed with guilt and bewilderment. I do not want to be called Lav. "My name is Lavinia—Lavinia Andrews. Scrap is a baby name—I'm old enough to be called Lavinia now," I say.

"Don't put on airs," my mother stares at me, just as she had on my first day at school when she told the teacher to call me Lav. Now she's pretending I want to be called this stupid name.

Neither woman notices my anger. Milady holds out an organdy thing that looks like a large, droopy, sunflower.

"It's beautiful," my mother says, "like something Scarlett O'Hara would wear." She sets the wide-brimmed hat on my head, tying the yellow ribbons in a stiff, scratchy bow under my chin.

I do not know Scarlett O'Hara. I fold my arms across my chest, "I'm not going to wear it," I say.

The women look down at me. Then they exchange foolish smiles. "Well—maybe she's right—it doesn't suit her, somehow," my mother is not really disappointed. She unties the ribbon, gives a small shrug and passes the hat back.

"No doubt she'll grow into a handsome woman," Milady says.

But my mother has forgotten me, she nods in an absentminded way and asks to see some white gloves.

When we go out onto the street there is a man in a dark suit locking the bookshop door, although it is only three o'clock and Saul always locks up himself. Then the man slips the key into his pocket, he turns towards us and I see that it is Saul. Saul with his hair flattened down and his beard trimmed straight across instead of wisping into the woolly grey sweater he usually wears.

Saul is smiling. He takes my hand, and without a word we walk down the sidewalk and around the corner to Mulgrove Road United Church. I am glad it is Saul who is going to marry my mother, not some dark, unknown sea-captain, even if he is my father. I reach up and slip my other hand into my mother's gloved hand and we walk along, all three of us holding hands.

That memory is more than thirty years old and probably no longer accurate. Lav has observed that memories take on a life of their own, pick up detail, evolve into stories with beginnings, middles and ends—sometimes even with morals. It crosses her mind that some dark, unacknowledged fear has caused this particular memory to suface today. She rejects the idea, pushes it firmly away, decides remembering that happy hand-linked family walking in sunshine to a wedding is an omen that today's business will end well.

Lav moves a little faster through the sea of people on the wide sidewalk. She feels confident, exhilerated, thinks how pleasant it is to walk in a modern city—especially on a day such as this—one filled with sunshine, with racing white clouds that are reflected a thousand times in the glass facades of buildings—so that the earth spins and the city spins and you are at its centre, heels clicking on pavement, skirt swishing, hair moving like silk against your neck.

Never mind those woolly winter jackets, those fur hats and cumbersome overboots already lurking in store windows. Today is sufficient, today the streets throb with energy, with secrets that vibrate up from the warm centre of the earth.

There is a poem, something about crowds upon the pavement like fields of harvest wheat. Lav tries to recall other lines but cannot. How accommodating, how well dressed and happy they all look, this great, golden wheat field of people moving with cheerful good-humour in search of food and drink served quickly enough to get them back to their desks by one-thirty.

Lav marvels at the inventiveness of the human mind—to have conceived of such varied things as air-conditioned coffee shops, carts piled with orange chrysanthemums, poetry and flex-soled high heel shoes and glass towers that reflect the sky. She recalls how her stepfather used to tell her about invisible energy that would one day fuse thoughts to paper, atoms whose vibration through length and mass would slow time, or speed it up, whichever you wished. According to Saul such things have existed eternally. From the foundations of the world, he told her, there have been secrets hidden inside the earth, just waiting to be discovered.

This view of science as the luring of secrets from earth, air and water was probably what led her to become a scientist. Religion had failed, Saul used to say, law and politics and philosophy had failed, even his beloved poetry had failed.

"But," and her stepfather would bend forward, holding out some book he wanted her to read, "Science will succeed, science will give us a world that is healthier, happier—a safe, productive world."

And perhaps Saul had been right, Lav thinks, as she hurries through the humming October city towards her mother's apartment.

Charlotte had moved downtown after Saul died. Without anguish or discussion she had sold the book store on Dugan Street and rented an apartment fifteen minutes away from the Department of Fisheries building where Lav works. At the time Lav wondered if this was an offer of friendship, an indication that she and her mother might see more of one another. But apparently not. There has been no casual visiting, they never drop in on each other, never shop together as Lav has seen other mothers and daughters do.

Now that Lav and Philip own a house in the Glebe they occasionally ask her mother to dinner. But Charlotte never asks them back. Charlotte does not entertain. Her mother has, in fact, never made such a statement though it is true. In all the years of her childhood Lav can not remember one visitor ever sitting at their table. Indeed she, Saul and her mother rarely sat there themselves.

Still, three or four times a year her mother cheerfully accepts invitations to dinner. Lav is surprised, really, at how well Philip and Charlotte get along, they are alike in some ways. Philip once remarked that Charlotte has a rational mind—a rare thing in a woman, he said.

Lav had shrugged. She has long ago grown tired of trying to decode her mother's mind, stopped trying to uncover her secrets, ceased to be intrigued by her silence. These days Lav lives happily in the present, she is indifferent to the past.

Today she is going to her mother for straightforward data. A security check of Department of Fisheries employees is being made. All she needs is her father's name, his birth and death dates and the names of her grandparents.

"I suppose I can have a look," her mother had said when she telephoned this morning. Charlotte had seemed preoccupied, had said she is moving to California. Her mother can still surprise.

Lav does not enjoy travel, feels apprehensive boarding trains, planes, even busses. Last spring, partly in memory of Saul, she had gone on a guided tour to Israel and Egypt, had become ill and cut the trip short. She has never considered living anywhere but Ottawa. "Why?" she asked her mother, "Why move? And why to California?"

"I've always hated the cold—I might as well move south permanently," Charlotte told her, so casually that she might have been talking about changing banks or the brand of tea she drinks. She suggested Lav come over at lunch time, before she begins packing.

When Lav arrives her mother is already searching through the big desk that once belonged to Saul. "What you need is in here somewhere," she says.

Charlotte's apartment is on the tenth floor and has a view of the river. Lav has been here only twice. She is still surprised that her mother has chosen to live in such a place, grander, more stylish than anything she would have expected.

Saul's desk seems to be the only thing Charlotte has rescued from the dark rooms behind the bookstore. Her apartment is furnished in black and white: heavy glass tables, white carpet, black steel dining room chairs and a black leather sofa set. Although Charlotte has lived here for almost four years, the place has the clean, uncluttered look of a hotel suite. The only colour in the apartment is a painting, one huge, blazing-red poppy hanging above the black sofa.

"I only had one letter from your father—no papers. I suppose some might have come after I left," her mother peers into the desk's pigeon-holes which seem to be empty.

"Left where?" Lav asks. It is an absent-minded question, she is gazing about, trying to reconcile how the woman who has chosen this decor could have been content surrounded by Saul's old books, his clutter of discarded furniture. She is wondering if her mother will offer her lunch, she sniffs, nothing is cooking but then Charlotte always hated to cook, there might be tea and toast, sliced fruit perhaps.

"Cape Random—you know that! I told you a dozen times I ran away from a place called Cape Random!" Lav turns and catches her mother regarding her with what seems to be dislike, dislike quickly concealed as Charlotte bends and, still talking, opens one of the desk drawers.

"That's if a woman with a three-month-old baby can be said to run. I never got in touch with his people again. I don't even know when his birthday was. Make up a date—what difference? He was between nineteen and twenty-one the year you were born."

The phone rings. Lav gathers from the conversation that Charlotte is selling all this sharp-edged furniture. "Practically new, hardly used," she is saying, "everything modern, top of the line at the Bay."

Lav stands in the middle of the room, her mother has not asked her to sit. I have never, never heard of Cape Random, she thinks. She culls through memory, through imagination, through a clutter of truths, half-truths and layers of lies—trying to sort one from the other. What had she been told? What imagined? What imagined being told? She reminds herself that she is a scientist, trained to observe, to test hypotheses, to identify truth—but in her own past there is no truth—nothing is labelled, nothing sure.

Listening to her mother negotiate with the furniture buyer, Lav marvels, as she has before, at the dispatch with which Charlotte disposes of things. My mother the minimalist, she thinks.

"Everything's new except one piece—a desk of no particular value," her mother says.

A desk of no particular value—her mother has peeled the past, made it flat, one dimensional. Nothing is left—no stories, no keepsakes, not one of Saul's tools, none of his leather-bound books, no wedding certificate, no box of faded photos.

Her mother replaces the receiver, bends over the drawer, flicking through file folders. Lav cannot see her face.

"What's become of that small picture in the oval frame—the one that used to be propped beside Saul's pen holder?" It seems a safe question.

Charlotte looks up, "The picture of the woman and two children," she says. Her face is blank, guileless "It's gone."

Lav feels a surge of anger. Who is this serene woman dressed in the pale wool, a silk scarf draped artfully around her neck, plain leather pumps on her small, neat feet?

The childhood Lav recalls as bare—whose very bareness has become the subject of anecdote, a source of shared amusement for her and Philip—this bleak landscape is suddenly crowded with a multitude of things Lav wants to see, wants to own, to touch, to smell. Where had her mother's velvet, wedge-heel slippers gone? What became of those bits of coloured cloth she used to tie around her hair when she dusted books? Where are the floral, wrap-around aprons? The teapot decorated with ugly purple roses? Where is the green desk lamp, where is the shiny fold-out holder she used to bring toast on? Most of all, where is the picture? The small, brown photo of Saul's first family, his foreign wife and children—dead, tragically dead, though how Lav knows this she cannot say—neither Charlotte nor Saul had ever spoken of the picture or of Saul's having another family.

As a child Lav had spent hours staring at the three faces contained inside that oval frame—a woman and two children. The woman wore a lacy summer dress. Her hands were beautiful, white, tapering, she wore rings, one hand was holding the hand of the boy who stood beside her, the other restrained a blonde baby who was squirming to be off her lap. The baby pressed forward, round-eyed, joyful, reaching towards the camera, toward Saul. The woman and boy are not quite ready. But Saul is looking at the baby, at the round beaming face, at the small fat hands inviting him into the picture—and this is the instant he chooses to capture. The boy wants to be gone, you can see that, see how he hates the starched shirt and short trousers he is wearing. He stands stiffly, impatiently, beside the woman, refusing to respond to the loving, half-coaxing smile she has turned on him.

Those people were her real family. She was the baby, the boy was her brother, the smiling woman her mother. She had known them, known the room—could see things that were not in the picture—tables crowded with keepsakes, an open window, many-paned with billowing curtains. Through the window had come the voices of children—children the boy's age, laughing, playing ball—calling her brother's name. She could almost hear his name.

"Why would anyone throw such things away?" she shouts, so savagely that her mother's head jerks up, hands fly to face, fingers are pressed against bottom lip. Losing her place in the files, Charlotte stares at her daughter with that familiar combination of bewilderment and annoyance, almost horror.

Lav closes her eyes, takes a deep breath: "I mean, if you didn't want the picture I would have liked to have had it. Didn't that even occur to you?"

"But neither of us ever saw the sky over the people in that picture..."

"What does that matter? I always loved it and I don't have anything of Saul's—not one thing!" Plopping herself down on one of the uncomfortable chairs, Lav folds her arms across her chest and stares sullenly ahead. Flushed and awkward, she bears no resemblance to the well-groomed, confident woman who, just minutes earlier, had whirled through fall sunshine admiring the world.

"I buried it with him. I think that's what Saul would have wanted—don't you?" Charlotte says—she who never hesitates, never makes a false step. Pretending to be unaware of her daughter's anger she returns to the drawer, pulls a folded piece of paper from a file. She looks smug, as if she has read Lav's thoughts, as if producing this scrap of the past negates all she has concealed.

"Here—this might be what you need. Anyway, it'll have to do. It's all I have—all I ever had—relating to David Andrews—David Andrews!" Charlotte repeats his name, the echo of a memory flits across her face but is gone before Lav can catch its essence.

"I don't even remember what he looked like—but then, I didn't know your father well." She passes Lav a single sheet of pale blue tissue, brushes invisible dust from her dress and goes to sit in a chair across the room.

It is a short letter, written on one side of the paper and folded to make its own envelope. It is addressed in green ink to Mrs. David Andrews, c/o Mr. and Mrs. Ki Andrews, Cape Random, Bonavista Bay, Newfoundland. Below the address two black-smudged marks indicate that the enclosed message has been read and censored by the War Bureau of Great Britain.

Lav unfolds the limp tissue and reads aloud: "My Darling Lottie." An unexpected salutation. She glances up, hoping to see some acknowledgement of this younger self, this darling Lottie, on her mother's face. But Charlotte sits unsmiling, detached. Her daughter might be reading yesterday's newspaper or a discarded shopping list.

> I know my darling you must have had a rough crossing. I did not dare tell you how rough it was going to be. But now you're home and it is such a comfort to me knowing you're there. I am sure Mamma and Pop will take good care of you. There is no safer place in the world than the Cape. It makes me feel better just to think about you there—looking out to sea from my room or walking up the beach behind our house. Sometimes I wake up thinking this is all a dream—or one of them stories poor old Sollie Gill used to read out to us in school. I wish it was. Tell Sollie I spoke kindly of him, that will tickle him.

Here at [a small hole has been razored out of the letter] we are still training and still all together but will probably be split up soon. The Limies have great sport making mock of the way we people talk and the things we do not know about. We Newfoundlanders can hardly wait to get them in boats—then they will see what we are good at! Tell Cle I said he is not to join up.

Tell Mamma I misses her meals. We're getting whale meat every second day. They calls it something else altogether—but that's what it is—whale meat. Jim Way says it must be stuff harpooned before we was born!

I think about you all the time—about being with you on the Cape when this is all over.

Love, David.

It is more than Lav had expected—much more. Her hand holding the blue paper begins to shake. She can see him—a boy, almost a child—tongue between teeth, considering each formal sounding word, scratching each round careful letter in green ink on the blue paper—probably both borrowed.

She reads the letter again, slowly. She feels old, tired—she is old—thirty-seven—infinitely older than this homesick, lovesick boy.

"Who was Cle?" she asks.

"His younger brother. Cle had already gone in to St. John's—lied about his age and signed up. That letter took five months to get from England to the Cape. You'd already been born and your father was probably dead by the time I read it."

"I see." She waits, hoping her mother will say something more. She doesn't. "Why did you leave?"

"Anyone in their right mind would have left."

Their business together has been attended to. Charlotte drops the empty folder into a wastepaper basket. "Keep the letter if you like. Your father's name was David Andrews, his father was Hezekiah—they called him Ki. His mother was called Cass—Cassandra. They had a liking for long names in that place. It was Cass who made me name you Lavinia—after some old aunt or grandmother who'd died donkey's years ago! Here, have this too." She slips something into Lav's hand, sliding it down behind the letter.

Without looking Lav knows she's been given Saul's folding bone, the little stick he used for bookbinding. She rubs the worn ivory across her cheek.

"Have a cup of tea before you go," her mother says.

Lav takes the cup and they sit, one on either side of the table that resembles a roughly hacked block of ice. She sips the tea slowly, holding the folding bone and the letter, muttering awkward thankyous. There is a long silence. Dislike of her mother has become one of the certainties of Lav's life and this kindness leaves her feeling naked.

Charlotte brushes thanks aside, "You might as well have keepsakes from both of them," she says. She is sitting like a school girl, feet together, back not quite touching the black leather.

Lav senses that her mother's discomfort is equal to her own, hears herself say: "I want to know things about my father. I want to know what he was like."

"Shouldn't you be getting back to work?"

Lav shakes her head, she settles down into the seat, stubbornly, permanently present. "This might be the last time I'll get a chance to ask—I want to know about him."

"There's nothing to know. No big secret. No story. I don't have any idea what you're talking about, what you're after," Charlotte says. She goes to refill their cups, brings apple and cheese cut up on a plate, sighs and returns to her chair: "What is it you want? What is it you've always been at me for? I've already told you I hardly knew the man—and what I did know I've forgotten!"

Questions swallowed since childhood fly, black as screeching crows, from her mouth: "Who am I? What am I? That's what I'm asking. How can you not remember? You must remember! For God's sake! What are you? Fifty-six—fifty-seven? Not old—not senile!"

Forgetting to be grateful for the relics in her lap Lav flings these questions at her mother. She longs to shake the older woman, to rattle information out of her, to once-and-for-all satisfy her famished curiosity.

"It was long ago—I was young, he was young—children, for God's sake!"

Lav is ruthless, she stares at her mother, stares silently, insisting that she remember.

"We were young," Charlotte repeats, she holds herself tight, shoulders pressed back into the chair, face turned aside. "We were a lot younger than you are now—yet in some ways we were old—hundreds of people our age were getting killed every night. My own mother had been dead since I was fourteen and my Da had gone off soon as the war started." She pauses and frowns, as if it really does take her an effort to remember.

"I'd been on my own for years by then—working in a boot factory in Portsmouth—stuck in a great grimy warehouse nine hours a day with no prospects of ever doin' any better. I was glad when war came, when they turned the old fort into a naval base. It was exciting, planes fallin' out of the sky, bombs burstin' down by the docks, thousands of sailors—young boys in uniform, bell-bottoms and tight jumpers—roving the streets. He was just like all the rest but something made me notice him—maybe the odd way his sailor hat perched on top of his great mop of red curls."

Charlotte's voice has changed, taken on a kind of careless harshness her daughter has never heard before: "He used to tell me stories about this wonderful place he come from—Cape Random. He used to call it 'The Cape,' as if there wasn't any other cape in the world. Not a bit like Portsmouth, he said—a clean place, with long empty beaches and sunshine and the sea rolling in. I thought it would be heaven—*it wasn't!*"

"You got married. Did you get married?"

"Of course we did—had to be married for me to be a Navy dependent and get passage over. He took all kinds of trouble to get me out of England before he was assigned to a ship. And I left, all hopeful, thinkin' it was a real lark.

Thinkin' I was coming to some modern place, a new world—some place like I'd seen in films—some little American town by the sea, with trees and white houses along the streets. Sweet God!"

Her mother is talking—sitting primly upright, feet together, hands clenched in lap, she is talking. Afraid to speak, afraid to move, afraid even to look, Lav stares at the great, blood-red poppy and listens.

"We travelled in convoy, zig-zagged across the ocean to keep out of the way of U-Boats. It took three weeks and I was sick as a dog—most of the women were, especially us who were expecting. The ones who already had babies were even worse off."

Charlotte tells of crying babies, of the dank hulk of the transport ship, the monotonous food—tinned tomatoes for almost every meal during the last week! Then, when they docked in Halifax and they all thought it was over, a Naval Officer came aboard to speak to the women who were married to Newfoundlanders.

"He got us together—not even sitting down, just standing around in a circle, fifteen women, some like me already pregnant, others with small children—told us we should think long and hard about what we were doing. Newfoundland was a day's voyage away, a strange place, a different country from Canada, he said. And once we got there, that would be it! Scared us half to death. Said we'd be going back to the last century—to this god-awful place where half the population had TB. Covered in fog, surrounded by fish and inhabited by fools, was how he put it. Then he looked at us and laughed, like he thought it was all a great joke."

"He'd been directed, he said, to inform us that there was no divorce in Newfoundland and we should think long and hard about that. If we got off the ship there in Halifax the Navy would try and help us but if we went on they would not accept responsibility. One girl went with him—got off right then and there. The next morning before we sailed two more left the ship."

But not Lottie Andrews. Lottie, seasick as she was, pregnant and frightened as she was, went on to Newfoundland, to St. John's, where she was transferred to a small coastal ship.

A month and three days after leaving England she climbed up onto the wharf at Cape Random—a sand-bar jutting out into the North Atlantic. She did not know it, but her husband's ship had already been torpedoed in the same ocean his darling had safely crossed.

"That's it—everything I can tell you!" the woman says. It is almost dark outside, clouds scud across the sky. Charlotte gets up and pours herself a whiskey, comes back and, unasked, begins talking about how she and the baby had gotten to Ottawa, how she found a room in the Petrassi house, got herself a job in Saul's book store. She talks about Saul, about what a good man he was, how fond he had been of Lav, how he had paid for her education, how proud he had been when she started working on a doctorate.

It seems ungracious, a slight against Saul, to interrupt her, but eventually Lav does—standing in the apartment doorway, pushing against the tide of words she asks, "What was Cape Random like, then? Was it really so bad?"

"It was awful—awful!" Charlotte rests her head against the door frame as if just thinking about the place makes her weary.

"But how? How was it awful?"

"It was the worst place I ever saw—the very worst! Cold—dismal—the sea all around, pounding away day and night. A god-forsaken strip of sand sticking out into the ocean with four or five crazy families living on it. No electricity, no plumbing—not even clean water to drink because the whole place was sliding into the sea. Seawater seeped in underneath and the wells were all salty. They had to cart water down from another place by boat—in big barrels—or else drain it out of the bog—brackish water you had to let stand in jugs overnight so the dirt would settle. And it would still be brown—cankery colour. I can taste it yet—brown and gritty, smelling of dead things!" Realizing how loud her voice has gotten, Charlotte pauses.

Her face has come undone. Just by speaking of Cape Random she has broken some taboo. Looking distraught, half mad, she darts up and down the beige carpeted hallway—as if expecting some neighbour to leap out and defend the place she hates so much.

After a long minute her mother continues, but in a whisper: "I remember the night you were born, the old woman washed you in that bog water. You smelled old, like something dug up. Frightened me, that smell did. Then and there I promised myself I'd get away from the Cape, away from Newfoundland, before you could walk or talk—before the place owned you like it did them. And it wasn't just the Cape—the whole island is a hell hole. Bleak and barren—the kind of place would drive anyone crazy—if it didn't kill them outright!" Charlotte leans forward, close to her daughter, staring up, hissing words into her face: "Don't ever, ever go there! Don't ever let anyone send you there!"

Lav does not move, does not say a word. The impossible has happened, her mother has spoken of feelings, of passion, of hate. Horror stories she has longed for are being told.

Charlotte looks exhausted, "You're satisfied now, I suppose!" she says bitterly. "Isn't that what you wanted? Isn't that what you've been pestering me for all these years?"

Falsely, Lav shakes her head. Her mother is not deceived: "Of course it is. It's just what you want—black stories, regret, easy regret. Milk as much sorrow out of life as possible—it's been your way ever since you were little. A lover of grief, you are, Lavinia Andrews—probably soaked into you from that bog water."

Charlotte shrugs, steps back. Reassembling herself she pats her hair, adjusts the scarf and without another word shuts the door in her daughter's face.

Philip's past, on the other hand, contains no murk, his story is history. From the beginning Lavinia has been impressed by the clarity of her lover's life.

All around the Bay of Quinte there are houses crowded with Philip's history. Houses where nothing has ever been lost: powder horns, cooking pots, family

Bibles, needlepoint samplers, jewellery, tools and enamelled pill boxes, lacquered tins that once held china tea, ivory buttons and button hooks, glass bottles, all polished and on display. Evidence not so much of success as of permanence, of permanence and responsibility.

And Philip's relatives are there too, of course, in those grey stone houses: parents, grandparents, aunts and uncles, cousins, nieces and nephews.

It seemed to Lav that Philip's family existed outside of time, beyond trouble. His older brothers are architects, they work in the family business, his sister's husbands do something nebulous in offices. The men do not discuss business at home. The women are well educated but seem without personal ambition. One unmarried aunt teaches at the University of Toronto. The wives, although they put in long hours fund-raising for community hospitals, symphony orchestras and art galleries, do not have paying jobs. Teen-aged nieces and nephews attend private schools. They do not do drugs, or at least not noticeably, do not hitch-hike across Canada or vanish into cults.

In Philip's world people never vanish—or even die. Not only are his parents alive, so are his grandparents, all four of them. Even those who disappear from most families, the dead and divorced, are very much present in Philip's. Sepia-faced ancestors stare down from the walls as if guarding their possessions, divorced couples stay politely friendly, the stone houses are always home to them and to their children. Families gather to celebrate Christmas, rally 'round for marriages, christenings, funerals. By not attending such gatherings, by showing anger, by refusing to maintain this family tradition of civility, Philip's wife Zinnie has disgraced herself since their separation.

It was those powder horns, those cooking pots and family Bibles, those button hooks and carved sideboards that kept Lav from hearing her lover when he told her he was about to leave. Philip's origins were visible and so, by extension, must his destinations be.

It was November and bitterly cold in Ottawa the night Philip made his announcement. He had suggested a fire—the first of the season. The dry wood caught at once and Lav settled down on the sofa with her mother's letter and a pile of papers she had brought home from work.

"Not going to bother with those tonight, are you?" Philip asked. He passed her a drink and went to stand, elbow on mantlepiece, sipping his whiskey.

Later Lav will remember how well this classic male pose suited him. Despite thinning hair, despite bifocals he is too vain to wear at work, Philip looked quite handsome, tall and loose-limbed as he stood there declaiming on the decline of significant research in Canada—a particular concern of his despite the fact that he himself had done no research for years.

Lav was reading a letter from her mother. A letter which contained an invitation to spend Christmas in California. Charlotte has now lived there for three years, has become the wife of Rick Cabrillo whom Lav has not met. The Cabrillos live in Bayside, in a house Charlotte describes as modern Victorian—a house festooned with fretwork and a front portico supported by cream coloured Greek pillars. Charlotte has sent a picture of herself and Rick standing beneath the portico, surrounded by pots of pink azaleas. They have their arms around each other, they are tanned, they smile, they look as if they have dressed to match the pink and cream house. Lav studied the picture, it might be pleasant to spend Christmas in California, she wonders if she should suggest it to Philip.

"...some remarkable work being done in Australia. After twenty years with Fisheries and Oceans I'll have a good severance package," Philip was saying when she began to listen. "I'll certainly be able to pay off my share of the mortgage on this house. So if you decide to sell we can divide the equity—I expect it's doubled in the nine years we've been here."

Could he really have said that? Could there have been no hint of defensiveness in his voice when he spoke the words "nine years"—the length of time they have been lovers? Could he have so brutally announced his intention, so quickly gotten on to the practical aspects of his leaving? Surely Lav misremembers.

Surely. Yet it is all so clear, how he stood, how he spoke, not guardedly but with care, pausing, just as he does when making a presentation at work—waiting attentively for questions.

Lav asked no questions. She sat, trying to control her face, examining the recent past for some omen that might have warned her this was coming—there had been a dinner party months before when the host and hostess ended the evening snarling at each other in the kitchen. Lav and Philip had been among the guests who slipped into coats and left as quietly as possible.

"Thank God we're not like those two—I cannot think why people stay in such relationships!" Philip said later, unknotting his tie in the peace and quiet of their house.

There was never any acrimony in their relationship—no embarrassment, no big arguments, no petty meanness. Lav and Philip had worked at keeping such things out, had come to an understanding about what their financial arrangements would be, whether they should have children together, how much privacy each needed.

It had taken a little time, a little care, but they had arranged a life in which each had freedom to indulge their separate interests—Lav did volunteer work at the National Gallery, Philip played squash and belonged to an amateur theatrical group—and enjoyed the civilized shared pleasures of a comfortable old house, good food, quiet conversation, friends, music, twice-yearly ski week-ends with his relatives, visits to galleries and theatres.

When Lav learned she was to be appointed Philip's assistant she had worried briefly, secretly, about how they would maintain this comfortable balance. Would it be too much—working side by side during the day, then eating together, talking, exchanging ideas, making love, at night? Her concerns had proven unnecessary, their work life flowed smoothly into their private life. Lav knew, and enjoyed knowing, that Philip's growing reputation for being a top-notch administrator depended partly on her approach to problems, which was, she thought, even more analytical than his.

She was aware, of course, had been given subtle hints, that certain people in the department considered her promotion unearned. Lav did not think this was so, she was good at what she did and knew it. Later she would wonder—she had, after all, done little original research, published no papers—could Philip have sometimes suggested her name to people at the top, given her credit for work that was really his?

"...and I'll make some kind of financial arrangement for Zinnie and the children—something I can oversee from Australia. Nat can set up a trust fund." Philip seems to be appealing to her for suggestions as to how he might best provide for his wife and children. And Lav sits there trying to look helpful—trying to look kind and caring—a civilized, modern woman. A woman who has learned to fit in, one who is never nasty, who never wails, tears her hair, never draws blood.

We are being unfair, of course—introducing you to Philip at a bad moment. He is in many ways an admirable man, a tactful, considerate man, a man with whom Lav has lived happily for nine years. From the beginning he was completely honest about Zinnie and his sons, who, according to Philip, live in squalor, surrounded by unwashed socks, unanswered letters and unkept promises.

Philip and his wife had been living apart for two years before he met Lav. They did not intend to divorce—Zinnie because it does not matter and Philip because this arrangement gives him free and open access to the three children, some chance of organizing his family's financial affairs.

Yet that night he spoke of his children with a kind of absent-minded nostalgia that seemed to relegate them, and Lav, to the past: "...dirty dishes and dirty laundry in every room—piles of papers, stacks of brochures and posters—wild stuff, she calls it—propaganda for that environment thing she's into...and cats—cats everywhere. I've seen my own children eat beans out of cans and I doubt there's a matching cup and saucer in the house."

Philip poked irritably at the fire, sparks flew upward. "Once—for a very short time—I thought living like that was exotic, now I see how squalid it is, how completely undisciplined Zinnie is—too undisciplined to ever achieve anything. Of course, her parents were the same—strange, arty people who expected their own daughter to call them by their first names—went off to Zaire in their sixties and vanished. The boys seem to have caught it—I used to hold out some hope for young Chris, but if this first semester is any indication I doubt he'll make it through the year at Queen's."

Philip has tried to direct his sons into professions, hoped the oldest boy would want to become an architect, join his uncles in the family firm. Now, for the first time, the possibility that his own children might slip out of the middle class occurs to him.

After Philip had gone upstairs—kissing Lav on the neck, mumbling that she was one in a million—she sat nursing her drink. She thought of phoning Zinnie, suggesting that she dump all three children on Philip and run. Taking dramatic licence, Lav imagined the boys much younger than they really are, contemplated with pleasure the havoc their day-to-day presence would wreak on Philip's life, on his escape plan.

She and Zinnie could drive south together, shedding clothes, becoming tanned, younger as the miles slip by. They might visit Charlotte. Lav poured another brandy and reread her mother's letter. She imagined arriving at the Victorian house—Zinnie would wear her yellow duck slippers, bring her stacks of inky brochures, her disgraceful cats.

A silly dream, a childish, self-indulgent fantasy, the memory of which will one day make it possible for Lav to find Zinnie and ask her for help.

In reality Lav and Philip parted with a minimum of fuss, choosing to say their goodbyes at the same Ottawa restaurant where they had eaten Boxing Day dinners for years. There were Christmas lights, a tree beside an open fire, there were bookshelves arranged at odd angles—the illusion of privacy, the illusion of home.

They had been exceedingly civil, very adult. Between courses they exchanged parting gifts: his to her a filigree brooch, 17th century Venetian—a fish within a circle of scrolled hearts; hers to him a small engraving called "Inuit Migration"—the backs of people walking in a long line towards the horizon, gradually disappearing into whiteness.

Not until they bid each other a tearless farewell outside the restaurant, not until Lav saw his taxi pull into the stream of traffic did a sense of wrongness, of having been cheated of an appropriately emotional ceremony, engulf her. Standing on the slushy sidewalk she had the mad desire to run after the taxi, to drag Philip out, to create such a scene that Christmas diners would rush from the restaurant, turkey bones in hand, red napkins aflutter, to stand gaping at their battle. Such shrewish behaviour suddenly seemed more human, more satisfying, more appropriate, than all the polite conventions they had observed.

two

Foolishly imagining that from the air she might be able to see the shape of Newfoundland, even identify Cape Random, Lavinia Andrews tries to stay awake. But the drone of engine, the knowledge that she has finally, irrevocably made a decision, relaxes her, and now, suspended above the vast grey Atlantic, she sleeps. Mouth slightly ajar, head wedged between hard seat-back and cold plexiglass, Lav sleeps.

She sleeps and dreams of fish. Even in sleep she knows it is not new, this dream in which she swims through watery canyons, through pale reaching reeds, through damp light filtering down from some unknown source—a moon perhaps or a dying sun.

There is a change in engine sound, the dream splinters. Jarred awake, feeling sick and chilled, Lav pulls herself up, takes a deep breath and buckles her seat belt.

Below is St. John's, a black and white etching. The pilot overshoots the city, circles out over the ocean, turns and, aligning the plane between cliffs, sweeps back in over harbour and town. They come down without a bump in a landscape as desolate as Siberia.

Outside the airport St. John's seems benign enough, mundane even. An uncomfortable taxi takes her to Hotel Newfoundland in time to have a swim followed by an excellent meal, some kind of thick flaky fish with a cream sauce and salad. Lav eats with relish, she enjoys food, especially when someone else prepares it. In the weeks since Phillip left she has neither eaten nor slept well.

Lavinia Andrews is a tall woman, graceful, inclined, now that she is nearing forty, to a certain thickness around the hips. She reminds herself she will have to find a place to work out. Meantime she drinks tea, eats jam tarts, muses on why, at this age, at this point in her career, she should have let herself be sent to the outermost edge of the continent.

She had been surprised, shocked even, by the wave of sadness that enveloped her after Philip left. At night, alone in their house, she was filled with despair. It was then the dreams started—dreams of a fish moving through ink-black water, cold, afraid—and alone. Dreams from which she woke feeling tired, disoriented—bereft.

At work everything changed. Some magnetic force her job held when Philip was there was now missing. And, or so it seemed, something unpleasant had been added. She was being watched. A new attentiveness emanated from her colleagues, an attitude that fell somewhere between concern and satisfaction.

During those weeks Lav took special care with her looks, went regularly to the Spa, a combined beauty salon and workout place located in the mall below the DFO building. She tried to focus all her attention on the project at hand, the final compilation of statistics on Zone PK3—a fifty mile square of ocean off the east coast of Canada. This project, a singularly dull undertaking, would have long since been jettisoned were it not for pressure from the Minister's office.

She thought often of Charlotte, wishing for her mother's ability to shuck off the past, to leave it behind, empty and forgotten as a shed skin. She thought of Charlotte but did not telephone or write, did not tell her of Philip's desertion though she might be interested, perhaps even sorry. Philip and Charlotte had gotten along—the gross inefficiency of the country and the world annoyed them both.

The last time the three of them were together, that evening Charlotte spent with them before leaving for California, the bitter conversation in her mother's apartment had not been mentioned.

Very little was mentioned. Having used up their small-talk at the dinner table, the three of them spent the rest of the evening watching television. A federal election campaign was in progress and they turned on a special edition of the Journal, Philip and Charlotte commenting as cabinet members made extravagant promises to their constituents.

Lav can recall the Fisheries Minister pledging that "...in-depth research designed to breathe new life into Canada's Maritime Provinces" would be undertaken by his department.

"Old fraud!" Philip and Charlotte muttered in unison at Timothy Drew's smiling face. His proposal had infuriated them both, though for different reasons, Charlotte being of the opinion that tax money should not be spent to maintain places unfit for human habitation, Philip saying that in-depth research means thirty percent of his budget would be siphoned off to fund some specious half-baked project that was probably only window dressing.

Lav has never paid attention to politics. Saul had dismissed all politicians, called them bankers' puppets—and that night she was only amused, glad for anything that would make conversation easy in the hour or so before her mother left.

Leavetakings. Charlotte's, Philip's—and now mine, Lav thinks.

She had not slept well last night—woke with a headache and the imprint of some unhappy dream flickering at the corners of her eyes. Only then did she begin to pack—stuffing clothing and a few books helter-skelter into suitcases. The department would have paid to ship the furniture, even dishes and bedding. But Lav wants none of it. Never again will she eat from the smart, deep blue dinner set, never again sleep between these Liberty-print sheets she and Philip have used for years.

She'd had a nine o'clock appointment with Nat Hornsby, Philip's lawyer—and now, she supposes, hers too. Lav reflects on why using plates and sheets she and Philip had shared seems odious while putting her affairs into the hands of his lawyer is acceptable. She left the house-key with Nat, told him Fisheries and Oceans was sending her to Newfoundland for a year, asked him to rent the house and to see that it was kept in repair. Anything left after expenses can be divided between herself and Philip. She gave him the Research Station's address so that he could forward her mail but did not ask if he had heard from Philip or what her ex-lover's Australian address is.

Lav is tired but she continues to sit in the hotel dining room, listening to three businessmen at the next table talk of contracts and government loans—dull stuff. An habitual eavesdropper, Lav wishes she were sitting beyond the men, near the corner table where an elderly couple is being toasted by laughing children and grandchildren.

She should phone her mother. The thought nags at her. She should stand, should go to her room and call Charlotte: "I've just had a swim in clear blue heated water," she will say, "I've eaten a civilized meal at a table set with linen and silver and am now lying on a posture-perfect mattress in a hotel room identical to a million others all over the world—I'm in Newfoundland." She wonders what her mother's reaction would be.

But it is too late—too late or too early to telephone California—and so she sits on, drinking tea, eavesdropping—brooding.

It was Ian Farman who had first mentioned the Newfoundland job. Ian was a good friend of Philip's—a friend of Lav's too, she supposes. One day in January he had stopped in the doorway of her office and told her he'd just stumbled onto something up above. Ian had rolled his eyes heavenward, as they all did when referring to the top floors of DFO's Ottawa building—offices from which the minister's staff operate, unnumbered floors to which the public is not admitted.

"They're upgrading the PK3 research, putting a new spin on it, calling it Oceans 2000," Ian said. "There's talk of seconding someone from here to pull the project together, head it up in Newfoundland—probably for the rest of this year. Someone who knows the scene here in Ottawa—someone with enough policy experience to oversee regional people—to work with them, pull the PK3 stuff into a cohesive package, something we can get a policy planning document out of before the next election."

Ian's voice dropped, "Well—listening to them talk, it occurred to me it might be just the thing for you. You're familiar with existing policy and you've worked with Philip long enough to know what's involved in producing an acceptable report. You're certainly qualified and," he gave Lav a half-sympathetic, half-rueful smile, "and maybe you'd enjoy a few months away from this place."

Lav had been non-committal, but really she was intrigued by Ian's suggestion. Although she had never been there, Lav knew the Fisheries and Oceans Research Station in Newfoundland was located in St. John's. Despite this, as Ian talked she was imagining a remote community, a light-house-like building clinging to sea-battered cliffs. A place of storms, fog and brown water.

The thought of how much her going to such a place would annoy her mother skipped unbidden across her mind.

She had probably smiled. Ian certainly seemed encouraged, told her he would put in a word should she be interested. "Think it over," he said, "there are a lot of plusses—your position would almost certainly be reclassified, upgraded, it would give you good experience in the regions. I'm reasonably sure the job could be yours if you want it."

It had seemed a casual, friendly gesture, nothing official, but Lav knew enough about the inner manoeuverings of the department to recognize the message: with Philip gone, her position was not as secure as it had been.

Even before Ian Farman left her office Lav had decided to try for the Newfoundland job. Go away. For the first time in her life the idea of leaving seemed appealing. It was just what she needed—a few months in a new place, a hiatus between Philip and whatever her future might hold.

Now, though, sitting in the almost empty dining room of Hotel Newfoundland, delaying sleep, icy loneliness breathes down Lav's neck: Philip has disappeared, has abandoned her for the warmth of Australia. Saul is dead, his shop sold, his books scattered. Her mother is gone, long gone—is now Charlotte Carbrillo. The new name, Lav feels, suits her better than those mundane, abandoned names: Charlotte Rosenberg, Lottie Andrews, Darling Lottie—folded like tissue and placed in some forgotten drawer with Charlotte Hinchley, the silly little factory girl who thought she was escaping to paradise.

Perhaps it is just as well she hasn't phoned her mother. Would it matter to Charlotte Cabrillo, smiling among her pots of pink azaleas, that on this grey February day, in contravention of the only piece of advice she ever gave, her daughter has flown eastward—eastward and northward—away from the light, away from the sun, away from the safe centre of the continent?

When she wakes next morning it is sunny. Looking down on snowy streets and out over the harbour, which is deep blue, Lav realizes she has slept without dreaming, has outdistanced her phantom fish, defied her mother, perhaps expunged Philip.

I am alive and well, forty is not old, I'm in a new place, a place where the past is unimportant—so she tells herself. Filled with energy, she arranges for a rented car, eats a huge breakfast and goes in search of the Department of Fisheries Research Station, which the desk clerk describes as: "that stunned-looking building up in the White Hills."

Driving up the steep, winding road, between hills that are, in fact, black, Lav comes upon the building suddenly. It is set in a hollow between outcroppings of rock, safely out of sight and sound of the sea. A stream splashes along between the road and front entrance so that one has to cross a kind of draw-bridge to get to the main entrance. The design suggests a walled castle, yet the total impression of the building—its curved concrete enclosure, its five towers capped with steel siding and linked by glass walkways—evokes something more bizarre—a space station perhaps, or one of those multi-tiered towers of Babel pictured in Bibles her stepfather used to rebind. Standing outside the building Lav visualizes airy laboratories, sun-filled spaces in which to work and socialize.

When the security guard leads her through strangely sloping passageways, the walls of which are painted deep blue, livid green and purple, she realizes there are no sweeping vistas, no shiny laboratories or comfortable lounges, no army of white-smocked research assistants. Inside, the Fisheries Building resembles a series of Quonset huts joined by awkward walkways, subdivided into cramped rooms.

Bundles of bedraggled blue notebooks tied with string are stacked haphazardly outside office doors. Since the doors are all open, Lav can see the occupants: most, dressed in cords and sweaters, tap data into computers; some make notes and prod thoughtfully at specimen trays, others stare into computer screens on which many-coloured graphs unroll endlessly.

She pauses beside the door of a darkened room inside of which a tall black man is explaining video image analysis to a group of young children. Lav watches the children, their eyes move back and forth from the man's face to the pictures of cells projecting onto the wall. She thinks the children probably feel frightened, but pleasantly so, safe and frightened at the same time—and mystified, trying to make some connection between the scientist's black face and the pale translucent images floating on the wall.

"They're too young to take it in," her guide shakes his head and beckons Lav onwards down ramps and around circular hallways where every intersection is blocked by huge, padlocked freezers. The contents of these freezers are identified and dated by tags wired onto the locks: scum-oil scraped off fishing nets, cod livers, gullets of sea birds, genitalia of seals—all oozing the smell of formaldehyde and death.

Far, far down, in what surely must be a bunker built into the cliff, she is directed to a windowless, kitchen-like room where a lanky young man is waiting. When Lav introduces herself he admits, as if every word is being forced out of him, that he is Mark Rodway, her research assistant "...and gofer," he adds, mumbling something about being a graduate student and only available three days a week.

Instinctively wary of this person, disliking the way he will not meet her eye, Lav turns to inspect the cupboards, poorly-built, makeshift affairs.

"I had hoped to have a full-time assistant, someone experienced," she peers into the cupboards—all empty.

Her lack of attention seems to loosen his tongue. "Oh I've got all kinds of experience," he says. "I've been workin' with DFO four years—laid off twice every year and rehired twice every year—every year since I graduated. They got no cause to complain of me here at Fisheries and Oceans—at the Department of Employment either—and they're ever so pleased with me at Statistics Canada. Yea, my name is gone abroad in all the land. You must have heard tell of me, Dr. Andrews! Why, I'm the man who's created eight new jobs in four years! Still, I let them all down—got pissed off—went back to do university last

September. Blotted my copy book, Nan says—been demoted from temporary-full-time to casual-part-time."

This is what Mark Rodway says—or what Lav thinks he says. She will have to listen more carefully in the future. He speaks so quickly, so softly, in a low, continuous monotone—seems slow, dull, almost uninterested in the words coming out of his own mouth.

Content does not conform to sound with Mark Rodway, listening to him is like watching a movie that is out of sync, badly written—or too well written. You never catch the sharpness, the stab of sarcasm until it is gone, flung over your shoulder, flung at the wall behind you—never, surely, flung at you. Such arrows cannot come from this handsome creature slouching against the wall gazing innocently at his hands.

Pondering the young man's speech patterns, Lav has already missed part of what seems to be a briefing on the building and its inhabitants. Mark Rodway is telling her that over six hundred people work in the five towers, that each tower is a world to itself.

"Like unto the tower of Babel this place is—it confounded all the earth," he says, echoing her own impression, though Mark is not speaking of spiral rooms but of the people who inhabit them. "Everyone in this building speaks a different language. Everyone sticks to his own little cubicle, guards his own little project, circulates in his own little clique. A guy I went to school with has been working in Allocations and Licensing for five years—swears he's never seen his boss or the front entrance. Of course, the senior types are paranoid as hell about their own bits of research and their own work space. They're up above holding onto all the outer ring of offices—the ones with windows. The rest of us scrunch down here in steerage. Everyone keeps their doors open—it looks friendly but really it's to keep from choking in the recycled formaldehyde they pump around to pickle our brains and keep us docile." All this is said in the same casual, apathetic monotone.

He glances up just once, probably assessing how far he can go with this middle-aged creature from Ottawa, this woman with her doctorate—this outsider.

Lav begins to pace slowly around the room, keeping her face as deadpan as possible, pretending she is not really listening. This appears to be the right approach, for he continues.

"Bein' casual part-time I don't qualify for a key to the supply room so you'll have to make out requisitions for every jeezely thing—for secretarial help, for computer software, for a phone, paper, even pencils and paperclips. There's no proper cafeteria and you notice we don't rate a perc—there's coffee in machines down the hall but you wouldn't wish it on your worst enemy."

He instructs her to buy a kettle: "We can make ourselves nice and comfortable down here. You get coffee and teabags and I'll bring in milk and some teabuns." This concludes the conversation. He straightens up, raises a finger to his forehead—a gesture that in generations past might have indicated servile cap tipping but has evolved into curt dismissal—and walks out.

He leaves Lav to contemplate the room, a marginally more comfortable occupation than dwelling on the character and background of her research assistant. There are two desks and two chairs, both chipped and worn. One computer terminal, one government issue filing case, unlocked and empty. Below the row of cupboards a steel sink is set into a wooden counter. On the opposite wall is a large, cracked cork board onto which one envelope is pinned.

All her years of work, all her dreams—all her stepfather's dreams for her ("If you are lucky, Laviniandruss, you will live to see the beginning of civilization...") have led to this room.

Clearly, Oceans 2000 does not carry much weight here. How long will it take for the data she needs to be transferred from Ottawa? How will she endure working in this broom closet? How will she manage with just one, part-time, certainly insolent and probably lazy, assistant?

In six months' time I will go back and discover I've been demoted to research assistant, Lav thinks. To distract herself she walks over and unpins the envelope from the cork board.

The envelope contains a note from the room's former occupant. Roger Martin suggests she might like to rent his house. It is a nice house, he says, and since he and his family will be in South America for the next eighteen months Lav should at least go look at it. The key is with the security guard at the front desk.

She feels grateful to Roger Martin. His note is sane, clear—a small, accidental welcome. Before dark she is ensconced in the Martin house.

It is narrow, squeezed between two almost identical houses, each with blanket sized front and back yards and no off-street parking. From outside, the house seems to consist of two storeys topped by a steep attic, but generations of floor levellings, ceiling lowerings, adjustments and additions have left every room on a different level so that Lav is constantly going up or down one or two steps.

It is a crowded, comfortable house, cluttered with the Martin family's belongings. The front hall closet is packed tight with winter jackets, heavy boots, wool caps and scarves. Shelves overflow with books, walls with pictures. Tapes and games, Monopoly, checkers, Scrabble, are piled in corners of the living room. The mantle is lined with garish, child-made ornaments and ugly souvenir plates. Sideboards contain unmatched china and tarnished silver.

The Martins are not neat by nature but have, Lav can see, attempted to make room for their unknown tenant. Ice skates, skis and tennis racquets have been tossed into a cupboard under the stairs. One bedroom has been taken for storage, filled with junk: piles of old records, stacks of magazines, *Atlantic, National Geographic, Chatelaine, Science Report, Owl, Canadian Forum*—there are even comic books—the Martins are eclectic readers. The bed in this room is piled with dolls, teddy bears, a wooden sailing ship and a hundred plastic toys. Cardboard boxes overflowing with school reports, letters, receipts, photos, cover the floor. The urge to rummage through this mass of unfiled history, this detritus of life, is so strong that Lav pushes a small bookcase across the door.

Having the Martin house to return to makes her unpleasant work-space bearable. At night she sits in Roger Martin's easy chair debating whether she has ruined her career, if she has been manipulated by Ian Farman into coming to Newfoundland. Eventually, she bores herself and stops debating, tells herself that she will make a success of her stay and produce a report that will bury forever any suggestion that she owes her position to Philip.

Holding to Philip's dictum—that a modicum of civilization makes all things possible—Lav spins off polite requests to Ottawa asking that all their PK3 data be transferred to St. John's, asking for more space and additional staff. She buys a kettle, she requisitions supplies.

She suggests to Mark Rodway, carefully staring into her cup as she dabbles a teabag, that the Oceans 2000 Report might be his golden opportunity to establish a name for himself, to get that permanent government job he has informed her is the lifetime ambition of every right-thinking Newfoundlander. After saying this, Lav glances up quickly enough to see Mark regarding her with a look of astonishment. "So!" the look says, "So, this mainlander is catching my throw-away lines!"

Lav congratulates herself. She is sure that up to now, Mark has thought her deaf.

They do not get any more space, but by the following Monday supplies have been delivered and Lav has a key to the office. Data from Ottawa has been transferred into their computer and several dozen notebooks, all filled with notations on Zone PK3, have appeared as if by magic in the hallway outside.

But, most important, they have been given Mrs. Alice O'Reilly. Mrs. O'Reilly is in her fifties, a formal woman who frowns on the use of first names or the wearing of cords in offices.

"I came to the Department right out of Commercial at Mercy. I was eighteen—standards were different then—if you had a Commercial diploma it meant something. That was just after Confederation—the Provincial Government passed over its Department of Fisheries, staff, files and all to the Federal Government. Everyone was getting jobs in federal offices that year," she told Lav on the day she arrived.

"There's no need for this," Alice O'Reilly said, surveying the depressing room. She set the potted plant she was holding down on a desk and began unpacking boxes, arranging office supplies in neat, labelled piles inside the cupboards. She sent Mark off in search of another desk and something she called a credenza, which turned out to be a kind of sideboard.

Lav recognized Alice O'Reilly at once—there are hundreds of women like her in Ottawa. Professionals, the glue that holds the civil service together. Given the opportunity, Mrs. O'Reilly could run the entire department, probably the entire nation. The minute she walks in, Mark's demeanour becomes less casual, less insolent—the room becomes an office and the maintenance staff begin to treat Lav as if she might stay.

In front of Mark and Mrs. O'Reilly Lav is on guard, alert, attentive to detail. Although the objectives of the project seem nebulous, although she is secretly appalled by the vast amount of random, uncatalogued material contained in the pile of blue notebooks, she takes pains to sound crisp and sure.

"We'll standardize this local material, format it into some kind of database and integrate it with Ottawa's material. Then, we'll see the shape of the Oceans 2000 report," she announces with great confidence. She can hear the pomposity in her voice.

Week after wretched week, three of them pour over the Newfoundland research. Mark and Lav analyze, code, transfer the information onto charts and graphs, measure figures against Ottawa baselines. Mrs. O'Reilly taps endlessly at the computer. It is the first time since university that Lav has done such work. She had forgotten how tedious it is.

On the stained pages of the blue notebooks fisheries observers, biologists and oceanographers have recorded years of work, thousands of nautical miles of research in Zone PK3. Every imaginable measurement has been taken: currents, seasons, salinity, phases of the moon, fish tagging data and blood samples, acoustic surveys, the spawning areas and biomass of twelve species, the presence of ice, of seals, caplin, plankton, of abandoned fish netting, of plastic debris, where containers of toxic chemicals have been dumped, the levels of dioxins and heavy metals. This, and much more, on-site scientists have monitored and written into notebooks.

Though the material numbs her, Lav is determined to finish, not to stop until they have coded the contents of every blue book into the computer. Each week she works longer and longer hours. After work she goes directly home, where she exists in a kind of timeless, mindless isolation, wandering through the house like a ghost, examining the Martins' belongings, idly speculating on what kind of family the Martins are.

She speaks to no one, does not telephone, does not write letters—not to her mother, not to Philip, not to anyone in Ottawa. In the mail Nat Hornsby forwards that there are no personal letters. Detached from her past, Lav drifts in a kind of hiatus. This time she has disappeared.

The only emotion she acknowledges during those first weeks is that twinge of disappointment she feels whenever she comes in contact with the town and its people. As if Newfoundland and Newfoundlanders have failed her. Nodding goodnight to the security guard—a friendly man, who, when she works late, walks her to the door and watches as she crosses the bridge to the parking lot—Lav feels judgment behind his kindness. She imagines the same suspicious watchfulness in shops, in restaurants, from Mark and even from Alice O'Reilly despite her friendly office demeanour. Sometimes she thinks she is not in Canada at all but in some dangerous, foreign country that will swallow her if she puts a foot wrong. Clearly these people do not trust her—and she must not trust them.

By April there is barely space in the office for the stacks of computer print-outs, the miles of statistics from which, no matter how Lav assesses and cross references, no perceivable patterns emerge. There is something deeply disturbing about the sight of all these figures, spewing hour after hour onto the floor. When she tells Mark this he understands.

"It's like a fortune cookie you can't read—a million fortune cookies," he says, then brightens, "No—it's more like poor old Belshazzar in the Bible!"

Seeing Lav's blank look, the young man explains that Belshazzar was a king who had to get someone out of retirement to interpret mysterious handwriting that appeared on the wall of his palace. "Maybe," he suggests, "you should go over to the Hoyles Home and find someone to read our print-outs—ask if they got some old fisherman in there we can have a lend of." Mark laughs at this joke.

Lav tells him to shut up.

Her unease has returned and with it the fish that swims through her dreams. Moving inside its flesh she feels the cold, the ribbons of water, the silence. Nights and days are filled with foreboding. No word has been heard from Ottawa, she has been forgotten, shelved. Lav has seen such things happen inside government departments—setting a bothersome person to work on some pointless project with no beginning and no end.

Mark turns grumpy, complains that he is blind with boredom. More to clear the air than with any expectation that he will find anything, Lav directs him to go track down the original statement of objectives for the study of Zone PK3.

He doesn't come back for two days. On Friday afternoon he appears, announcing, for once in a voice Lav can understand, that he is the Lord's messenger, come bearing Ottawa's commandments—the definitive document.

When Lav and Alice O'Reilly swing their chairs around to face the young man, Mark drops his voice, assumes what she has come to recognize as his mainland accent: "The study of Zone PK3 off the northeast coast of Newfoundland will be a coordinated marine science effort," he drones.

"Objectives will focus on improving government's ability to anticipate future oceans-related problems and respond before such problems reach crisis proportions. From this study the Department of Fisheries and Oceans will formulate a multi-year marine science policy paper, propose marine science programs and relate these programs to the priorities of government and the missions of line departments."

"Very precise, very clear! Don't you think so Dr. Andrews?" Mark stares, straight-faced into Lav's eyes as he passes her the paper.

They look at each other for a second, then they begin to laugh. The vacuous statement delights both of them. Surrounded by the bundles of blue notebooks, the miles of print-outs, the thousands upon thousands of statistics engendered by these empty words, Mark and Lav hold each other up and laugh.

It is the first time Lav has touched anyone in months, the first time she has laughed in months. Once started she cannot stop. Alice O'Reilly is mystified, then annoyed, but this only makes the other two laugh louder. Lav laughs until she drops, choking, into a chair and Mark has to pound her back.

"That's better. You should laugh more often," he says when she recovers, then he turns to Alice, "Dr. Andrews takes all this too seriously—she doesn't realize yet that down here in Newfoundland we can do anything, anything or nothing—because nothing we do counts. Not in the great scheme of things. Isn't that right Mrs. O'Reilly?"

Alice O'Reilly will not answer him. Her face tight with disapproval, she hands Lav a glass of water.

Lav sips and rereads the paper. Mark and Alice return to their desks. Except for the tap of computer keys, the office is silent. In other offices, telephones ring. Down the hallway there is a scraping sound, a man's voice saying sharply: "Hold her there! Steady now!" Freezers filled with specimens are being rearranged again.

What have I been playing at all these weeks? Lav wonders. Have I been trying to turn myself into Philip, duplicating his management style, his procedures? Trying to copy the absorption with which he tackles such projects, despite the fact that I am not in the least absorbed—neither by the hodgepodge of information nor by its source—a tiny bay somewhere on the northeast coast of Newfoundland. The priorities of Government and the mission of line departments indeed!

The entire project bores her. Mark is right, nothing done down here counts.

She pulls on her coat and leaves without a word. Outside, even the light looks unfamiliar, pale grey and damp. It is the first time in weeks she has left the building before dark. Spring has come to the rest of the continent but here fingers of ice still cling to cliffs and half frozen slush covers the parking lot.

Lav turns away from the research station, driving down, then up, up to the top of Signal Hill where she parks and sits staring out at the sluggish, half-frozen sea. She finds herself considering fish, not the mindless, boring statistics that fill her office but the graceful, lonely fish that swims nightly through her dreams.

Lav has identified her fish—a species of salmon, the female of which drives herself to premature senility in frantic determination to lay eggs on the same bit of sand where she had been spawned. Burdened with eleven million eggs, the great fish swims slowly through endless oceans, avoiding—or not avoiding—ghost nets, trawlers, sharks—moving towards the perfect time, the perfect place, the perfect other. How sensible, how dignified, how right such a search seems.

Beyond the dream, overshadowing it, is the knowledge that her salmon is doomed. It has ceased to produce fluids that let oxygen filter through gills into flesh and bone. Within days the fish's jaw will lengthen—in her dream this is already happening—soon the fish will grow a great jutting snout, scales will lose their shine, tarnish and turn rusty. When the salmon reaches the goal she has been seeking so resolutely she will spawn and die—inexplicably of accelerated old age.

The wind is strong on the hill, it pushes against the car, nudges it gently. Lav is half-asleep, lulled by thoughts of the ageing fish, by the wind and the sluggish movement of sea—wave after wave of grey, half-frozen water, cresting in white froth, retreating backward, unrolling towards some far off, invisible, English coast.

If her salmon should turn around, begin swimming the other way, would life-fluid pump through its body again? Would the natural process be reversed? Would flesh and bone regenerate?

Lav is jarred into reality by a loud tap on the passenger window of the car. Outside, a woman hunches forward, face pressed to glass. Her nose and cheeks are red with cold, wind is clawing at her black scarf and wispy grey hair. The apparition taps at the glass, makes an impatient gesture, telling Lav to roll down the window.

When she reaches across and opens the door the woman hops in, pulling yards of coat behind her, folding it blanket-like around her. She sets a pile of brochures on the dashboard and blows on her hands.

"There's only one way down—unless you're thinkin' of drivin' off the edge," the woman gives Lav a sharp, unsmiling look. "But I'm sure you're goin' my way—so you might just as well give me a lift." The woman's voice is brisk as the air she's brought into the car.

Feeling as if she has been rudely awakened from a deep sleep, Lav looks down at the dark water, at white foam and icy rocks, and shudders. Could she have been thinking of driving off the edge? Certain that no such thought had been in her mind she asks the woman where she wants to be taken.

"Oh, just let me off down by the foot of the hill—I'll be near home then. By rights I shouldn't be up here today at all—but I had to talk to Gus Whitten's grandson—he's workin' in the tower. Besides, I thought sure it was spring this mornin'—the cursed CBC crowd said we were goin' to have sun," she glares at the vast expanse of grey sky.

Here, Lav thinks, is a chance to talk to a real Newfoundlander, to think about something besides fish. She will kidnap this crony, take her to a restaurant, ply her with tea until she tells everything: who she is, how she fills her days, what makes her so fierce—what keeps her alive out here on the ice-crusted edge of the world.

"Is it always like this in April?" Lav asks.

The woman nods, "Always." She is not interested in small-talk, hardly looks Lav's way. She is talking to herself, muttering as she sifts through the brochures—glossy scraps of paper, resplendent with sunlit sea and blue skies. She snorts, tosses the collection of tourist material onto the floor of the car, sinks into her coat and does not speak again until they reach the foot of the hill.

"Right here!" she commands and, when Lav stops, immediately begins to scramble out. With one foot on the sidewalk she turns, "They used to hang people up there on the hill—it's a dreary place, a poor place to think things out." The woman nods, gathers her great coat around her and plods off down a sideroad.

The self-contained arrogance of the old woman does Lav good. On her way home she buys *The Globe and Mail, Ottawa Citizen*, fresh bread and a bottle of wine.

A pile of mail has accumulated on the floor of the front porch. Stuffing her coat into a space she's made amongst the Martins' winter garments Lav bends forward to pick up the letters. Doing so she catches an unexpected glimpse of herself in the oval mirror beside the closet. Startled, she holds her face up to the mirror and studies each feature, angling her head this way and that, eyeing the line of jaw, chin and nose—surely longer, more hooked than when she left Ottawa seven weeks ago? There is no doubt about the hair, it has turned rusty, brittle and fuzzed at the ends, no longer falls in a smooth auburn sheen around her ears. Her skin, however, is paler, finely lined, more transparent—yet she can detect no sense of movement, no urge to spawn. She turns away from the tired, defeated face—disowns it—it is not hers.

In Ottawa Lav had gone regularly to a place called The Beauty Boutique, a spa located in a mall directly below the DFO building. Each Tuesday and Friday she would leave the office early, have a swim, a sauna. Then, wearing a snow-white robe monogrammed B.B., she would have her nails, hair and face done. The attendant would usher her into a little room decorated to look like the inside of a jewel case, bring freshly brewed coffee which Lav would sip while sitting on a soft chair, listening to the soft music and the softer hum of voices from the other side of the wall.

Everyone at The Beauty Boutique knew her. The shampoo girl, when she came, would call her Dr. Andrews, make chirping sounds as she covered Lav's shoulders in a silk cape and gently eased her head back onto the cushioned edge of the peach-coloured sink.

This girl, whose name was Kyra, had dangerous-looking varnished nails but only the soft pads of her fingertips ever touched scalp. Kyra's fingers moved in hypnotic circles, circles within circles along Lav's hairline, back to the crown of her head, around her ears, down her neck, as oil, shampoo, warm water, conditioner and, finally, auburn gold rinse, anointed her head. Twice each week Lav would lie in this steamy, sleep-filled haze, the smell of crushed apricots scenting the air, mixing with the music, misting the birds and flowers that danced on the walls and ceiling.

Amazing, really, how such rituals comfort, contribute to one's total happiness. Thinking about it, Lav is convinced she misses Kyra as much as she misses Philip.

Resolving that on Monday she will ask Alice O'Reilly about fitness clubs and hairdressers, Lav picks up the mail, goes through the living room and up three steps into the big kitchen at the back of the house. She places the mail face downward on the kitchen table, pours herself a glass of wine and searches for a tin of Vienna sausage she remembers seeing somewhere in the tall old-fashioned cupboard.

Lav's eating habits have deteriorated along with her grooming. She takes wine, bread and the tinned sausage over to the stuffed chair by the kitchen window. With her back to the table and to the mail she eats supper.

Lav has always liked the worn, commonplace parts of cities, places like Dugan Street in Ottawa where she grew up—family houses such as the one the Petrassi family lived in, churches and grocery stores, repair shops and delis, book shops like Saul's, all crowded together. She likes the enclosed feeling of narrow streets, of sidewalks owned by people who live along the street.

From the Martins' kitchen she can look down on the backs of such streets, on a clutter of snow-covered roofs, at chimney pots, pigeons and sea gulls, down into tiny back yards where cats pick their way among rusting bicycles, discarded barbecue stands, car tires and baby carriages.

Between the chimneys and down across a back alley Lav can see the corner of Crotty's Convenience Store. In the window there is a sign saying, "Watered Fish For Your Brewis." Mysterious, hand-lettered words like those she used to watch Charlotte inscribe on Saul's store window. Tonight Lav cannot see the words but knows they are there since she often walks around the block after dark.

Most of the houses in this neighbourhood are built right at the sidewalk's edge. When people forget to pull their drapes Lav can look into kitchens and living rooms. If I were an artist, she thinks, I would want to paint these people, surround them with colour, with light and shadows. The families eating supper lean towards each other, towards the food which is heavy, earth coloured, unlike anything in supermarkets. Everything, the milk-white arms of women washing dishes, blue-faced lovers curled together in front of unseen television sets, the tired young mother who night-after-night spoons food into a baby's pink, smiling mouth, all seem from another century. Even the children, immovable as rocks, slumped on sofas, their eyes never leaving television screens, might be watching a cock-fight in some medieval marketplace.

Each lighted window is a picture, almost nothing changes from night to night, the colour of a shirt, a tablecloth, the arrangement of children watching television. The very monotony lends dignity to the mundane scenes. Lav herself is invisible. Only cats, surveying their street from window ledges, follow her progress with green gold eyes.

On these walks she passes Crotty's store window, reads the mysterious words, watches the clerk. Sometimes the woman is talking to a customer but more often she leans on the counter, a Vermeer, her placid round face cupped in her hands, engrossed in a magazine. Lav has considered going in to find out what the clerk reads with such deep, absorbing interest—and to ask what brewis is.

Far down beyond the store, beyond the houses and streets, Lav can see a scrap of harbour. It gleams steely grey in the cold April light.

"Can you see the harbour?" Mrs. O'Reilly asked when Lav told her that she was living in the Martin house.

Lav told her no, but Alice had insisted, "Surely," she said, "you can see the harbour from upstairs?"

Every day for a week or more, polite but persistent, she asked the same question—as if some miraculous good fortune came with a view of St. John's harbour. Then, one sunny morning, Lav realized that the bit of deeper blue between Crotty's two chimneys was the harbour.

"I knew very well you'd be able to see the harbour from that house!" Alice O'Reilly said with great satisfaction.

That very evening Lav had dragged Roger Martin's overstuffed chair from his study, pulled it across the hall, up the three steps into the kitchen. Chipping two white-enamelled door frames in the process, she installed the chair in front of the big many-paned window. Now, every night before bed, she spends an hour or so sitting in the chair. Only here does she have any sense of being in a different place—a place distantly akin to the island her mother described.

As she sits watching St. John's harbour fade from grey to black Lav feels very much a visitor, an observer, detached from the real life of the place.

I will do my job and leave, she thinks. It is foolish to imagine otherwise. I will make no real connections, never be invited into the houses I walk past, will not have conversations with people like the woman on the hill or the clerk in Crotty's store. The urge to do so seems unnatural, slightly vulgar, possibly dangerous. She will have to cultivate detachment. Reviewing those pleasant, well-ordered years with Philip, she decides that detachment has served her well.

She pours herself more wine and speculates on what she might do if there is a letter from Philip in the mail on the table behind her—a reply to her casually worded card telling him she has closed the house in Ottawa.

She imagines Philip writing from Australia—a wild, impassioned Philip who will surprise her—he has, after all, proven himself capable of surprising her. Lav amuses herself for some time conjuring up this new Philip. A man who, having cut himself adrift from geography, can now cut himself adrift from history, from order, from habit, from tradition—free himself to follow some new arrangement of urges, impulses more suited to Australian dust and sunshine, to heat and desire.

"Come at once—cannot live without you!" this most unPhiliplike man will write. And what of her? How will this Lavinia, this woman of rusting hair and lengthening snout, respond to his siren song?

It is almost midnight when, having finished the wine, she finally picks up the mail. There is no letter from Philip. There are bills for light and fuel oil, a scrawled message from Roger Martin reminding her to have the furnace checked and cleaned—a remarkable thing to have thought of in Caracas! There is a magazine, a flyer for Papa's Pizza and a brown envelope with "Delivered by hand—To Dr. L. Andrews, From M. Rodway" written across the outside. Inside there are three sheets of paper.

The top sheet is Mark's hand-written note: "I've come across something you might be interested in. Could you meet me at the University—in the Maritime Archives—after work on Monday? Oh yes, the attached telexes came in after you left. Me-ne, Me-ne, Te-kel."

A coded message from her research assistant—a warning, perhaps.

The second paper, just three lines typed under the DFO heading, reads, "To: Dr. L. Andrews, Department of Fisheries and Oceans Research Station, St. John's, Nfld. From: Dr. Ian Farman, Policy and Program Planning, Science Section, DFO, Ottawa. Puzzled by the implications of your preliminary report. Please reassess material keeping in mind the attached memo from Communications."

Puzzled indeed. What preliminary report? And, more disconcerting, why has Ian Farman, who must have eaten at her table a dozen times, not added a personal note to his nasty little memo?

The last paper is a copy of another office memo. This one is addressed to Ian Farman and signed by someone named Wayne. Wayne has given himself neither surname or title.

I am not going to like this—I know I am not going to like it, Lav thinks as, gripping the paper under her elbow like a handbag, she makes herself a cup of tea, takes it to the bedroom and, without undressing, crawls into bed where she reads the damned memo.

"Urgently suggest the following rationale be given to Dr. Andrews as a broad basis for her Oceans 2000 advisory report being finalized in St. John's, Newfoundland: The report on Zone PK3 should be regarded as just one model among many being used by government in developing a strategy that will promote science and technology as the driving force for economic activity on Canada's coastal waters. It is the Minister's hope to put in place a policy that will be responsive to the needs of the private sector and consistent with government's strategy to maximize development and exploitation of the resources of our oceans for the benefit of the people of Canada."

Below the cunningly worded paragraph, separated by three asterisks, its author has added a note, presumably to Ian Farman, "Will be in St. John's next week—think I'll check this Dr. Andrews out. Wayne."

Lav lies in bed holding the three pieces of paper. She studies the signatures, two of which are machine-printed, rereads each word. Uncertainty settles like a rock in her stomach. She suspects Mark Rodway. What has he done? Why has he dropped off this stuff? Who is Wayne? What does "developing a strategy that will promote science and technology as the driving force" mean? Why urgently suggest? What preliminary report?

She feels disoriented, ill, a tourist picking her way through some foreign maze. It is late, it seems like days since she left the office. She has drunk too much wine, is not thinking clearly. She tosses the papers onto the floor and falls into a fitful sleep.

All night long her ageing salmon swims, first through shifting, weed-filled sludge, then through computer printouts, along watery pathways that rattle with the tap of keyboards smelling of formaldehyde.

She wakes on Saturday feeling only slightly less ill—knowing the night has been fish-haunted, telling herself she should go straight in to the office, track down the mysterious report referred to in the memos. Over coffee she decides to try and forget the memos—after all, nothing can be done until Monday.

She will dedicate the week-end to her physical well-being, do something about appearance, about her face and hair. She consults the phone book, lists dress shops, makes appointments. She finds a fitness centre, has a swim and workout, a massage. She visits three dress shops, a shoe store, then a beauty parlour, gets her hair coloured and styled, has a facial, a manicure. She is cosseted, glossed, coiffed, complimented. At great expense she is pampered. Those who say money cannot buy happiness lie.

On Sunday it is pouring rain and windy. The three pieces of paper are still on the floor near her bed. Lav ignores them. Instead she tries on the dresses, the wool suit, the scarves and shoes, all her purchases of the day before. She admires her newly rinsed auburn hair.

Later she lights the living room fire, settles down with a volume chosen at random from the Martins' shelves. Called *Fallen from the Sky*, the book seems intended for children but is filled with clamourous, unchildlike tales. Stories of how the earth and sky, once one, were torn asunder, how gods and goddesses fell, became vulnerable to pain, to sin, to death.

All through the blustery afternoon she sits by the fire drinking tea, devouring crackers and cheese, reading of Zeus, Apollo and Aphrodite, of how they wreak ungodly vengeance upon one another and upon poor humans. Gods, like humans, seem driven to teach what they cannot learn, succumb repeatedly to the charms of mortals and sometimes suffer endless tortures to help them. Prometheus dares the wrath of Zeus to bring man fire, Pandora opens her cunningly contrived box, Balder the Beautiful dies, he sails out to sea in his fiery ship, "burning like autumn foliage and the earth wept for him and cold and darkness followed."

Lavinia wept for him.

The sound of her weeping shocks her. She had thought herself content, pleased with her own company, with the fire and the book. But she reads of Balder's death and is attacked by sadness. A shroud of despair, all-embracing impersonal sorrow, drops down upon her and she weeps. Beyond the edge of her weeping there is something else, something closer, more personal. But ice and sleet rattling against the window drowns it out and she huddles on the sofa sobbing for all the poor gods and poor humans who must die, their possessions scattered and their stories forgotten.

When the weeping stops she lies sniffling in misery until dark, until there is not a spark of fire left in the hearth—then she goes to bed.

three

"After that nothing was ever the same." People say such things. "That was when it all started," they say, "From that day on, everything changed," or "I knew right away." Conventional, comfortable phrases, phrases that give the illusion of order, of neatness, of one's ability to compartmentalize, to separate event from event, to disentangle.

But life will not be disentangled, has no pattern, and events are connected only in the random way of pebbles tumbling from a narrow-necked bottle—each pebble nudging the other, each one that falls making room for another to fall. For most of us—barring getting hit by a truck or having the earth drop out from under our feet—there is no moment, no hour, no day, when we can say "after that nothing was ever the same."

Yet that is what Lavinia Andrews will say.

"After that stormy Sunday nothing was ever the same," she will say. "After that night of weeping, events in my life did not wait upon one another, did not politely nudge one another into being. After that everything tumbled helter-skelter—past and present, public and private, reality and imagination melding together."

That is the way she remembers the days that followed—but of course, days and events must happen in some order, in fixed time—and we must recall them in that order.

On Monday morning Lav wears her new scarf, her woven jacket and the tight slit of skirt she bought on Saturday. She takes great care with her toffee-coloured hair, with makeup that must camouflage all signs of last night's weeping.

Alice O'Reilly, waiting in the lobby, pacing beside the security desk, notices none of this.

"They're moving us! Moving us! Without a word—without as much as a by-your-leave—we're being carted body and bones up to the top floor! And that's not all," she rushes Lav towards the spiral walkway. "Wayne Drover and his crowd'll be here before week's end. Won't say which day, of course, just, 'Arriving mid-week from Ottawa!'"

Alice pauses to assess Lav's reaction, apparently not as dramatic as she would wish. "You know who Wayne Drover is?" she asks and, when Lav shakes her head, looks shocked, "Sure I thought everyone in the department knew that one! Wayne Drover's special assistant to Timothy Drew—went to Ottawa with the Minister when he was elected. From here, Wayne is—grew up in the Battery—but sharp as a tack...."

On the way to the new offices Alice elaborates on Wayne Drover's career, the campaigns he has run for Timothy Drew, on his failed advertising firm, his failed marriage, his ambitions. The man appears to be something of a local celebrity.

The space they have been given is large and airy. Lav points to windows, closets, the corner countertop already holding a kettle and coffee perc—as evidence of their new status, tells Alice she should be pleased.

"I don't like the feel of it—never known anything to happen this fast—usually you hear about stuff like this weeks ahead. There's something queer goin' on—always is when the political people move in—and mark my words that's what they're doing. This space is too big to be just for support staff—me and Mark and whoever else we need."

"You're in that middle office over there," Alice points to five private offices that open on the reception area. "It's a nice office—you have a window and some new furniture's already been moved in. Maintenance says that office left of yours is for Wayne Drover, the others are for Drover's glow boys—which means they'll be staying a while." Alice suddenly notices her supervisor's newly groomed self and asks sharply, "Did you know about all of this?"

Lav assures the woman that she is as surprised as anyone, quickly asks if they've been told who will be travelling with Mr. Drover.

"Well, the Minister's not coming—thank God for small mercies! But Wayne'll have two or three of his own staff from Communications—Tony Mallard and Keith Laing more than likely—or perhaps that Chinese woman photographer he had with him last time." Alice frowns but not, apparently, because of the Chinese photographer but because of someone called Melba Summers who Wayne Drover always brings up from the steno-pool. "Melba smokes—do you object to people smoking in the office?"

Lav chooses to ignore this question, asking instead if Alice has seen Mark this morning.

"There's something on your desk—a report Mark dropped off, told me he might be leaving the project."

Alice gives Lav another accusing look. This move, Mark's talk of leaving—she knows Lav cannot be innocent. "This'll be a busy week—it would have gone a lot more smoothly if I'd had notice," she says before turning to a man who has come pushing a trolley piled high with boxes of their printouts.

The office Lav has been given is attractive. There is no computer, no clutter. The shiny, black surface of the desk contains a telephone and a file folder—nothing else. Behind the desk there is a rose-coloured chair. In the opposite corner a small coffee table, a sofa and easy chair, also rose-coloured, have been arranged beside a window that looks out onto the cliff face.

She sits at the desk and lays her hand on the file. It is quite thin, nothing is written on the cover, she has no doubt that it contains a copy of the preliminary report referred to in Friday's memos, that it will tell her why Mark wants to meet her after work, why Wayne Drover and his communication experts are so hastily descending upon St. John's.

Eventually she opens the folder. Inside is no handwritten note, no explanation—just fifteen Xeroxed pages, ten of which are simply a list of references and data sources.

Headed "A Preliminary Paper. From: Oceans 2000 Project, Policy and Program Planning, DFO St. John's," it is addressed to "The Director, Science Section, Policy and Program Planning, DFO, Ottawa."

Lav speed-reads through the first five pages. Certain phrases leap up, "...a steady, well documented and perhaps irreversible decline in the size and numbers of cod landed in Zone PK3. In nine years the number of 3-year-old cod entering this area has dropped by half...."

"The practice, by Canadian and foreign fleets, of dragging the ocean bottom has destroyed vast spawning areas...."

"The systematic harvesting of spawning caplin to supply the vast Japanese market has depleted the caplin stock and changed the patterns of cod moving inshore."

And so on and on, oil spills and the dumping of toxic waste, the trading of fishing rights to foreign countries, too large quotas, too small mesh size, gill nets, ghost nets, double nets, the warnings of fishermen, inappropriate, unanalyzed and incomplete research, inaccurate baseline data, improper monitoring.

Mark has missed nothing. For there is no doubt this is Mark's report—Lav recognizes the sonorous style, the apocalyptic view, the way bleak fact has been piled upon bleak fact, footnoted, annotated and lined up with the relevant research code.

All building to the final doom-ridden paragraph—which, to make sure no one misses, Mark has typed in bold face capital letters: "The data on Zone PK3 is almost surely applicable to neighbouring zones and indeed to the entire North Atlantic. The conclusion is unavoidable: unless immediate and drastic action is taken to stop all fishing for many years, this entire ecosystem will, within a decade, be completely destroyed. This will, of course, mean the extinction of several species, including Northern Cod."

When Lav puts the file down on her desk, her hands are shaking. Mark Rodway has probably ruined her career.

She has never been so angry. That a research assistant should take it upon himself to send out such a report is indefensible—outrageous. She walks to the window, takes deep breaths. Outside it is beautiful, spring-like, sunny. On this side of the building there is no sign of ice. The cliff facing her seems to have been landscaped, each depression in the wet rock is filled with moss, with fern and small, Japanese-looking evergreen.

Concentrating on the green, which is said to have a calming effect, she wills herself to breathe slowly, to consider her options. The damage has been done. Useless now to try and shift blame. Useless now to reflect on Mark's self-destructive character, on his lack of experience, his pessimism, his fundamentalist grandmother, his strange speech patterns. Useless to say that this young man has no authority to submit such a report. Ottawa, Ian Farman and Wayne Drover clearly attribute the report to Lavinia Andrews.

Is it within the realm of possibility that Mark's conclusions are correct? If so, why have others not seen the evidence? Why has she not seen the evidence? Because of her inexperience? Incompetence? Because she is from "away?" Because she is deliberately blind?

Slowly Lav rereads the report. The scenario suggested by Mark seems highly unlikely. Still, she gives Alice the reference list, asks her to bring whatever the DFO library has, along with any recent assessments of biomass together with their own print-out summaries on stock assessment.

She spends the entire day checking baseline data on various commercial stocks of fish, comparing indices of abundance, estimates of biomass. She cross-checks everything—research vessel surveys and catch information from industry, DFO figures and those received from other G7 countries.

All the papers are hopeful. In startling contrast to Mark's report they all end optimistically. One major study released by an internationally based fishing company just two months earlier concludes: "Since 1950 marine catches have grown almost fivefold to a world-wide industry that is now worth $30 billion, calculating that last year more than 85 million tons of fish were caught globally, and considering the scientific principles and international laws now in place, research suggests that a 100 million ton catch is both practical and sustainable."

These words, written by a world-respected stock assessment expert, together with a dozen other studies indicating that the seas of the world hold almost unlimited potential, convince Lav that there is no reason to take a graduate student's grim predictions seriously. Zone PK3 is one of the richest fishing grounds in the world and will doubtless remain so.

At day's end, more mystified than angry—perhaps the young man is mentally ill, depressed or revengeful for some imagined wrong—she leaves work and drives to Memorial University in search of Mark Rodway.

It takes almost half an hour to find the Maritime History Archive—an underground cavern just off a network of tunnels below the University. The low-ceilinged room seems empty. A young woman sitting at a desk near the door does not even glance up when Lav walks in. She wanders around and eventually finds Mark hidden in a cubbyhole, his chair tipped back, his feet resting on a heating pipe. His head, blonde hair falling forward, is bent over a large book he has propped open on his knees.

It is a pleasant sight. Despite her annoyance and unease (for that is what her anger has become, a kind of motherly frustration—she could shake the young man, demand to know what's wrong with him, what foolishness he's been up to), she stands for a minute studying the youthful face, the bony fingers resting on the book. The scene reminds Lav of a seventeenth-century painting called "The Young Student"—the same dark background, the long blue-clad legs, the worn leather binding of the book, the slanting light that touches the planes of face and hands. Only Mark's feet, in mustard-coloured work boots, red laces dangling, are at odds with the remembered painting. She is surprised by a rush of desire.

"Hallo," it is a kinder greeting that she had planned. Nonetheless his chair comes down with a thump and his look, a mixture of guilt and embarrassment, is disconcerting.

"Why?"

He blinks, as if he does not know what she is asking.

"Why in God's name did you send that stupid report off to Ottawa?"

"Because I knew you'd never send it," the surly look has returned.

"Of course I wouldn't have sent it—you stupid, irresponsible child! I've spent the entire day checking the so-called facts in your report—and not one of them can be substantiated."

"Depends who you ask," he says and mutters something about being weighed in the balances and found wanting.

Lav has no time for his silly jokes or the Bible riddles he is so fond of. She enumerates the many ways he has broken civil-service protocol, lists the documents she has combed through, in fact, delivers an exhaustive lecture on the North Atlantic ecosystem, throughout which Mark sits, head bent, book on knees, finger marking the page as if waiting to return to his reading.

When she stops talking, having pointed out that he may well have undermined his own future as well as hers, there is such a prolonged silence that she thinks he has fallen asleep. She begins to feel quite foolish. Towering over the slouched figure she wonders how much of her tirade the young woman at the desk has heard.

Eventually, without looking up, he says, "Not a fisherman on the water wouldn't tell you the same's in that report."

"Fishermen didn't tell—you did—and fishermen aren't the ones who will read the report," Lav snaps.

"No one ever reads our reports," he mutters.

"Obviously, someone read yours. Otherwise, why this sudden invasion by Wayne Drover?"

The name seems to bring him fully awake. "Wayne Drover—so that one got his slimy hands in the pie!"

He sits up straight, attentive, schoolboyish, ready to explain everything to the teacher, "That frigger's back and forth between here and Ottawa all the time—buttering up Timothy Drew's constituents, playing footsy with the Board of Trade, with anyone who'll do Drew a bit of good when election time rolls around—the university types, the church crowd, the Confederation Building boys—Drover's not a bit particular who he sucks up to. It all takes a lot of time but he loves it—grabs any excuse to come down here and play the king's messenger—'do' lunch with the lawyers and C.E.O.s, get invited to their cocktail parties, wine and dine their wives."

Lav has never heard such bitterness in anyone's voice. Why he hates Wayne Drover she cannot imagine, does not want to imagine. His anger drains hers, he seems very young—young and rash and perhaps a little crazy.

Mark stands, and clutching the heavy book to his chest as if it were a shield, gazes beyond her left shoulder and returns her lecture: "Wayne Drover knows all the right people, he's done them favours and they owe him favours. Never fear, the likes of him is losing no sleep over what a couple nobodies like us sent up to Ottawa. I knew if he got his paws on our report it'd be rendered useless—defused I think they call it."

When Lav interrupts to point out that it was not "our" report he sent to Ottawa, Mark ignores her.

"You'll like Drover," he says, "I've watched him work—he'll be ever so charming, ever so helpful. Before he even steps off the plane he'll have a new spin on our data—have it abridged, rationalized and deodorized, just like that stuff you spent the day reading—tarted up so it wouldn't hurt a fly much less a career civil-servant like yourself."

Lav can think of nothing to say. "We'll talk about this in the office," she tells him.

She is about to leave but he passes her the book he's been holding. "None of that was what I asked you to come here for—there's something I think you should see," he says.

The book is a ledger, on the leather cover, embossed in dulled gilt are the words "Ellsworth Brothers—Record of Shipping 1810 to...." The leather is worn through at the edges, the boards show. It is the kind of book Saul would have enjoyed repairing.

Mark turns the book over as he passes it—so that the blank back cover is facing upwards. It is a gesture that will, in memory take on a slow, almost ritualistic quality.

Years later Lav will think of herself standing like a novice in that low-ceilinged room, holding the open book and watching Mark Rodway's finger move down the stained page. Imagination again, imagination imposed over memory. She probably felt no premonitions as she peered down at the faded handwriting, seeing, just above Mark's finger, her own name—Lavinia Andrews—seeing it for the first time. She is pleased with the way it slopes hopefully upward away from the straight blue lines of the ledger.

Mark launches into a long, murmured explanation that Lav hardly hears. Something about looking through microfiche material on shipping in the main library, noting the Ellsworth Ledger listed as one of the source documents, deciding to have a look at the actual ledger, seeing that the shipping record ended in the fall of 1824 with not half of the book used, flipping to the back of the book, finding her name.

It occurs to Lav that Mark is more embarrassed about the document they are holding than he had been about his own treacherous report. She would like to know what has embarrassed this usually unflappable young man—could it be something he's read in the book?

She looks down at her name—Lavinia Andrews—written in a round, childish script. It is the name she had once wanted to be called, the name her mother steadfastly refused to use. On her first day of school Charlotte had conceded, in the face of a childish tantrum, that her daughter could be registered as Lav instead of Scrap—the hated name she had been called up to then.

"Is it possible to check this book out?" she asks.

"No—none of this stuff can be removed from the archive," Mark drops his hands from the ledger, reluctantly it seems, and steps back.

"Well then, I'll have to read it right here—maybe you'll let me have your chair," Lav moves around him to the straight backed wooden chair he has pushed up to the heating pipe. "How late does the archive stay open?"

"Two more hours."

She nods, says thank you, nods again. Mark doesn't move. Once again she tells him she expects him to be in the office tomorrow morning. "We'll talk then," she says, she even smiles. At last, somewhat reluctantly, he goes.

An awkward person. He must have expected something, some reaction she had not given—but what?

Lav dismisses Mark Rodway from her mind. Folding her coat into a cushion she sits down, tilting the chair back just as he had done. She is happy with this small, contained mystery, glad to be distracted from the larger, uncontained mysteries of fish and men. Pleased with the feel of the leather bound book, with its musty smell, with the square, solid weight of it on her knees. Lav rests her legs, unusually long for a woman, on the heating pipe and begins to read.

At first only her own name is legible. Then, slowly turning the pages, she deciphers other names: Meg, Ned, Ben—and the name of the place—Cape Random.

All the rest is a tangle of words, words crossing and criss-crossing, words over words, unrelated words twining, trailing between lines, twisting around margins, like a garden gone wild, a chaotic extravagance of flowers and weeds, shrubs, vegetables and bush, all growing together, covering every inch of paper.

She is almost ready to give up, to take herself home and to bed, to fortify herself for tomorrow. The book is half closed when her eye catches a fragment of sentence.

"...better off if Ellsworth hung Ned..." she reads—and words become voice. She hunkers down, tracking Lavinia's child-like hand, feeling along the stem, through the undergrowth, untangling her words from those others who have written around and over and through her story.

Much later when the smartly dressed attendant taps Lav on the shoulder, she has only gotten to the second page of the journal. Blinking myopically she swims up from the net of words, up through layers of years, up into fluorescent light and the faint smell of scorched rubber rising from her boots.

Lav has the impression that the librarian has been standing beside her for some time. Trying to assume a professional manner, she gets to her feet, explains that she has not finished, that she will have to take the Ellsworth Ledger with her.

That will be impossible, the young woman says. The archive contains only original documents and these cannot be removed. She might copy the section needed—but even that seems unnecessary since the material already exists on microfiche in the main library.

Turning the book so that the librarian can see the words "Ellsworth Journal" on the front cover, Lav explains that this material is invaluable—necessary for research she is doing on shipping in the 19th century. "I must have it in the original—I'll do whatever's necessary, sign for it, make a deposit." she produces a handful of plastic cards that identify her as a Canadian citizen, an Associate of the National Research Council, a contributor to Queen's Alumni Fund, an employee of the Department of Fisheries, a MasterCard holder, a member of some forgotten group called The Industry and Science Seminar, a volunteer at the National Gallery, a B positive blood donor.

The beautiful young woman will not be moved. She holds out her hand for the book, watches impassively as Lav struggles into her wrinkled coat, then walks her to the door.

Hearing the lock click behind her, Lav feels bereft—and guilty. She hesitates in the passageway, examining this feeling, thinking about the girl named Lavinia Andrews, about the family that may well be her family, wishing there was a way she could have taken the book home.

The journal has kept for more than a hundred and sixty years, it will keep until tomorrow. Even as she tells herself this, Lav knows she will have to go back, ask the librarian to keep the book on reserve. Of course no one can take it out, still, someone, maybe even Mark Rodway, might come in to read it. She knocks loudly on the door which is opened immediately by the attendant, obviously on her way out. With an air of one doomed to martyrdom she lets Lav back in, turns on the lights and makes out a "hold" card which she clips onto the book.

This time they leave together, walking in silence through deserted tunnels, up the echoing iron steps and out into the damp night. When Lav realizes that the attendant is walking, not to the parking lot but to a bus stop at the corner, she calls after her asking if she would like a lift.

The girl hesitates only a moment before coming over to the car. She smiles and shrugs, having dropped her official manner she seems much younger. "Might just as well—I probably missed the last bus on your account anyway," she says ungraciously—making Lav reflect that she must curb this impulse to give lifts to strangers.

Her name is Lori Sutton, a commerce student who has taken a night job in the archive. It's a good place to work, she tells Lav, hardly anyone comes in at night so it's easier to study than in the small flat she shares with two friends.

"On Saturdays I work in a shop in the Village Mall, they only pay minimum wage but I get a discount on clothes," she eyes Lav's rumpled coat and suggests she drop into the shop sometime. "We've got some beautiful coats in right now—that new shiny stuff—looks like satin but it's waterproof and don't wrinkle."

She continues her easy chatter, nodding to left or right as they come to intersections.

Lav is no longer listening. Her mind is filled with the image of a girl sitting beside the sea writing. She reflects on what she's just read, comparing Lavinia Andrews' arrival at Cape Random with the arrival her mother described. She speculates on how the Ellsworth Journal could have gotten into the Maritime Archives, remembers her mother's saying, "The child's father came from the Maritimes." Lav remembers playing with the word—merrytime, marrytime, maritimes...how romantic it had once sounded. She is dizzy with words, faint with hunger.

Lori Sutton shouts, "Stop!" and Lav manages to bring the car to a neck-jarring halt. Lori tells Lav she has just driven down a perpendicular hill and crossed three one-way streets—but it's all right, "We weren't caught and this is where I live."

They are parked in front of a row of narrow houses, all attached, all painted the same dark oily colour, each house has three concrete steps leading up to a peeling door.

Lori points at a house identical to its neighbours, "See, up there—that's our flat—the one on top. Next month we'll get drapes for that window. We're getting mats this month. It's a nice place, really—see how we even got a little balcony by the window!"

Lav glances up at the third storey, at the bright, uncurtained window looking out on a rickety wooden fire escape, knowing that what she sees is not what the girl beside her sees. Lav wonders if she had ever in her life been so young, so pleased with herself, so confident?

Having pointed out her apartment, Lori Sutton shows no sign of going into it. She leans back and continues the story Lav has missed the beginning of, "...but I couldn't see any sense to marryin' a fisherman—so I broke up with him. There's no life in Chance Harbour, no life and no fun. I tell ya girl, a person can't live without a bit of fun—a bit of fun and a bit of life around 'em. Now here in town there's always somethin' goin' on day and night," Lori gestured to the dingy street.

While Lori talks Lav looks at the street, which is empty except for two leather jacketed teenagers lounging on the steps of a house four doors down. Street lights cast an ominous mauve glow, barely penetrating the fog that seems to rise from the gritty sidewalks, from the filthy snow piled around each pole. On the opposite side of the street six boarded-up houses await demolition. A billboard proclaiming "Luxury apartments now renting" has been covered with fluorescent graffiti of the most unimaginative kind.

"Why not marry a fisherman?" Lav asks.

The question brings such an incredulous look to the pert little face that Lav wants to laugh—does laugh.

"What? Marry a fisherman—marry a fisherman and miss all this!"

Lori Sutton is enthralled, captivated by this place where streets exist, where there are sidewalks and street-lights, where there are jobs, money, men and little flats for girls such as herself—clever girls, girls brave enough to leave Chance Harbour.

The young woman radiates impatience, is frantic to learn everything and to learn it as fast as possible. She says so: "I got to catch up on the townies," she says with a laugh, ticking off the things she must catch up on: the proper way to talk, what clubs to go to, how to make salads from things she's never eaten, how to recognize the right kind of music. She must learn the names of popular musicians, learn how to paint her eyes, how to make money, how to choose wine, choose dresses, choose carpets, furniture—men.

Lav finds herself thinking uncharitable thoughts about Lori Sutton, wondering if she is this frank with everyone. She concludes that this young woman cannot be as ingenuous as she seems, has probably calculated the appeal of unguarded enthusiasm.

"...I wasted my first year— hardly left residence. I was a real mouse, but that was before I met Kim and Treese—before I got into Commerce and started going out with Darren...."

Lori has noticed Mark Rodway and is interested, "I saw you talkin' to him—he's gorgeous! I'm still not sure how serious I am about Darren. Anyway, he's up in Lab City on a work-term right now—besides, there's no harm in keepin' an eye out for prospects...."

She finally runs down. Momentarily self-conscious, perhaps regretting her frankness, she thanks Lav politely and gets quietly out of the car. As Lav watches the girl go into the shabby house it occurs to her that the conversation has been very like the one she hoped to have with the witch-woman she picked up on Signal Hill—a lesson on survival in this damp and dismal place.

As she turns the car around and retraces her way through the labyrinth of one way streets, Lav is not thinking of Lavinia Andrews the journal woman, nor of Wayne Drover the man from Ottawa, but of Lori Sutton and her philosophy.

"I tell ya, girl, a person can't live without a bit of fun—a bit of fun and a bit of life around 'em," she repeats the words aloud. Tired as she is they make her smile.

four

The power of imagination over memory, the power of choice over forgetfulness. Lav is sure, or tells herself she is sure, she has not imagined her past. She would like to be sure she has not forgotten important parts of it—but knows this to be untrue. She has forgotten—and deliberately.

In the days before the arrival of Wayne Drover the office takes on a life of its own. Under Alice's supervision desks, computers and filing cases, magically filled with files, roll into place. Melba, the smoker, is installed in the general office and the ragged collection of blue books is packed away in acid-free cartons.

On Wednesday Wayne Drover arrives, hurrying towards her, hand outstretched, saying "I'm only here to help," or has she imagined these words to fulfil Mark's prediction?

Trailing him are two younger men who look like junior auditors. Lav does not go towards them but waits in the doorway of her office.

She estimates Wayne Drover to be in his late thirties—probably a year or two younger than she is—and an inch or two shorter. His hair, longer than is fashionable, is untidy, his tie is loose. He carries an oversized briefcase, which, with his billowing trench coat, gives him the appearance of taking up more space than he does. It also makes the men behind him look tidier, smaller, more buttoned-down than they probably are.

"Wayne Drover and team," he announces, turning aside to plant a loud kiss on the cheek of Alice O'Reilly who, smiling and blushing, kisses him back.

Before Lav has time to register surprise at this he is shaking her hand, "Glad to meet you, Dr. Andrews—your friend in Policy and Programs suggested I drop by," looking straight into her eyes he smiles. His face is round and guileless.

"Have you read that preliminary report?" She asks this without a smile or a word of welcome. Mark was wrong about one thing—she is not going to like Wayne Drover.

"Not really," he says and follows her, standing in the doorway of her office, surveying the room. "Cheap furniture," he says, and indeed the sofa groans as he throws himself down on its dusty-rose cushions.

Lav goes to sit behind her desk, as far from him as she can get. Political appointees like Wayne Drover, Philip used to call them information managers, consider it a handicap to know what is contained in the packages they manage, and so, knowing what the answer will be, she asks if he would like to see their material.

"Wouldn't do any good. I'm no scientist—I'm taking Dr. Farman's opinion that the report you sent up to Ottawa is wrong, dead wrong. 'Basically flawed' was what Dr. Farman said—that's good enough for me. Mind?" he is patting his pockets in that absentminded way smokers search for cigarettes.

"There'll be an election this summer, you know—and I don't think the old man got the chance of a snowball in hell—people are barely over our givin' that extra quota of cod to the French, now they're all aflap about selling spawny caplin to the Japanese—spawny caplin for Christ's sake! We used to dump 'em on the gardens!"

He has found a cigar. "Mind?" he asks, lights before Lav has a chance to reply and smokes in silence for several minutes.

"Could be handled, of course. Could be controlled—most things can be if a minister sticks to his script. Trouble is, the old man won't what's more, he gets snotty with reporters. And if Timothy Drew goes, half the transfer payments coming down here goes with him—a dozen federal projects—all this!" He waves at the cheap furniture, cigar ash fluttering around his cherubic face. It is not clear what will be gone—the room, Lav, the Oceans 2000 project, the building—perhaps the entire province.

"Still, I'm an optimist!" abruptly he changes track, veers off in another direction. "The last optimist, that's me! An endangered species—I should be protected," he grins, "but then, where would they find another optimist for me to mate with?"

Recharged by his own wit he sits up and grinds his cigar into the pristine ash tray. "Who knows? Maybe Good Old Tim'll pull it off one more time—people owe him, lots of people owe him. Maybe he can convince the PM to have a word with them Europeans—keep in your own yard or we'll stop drinkin' your booze! Not worth much really, but a nice gesture—good copy. Then too, voters have short memories and that's all to the good!" He jumps up, walks to the window and stands looking out at the cliff face.

The man is a surprise, cruder that Lav had expected, more obvious. Neither intimidated nor charmed, she asks what he's come for.

"I'm no dummy about fish, Dr. Andrews. I may not have a doctorate in marine biology but I know more about fish than you'll ever find out by staring at scraps of cod gut from some little cove up on the northeast coast."

Wayne Drover does not turn around but his voice is cold and she knows his face has changed again. "I was born on the seaward side of those cliffs. My father fished outta' the Battery fifty years. Dawn 'till dark for fifty years—and he never made more than nine thou a year in his life. Stunned bugger!"

"Still and all, that's not what you want to know, is it? You want to know why I'm here," he turns to face her, beaming down, benign, boyish, sincere. "I'm here to help you prepare the Oceans 2000 Report. Not just me, of course—Tony Mallard and Keith, too—and a few others in three or four weeks time when we're ready to decide on presentation, layout—that kind of thing."

Lav protests, such a deadline is impossible, no fair assessment of the material can be made in three or four weeks—nor in eight or nine weeks. She mentions acoustic surveys that have not been graphed, material still coming in, blue books filled with uncoded data.

Wayne Drover doesn't seem to hear a word. When she has finished he walks towards the door, still smiling, shaking his head. "The Minister will be in Washington in May, after that he's coming straight up here. Big announcement, press conference, policy report on the fisheries—the works!"

She reminds him that she's been promised six months, maybe a year, in which to complete the final report—but he will not listen.

"Look, love, we'll be into an election long before then. Now I'm supposed to torment the life out of you—breathe down your neck night and day—but if we understand one another that won't be necessary. My boys will look after everything—analyze your material, compare it with other studies, even write a good first draft—that's what they're trained to do. So let's just relax and see what the experts come up with, shall we?"

Wayne Drover pauses with his hand on her office door. "Any questions?" he asks and looks relieved when Lav shakes her head. "That's it, then—now that you know how important this report is to Mr. Drew—and to me—I'll leave you to it."

And he does. Depositing his briefcase in the office next to hers, he vanishes.

For a day or two Lav ignores his directions. Applying herself to the data, she begins a review of everything she, Mark and Alice have done. She is soon discouraged. Tony Mallard and Keith Laing do not need her help, in fact, make it clear that they want her to leave them alone. Mark is rarely seen, Alice and Melba Summers, overwhelmed with the reams of paper being circulated by the men from Ottawa, implore Lav to ask for another assistant.

Lav's own working day shrinks. There is nothing for her to do. Soon she is leaving the office at noon, is spending most of the day at the university. Things she would have spent hours mulling over a few weeks ago—the constant busyness of Wayne Drover's assistants, their prolonged conference calls to which she is not invited, Mark's frequent absences, a chatty phone call from Ian Farman, his casual inquiries about how things are going—now seem unimportant.

Supperless, sometimes lunchless, she drives daily to the university, hurrying through cavernous tunnels to the unpleasant room that houses the Maritime Archives. The place is hot and airless, the Ellsworth Journal heavy and awkward to hold, but she is determined to find out everything the book can tell her about the Andrews family and Cape Random.

The careful script has quickly deteriorated into an uneven scrawl, Lavinia's letters becoming more and more illegible as they climb the page. There are many misspellings and many words scratched over. Sometimes complete lines are obliterated.

Lav learns to read like a blind person, using her fingertips to trace pen ridges along the underside of the heavy paper. She forgets her resolve to stay fit, stiffness develops in her neck, a dull ache in her left shoulder. The lovely toffee colour fades from her hair. She becomes more and more frustrated with the discomfort of the archive. She wants to give herself up to the book, to read without the distractions of a hard chair, of hot feet and a freezing back. Each night she tries to convince Lori Sutton to let her take the journal home.

"You know I would if 'twas up to me," the young woman has become familiar, seems to regard Lav's persistent requests to take the book as a kind of running joke.

Lori Sutton and Lav are almost friends, observers of each other, anthropologist and subject—though which is which would be hard to say. The young woman watches the older with a kind of puzzled condescension—trying to place Lav in the social order she is arranging.

Lav, for her part, watches Lori with fascination, intrigued with the process by which people invent and reinvent themselves. Why has she herself never learned this trick? The girl reminds Lav of her mother. How soft I've always been, how malleable, how conforming to any role life has assigned to me, Lav thinks.

But it is the journal that now occupies most of Lav's time and thought. Slowly, carefully, as she feels her way through Lavinia's story—avoiding the contradictory comments: "No!" and "I did not!" that spring up from the ends of sentences, ignoring the vine-like border that encircles almost every page, encroaching on the writing in a maze of curlicues, of maddening loops and swirls—the Cape Random people begin to be more real to Lav than Lori Sutton or the people at the Research Station. At home, after the archive has closed, she begins to draw a chart of the Andrews family.

One morning Alice O'Reilly passed Lav a note, "Mr. Drover was here yesterday, he left this."

Alice has become formal. She disapproves of Lav's new hours, is contemptuous of her for having given up authority without a struggle, for her continued laxness toward Mark Rodway. Alice lets those feelings be known without ever uttering a word.

So be it, Lav thinks as she reads the note, a command couched as a question—can Wayne Drover drop by her office at five thirty?

It is almost six before he arrives. Lav pretends to be reading, feigns surprise to find him standing beside her desk, smiling, asking how things are going. "Fine," she tells him, "Just fine," and he opens his briefcase and takes out a bottle of Scotch.

"We'll drink to that, Doctor Andrews—drink to everything being fine. Then I'll take you out for the best supper you'll ever eat."

The lack of response does not bother Wayne Drover. He searches in his huge briefcase and produces two glasses—large, thick glasses that carry a golf club logo. He looks happier, better groomed than when he first arrived—someone, doubtless some woman, is taking care of him.

How did she get into marine biology, he asks.

"By magnetic force," Lav wants to say. "Because of the power beneath the earth, the power beneath the sea, because of poetry and bookbinding, because of secrets...."

Instead she gives the expected answer—an interest in science, love of marine life. How, she asks, had he come to be executive assistant to the Minister of Fisheries?

"Oh, I got tangled up with the Drews when I was still in high school. Got a job working with Drew Construction one summer, renovatin' a building on the Southside—Drew's fish packing business—Ocean North it was called then. The family had just taken it over. That's how I first met Timothy Drew—he slipped all us students an extra twenty on the last payday—always good to their people the Drews were—anyone'll tell you that."

They drink and chat. At dinner he returns to the story of his summer with Drew Construction. Lav can see he enjoys talking about the Drews. Speculating on how a family acquires money and power is, for Wayne Drover, endlessly fascinating.

"We did a good job that summer, modernizing the Southside plant. The place operated hunky-dory for a long time—then Ocean North got tangled up with a Japanese company," he ticks each step off on his fingers. "Far East Cod sold the place to a group of St. John's lawyers—they had a government loan—was them that mothballed the plant. Been boarded up for years now—but the old man got his eye on the place—got this new company, Green Valley Holdings, based in Tennessee. Perhaps we can put a package together—you know, government backing, draggers, fish quotas, export licences, all that stuff!" Wayne Drover hums softly.

He is completely unselfconscious, uninterested in her opinions or background, so self-absorbed that he expects no disapproval and requires no praise.

After that he begins dropping by Lav's office every Friday after work. He is just the company I need, she thinks, just the person to keep me from vanishing into the journal, disappearing on Cape Random.

At work the whole ambience has changed. Wayne Drover is rarely seen but his underlings, Keith Laing and Tony Mallard, have taken complete charge. These two, so ambitious, so alert, so focused, have swept Mark aside. Uneasy and out of place he sulks in corners.

Alice tells Mark he looks like a wet rooster and, when it becomes obvious that Lav will not, tries to keep him occupied with mundane jobs: collecting mail, making coffee, sending off the dispatches that go hourly to Ottawa—communiques Lav does not read but which Mark tells her all end with the instructions, "Check!" or "Verify!"

Mark does not mention the archive or the journal. He and Lav never have their serious talk—it seems pointless—his report has been forgotten. They have both been replaced.

In a part of the journal written by someone called Thomas Hutchings, Lav discovers the name Drew and other names she recognizes. In contrast to Lavinia's erratic penmanship, Thomas Hutchings has written in a consistent, beautiful copperplate. Unfortunately, sometime in the years since, dampness has seeped into the book, diluting the ink and causing it to disappear entirely near the outer edges of many pages.

Lav searches for, and finds, a magnifying glass—everything exists somewhere in the Martins' house—and takes it to the archive. As she squints through it at the spider-like scribbles weaving in and out, between and around the lines, she finds a third story—a story that is not Lavinia Andrews' nor Thomas Hutchings'—a text existing beside the official text.

She recalls Saul telling her that such jottings are called marginalia—a beautiful word. In the marginalia Lav finds Mary Bundle. There is something about Mary's voice, so strong, so determined, that she is lost and stays hunched over the book until closing time.

Again that night Lav and Lori Sutton leave together. Having been in the archive since noon she is hungry and invites the young woman back to her house for a late supper. While Lav breaks eggs and grates cheese she is aware of Lori walking from room to room, standing, as if in a gallery, before some object that interests her, studying it from one angle, then from another, stepping back to appraise it through half closed eyes.

"You got some nice things," Lori says when they sit down to eat and for the first time Lav can detect a trace of respect in the younger woman's eyes.

"Nothing in the house is mine—even the pictures and books belong to the Martins—the people who own the house."

"But I bet you got—you have," Lori often corrects herself, "have things just as nice in Ottawa."

Lav nods. She has told the girl nothing about herself, has never spoken of Charlotte or Philip, of her work, or of Wayne Drover—never said why she spends so many hours in the archive.

"I've got a plan a schedule," Lori says. "I'm giving myself three years—one year to finish my degree and two years to get into a good job. By 1990 I'll have a place like this, and a business card. Do you have a business card?"

Why are we so curious about one another? Lav wonders. Why do I find the girl's unabashed ambition attractive—would I if she were old, or ugly, or male? What a pair she and Wayne Drover would make! The thought is followed by a twinge of jealousy that disconcerts Lav, and she asks Lori if she will go back home when she graduates.

"Good Lord, no!" Lori is appalled at such ignorance. "What would I go back there for? Nobody goes home to Chance Harbour after university—there's not a thing back there except fish."

Lori is quick—sees the thought that flickers across Lav's mind. "Oh sure! Fish is fine for the likes of you! Lookin' at fish through microscopes or readin' nice clean print-outs about fish. You don't have to haul it over the side of a boat, don't have to stand in a freezing fish plant—everything covered in slime—and pull guts outta' fish eight hours a day. I wouldn't mind workin' with fish in a lab in Ottawa—or on the Toronto stock exchange, now that'd be a great place to work—saw it the other night on tv—all the good lookin' men in white shirts with their jackets off and their cuffs folded back—some sexy!"

She becomes serious, "No one goes back to Chance Harbour, girl. Not if they can get a job somewhere else. Oh it's a pretty enough place in summertime, you should see people from away sayin' how nice it is when they visit—and it is, too—all sea and sky and green hills—but you can't live on that, can you? 'Tis something else in February with a nor'east gale comin' in the cove and not able to see a hand before your face for blowin' snow. No, Chance Harbour is no place to go back to. Me mother says the same—she's the one drilled into me that I had to get away—most of the women tell their daughters that. Who wouldn't after six weeks on some friggin' winter make-work project? I seen me mother down by the breakwater movin' rocks around by hand, another time she was cooped up in the school every night tryin' to learn typing she knew she'd never use." For a moment Lori seems on the verge of tears but she swallows, eats the last bit of omelette and asks Lav why she doesn't make herself known to her relations.

Lav doesn't understand what the girl means.

"Well, you said your father was a Newfoundlander—maybe you've got people here—why don't you make yourself known to them?"

"I don't think so—I hadn't even considered it. My father died in the war, before I was born, and I've never had contact with any of his family."

"For all that there'd be people here belongs to you," Lori is her businesslike self again. "You'd have no trouble trackin' your people down—just say you're tracin' your family tree. Mainlanders are down here doin' that all the time. Know your grandfather's name?" she asks, already leafing through the phone book.

"My grandfather's name was Ki—short for Hezekiah. My father's name was David," Lav tells her, casually as if she has spoken those names a million times.

"Well there you are, then! All you got to do is phone someone with the same name. I bet there's Hezekiahs in this book—there's still a good many of them old names around—I was named Dolores, for God's sake!"

She looks up from her search long enough to give Lav a half-ashamed smile. "Anyone 'round here'll tell you if they're related. Let's see, Anderson, Andres, Andrews—Sweet Lord, there's dozens of 'em!"

"You've been reading Lavinia's journal!" suddenly realizing this must be so, Lav snatches the phone book from the young woman's hands, pushes it back on the shelf.

"I'm sorry," Lori says but looks only slightly contrite. "I hoped you wouldn't mind—it was just that I got so curious about what you're reading all this time. Do you mind?"

"No—no, of course not. The Ellsworth Journal is public property after all." This is a lie, of course. She does mind, in fact Lav hates the idea that the journal should be available to Lori Sutton—to any curious person who comes along.

Tired of the girl, of her inquisitive little face, her reaching hands, Lav stacks the dishes and offers, too quickly, to drive her home.

Later, absently watching the news (always the same these days—clips of various men walking into meeting rooms, pausing sometimes in doorways to say that no, they have no comment, really, no comment at this time) Lav finds herself leafing through the St. John's phone book, reading down the list of Andrews names, dialing a randomly picked number, calmly asking some stranger if he knows of any Cape Random Andrews.

On her third call a man listed as Clarence K. Andrews, unsurprised by her question, tells her: "We people are Port de Grave Andrews—yer crew'd be the Bonavista North Andrews. But I'll tell you now the best one for you to get hold of'd be Stephen Andrews' boy—him that owns that place down in Davisporte."

At that point he calls over his shoulder, "Marg, Marg—you mind the name of that Andrews feller got the place we stayed at down in Davisporte?"

In a second he is back telling her that Young Alf Andrews owns a place, Lav gathers it is a motel, the man seems to have an aversion to the word, called Cat Harbour Inn.

"You'll be able to get the number from Information. 'Tis a queer old name but the place is respectable for all that," he says, and after wishing her every success hangs up.

Lori is right, it's not hard to find your people in Newfoundland.

But she does not want to call Alf Andrews—at least not yet. She is afraid to commit herself to relatives, living people who cannot be put back on the shelf should she grow tired or be repulsed by them. The knowledge that she is such a coward depresses her.

Still, she falls asleep thinking how pleasant it would be to own the journal, to have it here in the house. The next morning Lav swims up from dreams of fish with a plan to steal the journal blueprinted on her mind. From then on, stealing the journal is the last thing she thinks of before sleep, the first thing she thinks of each morning.

five

"Here's to Oceans 2000—the final draft!" Wayne Drover clicks his glass against Lav's.

They are in Lav's office, having their usual end-of-the-week drink before going to eat. Friday is now the only full day she spends at work—a fact she is sure has not escaped Wayne's notice.

Lav has come to enjoy his company, discovered that when relaxed Wayne Drover has a kind of naive innocence completely at odds with his usual abrasive manner.

"We'll go somewhere special tonight—next Friday we'll be having a little wrap-up party at the office—and the following Monday the Minister'll be in town for the Oceans 2000 presentation. Next week'll be hell!" Wayne is pacing, pleased at the prospect, the many strings he will pull before next Monday coiled inside him waiting to spring.

Lav does not comment. She has long since stopped objecting to Wayne's deadlines, relinquished all ownership of the project she is technically in charge of.

"You should read our final report," he tells her. "After all, your team did the groundwork, and when you get back to Ottawa you'll be expected to be familiar with it."

He stands in front of her desk, staring down at her: "What do you want to do when you go back? Want me to put in a word in the right places?"

She is dismayed by his question. What do I want to do when I go back? Gripping her glass she avoids his sober, judging gaze and stares past him out the window at the cliff. It is still light outside, late April, the days getting longer. It has not occurred to her that she will not be here through the summer.

The silence goes on for some time until Wayne realizes there will be no answer. He shakes his head, "People who don't know what they want never get it," he says. Then he shrugs, smiles, "Come on, this might be our last supper—I know a special place."

The special place turns out to be a restaurant set up in a beautiful old house that had once belonged to the Drew family.

"The Drews always had big families, sent their children to private schools, travelled, acquired a taste for beautiful things," Wayne tells her, pointing to the mahogany panelled doors, the Gibbons-like carving above the mantels, the marquetry along the front of a sideboard.

"Fact is, they owned half the town, rows of houses, shops, newspapers, factories and fish plants—shoes and ships and sealing fleets and councillors and kings." He likes the phrase and repeats it, "Shoes and ships and sealing fleets and councillors and kings—they still own a good bit of St. John's—of Newfoundland for that matter."

She has never told Wayne what she knows about the Drew family, about the part of their story written into Lavinia's journal by Mary, nor does she now. She has no desire to talk. The question he has posed is still echoing through her head, what will she do when she returns to Ottawa? To keep her future out of the discussion, to keep from talking about herself, Lav asks if the Drews are still fish merchants.

"Na—none of their money comes from fish these days, at least not directly. But every time anyone here buys a can of milk or a bottle of booze, every time we switch on a light or an oven, or even sign a petition for an environmental impact study, we're making a small contribution to the Drew empire. Today, of course, the Drew name is probably not even on the letterhead—but you can bet some uncle, some lawyer cousin or ne'er-do-well in-law got a finger in every Newfoundland pie from Hibernia to Hydro, from Doreen's Decorating to Dickie Dunn's taxi."

He smiles across the table, the smile implies knowledge of all the Drew secrets, "I, Wayne Drover, am as important as family, as necessary as graft to the Drews!" the smile says. And Lav wonders, not for the first time, why he lets her see these things about him—and why he has any need for her company.

"But enough of that old stuff! Eat up, maid, the boys are workin'!" he nods at her plate, refills her wine glass, asks if she knows anything about folk music.

When Lav shakes her head he proceeds to instruct her on the subject. Quoting from old ballads he traces the roots of Newfoundland music back to pre-Elizabethan courtiers and Irish bards. He has, he tells her, collected old broadsheets for years. To her utter astonishment—ignoring the waiter standing nearby, ignoring the regal, grey-haired couple seated in the corner—he begins to sing.

> As I walked forth in the pride of the season,
> Thinking some pastime there for to see,
> Who should I spy but a lovely fair damsel,
> Sitting alone 'neath a green willow tree....

Wayne Drover has a pleasing voice, he sings softly, holding his glass against his white shirt, staring down into the wine.

Lav feels relaxed, happy. Why grieve for the past or worry for the future when one can sit surrounded by beautiful things, can sip wine, eat good food—can, in the soft glow of candlelight, have a man sing you a lament about love and betrayal under green willow trees?

When they leave the restaurant Wayne suggests they go downtown, find some live music. He is still full of energy. It is a mild evening, they can walk, he says.

Down over the hill it's cooler, Lav can smell the harbour, feel the salt mist. Yet people lounge in doorways and the narrow sidestreets are crowded with university students moving from pub to pub in noisy, laughing groups. Most of the merrymakers are much younger than Lav or Wayne—and so is their music. They linger at one or two places, have a drink, Wayne waves to several people but never settles or stops to talk.

Lav expects to encounter Lori Sutton but they do not—maybe the girl works on Friday nights. In one bar they catch sight of Mark Rodway. He is squashed into a corner beside a pale blonde. Wayne sees Mark too, waves and smiles, "That laddeo got his own agenda, wouldn't trust him far as I could throw him," he tells Lav.

Back near the restaurant where they had left their cars Wayne stops under a street light, "Don't s'pose you're an optimist by any chance, Lav Andrews?" he asks.

The mist has turned to fog, so thick that they seem to be standing inside a hollow cloud. Fingers of fog, moist with sea salt, brush Lav's face and catch in her hair. She finds herself thinking that she probably looks quite nice. She is relaxed, slightly tipsy.

But she understands what he is asking, "I'll take a taxi home—there must be a phone in there," she says and turns, walking quickly down the side lane towards the restaurant.

He catches up to her, "Hey Lav—don't you tie green ribbons in your hair? Lie down under shady green trees?" He walks by her side, not touching her, not even turning to look at her.

"No, no I don't. I don't think many people do these days," she says matter-of-factly. The question seems so impersonal that she has no feeling of rejecting him.

"Oh," he says, thinking it over, "Too bad—yes—yes, I suppose you're right."

A fog-horn moans out and he stops again, listening, "Isn't that the grandest sound you ever heard? Sometimes I think I'll get one rigged up on my deck in Ottawa. I did tape that fog-horn on CBC radio—you know, the one on the special report for mariners and ships at sea."

He imitates the CBC voice, "'Freezing spray tonight off the Funk Island Banks. Navigation light number 046 off Gunners Rock is out. Drifting wreckage has been sighted east of Bankero'—wonderful stuff—better than poetry." Wayne Drover shakes his head at his own foolishness. He seems to have forgotten his proposition, if such it had been.

They walk on through the damp silence. Lav resisting the impulse to take his hand—the gesture would be misinterpreted.

That night, lying in bed planning the theft of the journal, she is aware of the foghorn's wail drifting up from the harbour. She will miss the sound. Were there foghorns on the Cape? If so why had Lavinia never mentioned them? What sounds had the Cape Random people heard—sea sounds and storm sounds, birds singing perhaps? Her mind moves back and forth between past and present. As she sinks into sleep, faintly, below the plaintive wail Lav hears a man's voice, he is singing about love and fair damsels sitting under shady green trees—the song is familiar and for a moment she is on the Cape, is Lavinia Andrews dancing around a fire, pining for Thomas Hutchings.

The next morning, driving through thick fog to the archive, she hears the foghorn and remembers herself in that moment before sleep when she had merged into Lavinia's skin, known Lavinia's body and Lavinia's longing as her own. The mixing of dreams and reality—the idea frightens her. Is it better to have no history or an imagined one?

What am I doing here? Lav asks herself. Why am I neglecting work to read about people long dead? Why do I phone people I have never met, people I never want to meet—confusing the past with the present—lay plans to steal some bedraggled old book no one in their right mind would want!

She turns the car around. She will not go to the archive. Vowing to forget the journal she drives to the Research Station.

During the next few days Lav weans herself back to reality. She pays bills, gets her hair done, listens to the news. She pretends involvement in the controlled confusion that engulfs the office in advance of the Minister's visit.

She sets herself to read the final version of the Oceans 2000 report, peruses the mass of papers Alice has piled on her desk: lists of events planned for the Minister's weekend, a speech at the Board of Trade luncheon, an interview with the local paper and another on national television, a quiet chat with the Premier, dinner at the university, a side trip, with photographers, to Petty Harbour. Items are added daily.

Other memos contain details of the major event of the visit, a ministerial press conference that will launch the Oceans 2000 report. These memos, many of them written by Wayne, outline everything from accommodations for national reporters to what questions Timothy Drew will find acceptable.

Suddenly Wayne is everywhere, perched on her desk explaining some point in the report, jabbing at a print-out as it sputters from the machine, pacing the hallway with consultants, yelling instructions over the telephone to his Ottawa office, slashing red lines through page after page of typescript.

Every day now new people arrive, people without surnames—Jay, the American, who says he is a writer, a stunningly beautiful photographer who wears white silk blouses and tight jeans, Clive the English graphic artist and three people calling themselves media consultants.

Surrounded by all this artistic busyness, Mark, Melba, and even Alice fetch and carry, and somewhat grimly arrange the office party Wayne decrees they must have before the Minister arrives.

To Lav none of it matters in the least.

Faced with the emptiness of her days, the doom-laden dreams of her nights, Lav becomes depressed. The life she is leading is not enough—she misses the

Cape, misses the Andrews and Vincents. She even misses Lori Sutton. She is lonely. She phones her mother.

Charlotte's voice is brisk, crackling across six thousand miles, ordering her daughter to get off the island at once. She is lost if she doesn't, her mother says.

Listening to Charlotte explain why this is so, Lav realizes that in some strange way Newfoundland is the source of her mother's strength—a place of mythical horror, a great, dismal swamp from which no traveller returns—no one but her—who, with the resourcefulness of Odysseus managed to rescue herself from this nether world. It was, Lav thinks, Charlotte's first and greatest victory—the one that made anything seem possible.

Lav hangs up. First pointing out that after three months her mother has not asked her one question about her work, about Philip—about herself. Shouting that her mother is a self-centred bitch, she slams down the telephone.

The office party begins badly. Wayne makes what he refers to as his Excelsior Speech, giving them all an overview of the Oceans 2000 project: "This most definitive body of research related to the North Atlantic fishery ever compiled, Oceans 2000 challenges us to increase harvesting operations to the maximum possible level."

"A golden era for the Atlantic Provinces—the most exciting plan ever put forth by any government for ocean management and global competitiveness"—sentences honed and polished for tomorrow's presentation to the press.

He goes on to outline Timothy Drew's career, quotes from his speeches—most of which have been written by Wayne himself. He tells them that the Minister is, at this moment, attending an international U.N.-sponsored World Oceans Conference in New York. Sometime today the President of the United States will address the Conference, he will say nice things about Canada, about Mr. Drew—he might even mention Oceans 2000!

All this will hit newspapers across the world tonight, will still be a hot story on Monday morning when the Minister flies into St. John's. "I tell you, when he gets here he'll be followed by reporters from across the country, from Washington, too. The place'll be crawling with politicians and bureaucrats—each with their little retinue of fund-raisers, scientists, secretaries and assorted consultants!" Wayne is jubilant, he pauses to acknowledge a cheer from the three media experts.

"By noon tomorrow every hotel room in this town will be filled with big spenders—please the Board of Trade boys to no end, that will. So will Oceans 2000! Spin-off from this incentive will bring big federal grants, funding for research on production, on marketing, funding for a five-million dollar study on the feasibility of that international landing and distribution port we've been talking about for years—funding for fisherman, for factories, for longliners, for marine-related courses at the university!"

Wayne Drover leans back, fingertips pressed into a tower under his chin, he beams at his people, "You should all be proud—I tell you there's no one won't be happy with this report!"

A male voice coming from the back mutters, "Your report is a crock!"

The smile drops from Wayne's face, he hunches forward, "What was that?"

"This report is a crock and you know it!" Mark Rodway's voice is still low but the words are quite clear.

Wayne turns white with anger. Lav expects him to jump up and punch the young man.

But he controls himself. "Oh grow up, for God's sake!" he tells Mark. "At your age we all want to make a name for ourselves—I can understand that—but this job is not the one you're gonna do it on. This one is for Timothy Drew—a man who's done more for the likes of you than you'll ever know!" he looks around the room, focusing on each one of them. "Timothy Drew is gonna get reelected 'cause if he don't everyone in this room—everyone on this island is up shit creek!"

"You're a liar, Drover—a liar and a brown noser!" Mark is shouting across the room. "You worship Drew and Drew's money and you'll do anything to please him...." The young man seems on the verge of tears.

People are embarrassed—emotion does not belong in a government office. The beautiful photographer is distressed, she leans towards Mark, touches his arm, whispers something in his ear and they leave together.

Wayne is smiling again, smiling all around, "So!" he rubs his hands together, stands and shaking hands as he goes, starts for the bar that has been set up in the reception area. "There'll be no time for fun and games after tonight—so let's party!"

Lav knows she should leave. Things are nagging at the back of her mind, a fur-ball of unpleasant thoughts, of suspicion, a feeling of discomfort and betrayal. Everything and everyone in this room is wrong—the lights are wrong, the faces wrong, the music someone has switched on is wrong—and Wayne Drover's report, she is now sure, is disastrously wrong.

Or are these forebodings something she has imposed upon the scene? She looks blasé, hardly disconcerted at all, as she stands sipping her drink, watching Mark Rodway leave. His outburst confirms the hostility, the basic surliness she has always sensed in him.

By now the rest of the DFO building is empty. The media consultants troop off down the hall, returning with chairs they have appropriated from other offices. People sit, drink and talk, Mark is forgotten, the Oceans 2000 report is forgotten.

The conversation becomes animated, ranging over a variety of subjects: the quality and quantity of the wine, the unbearable spring weather in both Ottawa and St. John's, advances in colour printing, the cost and wisdom of buying Canadian art, bilingualism, multiculturalism—and by this circuitous route shifts to a discussion of the contrasting cultures of provinces, more particularly of Quebec and Newfoundland.

"Newfies and Quebecois are just alike—neurotic as hell!" the man named Jay says. Alice and Wayne, being natives, try to moderate, dousing little arguments that spring up behind this statement.

Jay is right, one of the consultants maintains. He has been in Newfoundland before—flown in from Texas by an oil company after the Ocean Ranger disaster, damage control job—"Look," he says, "Newfies got bigger chips on their shoulders than niggers!"

Alice stands up and announces that she is going home before the Newfie jokes start. After she leaves everyone feels slightly guilty. There is a deliberate change of subject. The talk turns to places they have worked, projects and people they might have in common.

Lav has hardly spoken all evening. She is possessed by a terrible lethargy. What will I do? Where will I go when I stand up? she asks herself. And what about tomorrow and the next day?

She continues to sit—as the people around her run out of things to say, as the conversation winds down, as one by one they leave.

At last only Wayne, the Englishman and Lav remain, drinking, not talking.

"What shits Jay and Desmore are!" the Englishman says quietly.

But Wayne is not concerned, "Oh well—takes all kinds!" He gets to his feet and begins to pull on his coat, "Let's go find some solid food."

Clive says he can't. He still has to talk to the printers about the cover of the report.

Wayne's attention is immediately focused, "You don't mean to tell me the covers are not printed yet!"

"Not to mind, old chap—all is under control. They're working overtime—I want the covers plasticized."

Lav hears herself giggling. She has never heard anyone speak the way Clive does, like a stage Englishman.

Wayne gives her a sharp look, "Come on, both of you, we'll get soup and sandwiches down at the hotel. Then you can come back here and Lav and I'll find something to do—won't we, old girl?" Wayne mimics Clive.

Wayne is in high good humour. After they eat he wants to go on, to make the rounds of downtown pubs but Clive says no, no he must really get back—just in case there's a cockup.

"His heart's in the right place but with that accent he's likely to end up in the harbour if he tries bossin' a St. John's printer," Wayne says as the Englishman leaves. "We'll have one drink, then I'm going to take you somewhere interesting," he tells Lav.

Although it is already late she does not object. The hotel lounge is empty of people but comfortably filled with shadows and soft music. Beyond the tall windows, ribbons of light shimmer across the black harbour, waft in lonely sparks up the black hills. Lav imagines deserters, or smugglers—doubtlessly ancestors of Wayne Drover—climbing those cliffs, each one carrying a lantern. She is half-drunk, bemused, longing to confide in someone, has to hold herself back from telling Wayne about the journal, about her mother, about not wanting to return to Ottawa.

"It's not far to walk—and it's a nice night," Wayne says and to her surprise, (Have I been expecting to be invited to his room? she asks herself), he leads her out of the hotel by a side door.

It is a warm night—soft, filled with the smells of new grass and spring. They walk away from the hotel, east towards the hills, towards the water. Within minutes they are on a narrow, rutted path with no sidewalks and few lights. Cars, parked for the night, are pulled tightly in against foundations of houses or abandoned helter-skelter in the roadway.

There is no one about. On their left, wooden steps lead up to the houses. Houses lean, one behind the other, tier upon tier against the cliff face. Lights shine down, yellow from kitchens, blue from living rooms. By tilting her head back Lav can see lace curtains, bits of ceiling and on the railings of dangerous balconies, white cats perched like birds.

Wayne Drover walks on her right, holding onto her elbow. Beyond him there is nothing. Blackness and the sluggish, ominous swish of ocean brushing against concrete. "This is the Battery," he says—then a little later, "We're almost there."

They turn, climb sixteen wooden steps, cross a long veranda, open a door and step into a cluttered, overlit room. The face of Knowlton Nash flickers from a small television screen, his mouth moves but no sound comes out. Next to the television is an ivy plant that has been trained to grow up the wall, along the moulding, around half a hundred school pictures of two children, a boy and a girl evolving from childhood to youth. The television and the pot of ivy are both set on top of a huge wood stove. The floor is covered with piles of newspapers across which floor lamps trail black cords. There is a stairway, untidy bookshelves, a sofa, a rocking chair occupied by a cat, a refrigerator and a thousand other things.

Overwhelmed by the room, Lav teeters in the doorway until Wayne touches her back, urging her over the threshold, "Go on in, girl, no one's gonna bite you," he says, moving past her towards a huge window.

In front of the window is a table covered with newspapers. A floor lamp has been pulled over to the table where a woman sits, she is grey-haired, wearing glasses. She holds a pair of scissors, pointing them like a spear at the news item she is reading.

"Hi mudder," Wayne says but the woman does not look up, does not move. Despite her grey hair there is something childlike about her as she sits there, the picture of preoccupation, comfortable in her terry cloth dressing gown, her pink-slippered feet curled around the chair rungs.

"Hi mudder!" Wayne obviously enjoys his exaggerated pronunciation of the word. He bends forward, kisses her cheek.

She comes alive, jabs with her scissors at the news story. "See that! See what the buggers are doin' to us now? Takin' away the trains! Made them so uncomfortable no one could use them—then took 'em away because no one used em! Next thing the planes'll go, then the busses!" She glares up at her son as if he is to blame for this outrage.

Seeing Lav she says, "Sorry," but without conviction. When she stands and turns towards them Lav sees she is the witch-woman, the strange crone who had demanded a ride down from Signal Hill.

"Mom, this is Lav Andrews—Dr. Andrews, this is my mother, Verna," Wayne is very formal.

Both women nod, shake hands. "Uncommon name, Lav—not from here, are you?" Wayne's mother says.

Lav mutters some reply. She feels like one of those passive fairy-tale creatures she used to wonder at, silly, feckless girls who are led into the forest or abandoned on the doorstep of witches' huts.

Something about Lav puzzles Verna, perhaps she is trying to remember where she has seen her before. Lav braces herself for more questions but Verna turns to her son: "I'd given you up—thought you'd stay at the hotel tonight."

"Worked late, Mudder, both of us," Wayne tells her. He jiggles the rocking chair until the cat jumps down, "Have a seat, doctor dear," he grins briefly at Lav before lunging towards the television sound button.

The announcer's voice blasts forth, but Wayne, hunkering in front of the set, does not adjust the sound. "The Minister of Fisheries and Oceans for Canada today met with the President and his advisors. Both men report that considerable progress has been made on a bi-lateral agreement to promote understanding of the ocean environment off the coasts of Canada and the United States."

The voice comes over a clip of Timothy Drew shaking hands with Ronald Reagan then cuts to a scene of the President and Timothy Drew on the deck of a yacht. "This afternoon the Minister dined with the President," the announcer says and goes on to describe what was served.

"Two of a kind—too bad they don't fall in and drown, both of 'em," Verna scowls at the TV screen. "You want something to eat?"

"Wouldn't say no," Wayne says. He is still kneeling before the set but the announcer has moved on to another story, a barge has sailed halfway around the world trying to get rid of its load of New York garbage.

He snaps the set off. "Well! I'm glad we caught that!" he takes a notebook from his pocket, scribbles something down. "That was pretty good, better than I expected, really!"

Verna goes to the most kitchen-like part of the room, plugs in a toaster and kettle, comes back with milk, sugar, jam and fruit cake. She sets these things down on top of the newspapers, removing only the scissors and a pile of clippings which she drops into a Carnation Milk carton under the table.

"Mudder collects nasty yarns from newspapers—background material for the revolution," Wayne grins back and forth between his mother and Lav, as if expecting some immediate and entertaining reaction from one or both women.

Unable to formulate an appropriate response, Lav gestures towards the pictures: "You have a sister, I see." Even this sounds rude, rude and somehow strange—perhaps the sister has been eaten or turned into a cat.

But Verna answers quite cheerfully, "That's Kelly." She smiles towards the wall of pictures, "My change-of-life baby—almost ten years younger than Wayne, here."

She tells Lav that Kelly is a student nurse. She lives in residence, kept on a tight rein but well treated. "Not like it was in my day. I had a sister went into nursing, they were treated like skivvies back then." As she talks, Verna slices fruit cake, sets tea to steep, butters toast.

Just as they are about to eat, the phone in the stairway rings. Wayne answers—"Sweet Fuck!" they hear him say.

Verna clicks her tongue, "One word I cannot abide."

Wayne says, "I'll be right there," hangs up and immediately begins dialing. "I'm callin' Vic," he tells his mother. To Lav he says, "That was Clive—little emergency at the building. Nothing fatal—I'll be back before the tea's cold."

Apparently to avoid questions about the call he pulls on his coat and goes out onto the veranda. Verna moves from lamp to lamp, turning off every light in the room, "Can't see anything with the lights on," she says.

For a minute Lav thinks the woman really is mad, but understands when they sit down—the view from the darkened room is magnificent. They drink tea and watch Wayne pace back and forth outside the window, beyond him is the great dark pool of harbour ringed by the lights of the city. Then a horn blows, Wayne runs down the steps and they hear a car door slam.

"Vic brings his taxi home—that way we can get him any time of night." Verna seems unconcerned about her son's sudden departure. She licks butter off her fingers and gazes into the night. "You're the girl gave me a lift down off the hill that day," she says. "Knew Wayne in Ottawa did ya?"

Lav explains that she had only met Wayne since her transfer to St. John's. Then they eat in silence, watching headlights wind up the crooked hills, enjoying the heat of the old fashioned iron radiator below the window.

"I got used to sitting here in the dark during the war—we had blackouts. Couldn't see a hand before your face. There was no streetlights, of course, during the war—even the cars had little tin hoods over their lights—everything was black, black."

"Sometimes, though, in the moonlight, I could make out ships slipping into port. Shadows—hordes of shadows—like black whales, a pod of whales glidin' in under the cliffs. You'd almost think it was your imagination, but in the morning you'd look out and there they'd be, a convoy of ships right from here to the southside. A few days later they'd be gone. Wayne's Dad used to work longshore them times and he'd bring men home for supper sometimes. We both had brothers in the Navy, so it was natural—Canadian sailors, English and

American sailors. Portuguese and Spanish, too, before the war—and after, when the white fleet came back. Nice boys all of 'em, but we liked the Portuguese best—they seemed more like us, somehow. One of them wrote to us for years and years." Verna speaks as if she is alone, probably does talk like this when she's alone.

But then she interrupts herself: "Andrews is a Newfoundland name—I s'pose you got people here?"

"I could have." Lav does not tell the woman that she has been making phone calls, has already talked to Alf Andrews, to his mother, even to the old grandmother, Rachel. "Really, I was born here—in Newfoundland I mean. My father was in the Navy, in England, my mother came here when they married," she says.

"Your mother was a war bride?"

"I suppose, in a way—but my father died in the war and I grew up in Ottawa."

Lav begins telling Verna the good things she can remember about growing up in Ottawa, the small-town feeling of Dugan Street, Saul's shop, the bookbinding, her friend Audrey.

There is something about the warm kitchen, about the black night beyond the window, about the woman's attentive silence that invites confidences. Soon she hears herself talking about Philip and his precipitous leaving for Australia, about how she had come to be given this job, about how she's neglected it—things she's been wanting to talk about.

Verna murmurs, "Why ever not?" and "Never!" in appropriate places.

Thus encouraged Lav creeps up on other subjects. "My mother was probably on one of those ships you saw coming into port."

"She's still alive, I suppose, your mother?" Verna says idly, sympathetically.

"Oh yes, she's remarried," and Lav recounts the story of her mother's many reincarnations, from Charlotte Hinchley the factory girl to Darling Lottie, from Charlotte Rosenberg the stern, preoccupied wife to cute Charlotte Cabrillo living in her powder-pink house in California.

As the story progresses she becomes more and more upset. Knowing that she sounds childish, she trys to explain her mother, her coolness, her complete self-possession, how Charlotte has never confided in her daughter, not even letting her know when she was getting married. How she's never tried to make a home, never loved her, how her mother has even managed to obliterate their common past.

Even Verna's little sounds of sympathy are enough to undo Lav. Crying, sipping tea, gazing out the window and crying again, she tells her about the night she visited her mother, the night Charlotte passed over the letter Lav's father had written. She tells about their latest phone call—about the terrible things she has said to her mother.

None of it seems so awful in the telling as it did in the living, yet by the time she stops speaking Lav is sobbing uncontrollably.

Verna pats her hand, putters around the room, brings fresh tea, more toast. Lav is still crying, but comfortably so, when Wayne returns.

He seems unsurprised. "It's all right," he says, "everything is all right." He takes the cup from her hand, eases her to her feet and holds her. "It's going to be all right, everything is going to be all right...." Gently rubbing Lav's back he repeats the meaningless, magical, longed-for phrases again and again.

"We'll see you in the morning, Ma," he says and leads Lav up the stairs.

Cried out, past will, past reflection, she sits on the edge of the bed watching Wayne struggle to get the window open. After several blows to the frame he succeeds. Sea air sweeps into the room.

"Mother keeps the place too hot," he says. He comes back to the bed, kneels in front of her and pulls off her shoes. Then he removes her dress—red and navy print, the matching navy jacket she has carelessly left downstairs on the rocker now occupied by the cat.

It is Lav's only concern, this knowing, as Wayne undresses her, that she will regret her carelessness with the jacket. No thought that in the morning she may regret having gone, so pliantly, so passively to bed with Wayne Drover—no thought that he too may regret it—crosses her mind.

She awakes in the bright, light room and for a hairsbreadth of time thinks she is Lavinia. Sun and cool, salt air pour through the open window. She hears seagulls, sees reflections of water ripple across the white beams above her head.

Then she notices the faded chenille bedspread—and remembers she is in Wayne Drover's bed. Cautiously she moves a leg and discovers she is alone. She lies there for some time, curled up and comfortable, reflecting upon the consequences of this impulsive lovemaking—embarrassment, heartache, infection, pregnancy, even death, can result from such encounters these days. She considers the last three highly unlikely and decides she can handle the first two. And, of course, it will not happen again.

Whether from the sex or the weeping she feels refreshed, full of energy, confident enough to wrap herself in the worn bedspread and go in search of a bathroom.

The upstairs rooms are empty. The aroma of perked coffee drifts up from below. It adds to Lav's hopefulness. She bathes in the big, old fashioned bathtub, brushes her teeth with someone's toothbrush, pulls on her rumpled clothes and goes slowly, for she is reluctant to face Wayne's mother, down the hallway. From below she can hear loud voices and she starts down the stairs, walking quietly, shamelessly listening to Verna's angry voice.

"I know what you crowd are tryin' to do! Don't think I don't!"

"Sweet Christ, woman, what do you expect? You can't make an omelette without breaking eggs!"

"We're not talkin' about eggs—we're talkin' about people—about breakin' people!" A chopping sound follows Verna's words.

"You're paranoid—your mind's gone from listenin' to too many CBC documentaries, readin' too many newspapers. It ever occur to you half that stuff is made up to fill space between the ads?" Wayne sounds more annoyed than angry.

"What I heard on radio this morning wasn't made up—I heard Mark Rodway's name," Verna says.

Partway down the stairs Lav freezes, but they are too occupied with their argument to notice her.

Verna is standing by the table, a dark outline against the sunlit window. She is chopping furiously at something green while Wayne shouts at her back: "Look! It'll all be over by Monday—a case of mistaken identity—a screw up—charges dropped! Rodway'll be free to go his way, no harm done...."

"No harm done! No harm done! Hilda Rodway thinks the sun shines out of that boy—she'll be heartbroke hearin' on the radio her grandson's down in jail! And what about Mark—how'd you like havin' to spend the night in that hell-hole under the court house? Havin' your name spread all over town—have the world know you'd been arrested for break and entry, assault? Ruin a person, a thing like that could!"

"Go on with ya—it'll do the young nuisance good!" Wayne sounds conciliatory.

Then he hears Lav, looks up and winks, "Mudder's always expectin' the worst," he says and without missing a beat begins to explain what he calls Verna's theory of Confederation: "It was all a plot, you see—right from the first. A trick to get us Newfoundlanders off the island—starved out and resettled upalong. Accordin' to Mudder all Ottawa ever wanted was this big empty rock...."

Lav interrupts him, brushes past Wayne to ask his mother what she'd heard on the radio but Verna just keeps on chopping, the knife flashes up and down next to her fingertips.

"We'll talk about it later," Wayne says. "Come on over—come over here and have some breakfast. Mudder got you a special treat..." talking and humming, singing little snatches of song, he ceremoniously ushers his mother and Lav to the table.

He pours coffee and with a great flourish brings warmed plates and food, announcing each dish as he sets it down: "Fish and brewis! Scruncheons! And—as a special concession to Madam's mainland palate—chives in drawn butter!"

Hunger overcomes. Despite growing apprehension, despite the unappetising appearance of the food, Lav eats.

"Look out there! Look out there and tell me there's anything wrong with the ocean, anything wrong with the earth!" Wayne pats his mother's shoulder and gestures expansively towards the sparkling, sun-drenched harbour.

"You know what that harbour's full of!" Verna says, but she is relenting, succumbing to her son's charm and to the beauty of the morning—to the cliffs and sea, to the small red boat chugging out the narrows, to the ragged, slightly hazy outline of St. John's rising against the blue sky.

"Best view in the world out this window," Wayne says.

They eat and watch the fishing boat, trailing gulls and white foam, circle and come back in to one of the small wharves that cling to the Battery cliffs.

"That'll be Herb Pearcey out for his Saturday morning spin," Wayne says. "Must be eighty, but he's on the water every day of his life."

The fish and brewis tastes better than it looks. Lav has eaten everything on her plate before Verna, with a hard look at her son, says: "You goin' to tell her then—or will I?"

Wayne refills the coffee cups, lights his cigar, turns to Lav and says, "Mark Rodway broke into our offices last night—got himself arrested."

"But he's an employee! Why would he break in?"

"He's only casual—no DFO security pass. He got in though—tricked the guard into letting him right into my office. Looking for that report he sent to Ottawa— apparently he was too stunned to keep his own copy! Not only did he have the nerve to ransack my desk, when he found the thing he took it into the Xerox room and started making copies. That's what he was doing when Clive caught him. Lucky for us Clive went back—that report could scuttle the Oceans 2000 launch. And it could cost you your job!"

"But what's all this about Mark being in jail?"

"I had him arrested for break and entry, for removing documents from a government office."

"But why?"

"Jesus! Can't you just see it on Monday morning? The Minister holding a press conference inside the Radisson and that little snot outside passin' out his own version of the report!"

The man who sits scrutinizing her through a cloud of smoke seems quite different from the one she had made love with last night.

"Besides," he pushes his chair back and stands, "besides, he hit the security guard—hard! You don't do that sort of thing to union members. He'd have done better hittin' Clive or me—but that's them radicals for ya, no sense of class, no discretion!" Charming again he shakes his finger in mock horror at his mother, leans over and kisses the top of her head, "Never you mind, dear old mudder, I got a lawyer all lined up—the poor lad'll be outta pogey soon as Minister and media takes off for Ottawa."

"Don't dear old mudder me!" Verna pushes him away. "I hope Mark Rodway breaks out, hope he throws a bomb into the middle of your press conference. What's all this about him having a report of his own?"

"Nothing fit for the likes of you to know—don't want to give information to the resistance, do we?" Wayne smirks at his mother, then, with one of his quick changes of mood, becomes coldly serious. "Look Mother, don't embarrass me. Stay out of this. Timothy Drew is only trying to get a few jobs down here. Wouldn't your union friends like to get that fish plant across the harbour opened?"

"You don't have the gall to drag that one out again—next thing you'll be rabbittin' on about a Coast Guard station for the Battery and a big federal pen for Bell Island."

"It's the truth—Drew is going to see that plant over there is refinanced..."

"Refinanced!" Verna's voice vibrates with anger. "I've got a two inch thick file on that place—been refinanced more times than poor Patsy Carey down behind the post office!"

"Mother! I didn't know you knew such people! You really are going to have to stop going to Government House garden parties!"

The mother and son keep at it hammer and tongs. Verna shouting and waving news clippings even as they hurry down the steep steps to where Vic's taxi is waiting. Only at the last moment does she remember the demands of etiquette and call down, "Nice meeting you, Lav—come again!"

"What happened to Mark's report?" Lav asks as Vic manoeuvres his taxi around the dead-end street.

"Gone—shredded. Disk wiped—never existed." Arrested by a sudden suspicion Wayne gives her a sharp look, "You have a copy?"

When she tells him no, he smiles. "I'll drop you off at home if you like," he says, sets his briefcase on his knees, opens it, and begins leafing through papers. "I'm going on into the office—see how Clive made out, how the finished product looks. The rest of the day and Sunday I'll be checking around town—making sure everything's in place."

Wayne doesn't speak again until they get to Lav's door. "I'll be busy until Monday—but I'll see you at the Minister's reception—and at the press conference, of course!" Beaming like a child on Christmas morning, he kisses her cheek, waves, and as the car pulls away calls, "See you at the Radisson, luv."

part two
Mary Bundle

six

In her ninety-seventh year Mary Bundle woke one morning with the sure knowledge that she would not see another spring. The howl of wind, snap of frost and the clatter of icicles against eaves, sounds she had once slept through, now keep her awake most of the night.

The thought of death did not frighten the old woman, it irritated her. "Such a torment, the way things turns out—last year this time I'da been content to go." This is not true, of course. Mary had not been content to go, never would be content to go—certainly not now with Rachel's life fousted up the way it was.

Mary Bundle lies in her bed, feathered and curved down in the middle like a dory, thinking about her great-granddaughter, thinking about safety—about safe places. There are no such places.

"Safe as if you're in God's pocket," Meg used to tell the children when starvation and death seemed certain. And although Mary would never have admitted it, the words had always comforted her, too. She used to think about God's pocket, about how nice it must be, warm and dry and safe. Well, Meg is long gone, Sarah too, and most of the children they tucked into bed. Taken by the sea, by cold, by old age and sickness.

"I outlived them all," the old woman thinks, not without pride, "all them good women who knelt and prayed, knelt and scrubbed the splintered floors of the church, herded their men and children into that holy coldness every Sunday. All gone. If we're in God's pocket, must be like crumbs he's forgotten, some of us gets flicked about and blows away when he pulls his handkerchief out."

The thought of God's carelessness cheers her. Ignoring her stiffness she climbs out of the sagging bed, pulls a quilt around her shoulders and pads across the floor to the narrow window. With her fingernail she scrapes a circle in the frost and peers out to see what the day is like.

When Thomas Hutchings finally came to build a house for himself he certainly knew where to put it, up here by the old potato garden, good and high and safe, back from the water. Mary can see everything on the Cape from up here—or could see if her eyes were what they had once been. But the world is drawing in, circled by a milky haze like slob ice. Still, she can manage—sighting down the tunnel she can make out the dark shapes of houses, the sheds and flakes and beyond, the glittering grey sea. Right below her window is her own front bridge and hen house, and below that the slate roof of her grandson Calvin's new house. Over a ways she can almost make out the corner of the old Andrews place—the big double house where she'd lived all her married life, she and Ned and their children in one half and Meg and Ben in the other—used now as a barn and storage shed.

Nothing moves, not animal or bird, nor trail of smoke. The walls of the room and the window seem to breathe cold air but the old woman stands looking down on Cape Random, thinking about the people in each house. Last night she had tested herself, calling up the face of every person in the place, remembering who their parents and grandparents were, tracking those who were connected to her through her own three sons and through Fanny's son, Toma. Mary has noticed there are days when the past is all aslurry, frost forming around her mind too, she supposes. But last night she could remember every soul on the Cape, all one hundred and twenty-six of them.

She watches the sun come up, changing the sea from dark grey to pale blue, shimmering like a silk shawl Lavinia once owned. It is going to be a fine clear day, but bitter.

Shivering, she turns away from the window and gathers up her clothes: two flannel petticoats, a home-made canvas corset, knitted sheepswool stockings, heavy bloomers and the dress her grandchildren had ordered from St. John's for her ninety-fifth birthday. Mary has worn the dress every day since, ignoring Jessie's insistence that it is intended to be saved "for good." The dress is made of warm red cloth, store-bought wool, not the scratchy homespun stuff. It has a ruffle of black lace at the neck and two big V-shaped pockets trimmed with the same lace. It is the grandest garment Mary Bundle has ever worn. The feel of it, the thought that she owns such a dress, gives her immense pleasure. She has no intention of saving it to be buried in.

Clutching the bundle of clothing to her chest and holding onto the bannister, she slowly makes her way downstairs. In the kitchen she lays her clothes over a chair next to the fire, which, having been banked, still gives off a little heat. The cat slides out from under the stove to curl around her legs. Being careful not to waken the young woman sleeping on the couch, Mary feeds the animal and pours herself a cup of black tea from the teapot that has been steeping all night on the back of the stove.

She takes a mouthful of the hot tea, puts down the cup—large, with the word "Mother" and the likeness of stern old Victoria, whom Mary is proud to have outlived, painted on its side. Without taking any care she pulls on layer after layer of clothing, covering everything with an immense wool shawl that one of her daughters-in-law, she forgets which, crocheted years ago.

Once dressed, Mary goes to sit in a rocker by the couch. She sips her tea thoughtfully, looking down on the mound of quilts at the top of Rachel's dark head. She cannot—must not—die until something's been worked out for the child.

Rachel is fifteen, born the year Lavinia died. Mary had wanted the baby called Lavinia, but Jessie, the child's mother, objected: "Go on, Nan, if you had your way every young one on the Cape'd be called Meg or Sarah, or Lavinia and every boy'd be Ned. We'll call her Rachel, she can have Lavinia for a middle name."

In her heart Mary still thinks of her great-granddaughter as Lavinia's namesake. It takes some of the grief out of her friend's death to know there is another Lavinia Andrews on the Cape.

She had expected to see Rachel grow into a tall, loose limbed Lavinia, with foxy curls and Lavinia's pale complexion. Instead, the child stopped growing at five feet and is dark as a Turk. Rachel, although Mary cannot see it, is the spitting image of herself the day she came ashore on Cape Random.

The old woman rocks, pondering life's infinite capacity for surprise: "That terrible time after Ned was killed I thought I'd never know another day's happiness, still and all I did. Then, all them years later when Vinnie died I'da sworn I'd never laugh at another thing—but Rachel and me had a good many happy days together since then."

Part of her happiness these past years, of course, has come from the fact that she's abandoned responsibility, a strangely intoxicating experience that Mary had deliberated upon for some time before informing her children and grandchildren.

"I got it all hove over, all of it!" she announced on her eightieth birthday—or what they have come to celebrate as her birthday—really it is the date of quite a different event, but what they don't know won't hurt them. "I'll never dig another potato, nor chop wood, and I'm never again going to darken the door of the fish store nor gut a fish, nor even turn one—fact is, I never wants to see a fish again except on a plate!" she said, and she hasn't either.

"I got to say they takes good care of me," the old woman brags to anyone who will listen, pointing to the red dress, the laying hens, the good tea Tessa brings down from Greenspond. Last spring the boys got together and tarred her roof, and hardly a day passes but one of them doesn't bring in a rabbit, a wild bird, a fish or a nice trout, all ready for the pot. The women look after her garden and every time she comes in from the woods there's a jug of milk, a warm loaf or a bowl of soup waiting on the table. They're good to her and she would have been content—but she would not have been happy if it had not been for Rachel.

Year in, year out, from early spring when the first tiny white flowers appear until the ground freezes in the fall, the old woman and her great-granddaughter would be outdoors. Together they picked fairycaps, aspen catkins, maidenhair, heart's ease and alder buds, gathered kelp, moss and eel grass, dug up the roots of yellow pond lilies, of snap dragons and dandelion, brought home basketsful of bakeapples and rose hips, buckets of blueberries, marshberries, partridgeberries, pillow-cases filled with wintergreen and the buds and petals of a hundred plants that grow in the crevices of rocks and under the shadows of evergreen trees. Rain or shine they could be seen foraging in the woods and marshes or along the beach.

When snow began to fly they would move inside and work in the spicy warmth of Mary's kitchen, amid the clutter of things they had gathered. Roots must be dried and ground to powder, some for burns and others for stomach disorders. Leaves can be made into tea for the cure of rheumatism, earache and lung disease or sewn into pillows to ward off consumption. From rose hips and seaweed they concoct ointments for anointing the eyes in cases of snow blindness, salve to cure hemorrhoids, to stop bleeding, to heal sores. Together they brew tonics for canker, for spring sickness and women's complaints, drinks to ease childbirth, headache and death, and some that can even lift sorrow from your shoulders for a while. When the sideboard jars are again full, when all the little cloth bags are tied and hung in lines behind the stove, Mary and Rachel would turn to jam making, to bottling caribou, seal and wild duck.

Winters when there was a teacher in the place the girl went to school with the other youngsters, but even then she would come straight to Mary's the minute classes were let out. Sometimes they would just talk, considering every curious happening or bit of gossip either of them had heard during the day. Other times Rachel would sit by the hour listening to the old woman describe how to put warts away, make hot fomentations, cure Seal Finger or tie off a baby's cord. Over the years Mary has taught her great-granddaughter every old charm, spell and incantation she has learned in a lifetime of tending the sick. Sometimes it seems as if the woman is pouring her spirit into the body of the small dark girl.

"Far as Nan's concerned our Rachel's the sun and the moon, she got the young one pure spoiled," Jessie says in her pleasant, absentminded way, more because such remarks are expected than because she has any real concerns about her daughter.

"That child was born with an old head on her shoulders," Mary tells anyone who dares suggest she might be keeping the girl from more suitable activities. The woman who has never had one word of praise for her own children boasts that Rachel is the brightest, prettiest and smartest child ever born on the Cape.

"She was, too—is still—and I'd have died content just knowin' everythin' was goin' to be all right for her," Mary thinks as she sips her cold tea. "I'da gone without a word 'tho I never did get all, nor half, the things I shoulda got outta life." This last is a stern reminder to God that she is still able to bargain.

"Then that slack-arsed bugger had to come along and do what he done to her. Where was God's friggin' pocket then?" During the years Mary lived with Lavinia her language had improved, but after her friend's death she had quickly slipped back to her old ways and nowadays, as her daughter Tessa says, "Would make a holy show of us in front of our Saviour should he see fit to land on the Cape."

Stephen Vincent, the young man Mary is thinking of with such bitterness, arrived on the Cape in June. Unannounced and unexpected he came, carrying two big suitcases, leather with shiny brass corners, one filled with books and the other with clothing the like of which no one along the shore had ever imagined, much less seen. The men and boys hated Stephen on sight, laughed themselves helpless the day he tried to scull a boat and fell in arse-over-kettle. Almost drowned. Mary wishes he had.

Girls and women loved him, doted on him, said he was the face and eyes of his grandfather. Rachel's mother Jessie, who was old enough to have better sense, let him sit at her kitchen table and recite poetry by the hour. "I do wonder you don't like him, Nan, sure he reminds me so much of Lavinia the way he says them poems!"

Mary had stared at Calvin's wife. Sometimes she wondered if Jessie was weak minded like poor Fanny—who was after all the woman's grandmother. Lavinia had once pointed out that since Calvin was Mary's grandson and Jessie her great-granddaughter the two were first cousins once removed—"That's no reason for her to be so stunned!" Mary protested and Lavinia had had to agree that it wasn't.

"Hid behind the door when they passed out good sense, you did my girl," Mary told Jessie the day she suggested Stephen Vincent was like Lavinia. "How could nuisance-face be like Lavinia when his grandfather were Char Vincent what married someone in St. John's, then went off to convert savages in foreign parts? The young whelp got no connection with the Andrews."

"Far as I'm concerned Stephen Vincent's a black stranger. S'posin' he is Charlie's grandson—and we only got his word for that, I don't take to him," Mary said and would not be charmed.

She found it hard to put her finger on what it was she disliked so intensely about the blonde, graceful young man. For one thing he was a good ten years older than Rachel, who was barely fifteen and innocent as the driven snow. And there was something foreign about him, not just his unfamiliar way of talking, either, but his manner. He had a sharp, bright glitter that never went away, like he knew he'd just have to put out his hand and whatever he wanted would fall right into it.

Perhaps, like Jessie said, she was just jealous. Certainly she hated to see Stephen Vincent and Rachel together—and they were always together. Sometimes when Mary was out tramping the hills, she would come upon them, sitting in some mossy spot, their heads close, talking quietly, or him with a book open reading to the girl. For all her good sense Rachel was foolish as a kitten that summer.

Then, quite abruptly, unexpectedly as he had arrived, Stephen left. Got himself up to Wesleyville on Eldon Gill's bulley and caught the coastal boat to St. John's.

From Rachel's silent despair it was clear the boy's leaving had surprised her as much as anyone, but, "Good riddance!" the old woman said, delighted to have Stephen Vincent out of Cape Random. Now things would get back to the way they should be.

And it seemed this might be so. As fall came on, the girl rejoined her great-grandmother, foraging in the woods and along the beach. But it was not the same, Rachel seemed smaller, shrunken, all her bright exuberance gone. It was pure torment for Mary to see the girl's pinched face, the way she hovered, hoping for word of him whenever a ship came in.

Still, Mary thought, it will pass—she's not the first whose heart's been broke—she's only a youngster and hearts mend faster than heads.

In early November she found out different. Wesley Lush, working his way down the coast by dog sled, arrived in Mary's kitchen with the last mail for the year. It was a terrible day, fog and freezing rain had coated everything with glitter. Yet Wes barely had his backside on a chair when Pash and Tessa, who must have seen him pass their house, came floundering up the lane.

It was Pash, blind as she was, who clutched at the ice-crusted fence, pushing and pulling fat, arthritic Tessa along. They made so much noise that the dogs Wes had barred up under the house rushed out and knocked Pash right off her feet.

"I mighta' knowed them two old fools'd be the first here," Mary said and sent Rachel out to help the women up the steps.

"Don't s'pose Miss What's-her-face could pass out the mail, was Tessa Andrews not here to tell her how. Been twenty year now since Tessa taught school but she still wants to oversee all occasions—anyone'd think she was Meg's daughter instead of mine," Mary was muttering to no one in particular as the two women came puffing and steaming into her kitchen.

"Stop jawin', mother," Tessa said. She is the only person on the Cape who dares speak to Mary Bundle in such a tone. "I want to have me way with Wes before the place fills up," Tessa winked at Rachel, eased herself down beside the mail carrier and proceeded to question him on church attendance, the results of the Labrador fishery, the progress of courtships, the weather and ice conditions, sickness, births and deaths in the communities he's passed through on his way to Cape Random.

Right behind Pash and Tessa, six youngsters slipped quietly into the kitchen, and behind them came Rose and Willie Andrews with their youngest grandchild Ki—a young nuisance. Tessa directed the boy to sit on the other side of the kitchen from the younger children who have jammed down together on the sofa like a line of big-eyed puffins. Next came Toma Hutchings and his wife Comfort, then Floss Gill and Dorcas Vincent, each with a small baby in their arms, behind them were Ned and Greta Way, Aunt Min and Skipper Lem Hounsell—all tramping water in over Mary's clean floor, smelling of frozen fog and wet wool, drinking her tea and eating her raisin buns, which Jessie passed around without so much as a by-your-leave.

They surround poor Wes, a painfully shy man, who had pushed his chair further and further back into the corner behind the stove, stared miserably at his hands and answered their urgent requests for information with monosyllabic grunts.

When Miss Mugford, the schoolteacher, arrived, Tessa told her not to wait for anyone else and the teacher began distribution of the mail. Parcels first, as was the custom, with good long pauses so that the contents of each package could be passed around, examined and commented on.

There had not been a lot of mail in Wes's bag. Mary sets herself to remember each item: the door hinges Calvin had ordered two years ago from Curran's in St. John's, Jessie's church paper, the box of oranges Toma and Comfort bring in every fall for the youngsters' Christmas, a sample copy of the new Methodist hymnal—addressed to the church but Tessa takes charge of it—and a calendar for Rose from The St. John's Fine Art Emporium. The calendar had a picture of what Tessa said was the Colonial Building, all draped out in flags with some stuck-up looking men lined up on the steps. Apart from that there was just the package of crochet thread for Triff Norris, a big roll of newspapers for David and Sophie Hutchings—and two letters, which Miss Mugford gave out last. One letter was for the teacher herself, the other for Rachel.

The girl snatched the envelope as if someone had given her the keys to heaven. Then she pulled on her jacket and disappeared out the door, although it was still sleeting and already getting duckish.

Nobody else made a move to leave. Women took out their knitting and Jessie put on another pot of tea. The newspapers, some of them four months old, were distributed among the men, who passed them from hand to hand, taking turns reading out bits they thought the women might find interesting.

The Boer War is still going on, they were told. The export price of salt cod has dropped twenty percent in the last ten years, government is suggesting people get out of fishing and into farming. St. John's is being rebuilt again, bigger and better than before the latest fire, with boardwalks and electric street lights along Water Street.

At first the women and children listen attentively but the press of information became too great, too ominous. Rival conversations sprang up: Are "Boers" people or animals? What are boardwalks and how can you possibly have lights along a street? Incomprehensible, unanswerable questions—quickly dropped in favour of examination of a new knitting pattern or the bleeding gums of Floss's baby.

But when Captain Hounsell shook his paper, commanding them to hear what he called the latest bit of government skullduggery, they all became silent again. "'It has been revealed that A. B. Morine, Minister of Finance, who is negotiating Newfoundland's contract with railway builder R. G. Reid, is also solicitor for the Reid company and was last year paid a $5000 retainer by Reid's firm....' Now what do you make of that?" The old man held the newspaper at arm's length as he read.

"Go on, wasn't for Reid none of us woulda gotten a cent last winter—wasn't it him paid ta have all that lumber cut and hauled?"

Some of the men agreed, "What difference how much big shots skim off so long as an honest man can get a day's work out of it?" Others insisted it was barbarous how the likes of Reid can make fortunes off Newfoundlanders. "What gives that bloody clique in St. John's the right to run the government, anyhow?" one of the younger men asked—Mary had been pleased to hear someone besides herself swearing.

"Sure, everyone knows they crowd loots banks, makes fortunes off government contracts and rakes in money on every bit of food, fish or gear comes into or leaves the country," Captain Hounsell told them.

Having skippered schooners all over Newfoundland and even down to the West Indies, Lem Hounsell is listened to with respect but when he stopped speaking, a general argument, with much shouting and shaking of newspapers, had broken out.

One or two of the men, Toma Hutchings among them, thought it wrong to tar everyone with the same brush: "Take this man Bond for example—I allow he'll be the savin' of us!" Toma said.

Political talk never changes, Mary thought. She can remember Ned and Thomas and Alex Brennan sixty years before arguing about what could be done to save the country.

"Always in need of savin' and never saved, this place is. Waitin' for time, Ned used ta call it—'we'um just waitin' for time, maid. Just waitin' 'til our ship comes in,' he'd say. Well, I allow our ship got sunk off the Funks!" Mary had glared around the room, challenging any of them to argue with her.

When no one spoke she directed Tessa to read some advertisements out: "Least I can make some sense of 'em—know what people gets in wages and what they gotta pay out ta keep body and soul together."

Willie Andrews, who cannot read much more than his own name, passed the newspaper he was holding to Tessa. The men leaned back good naturedly and lit their pipes. They will talk about what they've read later, in tilts or down in the twine loft when the women are not around. One of the babies toddled over to Toma who lifted the child onto his lap, rocking her and warming her feet with the bowl of his clay pipe.

"Wharf labourers needed, steady work, 8 cents an hour for ten hour days," Tessa read out in her loud, school-teacher voice. "Sturdy single back chairs, hand-built by Ephraim Nichols, 55 cents each. Strong boy, willing to apprentice to St. John's printer, $6.00 per month, keep not included," and so on through paper after paper until Mary could stand it no longer. She told her daughter to stop showing off and ordered her guests home to their suppers.

For herself, she had not been hungry that night. She tried to settle down, to wait quietly for Rachel, but ended up pacing the floor, assuring herself her great-granddaughter was safe, that she had simply gone home to read her letter and was probably asleep in her own bed. Eventually the girl did come, as she always had when she was in trouble. Blue with cold and shivering she dropped into a chair and began to weep.

"Foolish as a coo—dawdlin' about outdoors on a dirty night," talking and scolding, Mary had combed ice out of the child's hair, wrapped a blanket around her, hauled off her boots and propped her freezing feet up on the fender of the stove. All the while Rachel sat like a rag doll, holding the crumpled letter in her hand, crying quietly. Much later, when her father came looking for her, she still had not said a word.

"Come on home now, maid, 'tis well past bedtime," Calvin spoke gruffly, pretending not to notice his daughter's red eyes and dripping nose.

"She's bidin' the night. Her feet are full of pins and needles—she can't walk," Mary gave her grandson a hard look, thinking for the thousandth time how much he got on her nerves. He looked so like her Ned with his round smiling face, his bush of flaming hair, that she wanted him to act like Ned. Of course he never did. Calvin took after his father Henry—no more spirit than a pan of dough.

That night Mary could have kicked him as he dithered by the door not knowing whether to go or stay: "Jessie says she wants the young one home—wants to know what's in the letter before she goes to bed."

"'Tis just too bad what Jessie wants!" Mary snapped. She had no time for Calvin or his wife—what could those two gormless dotes do for Rachel?

Mary had snatched the letter from Rachel's limp hands and lifted the stove lid as if to throw the paper into the flames. At the last second something in the girl's face made her change her mind and she pushed the letter deep into the pocket of her red dress.

"Now, go home and tell your wife she don't get everything she wants—'twill be a good lesson for her!" Mary said.

Mystified, as he often was by his grandmother, Calvin shook his head and left without a word. When he was gone, Mary studied the girl for a long minute. Then she went to the pantry, ladled milk into a saucepan and set it on the stove. She pinched bits of bread into a small bowl, crumbled a spoonful of brown sugar over the bread and poured the hot milk on top. This mixture, which the children called mush, was considered a treat and reserved for serious illnesses.

A feeling of inescapable doom and terrible sadness had overtaken Mary. It goes on and on, she thought, the only way not to be tormented like this is not to care about one living thing.

"What's all this falderal then?" she asked when the girl had eaten the bread and milk. Mary tried to sound sure and unafraid, the way she used to when Rachel was a child and rushed in with cut knees or hurt feelings.

"Oh Nan, I wrote him. I wrote to Stephen right after he left—I didn't say much—only asked him to write me..." her voice dribbled out.

"So then—wrote back, did he?"

"I don't know if he even got the letter I sent. That letter, the one come today," Rachel gestured towards Mary's pocket, "'Twarn't from him, Nan—'twas from his mother. He's—he's—Nan, Stephen's dead!"

This was not what Mary had expected. As she waited for Rachel's weeping to end she pulled the letter from her pocket, laid it on her lap and smoothed it out. She looked at the pale grey paper bordered in black, squinting at the thread-like marks some stranger had made to tell her great-granddaughter that Charlie Vincent's grandson was dead.

"'Tis strange beyond belief, the way things comes 'round," Mary thought as she passed the letter to the girl, "I'm sorry, maid, I wrinkled it all up on ya."

"You want to hear it, Nan? She calls me 'Stephen's little friend.'" Rachel began to read, slowly, sounding out the long words the way she had been taught.

> I write to acknowledge your charming note and to convey the melancholy intelligence that our beloved son Stephen passed away three weeks after returning home. He had, as you know, been ill for some time, yet we had hoped that a summer by the sea would restore his health. Alas, it was not to be. During the days before his death, Stephen spoke with great affection of his relatives on Cape Random and of his charming little friend Rachel. His poor wife, Melissa, who has only just recovered from the birth of their

son, is disconsolate and can undertake no correspondence. On her behalf, as well as for myself and my husband, I express our deep appreciation of your kindness to dear Stephen.

> Yours sincerely,
> Mrs. Paul Vincent,
> 1026 Riverside Drive, Boston.

"His wife Melissa—and a son! He never said one word about them Nan, not a word! He said: 'I'll be back for you Rachel, I'll be back next summer.' Oh Nan, he were so different, so alive—he'd been so many places and when he talked about them 'twas like I been there too." The girl gulped and closed her eyes but did not start to cry again.

"What was his grandfather like, Nan?" she asked after a few minutes.

Mary tries to conjure up a picture of Stephen's grandfather: "He was skinny like all the Vincent men, but he thickened out later, got stocky, more like Sarah. Smart as a tack, accordin' to Lavinia. He was still young when he went off to some kind of school for ministers. 'Twas Meg and Ben Andrews paid money so's Charlie Vincent could go—I knows that for a fact. Saved for years and years they did—set on makin' a preacher outta their Willie. Then Willie went and married Rose Norris who was a real flibberty-gibbet in them days. Meg was that miffed she just guv all that money to Charlie Vincent—so's he could be a preacher instead of Willie. And when he got his education, sure didn't Charlie go off to foreign parts ta be a missionary and was never heard tell of again?" Mary shook her head, unreconciled after all these years to such waste.

"Stephen is—was—smart too, different from the boys around here—you knows what I means, Nan...." For the first time that night Rachel looked up, meeting her great-grandmother's eyes. "Oh Nan, I'da done anything for him—anything." Her voice dropped to a whisper, "Nan—I got his baby—what am I goin' to do, Nan?"

"I knowed it!" Mary thought and snapped, "I tell you what you're goin' to do, we're goin' to be rid of it—and before this night is out, too!"

Mary had stopped, had made herself stop and wait. She studied her hands, thin and sinewy, spotted with age and criss-crossed with great knotty veins. "Done some hard things in their time, them hands has," she thought, remembering the births and deaths she had presided over.

But the girl had not spoken, had not said: "No Nan, I'm keepin' the baby!" So Mary went out to the back porch and brought in her big cooking pot which she filled with water and set on the fire. Choosing carefully, she pulled five bags from the line behind the stove measuring a spoonful from each into the pot. She set the girl to grinding roots of goldenthread, mixing it with seeds of Queen Anne's Lace, while she pounded bittersweet berries into a paste. For a little while, working together like that, everything seemed almost ordinary.

All through the terrible night Rachel had followed the old woman's instructions without a word or whimper. The girl did not flinch, not even when Mary made her swallow the bitter stuff until she vomited, forced her to pace back and forth until she was faint. The old woman held the girl's head over a steaming concoction of herbs, spooned glutinous black seaweed into her mouth, made her eat raw eggs and, in desperation, finally dosed her with castor oil. By then Mary felt sick herself and so tired that every bone in her body ached.

She went to the window, rested her head against the cold pane and tried to recollect if there was something more she could do. Outside, the night was black—"black as a cow's guts," Mary thought, "not a light to be seen on land or sea...."

There were other ways, hideous dangerous means of producing a miscarriage. Gruesome probings and piercings, things she and Sarah had only whispered of. Things she recoiled from even thinking of in connection with Rachel.

"'Tis no use, maid—I done all I knowed of—'tis meant to be...."

Mary had turned away from the window then—and gotten the fright of her life. Standing by the table, holding onto it as if she might fall, had been not Rachel, but Una—Una Sprig. Mary's mother, almost ninety years in her grave, stood there looking very much as she had on the last day of her life. The weary slump of shoulders, the dirty, damp dress, the matted hair, the deep lines from nose to mouth, the crazed look, were all Una's. Mary gasped. The figure moved, straightened, Una vanished, became again Rachel.

"So," she had thought, "that's who the child takes after!"

Never having seen herself in Rachel, Mary had often pondered on the girl's swarthiness, wondering secretly if people had been right after all, if Jessie did have Indian blood from her father Toma. But Mary could see now, it was Una's blood Rachel had. The blood of the old people—the only thing her mother had ever spoken of with pride.

Without realizing it, Mary started to cry. She'd walked over and kissed Rachel's cheek, something she had not done since her great-granddaughter was a baby. "Some things nothing can change, girl—there's some things is just meant to be."

"But Nan, what'll I do, what will Mam and Pap say? What'll I tell people?"

"Less said, soonest mended. 'Twon't be the first merrybegot born along this coast and I doubt it'll be the last."

She looked at Rachel's exhausted face and said more gently, "Never mind, girl, you'll be all right. I'll work somethin' out. Go on up to my bed and lie down for a spell, no doubt your mother'll be up here nosin' around at the crack of dawn."

Rachel nodded and, biddable as a child, went upstairs.

It had grown light, Mary blew out the lamp and looked around. The kitchen was in chaos, a chair overturned, a bucket of vomit by the door, the table littered with bags of spilled herbs and moss, spoons, saucers, cups and bowls, each containing the dregs of a different mixture. Some powder had tipped onto the floor and been ground in with their pacing. Pots of liquid still simmered on the stove, thickening the unsavory stench of vomit, the acrid smell of seaweed, sweat and fear. Everything must be cleared away. Jessie must not guess what they had tried to do.

"I'll work something out," Mary Bundle had promised—and she meant it. And for a woman nothing could be worked out without a husband—this lesson Mary had learned long ago. As she scrubbed the kitchen floor she was already running through a list of unmarried boys and men on the Cape, trying to think of one who might provide a name for Rachel's baby.

After that night Rachel seemed to give up. She just wrapped grief around herself, curled up on Mary's couch and slept for longer and longer periods each day. The girl became obstinate, she ignored Christmas, refused to join in the mummering or the carol service and would not talk about her now obvious condition even with Mary.

By then, of course, everyone knew that young Rachel Andrews was in the family way and that dead Stephen Vincent was the cause of it. It was whispered about, but there was no open talk and, as far as Mary could see, no one condemned the girl. Indeed, there was a certain amount of sympathy for Rachel, especially among the women. In death, Stephen took on an even more romantic aura than he'd had in life. His good looks, his fine clothes, his manners, his habit of tipping an invisible hat, his reciting of poetry, his lavish compliments, were remembered and expanded upon.

"I partly blames meself, so I do, after all's said and done he was me cousin's son," Mary heard Flora Vincent tell Jessie one day when the women met in her kitchen, each bringing a pot of rabbit stew. "I shoulda kept a closer rein on the lad—but my, he were that handsome and him and your Rachel did make a lovely couple—I'm sure, girl, he intended to come back and marry her!" Flora was clearly trying to pull Jessie's tongue. And Jessie nodded and smiled—ignoring the fact that the handsome lad had already been married.

"Stunned as me arse, both of 'em!" Mary thought, but she said nothing, sensing that such foolish embroidering of the truth might be of benefit to Rachel and the baby.

Now, in late January, Mary sits sipping her cold tea, knowing she has been able to do nothing to protect her great-granddaughter. The poor maid is going to have to face life with a baby but no husband—and Mary knows how that will be. She studies the shape under the blankets trying to think what she can do, trying to calculate how long until the baby will be born, how long her own dying will take.

It is near noon and the girl has not moved. "If she keeps on like this, sleeping half the day, not eatin' nor goin' outside the door, moping about like she don't care if she lives or dies, she'll do herself harm, and the baby too, belike." Mary has seen more than one die from not wanting to live, she remembers her own daughter Fanny and Ida Norris, poor mad women both of them, women who lived in another world.

Mary wishes Lavinia or Sarah, or even Meg, were alive to talk to, wishes her bouts of dizziness and forgetfulness had not started at such an inconvenient time, wishes she had the strength to pull Rachel from the couch, to drag her, body and bones, outdoors. A few days tramping through the snow would do the girl a world of good.

There is one thing she can do. This very night, Mary resolves, they will change sleeping places. From now on, she will sleep in the kitchen and Rachel must sleep in the bed upstairs. The top floor is so icy cold the girl will at least be forced to get up each morning.

Mary sighs, it's not much, but it's a start. She pokes more wood on the fire, adds water to the rolled oats that have been in soak since yesterday and moves the pot to the front of the stove. She leans over to study the girl's face, small and round with a little pointed chin, a child's face. Mary nudges her great-granddaughter awake, forces her to get up and eat.

The old woman spends the rest of the short winter day trying to coax Rachel out of her lethargy, mentioning things that are happening on the Cape: that Greta Way was sung-down at last night's prayer meeting, the number of traps Moses John has set for fox, the light one of the boys saw out beyond the reach, the "time" planned for Friday night in the school and the astonishing, or so it seems to Mary, news that Triff Norris is crocheting a twelve-foot-long train for her niece Joanna's wedding dress.

In the past Mary and Rachel could have spent any amount of time discussing these things. Today the girl shows not a flicker of interest. Mary, who considers curiosity well ahead of godliness or cleanliness, tries to hide her annoyance at the girl's languor, suggests Rachel go visit the schoolteacher who has come by several times. But she just shakes her head, crawls back under the quilts and appears to sleep, leaving the old woman to brood by the fire.

It is dark again before Mary thinks of something that might bestir the child. "I s'pose we could find out what Lavinia writ in her book about Charlie Vincent," she remarks, talking as if to the cat who has curled in beside the girl but is at least keeping one eye open.

Rachel does not reply but she does move slightly.

"It just come to me how we can find out something about Char Vincent, him that was Stephen's grandfather," Mary continued, carefully keeping any eagerness out of her voice. "I allow, though, you'd hardly be interested in them old things happened before your time."

The girl sat up. "What book?" she said.

"That big old book Vinnie wrote in for ages, said I was to take care of it for her," Mary pokes at the fire, holding her breath.

"Where's the book now?"

"Stowed away somewhere—up in Vinnie's room I expects, in that old sack hung on back of the door. You can go take a look if you got a mind."

Mary knows exactly where the journal is. She had taken it from beneath the pillow of Lavinia's deathbed and slid it into the worn and patched bag Lavinia had carried around for most of her life. Then, right after the funeral, thinking she might soon be dead herself, Mary tucked her own prized possessions down into the bag and hung it behind the door.

How often, during their last years together had she watched Lavinia turning the pages, reading and smiling to herself. It had infuriated Mary. She'd threatened more than once to burn the damned book. And Lavinia had known how she hated and distrusted writing. Still and all, a few days before she died, Lavinia told Mary to keep the book safe and pass it on to someone else who would keep it safe.

"Someday the Cape will be a big, important place, there'll be a town here with thousands of people and they'll want to know how it was in the beginning when we came. It's a testimony, Mary, to what we done. Like the Bible," Lavinia had said, giving her that great broad smile that had never changed from the day Mary first set eyes on her.

Rachel wrinkles her nose in distaste as she puts the sack down on the kitchen table. It smells fousty, damp and mildewed. A long, long time has passed since Jennie Andrews, sitting by the window on Monk Street, had pieced the bag together for her daughter. Rachel sits opposite Mary and watches the old woman taking things from the bag, laying them out, one by one, on the kitchen table.

The largest item is the journal, which Mary puts to one side. "Vinnie's book," she says, patting it, "I'll tell you about that after—first I wants to show ya what else is in here."

"Now this is some old," she pulls out a little sealskin purse, folded over and tied around with a bit of dirty twine, "I think your Great Aunt Jane gave it to me when she was learnin' to sew." Inside the purse are three gold pieces, looking like new, the head of George III still shining bright.

Rachel fingers the coins, examining them, "'King William was King George's son and all the royal race he run'—is this the king in that song, Nan? I wonder what the 'royal race' is?"

"I don't know, maid," Mary has no interest in history. "I only knows them's sovereigns, real gold, and the longer you keeps gold the more it's worth. Here, look at this," she unfolds a piece of flannel, "what you think of that?" she asks with glee.

The girl picks up the purple brooch, holding it with the same wonder and covetousness Mary once had: "Oh Nan, it's the beautifullist thing I ever seen! Who do it belong to?"

"'Twas Tessa's—not your Great Aunt Tessa—the Tessa who was my sister, the brooch were hers. Once I traded it to Sarah Vincent but I got it back."

Rachel sighs, "I never thought to see such a thing!"

"Never wore it, not once. I regrets that now," Mary says and leaning forward pins the brooch on Rachel's sweater. "Here, 'tis yours—wear it outside where people can see and know you owns somethin'."

She reaches into the old bag and this time pulls out a thin wad of paper money, wrinkled and soft as cloth and kept together with a rusty safety pin, it has "Newfoundland Commercial Bank" printed on it. A sheet of parchment is curled around the notes. Mary flattens the paper and passes it to Rachel, "Read it out!"

"This is to declare that the store and wharf formerly belonging to Caleb Gosse and latterly to Timothy Drew are hereby assigned to Mary Andrews nee

Bundle and to her heirs or beneficiaries in perpetuity," Rachel stumbles over the long word.

"In perpetuity!" Mary rolls the word over her tongue, "Means forever—means long as rivers run, long as fish swim!"

The girl puts the paper down beside the bank notes and stacks the gold pieces. She stares at her great-grandmother: "Why, Nan—you're rich!"

"No girl, not rich nor nothin' like it, what I got here wouldn't buy the horse and carriage off a rich man. Still, I'm not dyin' a pauper—and I'm the first in me family as can say that." Mary surveys the collection with pride.

The ritual of counting her possessions reassures her. It always has. But tonight there is something else, a feeling of comfort just from seeing the book Lavinia used to write in and the sack she always had slung across her shoulder. The terrible sadness that came over Mary the night she found out Rachel was pregnant lifts a little. She should have brought the bag down before, not let it hang untouched for fifteen years.

"First thing tomorrow I wants you to get the teacher. Bring her down here and tell her to bring ink and paper. I wants her to set down that you'll have this house and the store when I dies. And I wants nothing said of it, tell her that, too."

"You're not going to die, Nan—not forever and ever!" Rachel repeats the old words she used to say as a child whenever they'd gone to a funeral. In those days Mary had agreed with her great-granddaughter. Now she tells her not to be so foolish.

"I'm over ninety, child, nobody can expect to live forever—beginning to think I don't even want to." Even as she says this Mary knows it is not true. She does want to live forever—but not as an addled old woman. She wishes she could believe the things Meg and Sarah used to be always pratin' on about: streets of gold and robes of light, everlasting summers with Ned and Lavinia—with her sister Tessa....

Mary shakes off such fancies. "Must be gettin' soft in me old age," she thinks and continues with her instructions: "When I'm gone you got some things to do—I'm tellin' them to you now, so remember. When me time comes I wants you to go upstairs and hide the gold and the book away for yourself, let them find the bag and sort out who owns the rest of it, but remember, hide the gold and the book first."

There were other things that Rachel must do. Ignoring the girl's protestations, Mary lists them. She will go over this same list time and time again in the weeks to come: "Make Nan decent, go upstairs and hide the journal and the gold, put the bag back on the hook..."

"What do 'make Nan decent' mean?" Rachel recites the list twice before she has courage to ask the question.

"Cover me up, child, fix me hair and, you know, see me eyes is closed—I'll do what I can meself but I got to count on you to do what's necessary before they comes traipsin' in and sees me lookin' like a witch altogether!" Mary begins to cackle at this and goes into a fit of coughing.

"Don't worry about it," she says when she gets her breath back, "dead bodies don't feel nothin', just close me eyes and plait me hair—take me nice hairpins for yourself—plain ones is good enough for the grave."

Rachel's shudder does not stop Mary. "You'll be surprised how easy it'll be, girl—I done worse long before I was your age."

After the morbid conversation they became quite festive, treating themselves to leftover Christmas cake and syrup before settling on the couch like children with Lavinia's journal between them.

"It come to me today, now's me chance to find out what Vinnie put down about them all—about Charlie, and about his people, about Meg and Ben and Thomas—about Ned and me, too," Mary told the girl.

The old woman speaks casually, turning pages, reaming off names of people long dead, her excitement is growing—with Rachel here not only can she find out everything Lavinia had written in the book—she can write something of her own! For the first time the power of written words—words that can stay behind and talk, just as if you were alive—dawns on Mary: "Sure that's why Vinnie done it!"

"I'm going to have you write something down, something of me own—at the end here, maybe," Mary shows her great-granddaughter the empty pages and watches slyly as the girl picks up the book and squints at the lines of fading script.

"I can write, but I'm slow. Miss says I'm about the slowest in class for penmanship—and she says I writes too small."

"I allow now you're every bit as smart as Vinnie was. We'll do it a few words at a time. If I told you what to set down, couldn't you put it in the book for me?" There is not another soul in the world she would have, could have, asked such a thing of.

Writing certainly is slow work. Mary had never realized how slow but she holds tight her impatience, makes herself repeat and repeat each sentence, watching the pen move snail-like across the thick paper, and after a week three pages are covered in Rachel's fine web-like writing.

Except for the growing bulge below the girl's waist it is almost as if Stephen Vincent had never set foot on the Cape. Rachel and her great-grandmother are together all the time. Mary sits in the rocker they have pulled over to the front of the stove while Rachel, curled up on the couch, reads Lavinia's words. This, too, is slow. Lavinia's writing is hard to make out, there are many misspellings, lines scratched over and dribbling into illegibility.

All in all Mary is disappointed.

"'Tis like the Bible," Vinnie had said and Mary had believed her, had expected stories of giants and floods, of storms and bolts of lightning coming out of heaven, yarns with great ringing phrases, rolling words like those that leapt from Ned's mouth when he was happy or excited. Instead Lavinia has written of women clearing gardens, of making fish, or hay, or candles—mundane things Mary would not have given the time of day to.

"Whenever is she goin' to get around to somethin' happenin'?" the old woman would ask peevishly after Rachel has been reading about berry-picking or boat building for an hour. Yet, when they do come to one of Lavinia's accounts of something happening, Mary is no better pleased, interrupting the girl's reading to insist that Lavinia has lied or completely misunderstood.

"Put the rights of it down there," Mary orders. And pointing to the white space around the edge of the page she dictates her own version of the event.

Sometimes she feels the past pressing down on her like the lid of a coffin. All she wants is to sit alone and think about it, work out the way it really was. When this happens Mary says she is tired, wants to take a spell and contrives some message, anything that will get Rachel outdoors, breathing a bit of fresh air into her lungs. Cautioning the girl not to say a word outside the house about what they are doing, Mary sends her to borrow thread, to bring in wood or water, to check on the hens or shovel snow off the bridge.

Still, they spend most of each day huddled by the stove, reading and writing, so content that sometimes it is late evening before they realize they have not eaten since morning. Suddenly famished, they warm soup Jessie has brought or get cups of tea and thick slices of bread spread with molasses. Rachel brings the food over to the fire, carrying it on Mary's old tin tray. They eat in companionable silence, staring into the embers and thinking about Lavinia and Thomas, Meg and Ben, about Moses and Ned and the Vincents, who are becoming more real to them than the people in the surrounding houses.

And this is how Mary's part of the journal is written. All through those dim winter afternoons, as they sit, oblivious of snow hitting the window and piling against the storm door. The old woman remembering things she had hidden years before. The young woman forgetting things that had happened last summer—not thinking of the child growing inside her—not realizing that it, too, must be part of the story she is writing down.

seven

"I minds me mother well but I hardly remembers me father's face—he was about the place but I thought no more of him than I did of the horse or the pig we kept each summer. He moved around like a beast, sort of hunched over and wearing a shaggy old jerkin made of sheepskin, mud coloured it was, same as his hair and face. I do mind he always carried a stick and would take a swipe at me or Tessa and bellow something we didn't understand."

"Me mother's name was Una, thinkin' back on it I believe he beat her. When he was home she scuttled around the house, dodging out of his way like a dog who expects to be kicked. I don't know what her last name was—maybe she didn't have one—I doubt they were married, we didn't have nobody like Meg to make us stand up before a preacher." Rachel wrote down each word her great-grandmother dictated, even those she didn't understand.

Mary Bundle was born in a part of Dorset called the Shepton Hills during the reign of George the Third. Her father, Walt Sprig, hired out to large landowners as a shepherd. Each year, soon as the days began to lengthen, he would take sheep high up into the hills, bringing them down in late fall, fat and ready for market. He was a silent, disagreeable man and the lonely life in the hills suited him.

Una and the two girls lived in the hut built on a small plot adjoining acres of rye and oats belonging to Master William Potts, who lived in the village of Coltsford ten or so miles away. William Potts had many interests including a mill and brewery in Coltsford. He also owned the hut, but let the Sprig family live there on the understanding that they guard the crop and take care of his sheep.

Una (Mary had never heard of anyone else with the name and wondered if she had gotten it right) was a thin, wiry woman, well under five feet in height. She did all the work around the place, raised turnips, beet and cabbage, kept hens, rabbits and a pig and grudgingly took care of the skeleton horse which she considered an extravagance since it was only used in winter and then just to take her husband to the public house in Coltsford. Una rushed from job to job like a small brown scavenger, demented with fear that winter would come before she was ready, half finishing one job before seeing another more urgent; hacking at the dry earth around her garden, lugging buckets of water from the river, pulling up a handful of weeds, flinging them at the rabbits, scrounging the woods for nuts, berries, for fallen branches which she piled on a hogshide and dragged home, stealing hay for the horse, creeping carefully around the edges of the field lest William Potts, during one of his infrequent visits, should notice.

Una constantly patched the roof and walls of the hut, using anything she could lay hands on: sheep and rabbit skins, the hides of pigs, bits of wood, straw and sods. As a result, the house was infested with vermin and had the look of a large dirty animal squatting in the middle of a trampled piece of earth. In the fall she killed the pig, using every scrap of the animal, hooves, bones, skin and innards. What could not be eaten she rendered into oil to cook with or to make rushlight—which was not often needed, for Una went to bed as soon as it was too dark to work, mother and children falling together into a mound of ragged quilts, sheep and rabbit skins piled in one corner of the hut.

When Mary and Tessa were old enough, their mother made some effort at compelling them to share in the work. But the girls were wild as goats and Una lacked the persistence to keep them at a job. She resigned herself to doing all the work alone, making them care for each other and, when he was born, for their brother John Luke. The baby was small and peevish and never stopped whimpering except when his mother's nipple or a tea-soaked rag was stuffed into his mouth.

Year in, year out, the only people they saw were Master Potts' farm hands who came to harvest the crop, and the odd peddler or tinker who stopped to have a drink of water. They had never seen another female. Mary and Tessa grew like young animals, hide-and-seeking in the tall oats, playing at the edge of the wood and splashing in the river. The only unhappiness they knew was the surly presence of their father, which was infrequent, and the gnaw of hunger, which was so constant that they accepted it as a normal condition. They ate whatever they could find: nuts, mushrooms, berries, even seeds, and chewed on beet and raw turnip stolen from their mother's garden.

Mary was seven or eight and her sister two years older the spring after John Luke's birth, when their father abandoned his family to become a soldier. On an all-night spree in Coltsford, Walt Sprig met two men going to join the Duke in Spain, where England was fighting the interminable Peninsular War against France. Returning to the hut he told Una, in a few grunted words, that he was leaving, snatched up the quilt that was covering the girls and stuffed it, along with cheese, tea, his extra leggings and his knife, into his skin bag.

Mary remembered seeing him reach forward and lock his bony fingers around her mother's arm. Jerking the woman towards him he pushed his other hand into the pocket of her brin smock, pulled out the few coins she had tried to hide and transferred them to his own pocket. Una had pulled away and he let her go so suddenly that she fell atop the pile of rags and children. As he banged through the door, Mary caught a glimpse of his companions waiting across the garden. In the dawn mist they looked like men without legs. It was an image that stayed with her all her life, men moving legless through the grey light—moving away.

Mary and Tessa did not miss their father, but before many weeks passed it was clear they would miss the few shillings he had provided. Flour and tea ran out long before anything had grown in the garden and they were surviving on two or three eggs the scrawny hens laid each day.

Faced with starvation, Una took time to teach Mary and Tessa how to get fish out of the nearby river she called the Watt. She showed the girls how to make a trug, binding a bit of pig gut around a curved stick, rubbing the rim with grease, whispering a spell as it was lowered below the surface of the Watt. Fish, Una told them, belonged to the moon and must be caught at the first light of dawn when they were still moon mazed.

Tessa, usually the more adventurous of the two girls, simply sat on the bank, watching. She hated fishing, hated the cold water, the slippery fish, hated having to keep silent. The silence made her afraid. Una warned them if they heard anyone coming to drown the net, cover it in rocks, pretend to be just playing in the water.

But Mary was enchanted by this simple method of getting food. The knowledge that she was doing something Master Potts would disapprove of made it all the more enjoyable. She would stand knee-deep in the river whispering the words Una had taught her: "Cold of May, heat of June, send me fishes of the moon," and slowly lowered the net.

Holding the trug still and taut below the water, she would watch her hands and feet turn blue and wavy. The instant she felt movement, Mary would snap the net shut, jerk it from the water, snatch the glittering fish and toss it to Tessa. Watching the fish sail through the air in a silver curve, Mary thought her mother was right, fishes were bits of the moon and Master Potts had no more right to them than she did.

One day in late summer, after the oats and hay were harvested, after she had gone over the stubble gleaning every grain the men had missed, Una killed all the rabbits and skinned them. She pulled up most of the turnip and beet and collected eggs she'd been saving for weeks in a wicker basket lodged between rocks in the river. Then she harnessed the old horse up to their cart, loaded everything and set off with her children to Coltsford market.

Mary and Tessa, leaving home for the first time, were beside themselves with excitement. It was a warm day and the path twisting and narrow. As the cart creaked along between fields of oats, through meadows and around clumps of trees, dust rose in little puffs from the wheels. Mary could taste the dust, the sunshine and the warm, ripe grain. The horse plodded along, at a pace that was much slower than walking and the girls began to ask their mother questions. It was the first time they ever had the opportunity to do such a thing. Indeed it seemed to them the first time they had ever seen Una sitting still.

When Mary tried to describe her mother to Rachel, it was as she had seen her that day sitting atop the wooden cart on the way to Coltsford. Una, with her face leather brown from working outdoors in all weathers, with deep lines around her nose and mouth and her cheeks sunken where teeth had rotted away.

Only her eyes were beautiful, large and grey, sometimes reflecting the blue sky, sometimes the green and gold fields.

Una owned two items of clothing, a bag-like garment made of brin, which she wore most of the time under the dirty sheepskin jerkin her husband had left behind, and a worn brown dress she usually kept folded away inside a clean sack. That day Una had been wearing the brown dress. Sitting close beside her on the seat, Mary noticed for the first time that the dress once had a pattern of tiny roses, still visible under the collar and below the sleeves. Mary studied the small pink flowers and wondered if her mother had owned the dress when they were bright.

Tessa, holding John Luke and sitting behind in the wagon, had nattered the whole way. Lighthearted and more talkative than Mary, Tessa kept pointing to things, insisting her mother and sister look—look at the scarecrow fluttering in a distant field, at larks swirling up out of the corn, at butterflies hanging like small blue clouds by the roadside, at the spire of a distant church.

"Look! Look! Look!" Tessa squealed—the very stones on the road seemed beautiful and wonderfully different from anything she had ever seen before.

Eventually, in a pause, Mary said: "Ma, yer dress got pink flowers on it—where did ya get it?"

Una looked startled—maybe she had never heard her youngest daughter speak before. She looked down at herself as if wondering what she wore.

"I got this dress before I come here. I worked two summers in the dairy at Rogers's farm—it were a nice place to work, warm and pleasant."

She rubbed the worn cloth between her thick fingers. "We used to sing to the cows when we milked them."

Mary gazed in astonishment at her mother, who was looking off into the distance and smiling.

Think of wearing a pretty dress and singing to cows! "What did you sing, Ma?" Tessa asked. Never once had they heard their mother sing—not even to John Luke.

The girls took turns then asking questions, pleading for details. What had the farm been like? Who were the other maids who sang and milked cows? Were they friends? Did they too have flowered dresses? And, most mystifying of all, why had their mother left such a place?

But she would tell them no more. When they realized Una had gone into one of her trances, Tessa laid the baby on the pile of rabbit skins and both girls jumped down from the cart to run ahead, giggling together at the thought of their mother singing to cows.

It was well past mid-day by the time they got to Coltsford. The houses were so close together the girls felt penned-in. There were people and dogs and horses everywhere, and, because it was market day, sheep and geese being herded through the streets. The noise and confusion frightened the children, John Luke bawled and the girls became quiet and climbed back up beside their mother.

When they reached the market some people were already packing things away to go home. A large man, in a bright blue greatcoat that must have made him very hot, shouted that they had to pay him if they wanted to stop. Una fixed her eye on him, fingering the tooth she wore on a cord around her neck, and stared him down. Before Una's stare the man got smaller and smaller and then turned away.

"We traded the rabbits and eggs for flour and tea," Mary tells her great-granddaughter. "But no one wanted turnip so we had to take 'em back. I remembers gnawing on one going home in the dark. I allow the trip killed the horse, leastways I don't remember him after that. I knows he wasn't there next winter when things got so bad—we would have et him."

John Luke died. One morning Mary awoke knowing there was something different about the hut. She lay curled down against Tessa in the mound of dirty fur and wondered what it could be. She looked around at the rough walls, covered in white rime, at the shuttered hole where pale light seeped down around the edges of rabbit skin, at the small pile of brush near the firehole, at the iron pot, carefully balanced to protect a tiny flame that had smouldered all night. The room looked the same, dark and smoke blackened. As always, it smelled of oil and dirt, of sweat, boiled turnip and of the earth floor—a smell that was so much a part of her world that she did not notice it. That morning, though, something cold and strange was waiting in the room.

Then she realized that the strange thing was silence—there was no whimper, no mewing sound from John Luke. Mary neither looked nor moved, she lay curved spoon-like into Tessa waiting for something to happen.

Eventually Una stirred, woke, sat up and leaned over her son. She uncovered the miserable, yellow little body and cried. But only for a minute. Mary watched through half-closed eyes as her mother turned away from John Luke, stood up and started pacing around the room. She began picking things up, making a pile on the rough plank table, a mug, two knives, a small tin box she had pulled out from under a rock in the corner, the two remaining turnips and the flint. She put the last of the tea into the kettle, carefully shaking every grain out of the bag, poured boiling water into the pot and left it steeping on the hot ashes. Mary noticed that her mother was moving very slowly and that her hands shook as she poured the water.

"Get up," she told Mary and Tessa, who were still huddled next to their dead brother. Their mother took a spade from behind the door and went out, letting an icy blast of air into the room. Since the girls had been wearing every garment they owned to bed for a month, it took only a second to pull on patched boots and the heavy jackets their mother made by brailling rabbit skins together with twine. The girls went over to the fire and held their hands as near as possible to the steaming kettle. As they squatted there, sniffing the smell of tea, Mary whispered to Tessa that John Luke was dead.

When Una came back, her face and neck were wet with perspiration, but she had not been able to dig in the frozen ground. Without a word to the girls, their mother went to the same corner she had lifted the box from and began to dig in the earthen floor of the hut.

When the hole was big enough she returned to the bed and rolled a sheepskin tightly around their brother. She started to pick him up but stopped and went to the table, gesturing to the girls to join her. When they were standing one on each side, Una eased up the lid of the rusty box and lifted out a brooch—tiny stones set in a circle of purple light. The girls gasped. Mary gazed covetously at the pin that seemed to draw every bit of light in the dark room into itself. It was the most lovely thing she had ever seen. How mean her mother was to have hidden it all these years! Tears gathered in the child's eyes and rolled down her cheeks. "What would it have hurt if me'n Tessa had been able to look at it betimes?" she thought bitterly.

Una picked up the glowing brooch and pinned it into Tessa's heavy jacket—on the inside where no one could see—she patted the jacket.

Mary was about to protest, when her mother reached into the tin again and pulled out two long hairpins. The wavy spikes were amber coloured, ending in miniature fans shaped from mother of pearl—it would be thirty years before Mary learned the name of the iridescent material. Una pushed the pins into Mary's thick hair, one on each side. Then her mother patted the pins, just as she had Tessa's jacket, in what might have been a blessing.

Left at the bottom of the little box was a single button, silver with the outline of a large bird on its tarnished surface. Una Sprig picked up the button, rubbed it across her lips and put it back into the tin. She closed the lid, and, taking it over to the body, tucked the tin down inside the skin she had wound around her son. She picked up the small bundle, slowly carried it across to the hole she had dug, laid it in the ground and shovelled the dirt back over it.

Her mother had stood there a long time, leaning on the spade and looking at the newly turned earth. Behind her, Tessa and Mary waited. Mary was sure her mother was going to fall forward and die. She reached over and took Tessa's hand, wondering what they would do with their mother when she was dead. But Una had not fallen. She turned, laid the spade against the wall, went to the fire and carefully poured the tea. They drank slowly, warming their hands on the bowls. There was enough tea for them to have a second bowlful. When the tea was gone, Una told the girls to take a quilt each, tie it around their shoulders and to put on their heavy caps. She did the same and, after adding the kettle and bowls to the pile on the table, she pulled the corners of the old cloth together to make a sack.

"Where's we goin'?" Tessa asked. It was the first time she had spoken that morning.

"To Coltsford," their mother said, "there's nothing left to eat."

"But what'll we do without a house ta live in?" Tessa's bottom lip quivered.

"I don't know," Una looked around as if she might see an egg or bit of bread they had not eaten, but there was nothing. "Maybe I can get work in one of the big houses, or maybe the postmistress got somethin' for us from your father. We can't stay here and perish."

They walked all day. It was slow, cold going. The ground was rock hard and in places the path had turned to ice. Dark came and they had still not seen the church spire that was the first sign of Coltsford. They tried to continue but when Mary stumbled into freezing water up to her knees they had to stop for the night.

They turned into a field where stubble stood stiff against the sky, tinkling like glass as they moved through it. Mary's feet were freezing. They tried to make a fire with the flint and bits of grass, but it would not light and after a time they were too cold to try any longer. Tessa rolled their two quilts together and pulled Mary down beside her. She hauled the wet boots off and rubbed her sister's feet and legs until blood began to circulate. Then the children curled against each other and slept, no less comfortably than they had the night before.

When the cold, grey dawn came their mother could not walk. Again and again she tried to stand but the willpower that had carried her through the previous day was gone. She told the girls to go on to the village and ask after Master Potts. Surely he would send someone out for her. They wrapped their blankets around her and left without a word. It was a long time before they reached the village and longer still before they could get anyone to understand and go for their mother.

Una was dead when they brought her, stretched out on the back of a longcart, into Coltsford. The two girls and the body were taken to the house of Master Potts who disclaimed all responsibility for the wretched family.

"It was only out of charity that I allowed the Sprigs to live in the house for as long as they have. There's nothing I can, or should, do for them," he told the village constable who delivered the children to his door.

However, being one of the guardians of the poor for the county, William Potts did make arrangements to have Una laid away in a field behind the regular graveyard, a narrow strip of land where paupers, gypsies and others unworthy of the rites of the church were buried.

The girls were more difficult to dispose of. Master Potts gave Mary and Tessa a stern lecture on the trouble they were causing him and the village: "Coltsford is already supplying alms to a dozen families who, had they been provident, could have gotten along on their own. But no, they come to us saying it's the coldest winter in a hundred years—as if that was a reason why we should take in paupers from all over the countryside. Why, there'll be no end to it!"

The other guardians must have agreed with him, for the next day, after spending the night in a back kitchen of Master Potts' house (where the cook fed them the best supper and breakfast of their lives) Mary and Tessa were trundled off to Christchurch where the district workhouse was located.

The workhouse was a bleak two storey building with a graveyard on one side and a stable on the other. There was a church on the far side of the graveyard and a row of dingy houses facing. The girls were met at the front door by Mrs. Brockwell and an overpowering smell of disinfectant—the two were to be forever connected in Mary's mind.

Mrs. Brockwell had been recently appointed to her position as overseer of the workhouse after a bout of typhus had wiped out most of the inmates. She was well chosen, for never had such an enemy of dirt lived as Mrs. Brockwell. She barely gave Mr. Potts' driver time to deliver his message before she had the girls stripped, into a tub and scrubbed until their skin was raw.

Mary and Tessa lived in Christchurch workhouse for the next three years, scrubbing clothing, floors, dishes and the bodies of old, diseased and dying paupers who spent their last days there. The girls worked thirteen hours a day and lived mainly on watery soup and workhouse bread, which was made with flour the miller swept up from his floor each night.

"I s'pose you might think we were miserable, but you know, we weren't," Mary tells her great-granddaughter.

"Betimes we thought of poor little John Luke buried under the ground in Master Potts' hut, and of our mother, cold and alone outside the churchyard in Coltsford, but we never gave a thought to our Da, nor expected to see him again 'tho we told Mrs. Brockwell often that he would surely be back one day and pay for our keep like Master Potts' driver told her."

Although Mary and Tessa worked until their backs ached, until their hands were raw from lye and water, they were young and hopeful and still had enough energy to join a group of town urchins who congregated in the churchyard each evening at dusk to play toss stick, hoist yer sails and run, or to sit on fallen headstones eating food the boys had stolen.

"Me sister Tessa was all there for a bit of fun, she could get us all splittin' our sides pretendin' to be Mrs. Brockwell. The poor woman, who was not all that bad to us now I thinks back on it, had this way of rollin' her eyes up to heaven and moanin' about the sin and filth of the world. 'Twas a fair treat to watch Tessa do her."

A rat-faced youngster called Tim Toop, the smallest, although not the youngest of the thieves, became Mary's and Tessa's special friend. Mrs. Brockwell, who sometimes hired one of the boys to dig over the potato garden or do some job beyond the strength of even Tessa or Mary, refused to have Tim near the place because, she said, "He'd as lief steal from his friends as from his enemies, and cares not for God nor man!"

This was true. Tim was smart and quick, with darting little eyes and hands that followed in a flash. He could have a cake, a ribbon, or a coin, off the shelf and tucked into the folds of his ragged shirt without the person standing next to him being aware he had moved.

Tim was often in trouble with the band of thieves he ran with. He was greedy and liked to keep his loot to himself, sometimes refusing to relinquish it to the common pool the boys traded for clothing and food, or to pay the watchman who let them sleep in a shed down on the docks. Still he was perversely generous with Tessa and Mary, whom he called Blackie because, he said, "Ye're like a black cloud compared with Tessa."

When Tim was in rebellion against the bigger boys he would stay behind when the others left the graveyard and share some special treat with the girls. Once he had a bag of strange, sweet nuts, another time a small loaf of white bread still warm from the oven. One glorious night they sat around a headstone sharing a complete chicken, stuffed and roasted.

As the years passed without any word of Tom Sprig, Mrs. Brockwell became more and more impatient.

"Good nature can only be taken so far. There's no reason I should be responsible for two big girls like them, especially now they're comin' to the age when they needs to be watched," Mary heard the woman tell Reverend Wentworth, the pastor of Saint James Church.

"I can't be after 'em day and night, your reverence, they needs more instruction than I can give 'em, if you take my meanin'."

It was unclear what instruction Mrs. Brockwell was referring to, since her only communication to the girls was to tell them which floor to scrub, which old person to clean, or what vegetables to dig for tomorrow's soup. Tessa and Mary had never, as the old minister assumed, received any religious guidance, could not count or tell A from B.

The next time the minister and his wife came to do the rounds of the workhouse, Mrs. Wentworth spoke of a friend of hers who was going out to the islands of the new world, "Mrs. Armstrong is a gentlewoman, married to an upstanding Christian man who has made a good deal of money trading in cloth to the Army. It seems he has a mind now to set up business in this place called Newfound-land."

The minister's wife explained that her friend was in need of two or three maid servants to take along since the family had four small children.

Welcoming what she considered to be divine intervention, Mrs. Brockwell immediately arranged for Tessa and Mary to be inspected by the lady and her husband. She herself signed the necessary papers that bonded the girls into service for five years in exchange for their passage to the new world.

"Seems to me not right to be given over for five years just to get to some place we never heard of," Tessa said bravely.

"Altogether too flick with that tongue of yours, you are—it'll get you into trouble yet, mark my words," Mrs. Brockwell told her. "Why, there's hundreds paying pounds for the opportunity you girls is gettin' for nothing. I can't think why you're so ungrateful—but then I s'pose that's the way of it—we'll be rewarded in heaven."

Before they left, she took Mary and Tessa over to the church where Reverend Wentworth prayed for them and told them to be good girls.

Of the trip across the Atlantic Mary can recall little. She was very ill and would have died (as did a female servant belonging to another family on the boat) if Tessa had not taken care of her, seen to it that she got clean water and what food she could eat. Tessa herself was not ill but grew pale and exhausted from running between Mary and the four Armstrong children.

Mrs. Armstrong, a haughty stick of a woman with a gull's face, had a way of hitting the girls so that the large garnet on her finger made the blow much more painful than it appeared. She took a special dislike to Tessa and hit her often. More quiet and watchful, Mary learned quickly to dodge blows and keep out of the woman's sight when she was having one of her moods.

Mr. Armstrong was called Colonel and seemed, in addition to his business interests, to have some connection with the fort in Newfoundland. He was very different from his wife, plump and shorter, red-cheeked with a smooth shiny face, given to jokes and easy laughter. He was a great favourite aboard ship, talking business with other passengers and with the ships' officers, and spent little time with his wife and children. When they did see him, Colonel Armstrong was always jolly and agreeable, calling Mrs. Armstrong "my beauty" and Mary and Tessa, whom he seemed unable to tell apart, "my little dumplings."

Mrs. Armstrong's eyes followed her husband everywhere he went. She watched him as a child might watch a dish of sweets being passed around the room, with greed and love, and fear that someone else might empty the dish before it reached her hands. When the Colonel joked with the girls, Mrs. Armstrong frowned and told them they should have more respect for the master, although they never returned his pleasantries and shied away from his fat, damp hands that seemed always to be reaching out to pinch their cheeks or pat their bottoms.

During the second week out, the Colonel found Mary alone and slipped his hand, like a fat grub, into the neck of her dress, clutching at her small breast. She jerked away and ran to hide below deck, where Tessa found her vomiting behind a pile of salt pork barrels.

After that, the girls tried never to be where Mr. Armstrong could come upon them alone. They were helped in this by Tim Toop. Tim's irresponsible habits had finally antagonized his fellow thieves beyond bearing. They had threatened him with such violence that the boy stowed away in the hold of a ship about to leave port. Found the second day out, he was marched off to the first mate and forced to mark his X on a paper saying he would work his passage across and remain with the ship for two seasons.

The master pointed out to Tim that he could refuse, in which case he would be thrown overboard. Tim put a firm X down on the papers and watched as the mate wrote "Tim Toop" on the list of ship's crew. It was the first of many legal, and illegal, documents on which his name would appear.

Once he had signed on and become a member of the crew, albeit the most lowly, Tim had the freedom of the ship and was delighted to find the girls he had shared graveyard meals with. Whenever he saw Tessa or Mary he would wink or give them playful punches. Sometimes at night the three children would huddle in the shelter of the foredeck and whisper about the place they were sailing to.

"'Tis a place big as all England," Tim, who listened to the seamen talk, told them, "with woods goes on for miles and miles—miles and miles what no one owns, only Indians, and they're wild and will shoot arrows into ya! There's animals, too, jeezely great beasts, bears and wildcats and deer twice as big as the ones in England—and you know what? There's gold and jewels mixed in with the rocks!"

Tim's voice dropped so low the girls had to bend close to hear. "They can whistle for me once we makes land! I tell ya I'm not goin' back, I'm goin' to run away and get rich!" He let Mary and Tessa feel a coin he'd stolen from the cook when he was helping in the galley.

"By the time we gets there I'll have a good few—it'll give me a bit of a start. You two should do the same—that Armstrong woman'd never miss a ring."

The sisters piously assured Tim they would do no such thing. Tessa warned him that he would be hung from the yardarm if he was caught stealing.

The girls told Tim how their mistress hit them, showed him the bruises on their arms. Tim, who had been beaten most of his life, was not impressed. However, when Tessa recounted how Mr. Armstrong's hands had grabbed beneath Mary's blouse, the boy immediately recognized the Colonel's intentions. "Given a chance that old bugger'll have ye both knocked up!" he told them and went on to explain facts of life that Mrs. Brockwell had not seen fit to instruct them in. He offered to demonstrate, patting his crotch and laughing at the girls' horrified faces.

When the ship docked in St. John's there was pandemonium, families and servants rushing back and forth, calling lost children, searching for personal belongings. Trunks, hat boxes, tables, chairs, beds, books and even musical instruments were being lowered onto the wharf. Animals were led ashore, crates hoisted over the side, barrels rolled down the gangplanks. Noises everywhere: seamen shouting orders, creaking chains, screeching pulleys, dogs barking, babies crying, the neighing of frightened horses. In the swirl of confusion, Tim Toop disappeared.

The Armstrongs had rented a narrow house on the hill below the fort. Mrs. Armstrong was very disappointed with it. It was barely large enough for the family, she said, and completely unsuitable for entertaining. Mary, Tessa and the old woman hired to cook slept on the third floor under the peaked roof. The room had two tiny windows from which you could see the crooked street, other roofs and the harbour. The glass in the windows and the slate shingles on the roof clattered in the wind and for several nights the girls hardly slept.

Fall slid into winter and the attic room grew colder and colder. Some nights Mary was sure the whole house was about to blow away and tumble down the hill into the harbour. Mary and Tessa slept on straw on the floor with but one blanket between them. Mrs. Bowden the cook slept in the same room. The girls never found out where the woman came from. She used to keep a little brown bottle of medicine tucked into the cuff of her wool stockings and would take it regularly before bed each night.

"'Twas a good spell before it come to us it was the Colonel's Madeira. I don't blame her a bit, took somethin' to sleep in that room. She used to hide bits of bread and cheese in her pockets, too—for me and Tessa to eat in bed—and she kept three bricks near the kitchen fire all day to carry upstairs. Them bricks were the only bit of comfort we had, we'd try to get asleep before they got cold."

At the Armstrongs, Mary and Tessa worked even harder than they had for Mrs. Brockwell. They could not go to bed until the household was settled away, until guests left, dishes and pots were washed and the kitchen set to rights. Then porridge must be started for breakfast, candles trimmed, lamps cleaned and fires laid for the next day. Long before dawn they must wake and begin again. First they lugged buckets of water on a hoop from the well pump halfway down the hill, then they had to light four fires: one each in the kitchen, dining room, parlour and in Mrs. Armstrong's bedroom.

While Mrs. Bowden prepared the Armstrongs' breakfast, Tessa and Mary set water to heat, carried it upstairs for Mrs. Armstrong's bath. They emptied all the chamber pots, scrubbed them and returned them to their place under the beds, the cloth bag containing dirty pieces of silk was removed, taken downstairs to be washed later, a clean bag with clean silk scraps was hung on the rod near Mrs. Armstrong's pot. Next they woke the children, bathed and dressed them in front of the fire in the Armstrongs' bedroom.

Sometimes even Mr. Armstrong took a bath there. He liked to have Tessa or Mary bring extra buckets of hot water up from the kitchen to pour over his back as he sat in the tub. On those occasions his wife would sit at her little table in the corner, sipping tea. "You two will have the Colonel spoiled," she would chide in a high, false voice as if carrying water up a flight of stairs had been Mary's or Tessa's idea. She always turned her head away when they poured the warm water over her husband. He would chuckle and tell the girls they should get into the tub with him and make playful grabs at them with his wet hands. His wife clicked her tongue, pretending it was all a game.

Mrs. Armstrong hired and fired five nursemaids in quick succession. "Slatternly, stupid creatures who wouldn't have been let in the door of any decent English house," she told her husband, and arranged for the two older children be sent daily to an infants' school run by Miss Slater on the Upper Path. The younger children's needs must be cared for by Mary and Tessa, who, their mistress said, had little else to occupy their time.

Mrs. Bowden made trips down over the hill for vegetables, meat and fish, but Mary and Tessa were only allowed to go as far as the water pump. Mr. Armstrong told them the streets of St. John's were not safe for females at night. Since there was not time to go out by day the girls saw almost nothing of the town. One day Tessa came back from the well and told Mary she'd seen Tim standing in a doorway as if watching for someone, but when she waved and called out he hadn't seemed to know her.

Mrs. Armstrong spent her time sitting near the parlour fire, working red roses on a set of needlepoint covers for the dining room chairs. She complained constantly of the cold, the lack of good tea and congenial society. Her temper grew even worse when winter came and she discovered that every woman she accounted her social equals had returned to England for the season. She swore that she would die of cold before spring, if she was not poisoned first by the food, which had a rotten taste and was, she said, making her sick.

Every few days she took up and abandoned new ideas about the running of the house. One week she accused the servants of being thieves. For a short time after this she counted each item of food and watched as Mrs. Bowden locked it away each night. All to no avail. Mrs. Bowden's brown bottle was always full and there was always cheese and bread for the girls to gnaw on at night.

After the food counting fancy passed, Mrs. Armstrong announced that prayers would be read by the Colonel each morning at six. Then she decided the servants had to take a cold bath every Saturday night. Each practice continued for a week or so until she thought of some other way to make their lives miserable.

Only the woman's meanness was constant. When Mary's boots fell apart, Mrs. Armstrong made her wear a pair of her husband's castoffs. Although Mary stuffed rags into the toes they were still far too big and flopped up and down, rubbing her heels until they bled. Mary hated her mistress. She learned to choke down rage by imagining what colour the blood would turn the dress Mrs. Armstrong was wearing if she were to drive a knife into the woman.

Mrs. Armstrong's only pleasure came from the status her husband enjoyed with officers of the fort. Governor and Lady Hamilton having returned to England, she felt it fell to her to "bring a touch of graciousness to the poor men's lives." To fulfil this duty she gave a dinner party each week.

On these occasions Mrs. Armstrong was usually the only woman present. When the Armstrongs and their guests sat around the dining room table, which was too grand for the small room, Mrs. Armstrong, with her hair pinned up in elaborate curls, seemed happy, completely unlike the woman who had terrorized the servants all day. She would smile in the candlelight, the tops of her pale breasts pushing up above the dark taffeta whenever she leaned forward to speak to the officers. Tessa and Mary, bringing in food, would be surprised to see how young the woman looked as she sipped wine and flirted with the men in red uniforms.

"But she wasn't near as pretty as Tessa. Tho' we was half-starved and worked like dogs, Tessa was still pretty, taller than me, she was, with blue eyes and blue-black hair and white skin—not plain and dark like me," the old woman tells her great-granddaughter.

Mary and Tessa had to stand in the doorway between kitchen and dining-room waiting for Mrs. Armstrong to indicate when to serve something or take something away. In the kitchen behind the girls, the old woman would be watching pots, laying food out on platters and piling dirty dishes in a corner to wash later. Sometimes there would be one or two soldiers lounging in the kitchen waiting for the officers. They would help keep the fire going.

The night it happened, Tessa was moving around the table from place to place with a platter of baked hen. One of the young officers, as he served himself from the platter, looked up. "Uncommonly pretty maid you have here, Mrs. Armstrong," he said, smiling at Tessa.

Mrs. Armstrong shot Tessa a look of such hatred that Mary, watching from her place in the doorway, felt a chill of fear, like the cold tip of a knife touching her skin, tracing a line around her heart.

"We was done for, that minute we was done for and I knowed it. I saw it in the look the crow gave Tessa."

The guests were barely through the door when Mrs. Armstrong swept into the kitchen. She walked over to Tessa, who stood back on with her arms in a pan of greasy water, grabbed the girl's long hair and yanked her around. She pulled Tessa across the room, screaming that the girl was a dirty little slut and would not spend another night under this roof.

Mrs. Bowden rushed over and, with a good deal of courage, tried to calm her mistress down, pleading that she was sure the girl meant no harm. With her free hand Mrs. Armstrong struck the cook across the face and continued pulling

Tessa towards the door. The enraged woman's screeching grew louder until it filled the room. She called Tessa a wanton whore and said she'd tried to corrupt first her husband and now her guests, that she was not fit to stay in the same house with innocent children. Tessa sobbed and tried to pull away and Mary stood with her back pressed against the wall, struck dumb, knowing nothing could stop what was about to happen.

Mrs. Armstrong had gotten to the back door and was pushing Tessa, who was wearing only a thin dress, out into the snow, when Mr. Armstrong came into the kitchen asking jovially what the fuss was about. He tried to calm his wife, her voice did drop slightly, but she continued to scream that the girl was not spending another night in her house, that she was going to have her charged with disorderly conduct and insolence.

"All right, all right my love, you just go on up to bed," he managed to disentangle his wife's hand from Tessa's hair. "Go on up to bed now, I'll take the girl up to the fort—they'll hold her for the night and we can talk about it in the morning."

She was satisfied then and stood back while Mrs. Bowden ran for Tessa's old jacket. Mary, who hadn't moved an inch, watched dumbly as Mrs. Armstrong held the door wide and her husband hurried Tessa through it and into the night.

"Then the old bitch went up to bed without another word. Me and Mrs. Bowden cleared everything away and there was still no sign of Mister. It must have been hours later, I was kneelin' down in our room with me face pressed up against the window, when I saw him come back to the house by himself."

At this point in her story the old woman stops. She gets up, pokes at the fire, walks to the window to stare down at the frozen Cape, comes back to the stove and sits down. Finally she tells Rachel to go on up to bed.

Next morning when Rachel walks into the kitchen Mary is sitting in the same place, staring at the dead ashes.

eight

Sure that her great grandmother is about to die, Rachel tries to fulfil her promises. She puts the journal into the sack and hangs it back on the nail behind Lavinia's door. Then she goes to get her mother. The kitchen fills with women bringing food and advice. The old woman refuses to acknowledge their presence but takes a cup of tea when it is placed in her hands. Sometimes tears roll down her cheeks. It is the tears that frighten them, no one on the Cape can remember ever having seen Mary Bundle cry.

Then, just after dark on the second day, Mary shakes herself, looks around the crowded kitchen and, as though there has been only a minute's interruption in the narrative, speaks to Rachel: "For mercy's sake, what's the matter with ya, girl? Go get the book. And the rest of ye—get yerselves on home!"

When at last her children and grandchildren have gone resentfully back to their own houses, Mary keeps Rachel writing all night. Sometimes she pauses to repeat a name, or a sentence: "Make sure you marks it all down—all of it, every word!"

Mary's jet black eyes peer out from deep sockets, her nose and chin seem to protrude farther and farther as her face shrinks. For the first time, Rachel can see why people are afraid of her Nan.

Mary had not closed her eyes the night they took Tessa away. She was still slumped down against the window, half frozen, when the cook touched her shoulder and said it was time to go downstairs. For all Tessa was gone, there was still water to be lugged, youngsters to be dressed and breakfast to be gotten for the family. After breakfast, both Armstrongs left without a word. Dressed up in their Sunday clothes, him wearing his military jacket with a medal pinned onto the breast pocket, they went off to church.

Everything was just like any other morning—except that Tessa was not there. Mary was beside herself with worry. "We gotta do somethin'," she kept repeating but Mrs. Bowden said all they could do was bide their time and wait.

The Armstrongs did not return to the house until after dark. And they spoke not a word about Tessa. The next day, no one came near the house and Mary fancied people turned away from her when she went down to the pump. "I think me and Mrs. Bowden both knowed somethin' terrible had happened but we was afraid to bring up Tessa's name to the Armstrongs. Afraid to ask—so afraid I just kept on doin' for them, cleaning up their shit and getting their meals, waitin' on 'em hand and foot."

"You knows, maid, how good Christians is forever saying people is meant to be sorry for things they does? Well I tell ya, not many things I done I been sorry for! What I been sorry for all me life is things I never done—'specially what I never done them days after Tessa was took. Many's the time I wished I'd poisoned both Armstrongs durin' them two days."

After supper on Monday, just as they were beginning to wash up, there was a tap on the kitchen door. When Mary answered she found Tim Toop standing there. He stepped into the kitchen eyeing the cook warily, "She alright?" he asked Mary.

Mary nodded and went over to shut the door between the kitchen and the rest of the house. When she turned around Tim was devouring a large slice of meat he'd snatched off the sideboard. "You know what's become of Tessa?" he asked through the food.

Mary shook her head.

"Well, far as I can make out the Armstrongs lodged what they calls a complaint of insubordination and disorderly conduct again' her. Said she had to be put in her place—set on havin' her punished and sent back to England on the first ship sailin' in the spring. Anyways, she was brought in before this Lieutenant Emerson—a mean bugger what got a lot to answer for—and will some dark night if he ever ventures out alone...."

As Tim talked, Mary put her hands over her eyes and began to rock back and forth. Mrs. Bowden pulled the girl toward her so that her face was resting against the cook's grease-stained apron.

On the testimony of Mr. and Mrs. Armstrong, Emerson ordered that Tessa be taken to the foot of Garrison Hill and given twenty lashes by the common whipper. Tessa fainted after ten strokes were laid across her naked back. Tim had not seen the whipping, a soldier in the tavern told him it had been freezing cold and they threw water over the girl. When she came to, they continued the whipping. It was terrible to watch, the man said, the cold water froze to her bleeding back and when the lashing began again the caked ice broke, tearing flesh away on the whip.

Mary started to gag, pulled away from Mrs. Bowden and rushed outside where she vomited in the snow. When she came back to the kitchen, Tim was telling the cook that after the whipping Tessa had been turned away to fend for herself. A soldier took pity on the girl and carried her home to his wife. She was still there, in one of the houses out back of the garrison. He had heard she was in a bad way.

Before Tim finished speaking Mary was pulling him towards the door, but Mrs. Bowden made them wait while she fetched Mary's coat from the attic.

"You'd best be prepared for the worst. Take this—just in case you needs a bribe," the cook pushed Mary's shell hairpins and Tessa's brooch, which the girls had hidden in their bed straw, into the pocket of Mary's coat. Then Mrs. Bowden wrapped a loaf of bread and the rest of the meat in a dish cloth: "I'll leave the latch off this door so's you can get back in," she said and put the food into Tim's hands, "And here," the good woman turned her back, hoisted up her skirts and pulled the little brown bottle out of her stocking, "take this—it might help the poor child. I wish to God there was more I could do!"

The weather had turned milder. Outside, the night was thick with fog that blended with the snow turning everything into a grey-white cloud. The surface of the snow was melting and each footstep took Mary ankle-deep in slush. The freezing water splashed up her skirt and stockings so that she was wet to the waist before they got halfway up Garrison Hill.

She was sick with apprehension and bitterly ashamed for not having gone in search of Tessa. If only she had done something—spoken out, shouted, screamed, kicked, followed Tessa—even if it had not helped she would have felt better. They would have been together. The Armstrongs were going to pay for this. No matter if they killed her, the Armstrongs were going to be sorry for what they did to Tessa. Stumbling along the narrow path behind Tim, Mary promised herself that she would never again suffer in silence.

Tim led her around the crumbling outer wall of the fort to the back where married soldiers lived. The row of small houses built against the stockade wall were half-buried in snow.

Tim pounded on the door of the third house they came to, it was opened by a young woman holding a baby in her arms. She let them in without a word and nodded towards the floor where Tessa lay face down on a quilt that had been spread in front of a feeble fire. The girl's back was bare, raw and bloody with flesh hanging away.

"I did try to clean them cuts, but the poor lass screamed so I hadda' stop—maybe 'twill heal itself for there's naught we can do." The woman sounded weary, but brightened a little when Tim passed over the package of bread and meat. "There's little enough we could do," she told Mary, "Harry's only a regular soldier, he's on duty up on the hill and I got the baby to see to. Yesterday I got some milk into the poor maid but today she took nothing. She's burnin' up and moaned for hours before she dropped off to sleep."

A huge dog occupied the space between Tessa and the fire. There were no chairs in the room, just a table, a bench and a bed against the wall. Mary and Tim sat on the floor beside the sleeping girl. Mary leaned forward to study her sister's face, her skin looked blue and her breath rasped in her throat. The woman went and lay with her baby on the bed. After a time Tim moved around to sit by the dog where he too fell asleep, his head resting on the big animal.

Mary stayed crouched by the quilt, never taking her eyes from her sister's face and torn back. She had seen old people die in the workhouse and recognized the grating sound. After an hour or so she thought she heard a change in the breathing.

She put her face down close to her sister's, "Tessa—'tis Mary—can you hear me? Tess I'm that sorry."

Tessa's lids fluttered and she cried out, some word Mary did not understand. Then her eyes opened and she saw Mary: "Mary, Oh Mary he hurt me, he hurt me..."

"Wait, wait a minute," Mary searched the room, found a spoon and came back. She poured some of Mrs. Bowden's rum onto the spoon and held it to her sister's lips, but the thick liquid only ran down Tessa's cheek into her hair.

Tessa was mumbling about being hurt. Mary hunched forward, straining to hear the words, and slowly realized it was not the whipping her sister was trying to tell her about.

"Don't go back to that house, don't go near to him, Mary," Tessa was saying over and over. It took a long time for Mary to make sense out of what the dying girl was telling her, but eventually she understood.

Mr. Armstrong had harmed Tessa. On the night he took her from the kitchen he had dragged her into one of the abandoned powder sheds and raped her before taking her on up to the jail in the fort.

Tessa seemed to have forgotten the whipping. It was the rape that played on her mind, that, and the need to impress upon Mary that she must not go back to the Armstrong house.

Weeping, Mary promised. She would never go near the Armstrongs again. Immediately, Tessa became quiet and seemed to sleep. Mary sat on, for an hour, two hours—she was never sure how long—she only knew that sometime during the night there was no longer any sound coming from Tessa. But she still sat watching her sister's face, recalling all the things Tessa had done for her, the times she'd given her food, saved her from beatings, cared for her when she was sick—and what had she ever done for Tessa?

Sometime later, she became aware that Tim was kneeling beside her, he pulled the quilt up to cover Tessa's body. "Want to say a prayer or somethin'?" he whispered.

Mary shook her head. She reached over and touched Tessa's hair. Then they stood and went silently across the room and out into the sick white winter night.

"What'll you do?" Tim's rat face peered at her out of the fog.

"I don't know." Tessa had been the only person who ever cared about her. "I don't know," she said again, "I'd have been dead long ago if 'twasn't for Tessa—I s'pose I'll have to fend for meself."

"I s'pose worse comes to worst you could go back to the Armstrongs," he said.

She told him about the rape. By the time she finished, her teeth were chattering. It had gotten much colder, the footprints they'd made earlier were frozen into hard ruts and the path down the hill had become a glittering white slide.

"I promised Tessa I wouldn't go near the Armstrongs. What will happen—to—to her body?"

"Dunno—don't make much mind, do it? They can't hurt her now, the bastards," Tim's voice was matter-of-fact even when he swore.

Mary nodded. No, they couldn't hurt Tessa anymore. She thought of the Armstrongs, right now in their warm beds. They had killed Tessa, yet they still lay safe and secure. Tomorrow they would go about town all dressed in their fur coats with Mrs. Bowden's good breakfast warm inside them, just like Tessa'd never lived. A great red wave of hatred rolled over Mary.

"Mrs. Bowden told us she'd leave the back door unhooked," she said.

Tim understood immediately. At the foot of the hill he told her to wait and disappeared behind a shed. He returned in minutes with two brin bags, dirty and stiff with snow. The eerie light had not changed although it must have been near dawn when they let themselves into the silent house.

The big kitchen was empty, the fire out, the pan where Mary'd been washing dishes when Tim arrived was still there, the dishes covered in congealed grease.

Tim tossed her one of the bags, "Here Blackie!" he grinned at the name and gave her a push towards the pantry, "Fill this with stuff to eat—I'm goin' to have a look around."

Instead she followed him, down the hall and into the small front parlour, watching as he walked around the room dropping things into the bag: a small vase, the Colonel's gold watch, a set of candlesticks. He saw her and grinned, "Go on back and get that grub, I'm goin' upstairs."

She shook her head frantically. She was sure that any minute Mr. Armstrong would appear at the top of the stairway. But Tim took no notice, silent as a shadow, he crept up the steps. Mary went back to the pantry and swept butter, bread, cheese, fish and sausage indiscriminately into the bag.

But she had not come here to steal! Looking about, wondering what she could destroy without making any noise, she saw the supply of wine Mr. Armstrong kept beneath the butter cooler. Using the corkscrew just as cook had taught her, she worked the corks out of three bottles of red wine. Carrying them with care she went into the dining room and poured the contents over Mrs. Armstrong's needlepoint cushions. The act gave her such satisfaction that she decided to take more wine upstairs—to pour over Mr. Armstrong's jackets, over his wife's dresses, maybe over Mr. Armstrong himself.

"No, I'll not pour wine over him, I'll smash the bottle down on top of his bloody head—then I'll cut his thing off!"

She rushed back to the pantry and was just snatching another bottle from under the butter cooler when she felt a hand on her shoulder.

The bottle crashed onto the stone floor. She whipped around to face Tim, still grinning and holding a bulging bag on his shoulder. He paused long enough to snatch the two unopened bottles, dropping them neatly in on top of the food, he grabbed her by the wrist and pulled her behind him through the kitchen door.

Mary did not want to leave. She was riding a crest of exhileration. All she could think of was killing Mr. Armstrong. It was what she wanted more than she had ever wanted anything, more than she had known anyone could want anything! She tried with all her might to pull away, but Tim held on and hauled her down the street, around the corner, behind a tavern, through a series of yards and back alleys, until they were standing on one of the wharves that jutted out into the harbour.

"What ya think of that—pretty good what? Not another person in all St. John's coulda got you down here quick as that!" Tim waved at the dim outline of warehouses, the shrouded harbour, the sagging wharf, as though introducing her to some magical kingdom he'd conjured from a bottle.

Mary was not inclined to be grateful. She dropped her bag and began massaging her wrist—"Got me friggin' arm hauled off, ya stunned bugger!" She looked around, "What good's this? The harbour's the first place they'll look!"

"And that they won't!" Gesturing for her to follow, he climbed down over the side of the wharf and vanished. Underneath the wharf they began moving back away from the water, dodging between barnacle covered supports, climbing over slimy rocks and reeking garbage, towards the blackness. It was so dark that Mary bumped into the stone foundation and, although she was not really hurt, began to sob.

"Shut up for Christ's sake—we'll be inside in a minute," Tim said.

She heard him moving things away from a low door, then they had to get down on their hands and knees to crawl in. Once inside Tim lit a candle and with the same irritating pride he'd displayed on the wharf said, "See—it's all mine—snug as a bug in a rug!"

The room was no bigger than a small hen house. Most of the space was taken up with a deep shelf halfway up the wall that appeared to serve as a bed as well as a place where Tim stored his belongings.

"Sometimes the floor gets a bit damp, but 'tis always dry up there," he tossed both bags up onto the shelf and climbed up himself, dangling his legs over the side and grinning.

He explained that they were in a crawl space below the warehouse and cook room of Caleb Gosse's business premises. "I runs messages for him, see—and betimes I fills in for the old coot what does night watch up above. But none of 'em knows about this place."

Sometime in the past, he told her, the floor of Gosse's warehouse must have been raised and the space that had once made a back entrance forgotten. Although she would not let on—pointing out that they would both drown like rats if a high tide ever brought the sea in over their door—Mary was impressed with the warm, safe spot Tim had found. Too tired to think about the future she rolled up in one of the quilts and cried herself to sleep.

Mary and Tim were both awkward during the first days they spent together in the hidden room but once the strangeness wore off they got along well. They slept when they wished, never washed, rolled around in the dirty quilts discovering the pleasures of sex, and ate better than half the population of the wretched town.

For two winters and the summer in between, Mary lived in the tiny room with Tim. She went out only at night, when she helped him steal, "floppin'" he called it, from seamen who frequented the fifty or so public houses near the harbour. Tim never called her anything but Blackie. He hacked off her thick hair, gave her a pair of boys' breeches and an oversized jacket he'd flopped off a Portuguese and told her to pretend she was mute when they met up with other young cutpurses working the waterfront.

She tried not to think about Tessa—about what happened to her. But she often thought about the Armstrongs and wished them dead. Tim learned that they had gotten a warrant sworn out for Mary Sprig's arrest. For months every ship leaving port was searched for the missing servant girl who'd ransacked her master's house and made away with candlesticks, a gold watch and, it was said, "a considerable sum of money."

Tim delighted in bringing her stories about sightings of Mary Sprig who became something of a hero among the town's underdogs. Someone had seen her on the highway on horseback, shouting curses on the Armstrongs for having her sister whipped. Some said she'd run off to live in the woods with Red Indians. Any villainy that showed imagination was blamed on Mary Sprig, but the story she and Tim liked best was that Mary had all the time been the wife of Mike Morey, a pirate who had been working the Newfoundland coast for three summers. Now they had sailed off to Bermuda to live rich as lords on their loot.

Tim knew St. John's like the palm of his hand—was familiar with every fish flake, cow shed, cove, back alley, tavern and gambling room. He knew each ship that entered port and who the crews were, was acquainted with every night watchman along the waterfront and made sure that every thief, beggar, and drunk who slept under the wharves owed him favours.

"Them gobs in Christchurch was right—ya got to learn to bargain," he instructed Mary. His old mates would have been proud of him, he could not read but had quickly learned to count and could do business with the sharpest cutthroats in the place.

"Tell ya the truth girl, I relished it—if ya ever gets a chance ta be a boy take it—'tis more fun!" Mary tells her great-granddaughter.

She would have stayed with Tim forever, dressing like a boy, roving around the foggy streets at night, eating, sleeping and enjoying sex during the day. Only one day she discovered she could no longer button her pants and was brought to the truth by Tim's, "Gone and got into it you have!"

Despite his knowledge of sexual matters, Tim seemed completely taken aback by the consequence of their lighthearted romps. "Sweet Christ!" he said and disappeared.

Since he often stayed away for a day or more, it was not until the fourth night that Mary began to think he had left for good. It would be just like Tim, she thought, to stow aboard some foreign vessel and leave her alone under the floor boards of Caleb Gosse's warehouse.

She pawed around among the dirty quilts, feeling for the corner where Tim kept what he called his "go to hell" money. When she found it she unknotted the torn corner and extracted the gold coins one by one. There were eight of them, two large and six smaller ones, all of unknown value to Mary. The money reassured her that Tim would be back. She piled them into two small stacks with a large coin at the bottom of each pile, knotted four coins back into the blanket and tied a scrap of rag around the other four. She pinned the money into the pocket of the old coat, along with the purple brooch that had been Tessa's and the combs she could not wear now that her hair was short as a boy's. Having done what she could, Mary settled down to wait for Tim and to think about her future.

He came in, jangling money in his pocket and telling her about a group of sailors he'd taken up to the card game in Doyle's Tavern. In exchange for bringing in business, Rube Doyle had given him sixpence and a cold meat pie. He was cheerful. While they shared the pie Tim told her he'd arranged for her to stay out her time with one of the sailors' wives who, with her five children, was spending the winter in a tilt down in Logie's Bay.

"Deed I won't spend winter in no tilt with five bawlin' brats and some old bag you probably been messin' with!"

"Go on, you'd love it, Kate's good as gold and 'tis pretty down that way—nice little farms, with hens and sheep."

"I seen enough friggin' hens and sheep to last me lifetime—I can't abide them empty places where there's no people nor streets, nor even a place to hide," Mary snapped.

Then she told Tim her own plan, "If I was to get to some big town back home I'd be able to make me way. I could live like you do—floppin' things."

"Aw go on, a girl couldn't manage on her own, ye'd be caught and hung first day—or end up bein' a little whore—full of pox like Nutty Nelly down in Bates' Cove—that'd be some life, now, wouldn't it?"

"Better'n workin' for the likes of the Armstrongs and endin' up like poor Tessa," she said bitterly.

They argued for weeks as the days grew shorter and shorter and Mary's waist grew thicker. She still went out each night disguised under layers of rags but she was now so awkward that she could barely crawl in under the wharf.

At this point in her story Mary stops, considers the thickening waist of her great-granddaughter: "I was tryin' ta bargain like he taught me, but truth be told I was frightened spitless. Tim didn't want me around any more and I didn't know what was goin' to become of me."

"Then, one night—it was wintertime, we were sittin' round a tar pot the boys had a fire goin' in—and me time come. Well, you talk about a fuss! Here I was bent over double, this crowd of ruffians shoutin' and bawlin'. Thought I'd been poisoned from the bottle we was passin' around, they did—and Tim tryin' to haul me away afore I had the baby right there, back of Murray's sail loft."

Tim managed to drag Mary up to the street and into the first place he could think of, a room above one of the licensed houses where Fan Larkin and her sister Lol entertained ships' officers. He had often directed men to their premises and reckoned they owed him a few favours. With only a cursory explanation he deposited Mary in the hallway outside the women's small flat and started towards the stairs.

"We'll expect to be paid for her keep," Fan, already beginning to unwrap the layers of clothing that covered Mary, called after him.

Without even looking back Tim waved over his shoulder: "Aw she got her own money, by the time ya works down to the skin ya'll find it!" and with that, the only reference he ever made to the disappearance of coins from his hiding place, he raced down the stairs and out the door.

The baby was born that night, a scrap of a girl, so dark that Lol asked Mary if she'd been messin' about with a black man. Mary named the child Fanny, after her benefactor, and stayed on in the rooms over the tavern for two months. Despite their businesslike attitude, the sisters were kind enough but it was clear that their activities were somewhat restricted by the presence of Mary and the baby.

In March, Fan told her that she and Lol were giving up work to become ladies: "I'm bein' married to a gentleman and Lol will come and live with us. We got a bit put away and we expects to open a tea-room out on the new road goin' towards Topp's Hill." She suggested that Mary might like to take over their room and continue the trade.

Mary considered the idea. "But ya know, I always was plain as an old boot, not pretty like them," she says and seeing Rachel's shocked face, adds: "Yes, I can't tell you a word of a lie, I gave thought to bein' a whore. I knew Tim'd bring me business. But by then I had a chance to see what 'twas like and I didn't think I could endure earnin' me livin' on me back like that—almost bad as cleanin' chamber pots. Besides, like I told Fan, that's the only bit of fun poor people haves and I'd just as lief not make work out of it."

Mary declined their offer, gave the sisters her largest gold piece and returned the other three to the front of her secondhand dress, one Lol had discarded. Then she rolled Fanny in an old blanket and went out in search of Tim Toop.

Outside she felt exposed and vulnerable. It had been such a long time since she'd ventured out dressed as a female. She had heard that the Armstrongs had moved into a larger house and were being made much of by the governor and his wife—Mary wondered if they were still looking for her. She rearranged the quilt so that it covered part of her face as well as the baby.

Walking fast as she could through streets that were filthy with spring mud and garbage, Mary made her way down to the harbour. Any minute she expected to have a hand laid on her shoulder and be carted away to the lock-up. She could not find Tim in any of his usual haunts. Becoming more and more terrified that she would be recognized by a soldier or one of the tradespeople who may have seen her in the Armstrong kitchen, she crawled under the wharf and into the hideout below the Gosse premises.

She could see Tim still lived there. Quilts and clothing lay in a great soiled heap on the shelf along with a clutter of stolen objects, a rum bottle filled with cold tea and a tin of ship's biscuits. She felt around and discovered Tim's money knotted in a corner of the grey wool blanket—that meant he would be back. She left the money where it was, laid the baby down and spread her own belongings out beside the infant. She still had the flint her mother had taken from the hut in Shepton, she had the fine bone hairpins and the purple brooch that had been Tessa's, the clothes on her back, the three coins pinned inside her dress—and the baby.

What could she do? Considering the question, Mary concluded, as she had months before, that the only trade she knew was thieving. The baby was certainly a problem. Mary folded back the blanket and studied the dark little face. She wondered if she might feel more affection for the child had it been pretty like Tessa instead of looking like a small monkey.

"What's the sense of wonderin' how you'd feel if things was different. They isn't different and wishes don't make ringlets," she'd unbuttoned her dress and was just putting the tiny mouth to her breast when Tim's head appeared in the doorway.

"Sweet Jesus!" His face registered such dismay that Mary laughed out loud.

Before he could say another word she told him her plan for them to work together again.

"Yer out of yer friggin' mind, woman! What's wrong with ya? What about—that?" He pointed at the sucking child. "Anyways you'd be seen an' tossed in the clink."

"We'll work nights same as we done before. She'll be no trouble, she never cries—we could just leave her here in the blankets and she'd be alright!"

Tim only shook his head but Mary persisted. "Look ahere—stands to reason I can't carry her about whatever I does to earn a livin'. Nobody's gonna let me be a housemaid with a youngster strapped to me back! I was a big help to ya before—we done good between us and I don't see why we can't do the same now."

He would not consider it and when she kept arguing, told her callously that he wasn't responsible for her. "I took ya in for a night and here ya still is two years later—I'm not havin' it! I wouldn'ta kept ya around this long but I was sorry for ya. I got ta get on—don't want ta be running around coves floppin' off sailors all me life—no future in it!"

Nothing would move him, not her pleading or her angry reminder, "Was your cock made the friggin' baby!"

Tim had changed—not just grown taller, there was no fun in him, he'd gotten hard in the months she'd been away. "I'm not stayin' forever in this rat trap!" he said, looking in disgust at the room he had once been so proud of.

Mary knew it was useless but she kept on fighting: "You're only sayin' that, Tim Toop! Just tryin' to be rid of me. What can you do any more'n me to earn a livin'? You don't know nothin' but thievin' same as me!"

"That's what you thinks—I got lots of ways—lots. I knows some important men in this place. Got me eye on an old store further along the harbour, been empty ever since I come here, got half a mind to just move in and see what happens. Maybe I'll start buyin' damaged goods from the ships, and second-hand stuff, too."

"Stolen stuff ya mean," Mary snarled.

Tim didn't even blink, "Talk sense, woman—'tis no good for ya here—what's the use livin' in a place where ya can't go out in daylight? If I can get ya passage out will ya take it?"

Defeated, she nodded.

He went off and was back within an hour saying he'd gotten a place for her as cook on one of Caleb Gosse's vessels going up to the Labrador.

"Labrador! I thought ya was gettin' me passage back to England!"

"And who ya think would pay for that?"

"But I don't know nothin' about cookin' and I certainly don't want to spend the summer on a smelly old boat—I gets seasick—ya knows how seasick I gets," Mary wailed.

Tim ignored her protests, assured her that the *Tern* was so big that she would not be sick: "Sure I heartell there's hardly any seas up Labrador way, the ocean up there's smooth as silk. Ya'll get bed and board all summer and be back in time to sail to England—and with enough money in yer pocket for a nice start."

Everything was arranged with Captain Brennan, the *Tern's* master: "Told him I didn't know ya well—yer name was Mary somethin', ya'd just come from England and was lookin' for a summer's work on the Labrador. All he wanted ta know was could ya boil potatoes—glad enough to get a cook on short notice." Tim looked proud as punch, all she had to do was smuggle the baby on board, he told her. Once out of the narrows there was nothing they could do about the child, she could make up a second name and she'd be safe from anyone looking for Mary Sprig.

Mary studied Tim's face. "Some flick with his tongue," she thought. Aloud she said, "Why? Is anyone still lookin' for me?"

"Well not lookin' so much as keepin' an eye out—there was rumours goin' around last winter that Mary Sprig was a witch. People said she'd been seen peepin' into the windows of the Armstrongs' new house—'twas said she put a hex on Mrs. Armstrong."

"Too bad someone don't put a hex on her!"

"'Tis said somebody did—anyway she's on the verge of dyin' and if they ever get ahold of ya it'd not go good, not with talk of your bein' a witch goin' around." Tim sat back on his heels knowing by her face that he had won.

"I'm not goin' to Labrador unless you gives me somethin' when I comes back—I wants something to get started back in England—what become of them candlesticks you took off the Armstrongs?"

The candlesticks were long gone, traded to a cobbler in exchange for a good pair of boots, Tim told her. "I don't owe ya nothin', Mary Sprig—look how I sove ya the day Tessa died—I say 'tis you owes me."

They argued for an hour, Mary insisting she would not budge until he promised her something that would set her up as a respectable widow in some English town.

"Awright! I'll find somethin' for ya—somethin' good, by the time you comes back," he said at last.

But even this would not satisfy her. Finally, afraid the boat would sail without her, he pulled out a small leather bag he kept on a cord around his neck and showed her the watch inside.

He refused to let her hold it, but turned it over in his hand, showing her a circle of leaves with swords crossed over: "See there, that's what they calls a crest and them letters on each side is for old bugger Armstrong's name.

"Tis all I kept from the stuff we took from their house. I couldn't part with this—leastways not in this town—people would ha knowed where it come from, see? Tell you what—I'll give this watch to ya next fall."

Mary made a grab but he was too fast for her. "No, ya don't! You'll get it when ya comes back, not before!"

Knowing he had won, Tim's good humour returned, "I can see ya now, Blackie! A respectable widow, like Mrs. Brockwell I s'pose, in charge of the workhouse."

She gave him a long, hard look. "I got rid of the workhouse stink once, I'll not likely go back to it—but I'll be back here, so remember! Take good care of me watch or—" she searched for some threat to hang over him, "or I'll hex you just like I done Mrs. Armstrong." For an instant, just before he tucked the watch away, Mary had the satisfaction of seeing a flicker of fear in Tim's eyes.

Taking what comfort she could from the small ripple of power the threat had given her, she gathered her belongings together and followed Tim down to the *Tern* where he handed her over to the mate, dropped something into her pocket, turned and jumped down onto the wharf.

"'Tis a wonderful bad feeling bein' set down among strangers—all alone—not a face ya know anywhere. Tha's what the frigger done to me. Put me aboard the *Tern* like I was a piece of lumber or a dog. He knowed how I hated the sea—always hated it. There's no reason to the sea, no gettin' around it, no place to hide on it."

Mary might have added but would not, even to Rachel, that she was afraid of the sea, that she put no faith in boats—rotting, poorly built hulks, most of them—or in the seamen who skidded across decks and crawled up ratlines—half-grown boys pretending to know what they were about.

She had been very afraid that day Tim passed her over to the *Tern*'s mate, a man named Sam Ryan. Following him across the deck and down a steep ladder to the galley, Mary held her chin high and bit her bottom lip to keep it from quivering.

"We got no spare room aboard—fact is you'll have to dishup our meals topside—the men eats wherever they can. The regular cook sleeps with the rest of the hands, but," the mate looked doubtfully around the space between the bins and barrels, a narrow path from the ladder to the iron brazier, "I expects you'll be able to bunk down here somehow."

Clearly relieved at the young woman's silence Sam Ryan smiled and tapped one of the bins, "Everything you needs is right to hand. Matt Escott takes care of ship's stores—he'll have keys to them bunkers. I'll send him down so you can get started on supper." With that he muttered something about being ready to cast off and disappeared up the ladder.

Mary was weak with relief, the man had hardly looked at her, had not even realized that the bundle around her shoulders held a baby. "Supposin' buddy never comes with them keys, I'm not stirrin' above deck 'til we're out to sea," she decided as she unknotted the blanket, stowed Fanny and her few belongings in by the wall on top of the largest bin, and leaned back to size-up her surroundings.

A dark hole, smelling of smoke and grease and overhung with that fetid mustiness Mary recognized as rats—but it was warm and dry and she had it to herself. She fingered the hard round orange Tim had dropped into her pocket and tried to cheer herself up. The orange smelled clean and spicy, if she held it to her nose she might not get seasick. "If only I can keep ahold of me guts," she thought, "we might come through safe and sound."

But when she set eyes on Escott, Mary knew the *Tern* would not be a safe place.

"What's this we got 'ere then? A little bit of fluff—somethin' special for the men this trip," the seaman leaned back against the ladder holding out a key ring, swinging the keys back and forth, smiling, waiting for her to come within reach. One hand, with two fingers missing, hung by his side ready to grab.

He was tall but scrawny, Mary wondered if she was able for him. Resting against the charcoal burner was a pair of iron tongs, a long-handled thing with two sharp edges. Without taking her eyes off Matt Escott, she bent and picked up the tongs—they would serve nicely if she could get in one good swing.

"Gonna be like that, are ya?" the man's smile vanished and he lunged towards her, slamming the key chain down across her wrist. Pain shot up her arm and the tongs clattered to the floor.

"Don't think I don't know who you are saw Tim Toop sneakin' around, askin' if the Skipper'd take ya on. Screws for him I daresay—and helps him roll sailors too, I don't doubt!" He grabbed a handful of Mary's hair wrenching her back against the wooden edge of the bunkers.

He pawed at her and she fought back, silently kicking and scratching. He was strong, his knee was between her legs, his terrible breath in her face. He pulled at the neck of her dress, there was a ripping sound and small pearl-like buttons rattled across the floor. Mary clamped her teeth down on the man's bare arm.

A boot kicked at the trap door, "You down there, Escott? The old man's lookin' for ya."

"I'm comin'," he shouted, gave a final jerk to her hair and whispered "Cunt!" spitting the word at her.

Holding a hand against her mouth to keep back the sobs, Mary backed into a corner. She could feel the pain in her wrist and her scalp was bleeding where he'd pulled hair out. But suddenly she was more angry than afraid.

"You god-damned fucker!" she hissed. "If ya so much as comes down here again I'll kill ya—by hook or by crook I'll kill ya!"

Matt Escott picked the ring of keys up from the floor. "Don't think I'm scared of a little whore been with half the sailors in St. John's!"

Mary thought he was about to hit her with the keys, but just then Sam Ryan swung down the ladder. "Pass over them keys and get up above, Escott—that lumber's not been checked or lashed down!" the mate watched as Mary took the keys and Matt Escott clambered up the ladder.

"There's a good strong hook on that hatch if ya needs it," the mate said mildly before explaining again how she was expected to carry the cooking pot topside.

"Long as we gets fed regular we're not too particular—just bang on the side of the pot and all hands'll come runnin' with their plates. When it gets stormy you'd best dout the fire and we'll make do with hard tack and cold tea."

Mary listened quietly, searching the man's face, wondering how much he had heard.

"Captain Brennan's a decent sort, let me or him know if you haves any trouble," Sam Ryan told her before returning to the deck.

As the hatch dropped, Mary's courage drained away and she slid down, crouching against the bins of potatoes. The baby was crying, had been crying for some time. Mary ignored the child. She sat dabbing at her bleeding scalp, sobbing, staring down at the six small holes in her dress, wondering how she would keep the buttonless thing together. "I'da done better at fightin' the bugger if I'd worn Tim's old breeches," she bitterly regretted having let Tim get rid of her so easily.

She stayed on the floor until creaking sounds shivered through the planks and she knew they were moving. Then she wiped her face in the hem of the dress, picked the baby up and began to nurse. It seemed to Mary that days and days had passed since she walked down the street from Fan and Lol's place. She felt very tired. Lulled by the sucking of the baby and the gentle rocking of the ship she dozed and dreamt.

In her dream she and Tessa and were sitting in a wooden cart that rumbled along between mustard coloured fields. They were laughing and all around them pearl buttons fell from the sky, each button was a small, perfect moon. Tiny, glittering moons filled the wagon, touched the girls' arms and faces, caught in their hair—then the wagon lurched and Mary was awake.

Forcing herself to ignore the deep, steady roll of the ship she stood up and made Fanny a kind of nest on one of the bins. The child whimpered for a few minutes and then fell asleep.

It took some time to coax a fire out of the charcoal that filled the ugly squatting brazier. When it was finally burning she unlocked the bins, found potatoes and salt fish, and started supper.

As the *Tern* made its way north Mary went quietly about her business trying her best to be invisible. She often caught the Escott man's malevolent glare when she ventured above deck to get water or serve up meals, but he didn't come near her. Except for the mate, who checked the galley every day or so, the seamen hardly noticed her. Captain Brennan tried just once to engage her in conversation but appeared unconcerned when Mary shook her head in answer to most of his questions.

"What they don't know can't hurt us!" she told Fanny, and pretended not to notice when the hands started calling her Mary Bundle.

The sea stayed calm but Mary seldom went above deck. Nor did she go ashore in any of the outports where they dropped supplies. Out of the way places, all of them, with nothing but a wharf and a few houses set right down by the sea. She wondered what made people live so cut off from the world—depending on the sea to bring them everything. Mary promised herself that when she got back to St. John's, not Tim Toop, nor no one else, was ever again going to pawn her off to some out of the way hole.

She was less afraid of the Escott man when she discovered the hatch could be hooked from below, but she hated being barred in. She worried about the charcoal fire, imagining the galley in flames, herself and the baby trapped and screaming, pounding on the hatch. Although it meant getting up even earlier she began putting the fire out at night. After that she slept soundly, bedded down beside Fanny in the walkway between bins of salt fish, potatoes and hard tack.

In the middle of their sixth night out she was jarred awake by a loud rattling not two feet from her head. A sudden storm was pitching the *Tern* about, shaking the round-bottomed brazier inside its circle of bricks. Mary reached out in the blackness to make sure she'd replaced the iron cover over the charcoal. Satisfied that at least they would not burn to death, she lay down again—and there she stayed, holding the crying baby, rolling from side to side, listening to pots bang off one another, to the crash and scrape of cargo, to the shouts of men racing about overhead, but not really able to hear the sea. She was glad for that. She vomited into the bucket but did not stand up all night—not even when a large rat ran across her legs. Once someone pounded on the hatch. She did not answer—no matter if they were sinking—anything would be better than this.

Eventually the gale must have blown itself out, she fell asleep and was awakened by banging overhead. "For Lord's sake—are yuh dead or alive down there?"

Feeling stiff and sick, she got slowly to her feet, climbed part way up the ladder and undid the hatch.

"Jesus, Mary and Joseph I thought ya'd suffocated!" Captain Brennan's cheerful face beamed down at her as she stood, still dizzy, clinging to the sides of the ladder. "We're safe and sound on Cape Random—yuh can come on up now, Mary Bundle."

Fresh, cool air swept down into the hold. Suddenly, above everything, Mary longed to set foot on land. "The baby's sick," she said, "I got to have her seen to—any women in this place?"

"I heartell Josh Vincent's crowd are after movin' down from Pond Island—Sarah Vincent's a good woman, she'll help ya. Go ashore if ya got a mind to. But be quick—all hands is in need of a bite to eat and I wants to be outta here by nightfall."

Down on the wharf someone was singing: "I saw three ships come sailing in, come sailing in, come sailing in...." The singer, a man, repeated the refrain over and over.

"I'm stayin'," Mary said, "I'll not put another night over me head in this old hulk."

"Don't talk foolish! The *Tern*'s as sound a craft as you'll ever sail in!"

"I tell ya I'll not spend the summer on no ship! I'm goin' to bide here for a spell—go back to St. John's first chance I gets."

"You signed on for the season, Mary Bundle—anyways, what can a young maid like yerself do on the Cape? That was a hard blow last night but you'll be alright now ya got used to it." The Captain dismissed her fears with a shrug, "Sure ya got your sea legs now, Mary Bundle!" he grinned each time he said her name.

"Now, bring that pot and a bag of vegetables ashore, we'll have a meal on dry land and you'll feel better. Mind now—Caleb Gosse don't take kindly to havin' hands jump ship on him!" he went off, shouting orders at two seamen who were putting out the gangplank.

"How stunned was I at all—thinkin' I'd bide aboard a fishin' boat for the full season. That's what the sea does, makes ya forget how bad it is the minute you're off it! I didn't put much store in what Captain Brennan said—since I can't read or write I knowed that about me signing on was wrong. If I was signed on 'twas Tim Toop done it and 'twould be him, not me, old man Gosse'd be after."

"'I'll do what I likes and the devil take the hindmost,' said I to meself."

"And that's how I come to the Cape. I was seventeen—if I'da known I was never again to set foot out of this place I allow I would ha' gone back and faced up to the sea, bad as it is."

nine

Rachel was disappointed. She wanted to keep on writing out her Nan's story. She had been enjoying it, it kept her mind off the strange movements inside her belly, off her fear of childbirth, distracted her from thinking about the mixture of sorrow, pity and curiosity she saw in people's eyes.

But, "I'll have to think on it," Mary said. "Regards things happened here on the Cape, I expects Vinnie put all that down. Tomorrow we can start readin' what Vinnie wrote—and them pages Thomas Hutchings put in. No sense markin' down the same words over again."

So, the next morning Rachel settled the old woman comfortably in her rocking chair and began to read: "In the beginning we all lived on Monk Street in Weymouth and we was all happy...."

She read for hours. Sometimes Mary seemed to be sleeping but whenever Rachel paused she would give a start and without opening her eyes direct her great granddaughter to go on. The day was well along when Rachel came to the part of Lavinia's journal recording Mary's arrival on Cape Random: "Mary Bundle come ashore today, she's the nearest thing to a savage any Christian soul is likely to see," the girl read.

Mary sat bolt upright, made an unpleasant sound and jabbed at the book, "Show me!" she said, "Show me where that's writ to!"

Rachel pointed out the words.

"I can hardly credit Vinnie markin' such a thing down!"

The old woman stared into the fire, brooding on the treachery of her friend. The sharp, bony face peering out from the folds of blanket seemed hardly human, more like the face of a large bird guarding some mountain cave.

"I s'pose Lavinia Andrews never give no thought to what she looked like that day—nor any of them Andrews and Vincents. Just standin' there, twenty or so people lined up along the wharf, like an army of scarecrows they were—with a red haired imp of a man singin' some foolish song and dancin' in and out among 'em. Never in me born days did I see a more poor lookin' crew—skivver legged and pasty faced with eyes sunk into their heads. Apart from the dancin' man, not one of 'em was makin' a sound."

It was not just the appearance of the Cape Random people that made Mary uneasy. Their manner, the scrutiny of the children, the quiet appraisal, gave her the shivers. "I couldn't make out what kind of crowd I'd fallen in with, couldn't make head nor tail of 'em. Not Thomas Hutchings, though—I seen right off what he were!"

Thomas was the boss and in Mary's experience such people were to be watched and feared. Josh and Sarah Vincent referred to Thomas as "The Skipper," and the children, who called every other man Uncle, always addressed Thomas as Mr. Hutchings.

"Had it good, Thomas Hutchings did—the rest always took his word for everything—even when he were wrong. Went around with his nose up in the air like he owned the Cape—like a king. So there they were on the wharf, a rag-tag crowd of scarecrows and a devil, and, of course their jeezely king—all starin' at me."

Mary had stared, too—stared and watched and listened. That was her main occupation those first days on the Cape. She could see from their clothing, from the bareness of Vincent's loft where she and the children slept, how poor the two families were. Knew, by the way they held a bit of bread, savouring the smell and feel of it before putting it into their mouths, that the arrival of the *Tern* had saved them all from starvation. Despite this, Mary hoped to find something valuable on the Cape, something worth floppin', worth taking back to St. John's.

"'Tis a poor crowd don't own nothin' worth havin'," Tim used to say but during her first weeks on the Cape, Mary wondered if even Tim would find anything to steal in such a place.

"I got meself landed in the back of beyond!" she would think, lying in the loft with Fanny, the Vincent children sleeping around her. She would frighten herself imagining what it might be like to stay forever on this fog-shrouded shore, a place inhabited by creatures odder even than her mother. At such times Mary could only get to sleep by thinking about the coins she kept tied in her shimmy and the gold watch Tim Toop held for her in a little bag around his neck, by picturing some vessel that very minute making its way towards the Cape—a vessel that would surely give her passage back to St. John's.

But maybe the old woman misremembers, maybe her dislike of Cape Random was not so great. She and her child were taken into the Vincent household. No one was cruel, no one questioned her, and, at least during the summer, there was enough to eat.

And there was certainly enough to do. From dawn to dark no one stopped—men back and forth to the fishing grounds, hauling nets, heaving great piles of slippery, shining cod up onto the wharf—women splitting the fish, washing and salting it, turning and yaffling it. By mid-summer Mary was proud to be able to keep up with Sarah Vincent on the flakes. Every day she learned something new, how much salt to spread, when the fish needed turning or covering, how to render oil out of cod liver, how to gather mussels, cut out cod tongues, dry caplin, dig fish-guts and caplin into the potato garden, how to gut herring, fill their bellies with salt and pack them into barrels. She learned how to make soap and candles, bread and hay and rag mats—even how to mend nets.

"As time passed on I found meself gettin' more easy—saw them people was no more'n meself—nothin' to be afraid of. The work was no harder than I done in Armstrong's scullery and nobody was bawlin' at me all the time or hittin' me. For all nighttime was black and lonely, 'twas nice to be outdoors in the daytime."

Beyond considering her sister Tessa beautiful and herself plain, Mary had never given much thought to her looks. Yet the day she walked ashore from the *Tern* both Meg and Jennie Andrews had commented on her prettiness. Small and barefooted she'd been, her black hair all uncombed and blowing about in the wind like a gypsy, still wearing Lol's blue gingham dress that had pink flowers embroidered around the hem.

"A good bit of stuff in that dress—well made, apart from how 'tis brailled together in front," old Jennie Andrews, who had once traded in second-hand clothing, said.

"Been a spell, though, since her or the dress seen soap and water," Meg remarked when they saw the girl close up.

As soon as she arrived, under the women's direction, Mary's appearance began to change. Lol's castoff dress, declared too grand for the flakes, was washed, mended and carefully packed away to become the official wedding dress for a generation of Cape Random women. From somewhere Meg, Sarah and Jennie dredged up an outfit identical to their own, a shapeless black garment, rusty with age and darned beneath the sleeves, and a big white pinny. The apron was only for the house. Mary was instructed to replace it with a brin bag or a bit of sailcloth when she worked outdoors.

Although she was raging inside, ("The very nerve of em, takin' me over like I was a youngster—makin' me wash and comb—'tis a pure wonder they didn't scrub me with carbolic!") she saw the sense of looking like the women around her.

Even when Meg decreed that she had to put her hair up, Mary remained docile. Meg's smooth coils proved impossible to duplicate in Mary's wiry hair, so they copied Sarah's more careless arrangement, four long braids twisted into a bun and pinned in place with the fan-shaped clips.

"At least we got rid of the clits and them pins keeps it from streelin' down your back," Meg said, not satisfied with Mary's hair but agreeing, "'twill do 'til I gets a chance to stitch up a sunbonnet to cover it."

Mary was secretly pleased with the effect. The bun and black dress made her look old and respectable. No one would ever guess she was still three years short of twenty or connect her with the dirty pickpocket called Blackie. For the first time in years she felt safe.

With the feeling of safety came other, more subtle, changes. Instead of setting her gaze at knee level Mary began looking into people's eyes and, after a few weeks, when she knew no one was going to strike her, stopped dodging out of people's way. Although she never became a great talker (as she later said,

"Ned done enough talkin' for all!") the Vincents and Andrews soon found that Mary Bundle was not shy about giving her opinion.

"Young miss over there be some cute—have us all dancin' to her tune before the year's out," Meg told Jennie one day as they watched Mary instruct Meg's oldest daughter on the best way to stack dry cod. "And to think I allowed first off she were shy!"

"That twarn't shyness my dear—that were townie sauce. Just bidin' her time 'till she could start orderin' us around."

Moving silently around the place, constantly eavesdropping: "I soon found out who was who—that's what you got to do, see!" Mary, who had unknowingly absorbed the Methodist dictum that all stories must have a moral, tells Rachel. "Keep your mouth shut and your legs crossed 'till you finds out who's to be trusted—more 'specially men. Times them first months I pure thought me ears would drop off and me eyes pop out from the strain of findin' things out!"

For all her curiosity there was much Mary could not discover. She could not find out who these people were, where they came from, why they stayed.

Strangely familiar and still strangely different the Cape was. Filled with secrets. Sometimes it seemed to Mary she had travelled around the earth only to arrive in the country of her childhood. Digging in the thin soil of the Cape, memories of the hut and dirt garden below Shepton Hills rose unbidden to her mind. Words she had forgotten echo in Sarah Vincent's queer sayings, in her cautions about spirits that live in bogs and woods and ponds. The barefoot children and the way they gobble anything edible reminds Mary of herself and Tessa. She sometimes dreams of conjurors, of pirates and imps, of devils and fawns—and wakes wishing for Tim Toop whose motives are as clear and uncluttered as her own.

Of all the Cape people, the young woman Lavinia mystified Mary most. "Went around in a daze, traipsin' off with the children. She might ha' thought me a savage but I tell you, I thought she were mental—moon mazed, star crazed or some such thing!"

"That first day when I saw her coochied down beside Hazel I wondered how she could stand the stink. Hazel was Ned's first wife and she died the very next day. The Andrews were all livin' together in the fish store and soon as I come in I got that sweet, rotting death smell I remembered from the poor-house. Yet Lavinia were right over alongside Hazel, hunched up, pretendin' to write but I could see she were watching' me."

Mary expected the young woman to tell on her—to shout out that Fanny was hidden in the store—that Mary Bundle and her baby were jumping ship. She hadn't, though, and after the *Tern* sailed away Mary came out of her hiding place and passed Lavinia the orange: "Never expected anyone ta do me favours for nothin', I didn't. Vinnie took the orange like she never seen such a thing before—then she divided it up between three of us. Not greedy, I'll say that for her. She fed most all of the orange to Hazel. Strange now I thinks on it—Tim Toop's orange were the last thing the poor mortal et."

"For all Lavinia Andrews seemed meek as milk she were contrary regards some things. Never did a tap around the house, no scrubbin' or cookin' and she only turned up to make fish the scattered time—when the rest of us was beside ourselves with work."

"She was a big gangly girl, near the same age as me and she had some kind of grudge against Thomas Hutchings just like I did—so we coulda been friends if she had a mind. But no, she were content enough scribblin' in her book and traipsin' off across the bog with the youngsters. Didn't care where night overtook her, Vinnie didn't!"

Although no one was friendly, by summer's end Mary knew she had gained their grudging respect. "No more than I should, for hadn't I worked harder, and longer—yes, and better, than any of 'em?"

The simplicity of fishing, the order of it, the sense of it—catching something wild, something wasted, and turning it into food, without the worry of caring for pigs, or chicken, or sheep (the stupidest creatures God ever put on earth!), without the nitpicking details connected with cooking meals or cleaning houses—appealed to Mary.

Not that it wasn't hard to start work at dawn and spend the day bent over, turning fish, spreading salt, lugging fish and salt back and forth between store and wharf. By nightfall it would be pure agony to stand upright. The heavy black dress, sweat-soaked and salt-crusted, would be a dead weight around her legs, eyes grew red rimmed and sore, hands bled, feet and ankles became swollen. None of this was enough to keep down the exuberance Mary felt every time she surveyed the dry codfish accumulating in pungent, golden stacks inside Thomas Hutchings' store. Whenever she brought fish into the store she studied the stacks. Head back, turning slowly, she would try to guess how much the labyrinth of stiff, flattened cod was worth.

Somewhere in her brief childhood, playing jacks in Christchurch graveyard perhaps, Mary had learned to count to ten. She knew two tens made twenty but was vague about what came between. On her fingers she could keep count of ten tens, which she knew made one hundred, before going hopelessly astray.

Alone in the fish store she often counted, naming every person who worked at the fish: Josh Vincent who fishes out of his own boat along with the Andrews brothers Ned and Ben—though by rights Ben shouldn't be counted for he spends more time working on the Andrews house than fishing. Thomas Hutchings fishes alone in his dumpy little boat. That's four. Then there's the women—Ben's wife Meg and Sarah Vincent work like dogs, and even Old Jennie Andrews puts in a good day on the flakes. Mary decides not to count Lavinia who is usually off gallivantin' with the children. Nor can you count young maids like Annie Vincent, or Meg and Ben's Lizzie. Nor can the older Vincent boys be counted, Young Joe has run off somewhere and Peter is a proper nuisance, hangin' 'round the flakes all day, more a hindrance than a help.

Mary calculates that the bulk of work on the Cape is being done by Thomas Hutchings, Ned, Ben and Josh, and Meg, Sarah, Jennie and herself. Eight people—one for each finger! Standing in the store room she imagines the great piles of salted cod divided into eight stacks. Although she has no idea what price fish is sold for, she tries to guess what her stack might be worth. How much will it make added to her coins, to the watch Tim Toop is keeping for her?

"It all come to nothing in the end! My fish and Sarah's, both got counted in with Josh Vincent's. And even he got no money—only marks scratched down in Thomas Hutchings' little book!" After all those years memory of this disappointment is bitter to Mary.

Rachel nods. The outcome had been perfectly predictable—would be to the youngest child on the Cape. "Sure Nan, anyone'd know them marks was credit for gear and salt and such. And 'tis only proper all hands works together for their own crew!" The girl is hard put to believe that her wise grandmother could ever have been so foolish.

"Proper is it?" although Mary's voice is gruff she feels sad, "Ya poor stunned mortal! How are ya ever goin' to make out at all, at all?"

What will become of the child when she's gone? Mary searches for something she can tell her great-granddaughter, something about the world outside the Cape, some scrap of wisdom gleaned from so many years on earth.

"Too soon old, too late wise! Sarah used to say—if only 'twas true! If age made people wise I'd be able to tell the poor maid things would save her the trouble of makin' the same mistakes I made."

This helpless waste of experience vexes Mary so much that even knowing the futility of such action she tries to explain things to the girl: "Ya poor foolish mortal! How you think nuisance-face got his silk ties and them shiny shoes? Where did that big trunk with the brass trim come from? You think someone guv him them things in trade for fish? He bought 'em, girl—bought 'em with money! That's how 'tis in big places people gets paid in money—in silver and gold—not in numbers squiggled down in a little book!"

Rachel no longer pretends not to know who nuisance-face is. It has become Mary's accepted title for Stephen—it is easier to hear than his name. Sometimes it even makes the girl smile. "His father owned a shop, Nan—he traded ivory for money."

"That's how it is in sensible parts. That's how it should be, too. No one with the sense of a jellyfish should trade for anything but money!"

"Why didn't you leave, then? Why didn't you go back to some sensible place? You knowed that first fall there was no money to be had here."

The question stops the old woman for a minute—then she begins to cackle: "Because by then I'd set me mind on having Thomas Hutchings—tha's why!"

"Queer a stick as you'd ever meet, Thomas Hutchings were. Deep. Nighttimes all hands'd be listenin' to Ned sing or tell stories and Thomas'd be off by himself in a corner readin', like he grudged us havin' a bit of fun. Close, too—I mind he used to eat supper at the Vincent place and ya wouldn't get a word out of him. Not even Sarah, who could talk the legs off an iron pot, could get anything outta Thomas Hutchings. Still, he were the one had all the say about the fish—say over what was taken from the store, say over what supplies was ordered from St. John's—and he kept account of what was credited to each crew. Gosse paid him ta do it. Paid him real money!"

Mary had seen the money. By the end of that summer, she knew precisely what every person on the Cape owned. She had rummaged through the Andrews barrels, turning up her nose at their bundles of gaudy cloth and bedraggled costumes. "Never credit anyone'd be foolish enough to lug fousty old gear half 'round the world."

Folding the secondhand dress away, she had discovered the hiding place of poor Hazel's boots and the blue china cow—into which Meg had even then stored one coin. Mary had peered under mats, into cups and crawled under flakes. Remembering her mother she had poked at the earth around fireplaces and in the corners of rooms. She had looked carefully through Lavinia's bag, flipped pages of the Ellsworth Ledger, run the bit of green velvet ribbon between her fingers. She searched the Vincent house and the Andrews men's pockets without finding one thing worth having. Only in Thomas Hutchings' store was her diligence rewarded.

On a shelf above Thomas's desk several books were wedged in place between a rusting tin and a red plush box. Mary had no interest in the books, or in the old tin, but she was sure the red box contained jewels.

One day, finally alone in the store, Mary had taken down the plush box, held it in her hand, half afraid to open it. What if Thomas Hutchings was really a pirate? Mike Morey perhaps, hiding out on the Cape with his loot? Pirates put curses on their stuff—what might happen to her if she opened the jewels? Even then Mary had known the Cape was filled with secrets: dark things and foolish things, hidden and forgotten things—things that would be harder to find than jewels or money.

Mary released the silver hasp and the cover popped up. Inside was a string of black beads with a black cross attached—worn, dull looking things. Bitterly disappointed she snapped the box shut, pushed it back on the shelf and lifted down the old tin. It was much heavier than the plush box. She eased off the lid and gasped. Inside were gold and silver coins—more coins than Mary could count—more coins than she could imagine one person owning! She wondered if Thomas Hutchings had counted them. Would he notice if she took one, or even if she took two—or three? Maybe she would take them all. She could put stones in the box to make it heavy. How often did Thomas Hutchings look inside?

She stood beside Thomas Hutchings' desk mulling these questions. Mary can still remember the rich smell coming from the golden stacks of dried cod, the sound of flies buzzing in the dusty sunshine, the glee she felt as she sank her hands into the coins, thinking what they would buy—a house perhaps, or passage to England. Imagine Tim Toop's face when she gets back to St. John's with a bag of gold and silver!

The day-dream was short lived. Of course Thomas Hutchings had counted the coins! Not only that, he doubtless had the number marked down in his tally book. Mary had barely reached this bleak conclusion when she was jerked out of her reverie by the familiar "thwack" a yaffle of cod makes when it is dropped.

"And what might you be doin?" Jennie Andrews stalked over to the desk.

When Mary didn't answer Jennie reached forward, pulled the younger woman's hands out of the box: "One friggin' shillin' be missin' and I'll tell Mr. Hutchings you done it—I'll not have one of my crowd blamed for your thievin', Mary Bundle!" Jennie banged the cover back on the tin and shoved it back beside the books.

Mary had marched out of the store without a word. For a time she stopped looking through other people's belongings, kept out of Jennie's way and lay awake worrying that the old woman would tell her family or Thomas Hutchings what she'd seen.

Shamelessly, Mary tells her great-granddaughter all of this, of searching the Cape for something to steal, of being caught with her hand in the money box.

She does not breathe a word of how she pursued Thomas Hutchings: of the weeks she spent watching his comings and goings, of how she sat beside him at the Vincent table smiling like a fool. She does not tell how the thought of Thomas' tin of money filled her mind day and night: how she had swayed her hips, pinched her cheeks, simpered and tried to catch his eye, how she had even bribed Sarah to cast a spell on Thomas, how lying awake at night she'd considered creeping up to the fish store and slipping into his bed. She does not confess to Rachel that one day she had taken bits of hair Thomas had clipped from his beard, mixed the hair with her own menstrual blood and smeared it under the boards of his bed. Does not say how useless all her efforts had been.

"Thomas Hutchings was right on the hand of proposin' to me when your great-grandfather come courtin' and I chose him instead," Mary says. She instructs Rachel to write this all around the margin of the page where Lavinia described how her brother Ned came to marry Mary Bundle.

For of course it was Ned Andrews she had married—foolish Ned, the dancer, the singer, the liar—Ned who would never in his life own one gold piece, much less a boxful.

He had been one of the people on the wharf the day she arrived. Mary remembered his red hair and red beard, the grinning devil weaving in and out among the dour, silent people. He'd been dancing his small daughter around the wharf, warbling some foolish song about ships filled with diamond rings. His voice had wafted up to the deck, mingling with the smells of spring, bright with promises of wealth, of security, of fine clothes and jewels, of ships laden with everything Mary had ever wanted. And she, soft and sick from a night locked in the fetid galley, heard the promise, picked up her baby and marched ashore.

In her haste she had not noticed how the little point of sand with its rock spine jutted dangerously out into the sea, did not see that it held but one fish store and one lonely house, could not know that these people, looking as if they had grown out of the rocks, had themselves newly arrived, had spent one winter in the place and almost died of it.

Unbeknownst even to himself Ned Andrews had lured Mary Bundle onto the Cape and for a long time she held that against him.

After the fish had been culled and counted, loaded aboard the *Tern* and sent to St. John's, when the only proof it had ever been taken out of the sea was a briny crust on the store floor and a few marks in Thomas's account book, when the last ship had left the coast and the first ice had glazed over fresh water, when Mary knew her decision to stay the winter could not be changed; during that period, when her thoughts were continually occupied with Thomas Hutchings' coins and how she might lay hands on them, then, sometimes, she slipped into the store. It was empty of fish now, holding only their winter supplies and Thomas' belongings, a desk, a chair and a bed crowded around the fireplace, and, at the far end, the long keel of a boat Ben Andrews had started to build.

One day when she was alone in the fish store—staring at the tin filled with money she dare not touch, thinking dark thoughts about Caleb Gosse and the piles of dried fish now stacked in his St. John's storerooms, or in the hold of some ship already sailing to England—Mary became aware of a great commotion on the wharf attached to the store.

"The last ship," Mary thought, "the one that'll get me out of this place!" Her escape—coming late from Labrador—sailing just ahead of ice that will soon freeze the sea solid as lead.

She did not stop to consider. Never for a instant asked herself why such a ship would turn in to the Cape, where it might be going, or if she would be let aboard. Lifting her brin apron so that it covered Thomas Hutchings' desk, she pulled down the tin and upturned it, spilling a glittering pile of gold and silver onto the brin. Quickly she folded the brin over the money, knotting it onto the rope that kept the rough apron tied around her waist. She dropped the empty tin and picked up Fanny who has been sitting on the floor nearby. The child, so used to being jolted about, only blinked as Mary raced out onto the wharf.

Outside, every youngster in the place, even staid Annie Vincent and her surly brother Peter, even Ned's sooky son Isaac and Meg's Willie, were skidding across the wharf, screeching and yelling, slipping about on their arses and bare feet. Ned was there, of course, flinging dippers of dark blubber about and singing. Each dipperful, which he scooped out of the barrel of cod livers that have been bubbling in the sun all summer, slopped half its oily contents down the front of his jacket and pants. Unconcerned, he danced about like a lunatic, spreading the cod blubber on the boards in front of the crazed children.

As Mary rushed through the door, Ned slipped and tumbled onto a great moving mass of children. Mary was barely aware of the noise, the shouts, the swirl of arms and legs gliding towards her. She saw there was no ship. In the instant before Mary fell her mind registered that—and nothing else—that beyond the wharf the sea was steel grey, cold—and empty.

Then she is off her feet and sliding. The world was a noisy blur. She hit the water—hard—as if it were already solid. But it was not solid and she sank. The baby, the tangle of skirts and apron, the weight tied to her waist, pulled her under. Water and terror filled her mouth, her eyes, her ears. Everything was silent.

The rope around her waist was being tugged, it cut into her body. There was a hand under her jaw, her head was pulled around. Face up, she gulped air, saw the sky.

Mary remembers it all, every detail. Although years later, Annie Vincent will swear that Mary did not even ask what had happened to her baby, Mary knows she was calling Fanny's name as they hauled her out of the water.

"Steady on, now—steady on," someone is saying, "steady on—while I gets ya aboard."

She is hoisted over the side and flops into the dory like some large, wet fish. The boat has not even been untied, it bangs against the stagehead. The man in the boat hoists her up, children reach down, dragging her onto the wharf where she sprawls on her knees and vomits. Groaning she rolls onto her back, lies in a spreading pool of seawater, kelp clinging to her hair, tangling in the rope and brin knotted around her waist.

Mary sees that the man who has saved her is Ned Andrews, fighting to hold back laughter, he stares down at her. Silent, wide-eyed children peer into her face, one of them begins to giggle.

Mary wishes the little brats would die—or she would die.

"Shag off!" she mutters when Ned reaches out a hand to help her up. Ned Andrews had laughed out loud. "Such words to come out of the mouth of a lady!" he said in mock horror. Then, "Thomas's after savin' your young one," he nodded towards Thomas Hutchings who Mary could see climbing onto the wharf holding Fanny under his arm as if she were a sack of flour.

"Some good dive!" Ned calls to the dripping man.

Thomas glowers. "You'll kill someone yet, Ned Andrews, with your carelessness!" he says and without a glance at the woman lying on the wharf he strides off towards the Vincent house with the squalling baby.

"By the sound of her she'll live! Come on maid, let's get ya inside before ya catches your death," Ned grabbed Mary's hands and pulled her to her feet, then ordered the children to go get Meg, "and tell her to bring some hot tea and a quilt," he called as they raced away, each one eager to be first with the story of Mary Bundle's plunge off the wharf.

Inside the fish store Ned propped Mary in a corner as if she were something made of wood, an oar or boat hook perhaps. Then he looked around, went over and picked something up from the floor. As he walked towards her, Mary saw that he was holding the money tin in one hand and a knife in the other. Numb with cold and fear she wondered if Ned Andrews was going to kill her.

But the red-haired man stands in front of her smiling—smiling and humming, singing softly:

> My mudder says I never should,
> Play with the gypsies in the wood,
> If I did she would say,
> 'What a bad boy to disobey....'

"Gypsies should be smarter," he said and slashed across the brin apron.

The coins clattered into Thomas Hutching's tin and Mary began to cry. She is never going to get the money! Never going to be rich! Never going back to St. John's, much less to England! She continues to cry as Ned puts the box back on the shelf. So he held her, rubbing her cold arms, blowing on her hands, pulling bits of seaweed and cod-liver from her streaming hair. And she kept on weeping as if her heart would break.

Throughout that winter Mary had reasoned with herself—sometimes even when lying in Ned's arms: "A person'd be some stunned to make fast to a man don't have n'ar thing to his name, not boat nor house, nor pot to piss in. A man what don't even care!"

It was the not caring that had bothered Mary most, it was what made men die paupers, the not caring. It was what made Ned so different from men like Tim Toop or Thomas Hutchings, men who tallied up every coin, men who had little hoards of gold.

"Was Meg of course who tormented Thomas Hutchings into sayin' words over Ned and me. Meg talked to God—told us he spied on the Cape through a hole in heaven. And she thought a wonderful lot of Thomas, wouldn't hear a word against him, even later on when we all knew what he done."

But Mary let it happen, had gone quietly to the altar—or to be more precise to the cloth covered splitting table Meg had improvised as an altar. Because she saw that to own anything on the Cape a woman must have a husband, because sleeping with Ned Andrews had been enjoyable—infinitely better than spending another winter in the crowded coldness of the Vincents' loft.

That day, watching Thomas Hutchings write the names Mary Bundle and Edward Andrews in his little book, her feelings had been a strange mixture of apprehension and happiness. Thomas had drawn a swirl below the words. "There," he said, and shook Ned's hand, "The first marriage on the Cape. Congratulations, you're a fortunate man, Ned!"

"Liar!" Mary had thought. But she held her tongue and smiled, still clinging to the hope that the money in Thomas's tin might somehow, someday, belong to her.

ten

The last winter of Mary Bundle's life is the stormiest she has ever known. In notes that her great-granddaughter Rachel scratches around the margins of Lavinia's journal, the sky is always dark, the sea rough, the wind always blowing a gale.

In the dim, over-heated kitchen the girl and old woman lose track of time, morning blurs into evening, evening into night, days run together. Mary talks quietly to people long dead—asking questions unthought of until now. The small room is full of ghosts, sometimes Rachel can see them—beautiful Lavinia smiling mysteriously from the corner, Ned sitting astride a chair, chin resting on his folded hands, eyes focused on Mary's face. It seems to the young woman that she has been sitting here forever, that the past, the present and the future are all one—like a shell curved in on itself so you cannot see where the outside ends, where the inside begins.

"You done that on purpose—just for badness, didn't ya, Ned Andrews?" Mary says one day. Then she smiles, begins to cackle and, for the first time in an hour, speaks to the living person who sits beside her in the shadowy kitchen: "I were so contrary that first winter me and Ned was married 'tis a pure wonder the poor man didn't run off," she says.

"All the Andrews—Meg and Ben's four youngsters, Ned and his children by Hazel, a daughter named Jane and Isaac, his nuisance of a son, even Lavinia and the old Missis, along with me and Fanny—thirteen of us all cooped up together in somethin' no better'n a tilt, for all Meg called it a house. Bread and potatoes, salt fish, rolled oats, molasses and partridge berries was what we had to eat. Enough ta keep us from starvin' but some tedious. Nowhere near as good as what me and Tim used to eat under Gosse's wharf!"

"Jane was a good enough young maid but Isaac was forever bawlin' and clingin' onto his father so as me and Ned was never alone for a minute. Fanny was cuttin' teeth, Meg's oldest girl Lizzie almost died of fever, the baby Willie along with Pash and Emma all got some kind of croup and every mortal one of us had chilblains."

"On top of that Meg kept Ben poundin' and hammerin' all day and half the night. I were fair out of me mind thinkin' on what I'd gone and done by marryin' in with such a crowd. I didn't have a civil word for any of 'em—especially not for Ned—for all he were good as gold."

One day that winter Mary told Ned she had never been hunting and why didn't they go. "Maybe we can find a fox, or duck, or even some salt-water birds like Josh Vincent's all the time bringin' home," she said.

"No fox hereabouts, maid. Anyhow it'd freeze the arse right off ya out there t'day—and we don't want that, do we?" Ned gave her a wicked grin and made a grab at her behind.

They had gone, though. When Ned saw she was desperate to get out of the house he capitulated, became enthusiastic, sent Jane off to borrow two pair of racquets from the Vincents and went himself to get the old gun Thomas Hutchings kept in the store. Mary stuffed bread and roasted caplin into a sack and told Jane to keep an eye on Fanny.

"Better you stayed home and looked after your own youngster, Mary Bundle! Never heard the likes—a grown woman traipsin' about this time of year!" Meg glared at Mary who was wrapping her skirt around her hips and hauling on a pair of woollen leggings.

When Ned came back with the old muzzle loader and powder bag, Meg started in on him, "Haven't got a mortal grain of sense, neither of ye! Can't put your trust in weather this time of year—civil enough now but s'posin' the wind comes up, or ya comes across some wild creature—a bear, or even a wolf? Ye'd both perish and who'd be left then ta take care of Fanny—or of Isaac and Jane, comes to that?"

"Don't worry, Meg girl, I'll make sure no wolf don't eat sweet little Mary," Ned made a terrible face, growled and dashed at the children, sending them into the corners squealing—all except Isaac who grabbed Ned's leg, whimpering that his father was not to go.

He picked the little boy up and danced him around:

> Isaac Andrews went a-hunting,
> For to catch a hare,
> He rode a goat about the street,
> But could not find one there.
> He went to shoot a wild duck,
> But the wild duck flew away;
> Says Isaac, 'I can't hit him,
> Because he will not stay.'

Ned gave his son a great smacking kiss and planked him down on Jane's lap.

"Grease up the bakepot and keep the fire goin'," he told Meg as they went through the door. "We'll be back by dark with a feed of duck."

"Nomedoubt!" Meg's voice was tart but she rolled a flint and a candle inside two pair of knitted socks and stuffed the bundle into the sack Mary was carrying.

It was bitterly cold outside, but sunny and still. Along the beach frozen spray covered everything. Driftwood, upturned boats and rocks glittered in the sun. Above the beach, where snow had swirled into great looping drifts, Ned and Mary laced the racquets onto their boots and waded back through small woods and over snow-covered marshland.

Neither of them had ever worn snowshoes before, but Ned seemed to know instinctively how to swing his legs in a wide arc, breaking a trail across the powdery snow. Mary wallowed behind, stumbling and cursing for an hour before she fell into a rhythm that accommodated the awkward foot gear.

Only then did she become aware of how silent the world around her was. All she could hear was the whoosh of snow underfoot and her own gasping breath. She could see for miles across the frozen bog to a line of spruce-covered hills on the horizon. Nothing stirred. Not bird or animal, only Ned, a large dark figure well ahead of her, moving gracefully despite the muzzle loader and powder bag slung across his back. Ned, moving silently, swiftly away from her across the vast whiteness, a white mist rising around him as he plowed into the snow.

Watching him, a sudden sense of loss, of abandonment, hit Mary like a blow. Without thinking, she screamed his name. He stopped, swung around. She saw his face, and the panic, or whatever it had been, left.

"Look!" he yelled and pointed to a clump of alder on their left.

A great flush of birds rose towards the sky. Brown, hen-like creatures, speckled, with white underbellies, cackling in fright over their heads.

"Partridge!" Ned said, dropped to his knees and began scravelling through the powder bag.

It seemed to take him forever to find a paper of powder and a piece of greased rag, to slip the powder and the rag down the barrel of the rifle, to pack in the shot and ram it home. Mary had watched Josh Vincent show Ned this method of loading a dozen times but never had it taken so long.

The birds collected their wits, stopped bawling, their flying became orderly but Ned kept frantically pushing more and more shot into the muzzle loader. Some of the birds disappeared back into the clump of bushes. Still, others—many, many more than Mary could count—swooped and circled overhead.

Finally Ned rolled onto his back, pointed the long barrel skywards, braced the stock against his shoulder and fired straight up into the cloud of birds.

The gun roared. Not one bird fell but the sky was instantly empty. Everything became silent and Ned lay sprawled on his back with the rifle in the snow beside him.

"Ned, Ned for God's sake!" Mary floundered towards her husband. It seemed to take years to get to where he lay in the snow surrounded by a black circle of burnt cloth and gunshot.

His eyes were closed and blood dribbled from between his lips. Certain he was dead she fell to her knees, grabbed his shoulders, pulled him up to a sitting position and screamed: "I've gone and loved ya and now look what ya done—killed yerself! Ya stunned bugger!" Half mad with fear and spite she kissed his blackened face, cursing and shaking him by turn.

Ned's mouth opened and two teeth dropped out. Mary stopped shaking him. His eyelids fluttered, he began to groan. She eased his head down on the powder bag, got a handful of snow and began rubbing it into his face.

"Lord, girl! What ya trying to do, kill me altogether?" the words came out of one corner of his mouth. "How's about a bit more of that lovin' and kissin'—fair warms the cockles of me heart that stuff do," he lay there a few minutes more as if hoping she would kiss him again.

"Got the guts frightened half outta me you have!" she said and made as if to rub more snow in his face.

He pushed her hand away, got slowly to his feet and touched his cheek gingerly, "Friggin' gun slammed up agin' me face, wouldn't doubt but me jaw's broke!"

"Serve ya right, Ned Andrews! Rammed in too many fingers a powder, ya stunned arse! How's about you call out and I'll shoot—allows I'll make a better job of it."

Ned didn't seem to hear, he was studying the two teeth he'd picked up from the snow, "Too bad we can't figure out some way ta mitre 'em back in me head!"

"Here—give em to me," Mary shook what was left of the old priming out of the gun, rummaged through the gunny sack, found another scrap of greased cloth and in a minute had the muzzle packed with powder and teeth.

She stuck the stock of the gun in the snow and wedged it in place with the bags so that it pointed cannon-like towards a spot just above the alder bushes. "Now," she commanded, "Shout!"

Ned yelled, "Mary loves Ned!" Twenty or so birds, wings pounding, rose into the sky. She fired and two birds fell to the ground like rocks.

Mary let out a shout, and moving faster that she had all day, flung herself through the snow to the dead birds.

"Fair exchange I'd say—two birds for two teeth," she gloated and did a little dance, jumping up and down on her snowshoes.

"Might seem fair to you, 'twarn't your teeth," Ned gave her a reproachful look and tugged at her hand. "Come on, Mary maid, we'um both half perished with cold. There be an old tilt just inside them woods," Ned nodded towards the few scrawny trees beyond the alders.

"Last fall Josh daubed up a chimney out of rocks and mud so's we could have a fire."

"We're not going to eat them birds 'till everyone sees em!" Mary said as they clumped in the direction Ned had pointed.

"I s'pose now you're gonna stuff 'em and hang 'em over our fireplace so's you can forever tell people how smart you are ta get two birds with my teeth," Ned teased.

Mary remembers that day as being one of the happiest of her life.

When they reached the tilt they had to use the racquets as rakes to clear drifts away from the low door. They crawled in on hands and knees, lit a fire with wood stacked below the bunk, filled a dented bucket with snow and made tea. The tiny room became very smoky but it did warm up. They took off their heavy clothes and arranged sweaters, caps, cuffs and leggings around the fire on sticks. Mary thought the bread and roasted caplin was the best food she had ever eaten. When it was gone they made love on the hard slatted bunk surrounded by smoke and the stench of scorching wool.

"And that, my maid, was how our first, him was your Grandfather Henry, got started—in Josh Vincent's tilt—always found that part easy. Henry were born nine month to the day after I shot them birds. Meg worked it out—said that's what come of me goin' around the place got up like a tinker. Betimes I use ta wonder if Meg knew where babies come from!" Mary says and then, brazen as brass, asks where Rachel and nuisance-face started the baby her great-granddaughter is carrying.

"Never mind that, Nan," the girl says.

Love has been mentioned. Rachel wants very much to ask her great-grandmother about love: "That day, the time you was huntin', you said—said you loved him?" The girl turns away to poke at the fire.

"I were thinkin' on that t'other night—queer old things comes into a person's head nighttime! First time I ever remembers hearin' talk of love were once when Jennie Andrews, Meg, Sarah and me was burnin' roots up in the potato garden. Old Jennie started ta tell us how much she and her husband, Ned and them's father, loved one 'nother. I thought it were the most outlandish thing I ever heard tell of."

"Back where Jennie growed up there'd be one night each spring before the fields were planted when they'd have big fires. Boys and young maids would pile up dead wood, roots and dry grass, after dark they'd set it alight, stay out all night playin' games and dancin' 'round the fires."

"This was first when I come to the Cape—before ever I thought of marryin' Ned. Meg was mortified, she kept tryin' to hush Jennie but the old woman wanted ta tell us. What used ta happen was half the unmarried girls'd be knocked up by morning, then all hands'd get married after the harvest. Accordin' to Jennie that was how she and Ned's father got together: 'I loved him from the minute I clapped eyes on en', she said. Stuck in me mind, that did."

"For meself I never seen no signs of love around where I come from, certainly not between me mother 'n father. Nor thought on it when I bedded down with Tim Toop—for all I enjoyed it much as he did."

"Once I started listenin' to Ned though, seemed love were the most common thing in the world. In all them stories he told there'd be princesses and beggar maids in love with some man. He'd turn out to be rich—a pirate king or a prince—and they would live happily ever after. Tha's how Ned's stories always ended—happily ever after."

"For all I shouted out that I loved Ned that day in the woods, 'twarn't something I ever thought about. Love and happily ever after were things in stories. Words! Words nobody but an Andrews would ever say out loud." Mary pauses and Rachel waits, not daring to move for fear her great-grandmother will lose the thread of thought.

"Summertimes'd be best. In summer I'd think 'twas only a matter of bidin' me time and we'd all be rich, never again know want. That's what 'happy ever after' was, far as I was concerned."

Seeing the sea for miles around the Cape foaming with caplin, having the men returning trip after trip from the fishing grounds, their boats loaded to the gunwales with cod, helping to gut, wash, salt and turn hundreds of quintals, watching the stacks of salted cod in Thomas Hutchings' store grow taller and taller—these things filled Mary with energy and hope. Surely such abundance, such industry would bring its reward!

Then the fish would be carted away, the days would grow shorter and her fear would return. In the dead idleness of mid-winter she would become frantic. Cooped up in a dirt floored house with another baby on the way, watching the food supply go down, always down, seeing Ned's hands getting more and more crippled each year, listening to his tales about gold, watching the pinched winter faces of the youngsters, knowing another yaffle from the woodpile was going up in smoke, turned Mary into a black wrath.

"Many's the winter we barely kept body and soul together. Yet they'd call me greedy when I'd try ta figure out some way ta make a bit of money. Only real money we ever seen them days was what the men brought home from the ice—and God knows that were little enough!"

"Still and all, in between workin' and havin' youngsters, between shiftin' rocks, haulin' water and curin' fish, I stopped thinkin' it'd been a mistake ta marry Ned, stopped wantin' to be somewhere else. Lookin' back I can see clear as day that for almost fourteen year, all them years we was workin' like beasts, all them years I never stopped worryin' about havin' enough to eat—all that time I was livin' happily ever after. And I didn't even know it!"

The old woman looks straight at the girl: "Ta tell ya the truth, maid I'd give anything ta be in that old house again—a nor'east gale blowin' outside and me snug in bed havin' a bit of fun with Ned."

"Weren't only the bed thing either," Mary daubs at her eyes with the sleeve of her red dress. "Ned were all the time doin' things for me or showin' me somethin'. Most times 'twould be nothin' at all—a strange shaped tree, or seaweed curled 'round rocks—or just rocks! Ned could look at rocks by the hour!"

"I minds once he got me up in the middle of the night—wrapped a quilt around me and took me down to the wharf. Late fall it was and cold as the devil but we lay on our backs and watched the northern lights—right overhead, like you could touch 'em, or they might touch you! Little coloured fingers going around and around in circles, red and purple and green twinin' in and out like a maypole dance I saw once in Christchurch—coloured ribbons goin' round and round over our heads. And you know, every time they started to fade Ned'd whistle 'em up again. Never saw the likes of it, like they were dancin' for him."

"Sometimes on a warm summer's night when all hands'd be abed, Ned and me'd go out around the point in boat. Just easin' in near the shoals, everythin' still and the moon shinin' on the water. Sometimes he'd tell me things. Sometimes he'd sing—sea songs and old rhymes he learned in the streets when he were a boy. Had a nice voice Ned did...." The old woman rocks and smiles, "Vinnie used ta say Ned were a fair miracle. He were that—a fair miracle!"

Thinking Nan is going to cry, Rachel reaches out and takes her hand. "After you was married I s'pose ye got to be friends, you and great-grandfather's sister?"

"That we didn't! For all they got more easy with me after I married, there wasn't one woman in the place I'da gone to for anythin'. After I started makin' up cures I found the difference. Wasn't something I looked to do, just come to me. Had a knack for mixin' up tonics, poultices for snow blindness and salve to cure sore hands—anythin' like that. 'Tis in the blood—you got it, too," Mary tells her great-granddaughter.

Over the years, tales of the old woman's healing skills have become legends along the shore. Rachel has heard of the time Mary sewed Young Joe Vincent's finger back on, of the many women Mary nursed through difficult births, of how her Nan can put away warts, cure scurvy, stop bleeding. The young woman has noted that there is more awe than love in these stories—which often end with a recounting of Mary's monumental rages, of her ambition and acquisitiveness.

"My mother never was a woman you'd cuddle up to," Rachel has heard her Aunt Tessa say, and she wonders if anyone but Ned ever loved Mary.

"Bit by bit the women got used to me—but I can't say they got close ta me—not even Vinnie. No, maid, Vinnie'n me never got ta be friends, not 'til long years after. The truth is all hands thought I were greedy—covetous, Meg used to call it. Seemingly every trouble in the world started with greed and covetousness—accordin' to Meg 'twas what sent the devil down to hell. I s'pects me and him'd make a grand pair—seems to me, though, 'tis only natural to want stuff."

"Take that summer Frank Norris come to the Cape and started buildin' his house. I know now I weren't the only one envious! Green we was, all of us!"

"Frank had coloured glass put in the front door and proper stairs built, had everythin' moved in before his wife and young Rose set foot in the place. Set the rooms out just so—rockers and chairs, lamps made out of glass and everythin' accordin' to."

"I can see us now, me and Meg and Sarah, helpin', the day Frank papered them bedroom walls, lovely stuff with roses all over. If I coulda' got that house by pushin' Frank Norris off the wharf I'da done it in a minute, hell or no hell."

"In the end 'twas all for nothin'. Never a peaceful night did he have in that house. His wife Ida turned out to be crazy as a loon—let goats in downstairs, locked herself upstairs, screeched and bawled and scraped paper off the walls 'til her fingernails bled. Years after, when she died, they burnt the place down—only thing to do. Young Rose Norris kept the four little squares of glass, two red and two blue. When she married Meg's Willie they built on the very same spot and that glass is the same what's in their door to this day."

"Apart from Ned there was only one person I could pass the time of day with. 'Twarn't nobody you'd guess. None of them ever guessed either!" Mary Bundle cackled as if she had played a wonderful trick on the people who had treated her so coolly.

"You can mark this down—'tis nothing Vinnie woulda knowed about," she says, considering how best to begin.

Mary admitted that the Vincents had done more for her than anyone else. It was Sarah who had taken her and Fanny in when Thomas Hutchings wanted nothing to do with them, and it was Sarah who had first showed her how to make cures out of weeds and roots.

Josh and Sarah Vincent were good people, but Mary maintained there was something strange about the way they treated their middle son, Peter.

"Sarah was always talkin' about changelings and I wondered sometimes if Peter wasn't one of them. Different as night and day from the rest of the Vincents. People didn't take to Peter. He were about nine or ten when I come and I remembers noticin' how Sarah'd always be after him for somethin' he done—or didn't do. Scowlin' little bugger and fidgety as a blue-assed fly. Never settled. One minute he'd be there, gone the next—right in the middle of eatin' or doin' some job. Say all hands be hove to haulin' up a boat or nailin' down a roof—halfway through the job Peter'd vanish."

Josh and Sarah had four children. Charlie, the youngest and the first baby born on Cape Random, was sickly. More sooky than sickly, Mary said. "Spoiled by all hands just like his grandson nuisance-face," she tells Rachel.

Even Lavinia, when she started teaching the children, favoured Charlie. It was no wonder the boy learned to read so fast, much faster than Ned and Mary's three sons—Lavinia spent more time with Charlie than with all her other students put together.

Young Joe, the oldest Vincent boy, was the face and eyes of his father. Joe had stowed away aboard the *Tern*, given Sarah a year of misery and she never said a cross word to him after. He came home, went fishing with Josh, and a few years later settled down with Meg and Ben's daughter Lizzie.

Annie, the Vincent daughter, was what they called a "home girl." Good around the house and never seen outdoors without someone's baby on her hip. After her father died, Annie surprised everyone by going on the water with Young Joe. And Sarah never said one word against it, although it should have been Peter who got the place in his father's boat. Dressed in oilskins, Annie had, and fished with her brother for years and years—until Ida Norris died. The day after the mad woman died, Annie Vincent put on a dress and married Frank Norris.

After the great row on the day he chopped Young Joe's finger off, Peter became more and more aloof. The ugly bite the dog had made on his cheek did not help. When the youngsters teased him about the purple mark he began going off by himself. While he was still a boy he would go in the country, travel for weeks with a few cakes of hard tack, a piece of canvas and Thomas Hutchings' old gun.

"Many's the winter 'twas fresh meat Peter brought home kept us from perishin'. He'd be gone for a month—sometimes more—then one day he'd open your door and toss in a leg of caribou, a brace of rabbits, a wild duck or goose. No matter to Sarah—she still favoured t'other three."

"When every mortal soul in the place knew Annie was sleepin' with Frank Norris—who had a wife, mad as a hatter but alive as you or me—Sarah would still be tormentin' Peter, prayin' for him to join the church like Annie, naggin' at him to cut his hair like Young Joe or learn to read as good as Charlie. And she were forever after him to tell her when he was comin' and goin'. I never done that with mine—never made chalk of one and cheese of t'other," says Mary who has long since forgotten how little attention, good or bad, she bestowed upon her children.

Through all these years Mary had hardly spoken to Peter Vincent. He was just a boy—one of the crowd that tagged after Lavinia Andrews—and Mary was a woman. Sometimes, when she was out searching the countryside for an ingredient to use in her cures, Mary would see him. They would nod to each other, no more, then go silently about their business. Until one day, years after the finger chopping incident, when she found Peter in the woods with a deep cut in his leg.

It was the same year he started building a house. Without telling anyone his plans, all alone, the young man cobbled together some kind of foundation and uprights on the hill overlooking the Cape, an odd, mysterious structure looking as if it would be one room wide and three high—if he ever decided to add walls and a roof. Peter was a young man by then but he had no sweetheart, so everyone wondered why he was building a house. Or maybe it was a lighthouse or a lookout of some kind, or just a place to get away from his family.

"Ever notice how people only asks questions about things they knows? Seems to me when people don't have one blessed idea about a thing, they're afraid of what they might find out. That's how it were with Peter Vincent's house. Anyone else'd be harrished with questions 'bout them big tall posts stuck up against the sky—but no one said a word to Peter—apart from Sarah, and I doubts even she ever come right out and asked. No one offered to help him either, for all everyone helped his brother Joe when he'n Lizzie built their house."

The day Mary got to know Peter Vincent, his foot had gone down into a boghole and a pointed branch had scraped a deep cut up his leg. Mary told him to go on home and get the cut cleaned before it got infected but he shook his head. He had only just started out and wasn't going back until he'd made it around his six mile circuit, checking traps and rebaiting them with bits of seal meat. "Got somethin' to tie it up with?" he asked.

Mary squatted down, rooted in her gunny-sack. She, too, had just started out so there was not much to choose from. She poured lukewarm tea over the cut and stopped the bleeding with moss.

"I knows one or two things about you, Mary Bundle," Peter said quietly.

Mary was wrapping his leg in a bit of cloth ripped from her petticoat. She kept her face down, took her time knotting the ends of cotton carefully together, and hoped he could not tell how afraid she was.

For years she had expected this. Every spring when ships started to come in to the Cape the same chilling thought had whispered through Mary's head—someday, someone will walk off some vessel demanding that she go back to face those magistrates Tim Toop had said were looking for her. A thousand times she had imagined Ned's face as he watched her being dragged away. She would be taken to St. John's, thrown in jail, whipped perhaps—the very thought made her sick—or transported back to England.

The fear had not disappeared but in later years it had grown dim. Her new name, the births of her children, the circle of people who knew her, whom she knew, the work, and most of all, life with Ned, had made her feel safe.

"More fool me," she thought as she yanked at the strip of dingy cloth. "Must be soft, thinkin' there's a safe place for the likes of me."

Mary decided she would not say a word. Would not give Peter anything to hold over her. She rocked back on her haunches, looked the bearded young man in the eye and waited to hear what he wanted in exchange for silence.

"Know a feller by the name of Matt Escott?" Peter asked.

Mary did not move. The two stared at each other, so still that from a distance you would have thought they were wild animals hunkering there among the brown, fall brush.

"Ever hear tell of somethin' they calls surrogate court?"

She stayed silent and after a few minutes he began to talk. "A month or so ago, around late August, I were up by the Red Hills in back of Pond Island and I had a mind ta go down and spend the night with some of Pap's people. Uncle Ezra Vincent maybe, or one of the cousins," Peter said.

"But I never got to Pond Island. I dodged down, in no hurry, goin' along nice and easy, keepin' me eye out for the odd bird or rabbit. I was right down handy to the gardens when I come upon this stranger sittin' on top of an old cellar. Looking out over the place, he was. Seemed I shoulda knowed him. But I couldn't put a name to him 'till he told me he'd been in Cape Random plenty of times—sailed for years on Gosse vessels under Captain Brennan," Peter paused in his singsong recital and studied Mary.

"Said his name was Matt Escott—asked if I knowed a Mary Bundle. When I asks what Mary Bundle was to him that he should be askin' after her, he just smiles, cocksure of hisself, and points off to this friggin' big man-o-war hove to, way off shore. 'See her?' he says. And 'course I did—pretty hard to miss. So I nods and he tells me she's the H.M.S. *Valiant*—the Governor's very own flagship."

"'Think o' dat!' Escott says, tryin' to impress me—and I thinks about it. Still do. Some English shagger havin' a great bloody flagship ta tout about in while us people barely keeps body and soul together."

Peter paused, shook his head and pulled a plug of tobacco out of his pocket. He cut a lump, popped it into his mouth and held the tobacco and knife out to

Mary as if she were a man. When she shook her head he returned the tobacco to his pocket and continued.

Escott told Peter Vincent that Governor Cochrane had sent the *Valiant* out under Captain Upshall on a three month tour of the northeast coast with the task of bringing British justice to the outharbours. Captain Upshall had been made Surrogate Judge for the duration of the voyage. He had power to take complaints, arrest, examine, sentence, and punish by whipping if necessary.

The Captain had also been furnished with the names and descriptions of rogues who had committed a variety of crimes, ranging from murder to the theft of an eiderdown valued at tenpence. These fugitives were thought to be hiding out in lawless fishing communities and the Captain was instructed to bring them back to St. John's for trial.

"Seems him—Escott—were toady for the Captain. Clerk, he called hisself, s'posed to go round the different places, find out about lawbreakin' and nose out anyone they'd hidden away. Their three months was about up and they'd only found two people to whip—some old man and wife who'd been brewin' sprits up in Fox Cove. And they had one old feller in the hold for jumpin' ship in Bonavist'. Escott was that put out! Criminals were bein' hid, he said. Said 'twas a pure scandal the lack of respect we'um bay people had for the Governor. Been promised a bounty, this Escott had, for catchin' them with names on the list—and here they were almost ready to turn back for St. John's without a one!"

"Brightened right up when he seen me—pulled this paper outta his pocket and read out the lot. But the one he was most particular about was this Mary Bundle—who he said were really Mary Sprig—he had a lot of stuff about her."

"What?" It was the first word Mary had uttered since they squatted down. Cold bog water had oozed into her boots, her knees were cramped and her back ached. She wondered how Peter could look so comfortable.

"I'll read it to ya," he said and pulled a dirty piece of folded paper out of his shirt pocket: "Mary Sprig—A small, dark complexioned female servant. Escaped service without working out her passage, has maliciously destroyed her master's property, stolen food and household goods including gold candlesticks and a watch, valued at a hundred pounds each. May be armed. Dangerous and a thief, Mary Sprig is thought to be hiding in one of the outharbours near St. John's."

Mary was frightened—and astonished, not just at the words on the paper, but that Peter Vincent could read them. She had often heard Lavinia complain that Peter never showed his face in the schoolroom. "Don't s'pose you're makin' that all up?" she asked, partly to give herself time.

"No that's what the paper says—'tho Escott told me it was wrong. He knew the Sprig woman wasn't anywhere near St. John's 'cause he himself had come down the shore on board the *Tern* with a Mary Bundle—said he knowed she were a girl who'd been thievin' along the St. John's waterfront, besides, she answered to the description. Told me this Mary Bundle was so vicious she'd attacked him, then she was put ashore on Cape Random. Accordin' to Escott they'd be puttin' in at the Cape in a day or so—Mary Bundle were the one person on his list he was countin' on takin' back. I could see how it'd be with her if he ever got her on that ship."

"What did you tell him?"

"Nothin'" Peter said, "I told the bastard nothin'—then he got dirty with me, said he could charge me with shelterin' a fugitive or some such foolishness."

Peter stood up and stretched. "So I beat the shit outta him. When I'd finished I told him there was no Mary Bundle on the Cape and if anyone, anyone ever come lookin' for such a person I'd be inta St. John's on the next vessel and finish him off." He smiled and spit a glob of tobacco juice over his shoulder, "I think he took it as truth," he said with satisfaction.

Mary tried to stand but could not and Peter had to pull her to her feet. The pain in her legs was terrible and water had soaked up into her skirt. She was cold and frightened.

"So then?" she asked, trying to make her mouth stop bivvering.

"So then, what?" Peter folded the paper and tucked it into his pocket. "I'll be off now—only two hours of daylight left," he said and began trotting away from her in the opposite direction.

"Wait!" she called after him. "Why'd you do it for if you don't want nuthin?"

He stopped and scratched his head, "Dunno—cause Mudder likes ya, I s'pose," he said. Then he vanished.

After that, whenever Mary and Peter met they would take a spell together. Sometimes they would just sit and chew tobacco, sometimes Peter would talk, for the young man was more inclined to conversation than anyone on the Cape would have guessed.

"He'd be always showin' me how to do somethin'—I s'pose I were the only creature he got a chance to show off to. Taught me how to set a snare and how to toss a net to catch birds—he knowed everything regards the country roundabout—had walked to every hidie-hole for a hundred miles, knew people all along this shore, Peter did."

"Sometimes seemed like he thought I was gettin' too friendly, or too nosey. Soon as ever that happened he'd jump up and walk off. One minute we'd be squat down talkin', the next he'd be gone—vanished like the snow that fell last winter!"

Peter was right in thinking Mary Bundle nosy. She collected information and stored it away. She was patient, she trusted Peter and over time he came to trust her. Although he would never say why he was building the house, he did tell her other things, things Mary now tells her great-granddaughter.

"Peter Vincent were the only soul I ever heard tell really talked to Red Indians. Told me they were cute as Christians—had secret places in tree trunks or under rocks, where they hid messages so's they could get news to one 'nother across hundreds of miles—each one passin' it along to the next message place. That way they'd know well ahead if white men were comin' and they'd hide."

"For all that, Peter got to know some of 'em—lived with one crowd for a full winter. Said they could cure fish without salt and made catamarans with runners covered in seal fur so's they'd slip along on snow. Indians had their own medicines too, concoctions of dogberry bark, beaver root and suchlike. I still makes some of them mixtures Peter told me about."

After they had known each other for some time, Mary persuaded Peter to read the descriptions of all the fugitives listed on the paper he'd taken from Matt Escott. Apart from Mary Sprig there were four other names: Nell Sheppard, the poor creature who was wanted for stealing a counterpane; one Father Commins, an Irish priest who had gone mad and murdered some Englishman; Bertha Putt, a servant girl said to have smothered her infant child and buried it beneath the doorstep of her employer's house, and George Gipps, a one-eared thief who had escaped from gaol in St. John's while awaiting hanging.

"That all?" Mary was disappointed, having hoped that Tim Toop, or even Thomas Hutchings' names might be on the list with her own. Still, you never knew, one day the piece of paper in Peter's hand might be useful.

"What you gonna do with that bit of paper—no use your keepin' it now, is there?" she asked.

Mary tried to keep her voice casual but Peter had been alerted. His eyes got that far-off look, as if he were listening to something inside his head. She had expected him to get up and walk away. Instead he put the list down on the ground between his feet, pulled a plug of tobacco from his pocket and holding it over the paper began peeling off bits of tobacco with his knife. When the paper was covered, he picked it up and, holding it between the fingers of both hands rattled the shreds of tobacco to the centre. Then he rolled the list into a tube and, using a flint, set it on fire.

"He puffed away at it pretendin' like 'twas a pipe and laughin' to hisself. Had streelish hair, Peter did—almost caught it afire that day. Not many on the Cape had a decent word for Peter Vincent but he were a good friend to me."

eleven

"Once them preachers started comin' to the Cape things was never the same. Not ever!"

Rachel smiles at the venom in Mary's voice. She has heard Nan express this thought many times, usually to some unwary missionary come to pay his respects to the oldest woman along the coast.

"No need ta sit there grinnin' like a cat, Rachel Andrews! I'm not foolish yet—though Lord knows I should be, livin' among ye crowd all these years! A pure plague, ministers is!"

"I minds that old one come first, Reverend Ninian Eldridge. Like a dried up stick he were, creepin' up from the boat with Meg holdin' onto his arm for fear he'd break or get blowed away in the wind. Too bad he didn't!"

"Before the week was out he had all hands, even my Ned, yammerin' on about things ya can't see—souls and angels, heaven and bein' saved. Does no mortal good ta talk about such stuff. Turned everything 'round, Ninian Eldridge did."

"'Twas his pratin' on about foreign places put the idea of St. John's in Jane and Emma's head. I never trusted Meg's Emma, but Ned's Jane was a good, biddable maid—got along better with her than I ever did with me own Fanny who was useless in the house. After listenin' to the minister Jane and Emma made it up between them they'd traipse off to St. John's, go into service, make money, buy pretty things, marry rich men. 'Course I knowed how foolish such notions was but I had no say—the rest were content to let 'em go—said Jane and Emma'd just been saved, were big, sensible girls, and besides, Captain Brennan promised us his wife would keep an eye on em."

"I wondered after, when Emma had her two merrybegots dropped off on the Cape like kittens, if Meg or Ben remembered all their talk about the girls bein' wrapped in a cloak of righteousness. Coulda thrown it in their faces then—I didn't though," the old woman's look of piety is quickly replaced by a scowl, "but was the friggin' minister's notion to build a church on the Cape drove me to distraction!"

It was certainly Reverend Eldridge who put the idea of building a church into Meg's head, along with the idea that she could make a preacher out of her son

Willie—despite the fact that the boy hated schoolwork and had little interest in anything except Rose Norris.

By then the two Andrews families were living in the big double house. Mary's and Ned's side never changed, one huge downstairs room with their curtained-off bed and an open loft up above where all the children slept on the floor.

Ben and Meg were different. Meg's floors were boarded over, oiled and covered with the mats she had hooked. In wintertime she hung a mat inside the door and another over the glass window she was so proud of.

Ben was the same—was, as Ned said, "Forever addin' a fig to his cake." Whenever he was not repairing wharves or flakes, or working on a boat, Meg had her husband putting up partitions, adding rooms, building shelves, tables and chairs, blanket boxes and washstands and footstools.

Meg had a big sideboard against her kitchen wall, little seats on each end of her fireplace; and Lizzie, Pash, Emma and Willie slept in proper beds Ben had made. At night, while Ned was mending nets and telling tales, Ben would be whittling something: candle holders or spoon holders, toy boats for the boys, dolls for the girls, or frames for little pictures Meg worked in brin.

"All the men useta help get wood. Even then there were no trees on the Cape—even for splits you had to go well back in the country. All hands'd be cuttin' in the fall and wintertime, drag logs out on dogsled or else cruise 'em down by boat when the ice was gone. Bit by bit Ben got tools, first he had a regular saw and woodhorse but in later years he got a pit saw. And the men always let him have the best wood for lumber. Idea was Ben'd give us a hand with our place—for all Ned was willin' he warn't handy with tools."

"Once Meg got the idea of buildin' a church I hove over all hopes of gettin' our floor laid or partitions up. Took years and years ta build, that church did, great jeezely place!" Mary snorted and spat out her worst insult: "Pure useless!"

But even this waste of work and time was not the root of her bitterness against ministers. In Mary's mind something like a curse had settled on the Cape after Reverend Eldridge sailed away, a fog-like miasma that seemed at first harmless but in the end crept up, covering the familiar landmarks, changing everything so that a person's own yard could become a strange and dangerous place.

For a while after Jane and Emma left, everything seemed lovely. It was the best summer anyone on the Cape could remember, gardens were good, berries plentiful and the sea boiling with fish. By then Ned and Mary had four sons—the older boys, Henry and Alfred, along with Ned's Isaac were all able to fish alongside Ned. George was about six and Moses just beginning to walk.

"Thought I'd finished havin' babies but by the time that summer was out I was in the family way again. According to Meg all of it—fish, berries and babies, were God's blessings come about by so many of us havin' been saved. She and Sarah used to take turns bawlin' out hymns and preachin' in their houses on Sunday—only people in the place didn't go were poor foolish Ida Norris, me, and Thomas Hutchings."

"Bein' saved changed people, the scattered time Alex Brennan brought a bottle ashore none of 'em would take a drop and they stopped swearin' altogether—got right holy. Charlie Vincent started off preachin' for all he were only a boy. Bein' saved made Fanny queerer than ever but Vinnie come out of her daze and started makin' sheep's eyes at Thomas. Didn't change Ned—he knew all the words and all the hymns but in hisself Ned was same as ever."

"That were the summer Ned told me 'bout Thomas."

It had been a Sunday and warm for all it was October. Ned loved both the singing and Bible stories but had left the service to sit on the beach with his wife. He hoped to beguile Mary out of the black mood she'd been in for weeks.

From where they sat, clean empty sand curved out on either side, on their left the tall black rock called God's Finger pointed up at the sky, far down up on their right was the wharf, the fish flakes and the store—now holding only the Cape's winter supply of salt cod, the summer's catch having already been shipped in to St. John's. Potatoes were still being dug in the garden and every family had a cellar of turnip, carrot and cabbage. Barrels of wine, red partridge berries and tubs of blueberries stood in lofts and back porches. Despite the stacks of fish in the store and mountain of firewood behind each house, the men would continue to catch fish and cruise wood down around the point as long as the weather held. If tomorrow was fine Mary would do a second cutting of grass for her goats, other women planned to dip candles or turn out their houses one last time before winter set in.

Ned lay on his back, arms folded behind his head, watching gulls screech and dive around God's Finger. "Mary girl, I allows this is the year we cleans her—pays up ever'thing we owes and has to spare."

"More'n thirteen years you been tellin' me that and never happened yet—nor likely to, long's we depends on black strangers for everything we needs from rope to needles." Mary was out of sorts, having spent the better part of a month trying to talk the men into beginning work on a boat big enough to cart fish in to St. John's.

"Give over, girl! We'um wonderful hands at skiffs and dories—and I allow Ben'd got nerve ta build a good size bulley—but not a man jack of us'd want ta tackle a vessel big enough ta load down with salt cod and sail in ta St. John's."

Ned reached for his wife's arm and tried to pull her down beside him on the sand. But Mary stayed, sitting stiffly, half turned towards the sea, nursing her disappointment. This year for the first time the men could have started on a large vessel. The Cape had never seen such a fall, not a sign of snow and not one northeast gale had yet swept down the coast. There had been lots of time, Mary argued, to lay a keel, get ribs in place, maybe even plank down the deck before it got too bitter to work. She knew that Ned could have coaxed Ben around if he had only tried harder.

"What's the use persuadin' a man ta do something he got no heart for," Ned said. "And besides, ya needs more'n wood ta build such a ship—I doubt there's enough money in all the northeast coast ta fit out the vessel you're talkin' about."

"Would be if ye crowd hadn't been so stunned all these years—lettin' Thomas Hutchings say what ya owes and what ya don't owe!"

One of Mary's long held desires had been to control what is marked down in Thomas's account book. Since neither she nor Ned could read she had always been after her husband to recruit Lavinia into the plan.

"All Vinnie'd have to do is change a few of them numbers, or scratch things out," she'd explained again and again.

Ned would not hear tell of such a thing, "That man been a good friend to us Andrews ever since we set foot in the place. Let us live off him that first winter, he did—and look at how he got books for the youngsters in Vinnie's school and how he lets us use the wharf and flakes, for all 'tis him pays Ben ta keep 'em in repair. No girl, I puts great faith in Thomas Hutchings!"

"Go on, Ned ya don't know one thing about him. For all we knows he might be cheatin' us blind—might be the worst kind of crook ever lived!" Mary had made her usual retort. She was wondering if enough money remained in Thomas's tin to fit out a vessel.

"I'd trust Thomas Hutchings with me life, Mary. So could you—so could any of us! No better man on this coast for all he's one of them Papist priests."

Mary had been shocked into silence. In all her speculation about the man she had never considered such a thing.

"Lookin' back on it now I wonders anyone could ha' been so stunned," Mary tells her great-granddaughter.

"I didn't let on to Ned, but I knew right off Thomas Hutchings were really Father Commins, the murderer Peter told me 'bout years before—the very man Matt Escott and that judge were lookin' for—the mad priest who killed an Englishman and ran away—that were Thomas! And him all the time livin' here, lordin' it over us!"

"Soon as the words were outta Ned's mouth I could see he was sorry. Got right flustered he did—made me promise not ta tell a soul. Never did, neither. Apart from Thomas hisself, you be the first person ever heard such things from my lips. Years and years after, when Vinnie told me all about it, I acted like 'twas somethin' I never heard tell of before."

After swearing Mary to secrecy Ned had tried to change the subject: "I got a feelin' this one's gonna be a girl—let's get a good name for her," he reached out, patted Mary's belly and began rhyming off a list of improbable names.

But Mary was not to be coaxed out of her sombre mood. "What difference what we's called, any of us? All we got to do is live and die—work like dogs when them rich buggers needs us, and starve when they don't have no more use for us—and never in our lives havin' enough ta fill our guts or cover our backs!" she had started to cry.

"Never trusts me, do ya Mary? Never thinks I'm able ta look after ya?" Ned said. She remembers the hurt pride in his voice. "There must be somethin' we can do, Ned—somethin' so's we'll never be in want again!"

"No girl, I don't believe there is, don't believe there's a mortal thing people like us can do. 'Tis all fate, see—all fate!"

He pulled her head down onto his chest and stroked her hair: "All fate, all fate! Like Young Char read out this mornin'—'By fate Abraham, when he were called of God to go into a land he would after receive for an inheritance, set sail not knowin' whither the wind would take him.'"

Ned's ability to memorize such things always astonished Mary. She often wondered if there was a living in it—could money be made from such a talent? But that day she would not be distracted, "You mean ta tell me this God feller expects people ta go off without makin' a plan?"

"Yes girl—where the wind takes us—whenever the spirit moves us—just like I been doin' all me life. Same as you done, Mary—same as we does when we keeps on havin' youngsters. Like the sands of the sea our youngsters are—like the sands of the sea we are—comin' and goin' and not knowin' whither we went," Ned rolled out the words, repeating them again and again as he dribbled a handful of sand into Mary's hair.

"That how you screedless crowd got here, then—by fate?" Mary has often asked how the Andrews family had come to be on the Cape but had never gotten the same answer twice.

"Yes girl tha's how 'twas—by fate. Not knowin' whither we went—that was us Andrews. Followin' promises we was—followin' the promises of God."

"What promises?" asked Mary. Although she rarely listened closely when Ned was entertaining a crowd she was always delighted to have him telling stories just to her. "What promises, Ned?" she said, urging him on.

"That old man I met in St. John's—the one I told you 'bout before?" Seized by some new thought Ned sat up, "I'll be damned!" he said, rolled over and resting on one elbow looked her in the eye: "Mary, that man musta been God!"

Her husband's face changed from awe, to astonishment, to delight as the idea took root and blossomed. Mary felt the familiar glow that overcame her whenever she let down her defences to Ned, not in their wildest lovemaking had she loved him as much as she did at that moment. Certainty shone in his face and ever so briefly the possibility of God—a God who would come down and talk to someone in a potato garden—seemed right and natural. The thought had left her breathless, wordless.

"Yes girl—God hisself in St. John's! Don't that beat all!"

Doubt swept back, "God in St. John's!" she laughed out loud and the world returned to normal.

"That He were—though I shouldn't blame meself for not knowin' at the time. Far as I could see He were just an old man diggin' up potatoes—strange old bugger, looked like He been dug up Hisself. Had this dirty beard, same colour as the brin bags tied around His shoulders. Often wondered why I even stopped to talk to Him, instead of goin' on to the grog shop with the rest. I sees now 'twas fate—'twas meant to be."

"Go on boy, you'd talk to cats if they'd listen!" she had said, but Ned didn't hear.

"Yer seed shall be as the sands of the sea, tha's what He told me. Right about that, weren't He! Reamed off a lot more old stuff while we grubbed up potatoes—told me I were favoured by fortune. Them were His very words—'favoured by fortune.' Told me I'd go to a place that wasn't a cape nor an island but a bit of both. Said we could go together, Him and me—that there'd be a gold casket filled with jewels handy to where we'd land. He called it the place of turrs, wanted me ta jump ship and go with Him right then and there!"

"Why didn't ya, then?"

"'Cos I had Hazel and Mam and them waitin' for me back in Weymouth. You knows I couldn't just vanish, never be heard tell of again, sure it would ha killed Mam. Still'n all I had it in mind ta go back the next year—promised I would, in fact. Before I left He rolls out this barrel of fish for me—then He give me a token."

The sand was warm, and the children all barred in Meg's house listening to Bible stories. Mary was enjoying herself, feeling happier than she had in weeks. "Shoulda got a map from Him—made 'im mark out where that casket was. Woulda done ya a sight more good than that barrel of fish what got ya into so much trouble."

"Na girl—ya don't understand how God works—He don't give out maps, He teases us like He done with Abraham that time pretendin' He wanted him ta kill Isaac. Teases us with fate, God do. We don't have to do nothin', it just sweeps us along, like an undertow—we got no control over it. Only God knows how 'tis—He's it!" Ned pauses, struck by his own brilliance, "Ya s'pose I should change me name to Abraham?"

"What foolishness you goes on with—enough people in this place already changed names seems ta me! I s'pose fate found ya that gold casket and all them jewels? S'pose ya got it hid away all this time have ya, just waitin' for God ta tell ya what to do with it?"

"Na girl, never seen hide nor hair of it. But 'tis out there somewhere!" Ned sighed. "Like Meg says, God's ways is not our ways. Them jewels still tucked safe away in some crack or cranny on Turr Island. But don't worry, maid, we'll have it yet—if time should last He'll make sure we haves it all."

"Maybe yer old God wants us ta give Him a hand—ever think that? Maybe we should all be out there haulin' the friggin' place apart rock by rock," Mary nods towards the tiny island, shrouded in a mist that is rolling slowly in towards the Cape.

"Wouldn't do one bit of good—with God ya got ta have patience—patience and trust—things you're shorthanded in, Mary me love. He brought me here and someday I'll get a sign showin' me where that gold casket is—maybe I'll see it in a dream—or maybe a seagull'll drop a ruby or diamond right down on me head. Imagine that, Mary—us lyin' here and this dirty great gull swoopin' straight down—sent from God ta show us where that casket of gold is!"

"Shit on us, more likely," she said, watching the white birds criss-cross the sky, dropping mussels on rocks then diving for the tiny, soft bodies inside.

"What token did he give ya?" she asked.

There was no answer, Ned had fallen asleep. He smiled in his sleep, dreaming no doubt of diamonds spiralling downwards, glittering and turning in the sun. He was like a sun himself—his round face open and trusting as a child's, surrounded by orange hair and beard. Mary leaned forward awkwardly and kissed him, then, moving her lips to his ear, she hissed: "What token?"

He woke with a start, "What token? What token?" he blinked and muttered the word 'token' several times. "What token?" he asked again.

"The one you said the old man give ya along with the barrel of fish—God's token!"

"Ah yes. God's token," for a moment Ned seemed at a loss. He began searching his pockets, "Let me see now—I had it in here—seen it a fortnight ago...."

One by one he pulled things from his pocket: a shard of pink glass, smoothed by the sea but still holding the faint outline of a five petalled rose, two flint arrowheads, three fire blackened nails, the shell of a sea urchin and a dull metal thing that was beginning to rust. Holding these objects in his cupped palm he squints at them.

"Here 'tis! I was afeared I'd lost it," he beamed and held out what looked like a belt buckle, "See? A token!" he traced a design incised into the rusty metal.

"'Tis only an old buckle—broke too!"

"You got no reverence, Mary! See them lines?" he traced the design, "them's God's name—you know's yourself God'd have a belt buckle with his name on it."

"What's his name then? I allow you don't even know his name."

"God of the land, god of the sea and god of the land under the sea," Ned intoned.

The words had sent a shiver down her spine but she had not let on, just asked, "If yer so smart why didn't ya go find him then—them times ya been to St. John's?"

"He's gone, girl. Vanished. Every time I goes to the ice I asks after him—not a soul from town ever heard tell of 'em—Godforsaken's what St. John's is."

"Make no wonder we never gets ahead—after you breakin' a promise to God!"

"You're a scoffer, Mary." Ned had slipped the piece of metal back into his pocket, reached out and placed a loud kiss on her lips, "For all that I forgives ya. When I finds me casket 'twill have a buckle just like this one—and I'll give ya half of all the stuff inside, rings for your fingers and bells for your toes, Mary Bundle—you'll hang gold in your ears and stick jewels in your belly button like a real gypsy."

"Found his casket all right," the old woman in the kitchen says with great bitterness.

"Next spring he was lyin' in it—out on the point beside Hazel—no gold, no jewels, no token from God. Unless bein' put down in the ground is a token, unless bein' tore apart by a beast is a token."

It is the first time in all the years since that Mary has ever spoken of Ned's death. It still angers her. She orders Rachel to write around Lavinia's account of Ned's death that it was Thomas Hutchings' fault.

"Them days was hundreds of wild animals about—along with Indians and pirates. Strangers, too, the youngsters'd always be seein' strangers in the woods. Meg would chastise hers for lyin' but I believed 'em. Stands to reason me and Thomas Hutchings wasn't the only two villains hidin' out along this shore. Time and time again I got after Thomas to get us something better'n the old muzzle-loader. All that money he had in the tin he coulda got a good gun from St. John's—but he didn't and was his fault what happened to Ned and Isaac that day."

Mary describes for Rachel how it had been. The land and sea all frozen, the huge animal, dirty white, reared up on its hind legs, pawing at the two bodies—the blood and the terrible silence when she stopped screaming.

"It wouldn'ta happened if Peter Vincent'd been in the place. But Peter were gone and the muzzle-loader along with him. Us people left defenceless as babies—all through Thomas Hutchings' carelessness!"

That night Mary rants on for hours, weeping for the ancient grief, pouring out her rage at having lost Ned, at having been left with a crowd of children and pregnant.

"Think on it—we was married only fourteen year and I been more'n sixty year without him! Beside meself I was. Then, the very day Ned and Isaac was buried I found out Fanny were knocked up—big as a barrel with Thomas Hutchings' youngster in her! I made him marry her, though—you can mark that down in Vinnie's book. Mary Bundle made Thomas Hutchings marry her daughter. Told him I knew all about him and I'd have him carted away in shackles if he didn't!"

Rachel protests, surely the child had not belonged to Thomas, "Lavinia wrote out that it were the Red Indian was the father of Fanny's youngster!"

Mary gives the young woman a scathing look: "Don't pay no heed to that—that were Vinnie's romancin'. She didn't want to think her darlin' Thomas done such a thing to a young maid like Fanny."

"But Nan, what about that day on the beach, the day Grandfather Toma were born? The book says the Indian come that day and tried to drag Fanny away!"

"Some poor lost savage, half-mad with loneliness, his own people perished or slaughtered. Crowd in St. John's used to have a bounty on Indians in them days. Used to catch 'em alive to show off to the King or some such thing—always the women they used to get like that. I s'pose the poor mortal saw us on the beach and went out of his mind—tried to drag off a woman just like his own been dragged off more'n likely."

Mary studies the sad little face of her great-granddaughter, who is a granddaughter of the baby born on the beach that day: "Don't pay no mind to that stuff Lavinia wrote down. Though she was forever after poor Ned for tellin' yarns, Vinnie handled the truth careless herself betimes."

But Rachel has heard many versions of this story. She reminds Mary that the Indian who had tried to drag Fanny off just before she gave birth was also called Toma: "My Grandfather Toma—how come he got named after the Indian if 'twarn't his father?"

"Toma were just a name Vinnie dreamt up—out of them old plays more'n likely. Ever come to ya, Toma sounds a lot like Thomas? And why would Thomas Hutchings rear the boy like his own? Sure your Grandfather Toma's the spittin' image of Thomas, sober as a judge. Not a bit of fun in 'im. Comfort herself told me she useta have to hide his books ta get him into bed with her."

"None of we crowd is related to Red Indians, then?" Rachel sounds wistful. "I told Stephen I got me dark skin from the Indian who was me grandfather's father—he liked that."

Mary picks up the girl's hand, small, rough and bony and very brown. Like her own hands before the joints thickened, before heavy veins and dark splotches appeared. She runs her hand over Rachel's. "No maid, yer just like me mother Una. I seen it t'other night—you standin' by the table for all the world like me mother. She were one of them old people, them what used to own England afore the tall fair ones come. She was proud of that—said it gave her second sight," Mary pats Rachel's hand and tells her to go on up to bed.

Mary has not told Rachel everything she knows about that day on the beach, the day Fanny died and Toma was born. She sits up half the night wondering how much of the story can be written down. What use to speculate now about who Fanny had made fast to? To wonder if she'd done right forcing Thomas to marry her poor foolish daughter? What use to tell Rachel how she had found Peter Vincent that night, holding Fanny's body, weeping like a lost, frightened child?

Peter had looked wild, more animal than man with his long, dirty hair and matted beard and the smell of woods and earth and dried blood on him. "I always loved Fanny—anyone coulda seen that—anyone looked at me. 'Course no one ever did," he said fiercely.

He had eased Fanny's body down onto the table but kept her hands folded inside his as if he were holding a small bird, "That Indian who tried to take Fanny away today—him and me been friends since we was boys," he told Mary.

Those two, first as children and later as men, met secretly summer after summer. They had roamed the countryside, hunted together. One winter Peter even travelled into the interior with the Indian, met the rest of his family, two men and a woman, the last survivors of the tribe.

"No one ever took no heed of what I done," he said. "Then, this fall, when I got home I saw right off how 'twas with Fanny—knowed you and Mudder and Meg'd gotten her married up with Thomas Hutchings. I'd like to have made away with the whole lot of ye." Peter was trying to whisper and his voice came out rough and rasping, thick with menace.

Gave me the shivers, he did that night, Mary thinks, remembering how Peter was always the one with the gun, how he had attacked Thomas Hutchings that day on the wharf. And here he was standing over Fanny's dead body saying he'd had a mind to kill them all.

Never flinched, I didn't, not even when I saw he was out of his mind—just stood alongside him listenin'. Mary would like to tell Rachel this, to have the girl record how brave she had been—but no, too many threads run out from that night, untied, unconnected threads that will do no one any good.

"I see now 'twas him—the Indian—all the time," Peter said. Then he described how after he and the Indian fought on the beach he had tracked the man, bashed his head in. He told her where to find the body. The young man had spoken matter-of-factly, as if he were talking about something that happened a long, long time ago instead of that very day.

Mary said she didn't care where the body was, didn't care what he had done, or why. She advised him to get away from the Cape before light, gave him Ned's heavy coat and watched as he walked away up the path that led back through the marsh. She never saw him again and never told anyone about their meeting over Fanny's body. Nor will she tell Rachel now—some things are better left unsaid.

Next morning, when Rachel wants to return to the subject of the Indian on the beach, Mary says she has no idea who he was or where he came from.

"Thomas and Dolph Way found the Indian's body. Then there was a great fuss about where to bury him," she tells the girl. "Meg said he were a heathen—leastways we s'posed he were heathen—so 'twould be wrong to put him in what she called consecrated ground—whatever that means. But Thomas were set on the savage bein' buried out on the point with all the rest. I didn't care one way or t'other. In the end Thomas got his way—like always—Fanny and the Indian was buried alongside one another. Young Char cut words into two wood markers."

"I never seen no marker for either one of em."

"No girl, been gone for years and years—under the sand or under the sea. What difference does it make in the end?" Mary sighs with great sadness. Then, brightening, she says, "I s'pose now when I dies they'll say I was a heathen and bury me outside the churchyard!"

"Go on, Nan! You knows right well they won't—you'll have the biggest funeral the shore ever seen!"

"No more than I should!" Mary says and spends a good hour reminding Rachel of what must be done when she dies. When she is sure the girl understands how each detail of her funeral must be arranged, Mary tells her to write down what happened after Thomas Hutchings left the Cape.

"Can't say I was sorry when Thomas left," Mary says. "He never told us nothin' but 'twas understood he were goin' back to St. John's to some old life he'd left behind. Before he went I asked for his money tin but when he passed it over to me 'twas empty—not a shillin' in it! I did get this understanding with him, though—'bout me and Vinnie keepin' on with his job—sendin' the tally of fish and orders into Caleb Gosse and keep the wharf fixed up, stuff like that. 'Twas only right after what he done to Fanny—and the bit of money we'd get from Caleb Gosse'd help with the baby he was leavin' behind."

"You'd think the way Meg carried on we'd all perish and blow away without Thomas Hutchings but I tell you 'twasn't like that at all. The person missed most that spring was Ned—was like the heart was gone out of the place. Isaac was dead too, of course—and Josh Vincent—Josh died the fall before, with the same sickness took our Moses and left Pash Andrews blind."

The first part of that summer had been terrible. Fish was plentiful but there were not enough hands to bring it ashore. Mary drove everyone so hard that no one had a civil word for her. Her own three boys would run away and hide in the woods to get a bit of rest. But Jane's new husband, Dolph Way, was a big help and in July a new family named Gill settled on the Cape.

"They was always a good, hardworkin' crowd, the Gills. Brose was a grand hand with the fish. Still, when fall started to close in, I was not satisfied in me mind we'd get safe through winter."

She had been sick with fear—used to go down to the store and count the barrels of flour, the caplin, salt fish and vegetables, and then count the people who had to be fed.

"'Twas the same every year, no matter how hard we worked, we barely made it through the winter—but that winter was worse because we had less fish to trade with Gosse. I'd lie awake nighttime tryin' to figure some way we could make money above what we got for the fish."

Mary had tried remembering the ways she'd seen people earn money in St. John's and in Christchurch. But none of the things she remembered would work on the Cape, where everyone made what they needed, where everything was patched and mended until it fell apart. People on the Cape did not buy lumber or splits, everyone cut their own, they did not buy pots or kettles, there was one of each in every house, heavy black objects that lasted for generations. Everyone grew their own vegetables, made their own bread and soap and candles, rendered out their own oil. Mary would fall asleep naming things they had to buy from Caleb Gosse—salt, needles, molasses, flour, flannel, nails—but never anything they could make on the Cape.

One night she sat up in bed. Barrels! She could see the *Tern* with a hundred empty barrels lashed down on deck. Alex Brennan would drop a few off at each place the ship stopped, then pick them up in the fall filled with berries, caplin, pickled herring. Each year three or four barrels were kept back to hold their own berries, the salted cabbage, the trout and salmon.

"I worked it out we could make our own barrels! Don't think I closed me eyes the rest of that night for thinkin' about it. Seemed good sense—'twould save bringin' barrels in—and why shouldn't Gosse pay us for 'em same as he paid someone in St. John's? Would mean he'd have more space for gear and salt on each vessel 'comin down the coast."

At first light Mary went next door to ask Ben Andrews if he knew anything about making barrels. Her brother-in-law had never seen a barrel made, but said he'd study it. He immediately began drawing little pictures, which was the way Ben always worked. The following day he pried a barrel apart and laid out the staves, measured them and worked out how they had been put together.

"I allow we could make barrels if we can get the wood dried for the staves and cut small birch for the hoops. We'd split them and soak 'em in sea water same as I did for the rungs of that chair I made," Ben told Mary. "But then you knows how far we got to go to get decent wood, and I'm not real sure the tools I got could do such a job."

"Ben never had much spunk in him—'tho I must say he could do anything he set his hand to on land. I told him a man who could make boats could make barrels—kept after him day in, day out 'til he went down to the store and started working' on some dry wood Thomas had pushed out under the loft.

"You know, by spring Ben had a watertight barrel! He was good like that, once you set him to it he'd keep tryin' till he got a thing right. You mark that down, my maid—'twas Mary Bundle started them makin' barrels along this coast."

When they got into barrel making Mary would go down to the store each morning before anyone was stirring. She'd count the barrels finished the day before, sweep up the shavings, sort out the right number of staves and arrange the hoops so that Ben and the older boys who helped him would have everything to hand.

Meg heard her leaving the house while it was still dark, and one day scolded her for roaming around in the middle of the night.

"Only two things bed's good for, and since I'm not doin' either of 'em I might just as well be up and about," Mary snapped.

She liked being alone in the store in the cool pre-dawn. "I used to think, them mornings, plan out me day," she told Rachel.

Since no one now lived in the store the fire was allowed to die each night. Mary had pushed Thomas Hutchings' few belongings up against the bunk where he had slept to make room for woodhorses, tools, staves, drying lumber and the old puncheons Ben used to shape the wet hoops around. For the first time the store was just that, a storage space and workroom, the smells of cooking and living all gone, only the clean smell of wood, netting, oakum and rope remained. It was quiet there in the mornings, just the soft swish of sea washing in below the floor and the muted rattle stones make when the sea recedes.

"We had almost fifty barrels that first year Ben was at it—and that was with Meg forever draggin' him off work to go at something else. When Alex Brennan come down I told him what I wanted and he was satisfied to bring it up to old skinflint Gosse. I figured we could make twice fifty if we got things planned proper."

"We was gettin' along! I could see that, anyone with eyes in their heads coulda seen it. The second summer after Thomas left we done better with the fish—and that fall we all had goats, sheep and hens, and only the Norris family didn't have a pig. We women all done our own cardin' and spinnin', grew vegetables, and of course we had the fish, and sea birds was plentiful them times."

Just as Meg and Sarah had never grown tired of reciting Bible verses, so Mary never stopped tallying things up. How much did they have stored away? How much did they have to trade?

But there was never enough to satisfy her. She was always thinking ahead, always planning, not just for next winter, but for the one after. She would never give herself nor anyone else a minute's rest, would go for days without speaking to a soul, then fly into a rage at the sight of a misplaced tool, a child skipping rocks, or an adult gazing out to sea.

"Every minute ye wastes in summer is a spoonful of food you're without in winter!" she repeated so often that the children would whisper it to one another when they saw her coming.

The youngsters grew sullen, muttering against her heavy hand. Her own sons most of all: "Mudder'll have our backs broke afore we're half growed," Henry, George and Alfred would complain and hide when they heard Mary's voice or saw her shadow.

It was a common sight in those times to see Mary Bundle stalking about the place, shouting orders at rocks and bushes behind which she knew her sons were crouching. She had become the overseer of the place. Without any inclination to cajole or charm, without any authority to command, she had only brutish determination to bend their will to hers.

"All hands went by what I said in them days. They might grumble and complain behind me back, but to me face they done what I wanted—they had good sense," she told Rachel with pride.

The second spring after Thomas left was a long, wet season. The coast was continually shrouded in mist, damp seeped into the houses, clothes and bedding smelled fousty and the feel of sunshine was all but forgotten. The caplin came, were spread on flakes to dry, and then turned maggoty, fit only for dog food. This was a huge loss, since barrels of dried caplin could mean the difference between survival and starvation at the end of a long winter.

Mary decreed that more caplin would have to be caught and spread. Everyone kept watch for the flick of silver and the familiar black shadows just below the surface of the water. Day after day passed, when the sun finally broke through the mist they concluded that the small fish had struck off.

Then one morning Mary looked out from the store and saw a ripple on the water, saw small silver crescents on the beach. Snatching a casting net off the wall she raced from house to house, banging on doors, calling: "Caplin, caplin, caplin in!"

She had just lifted her hand from the door of Meg's and Ben's house when it opened and Meg stood on the step looking at her with grim disapproval.

"Don't you even know what day this is, Mary Bundle?"

Her sister-in-law's face and the sound of Charlie Vincent's voice made Mary realize why no one was about. It was Sunday, the day for service, the day when everyone sat on chairs and benches in Meg's kitchen to pray and sing hymns. Every Sunday, apart from the warmest days of summer when they held services inside the roofless walls of their church, all hands gathered like this—but Mary never went and never remembered.

Meg tried to make her son Willie take turns reading out, but it was almost always Charlie Vincent who did it. That morning they were working their way through the book of Matthew, Mary could hear every word clear as a bell, "...every one that hath forsaken houses, or brethren, or sisters, or father, or mother, or wife, or child, or lands for my sake, shall receive an hundredfold, and shall inherit everlasting life...."

Mary remembers still the numbing effect the words had on her, remembers wondering what a strange religion they had that encouraged men to abandon their families. Before she even opened her mouth she had a premonition of defeat, an unfamiliar and unpleasant sensation which she ignored.

"Caplin's in, Meg girl! Leave off this foolish rigmarole and come on down—might be the last sign we'll have of 'em this year!"

"No one in here will cast for caplin this day—we're not going to break the Sabbath for you, Mary Bundle. You might think you owns our bodies but I can tell ya, you don't have no claim on our souls!"

Meg looked down at her from what seemed to be a great height, very much as she'd done the night so many years before when she'd turfed Mary out of Ned's bed.

"Ya stunned bitch, we'll likely all starve next winter 'cause of you!" Mary had screeched.

Meg remained icily calm. "The Lord will provide for his own, now I'll take no more of your brazen tongue," she said and closed the door.

"Stunned bugger—where was the Lord last time we starved?" Mary howled at the door. She thought of barging in to drag out her own crew. Instead, she gave the door a childish kick and stalked off down to the landwash.

On the beach Mary pulled off her boots and wool socks, knotted her skirt up around her waist and waded into the icy cold water with a casting net.

She worked for an hour or more, enjoying the way she could whirl the net out over the moving shoals of fish that swirled around her, revelling in the pile of silver bodies she was collecting above the water line, remembering how she and Tessa used to fish in the Watt with the little underwater net. Hypnotized by the shining water and circling fish she forgot her anger, completely forgot the people up in Meg's house.

"Cold of May, heat of June, send me fishes of the moon," she chanted. Then, suddenly as they had appeared, the caplin vanished.

The harvested fish now had to be salted and spread out to dry. When Mary turned to estimate how long this tedious job would take she saw a figure bending over the great silver mound, picking fish up one by one, gathering them in her arms as if they were flowers. Mary thought she was seeing some spectre, the spirit of all the murdered fish, a woman with waist-length hair, stringy grey hair, grey face, and tattered grey clothing to which glittering fish scales clung. The creature moved without a sound, carrying each armful of fish up to the flakes, carefully spreading them in the pale sunshine, returning to gather more from the pile.

"Frightened the life out of me, it did, 'til I saw 'twas Frank Norris's wife, Ida. It was the way she moved sort of lop-sided that made me realize who 'twas," Mary tells Rachel.

For the first time since the day she arrived on the Cape, Mary saw the mad woman close up. The doll-like face was faded to a flaky grey, like old chalk. The blue eyes did not focus and the once pretty mouth hung slightly open. Ida's dead foot made strange patterns in the wet sand as she dragged it back and forth between the flake and the pile of caplin.

They worked in silence until the beach was bare and caplin lay row upon neat row on the flake. About five barrels, Mary calculated with satisfaction. She turned to tell the apparition this but Ida was gone—vanished as completely as the caplin scull.

Later, when the worshippers came pouring out of Meg's door and down to the landwash, they allowed, a bit shamefacedly, that Mary had done a good morning's work. Although she was in fine humour by then, Mary was not to be placated by their compliments. "The better the day, the better the deed!" she shouted and marched away without mentioning Ida.

"In late years I thought about Ida Norris, maybe she wasn't pretendin' after all. I seen other women go strange like her—Rowena that time she heard Samuel Blackwood's schooner'd gone to the bottom with two of her sons on board, and Jean Loveys after her little girl were lost in the woods—maybe such sickness is real."

"Anyhow, I never saw Ida Norris again after that day, not 'til the day she died, and that was a good spell. Just before she died she started doin' them foolish things again, same as she done when Annie and Frank were goin' at it, puttin' salt in sugar, pissin' in the water bucket, them kinds of things. Then, one day she died. Just died in her sleep like a baby."

By the end of January both Mary and Rachel were finding it difficult to get around. The girl because of her increasing girth and Mary because of sleepless nights and daytime spells of dizziness that washed over her like dark waves.

"Don't dare tell your mother I'm not well, or Calvin either, none of them. I plans ta leave this world me own way, not with that crowd up here pickin' at me!"

"But Nan we got ta do somethin'—maybe it can be cured, maybe Aunt Tessa or Mamma knows...."

"Stop mewin' or I'll send you off," Mary said sharply. "'Tis old age, girl—not a thing in this world ta be done about it!"

After that, Rachel began making the hot drink she gave her grandmother stronger, mixing ground-up lily root with herbs so the old woman would sleep at night.

twelve

"Thomas Hutchings was gone three, four year—no I thinks it was three—write down three," Mary directs Rachel.

The old woman has a sense of urgency, is trying to hide from the girl how little help the lily root is, beginning to think she will not be able to hold on until the baby is born. But she is determined to get all of her story written into Lavinia's book.

"Everything were strange the day Thomas Hutchings come back—I kept feeling it were all set out, learned off beforehand like them recitations people gives Christmastime. I often wondered if there were one grain of truth in anything Thomas told us that day. Regards him and Vinnie, I can only go by what she told me years and years after."

"So we can't write it down then 'cause you don't know," Rachel is disappointed.

Mary cackles, "Oh I knows all right, well as anyone could—and yes, girl, we'll write it down. Vinnie was fleck enough to write down all that stuff about me'n Ned, wasn't she?"

Brighter than Rachel has seen her for weeks, Mary recalls the time just before Lavinia's death when the two old women spent hours talking about early times on the Cape.

"One day we was rhymin' off every ship ever come into the Cape—the Tern, the Molly Rose, the Seahorse, the Charlotte Gosse, and so on—remembering how the youngsters'd go around bawlin' out 'Ship ahoy! Ship ahoy!' So's all hands would be down on the wharf waitin'. When we finished namin' off all the ships we could think of I asked Vinnie right out what she remembered about the day the Seahorse brought Thomas Hutchings back to the Cape."

"Everything, she said—the colour of the sky, the two crackie dogs runnin' around the wharf, the hole in her sock and the raw spot on her heel, the smell from the landwash where someone was barkin' nets, the fancy stitch in Meg's knitted shawl, the way Pash held both Lizzie's babies 'tho other people kept offering to take them—everything. Vinnie was like Ned that way—everything ever happened to her was stored away so's if she had a mind to tell about 'twas like you been there."

Gosse's new vessel was a beauty. The great four-master came billowing in towards the Cape like a white cloud on the water. There was a sigh of disappointment when, well back from the sunkers, she struck sail and lowered her anchor.

"Can't say as I blames him—ya wouldn't want to take a chance groundin' the likes of that," Ben said.

As they watched, a small skiff with a man at each oar was lowered over the side and held fast while two boxes were eased down on ropes. Then a man carrying something in his arms climbed down into the skiff.

"Might be Joe and Frank comin' home," Lizzie guessed. Since her little girl's death she had given birth to twin boys, had a miscarriage and was now pregnant again.

Brose Gill shook his head, "They'd not get free passage on a vessel like that—and I doubts Frank or your Joe'd be parted with sealin' money just to sail home."

"Young Joe's too close to do such a thing, not while he got feet under him to walk," Sarah chuckled. Then, as if realizing what she had said, a queer look came over her face, "Them boxes—them boxes looks almost like coffins."

"It's Joe, I knows it is," Lizzie whispered and crumpled in a dead faint. Meg knelt and pulled her daughter's head into her lap but no one else stirred or looked away from the small boat rising and falling as it came towards them.

When the skiff got close they could see that the passenger was Thomas Hutchings, that he was holding what seemed to be a baby in the crook of one arm and had the other arm around the waist of a small boy.

"What's this, then—Thomas Hutchings with a new family?" Mary said and Lavinia, who had been standing right next to her, slipped back to stand behind the Gill family at the edge of the crowd.

The boat nudged against the wharf. Thomas stood, looked up and passed the baby to the first person he saw—Annie Vincent. She took the infant and, clearly not thinking of her brothers, asked only, "Is Frank Norris in one of them boxes?"

Thomas shook his head. Someone held out a hand to help him and the boy climbed onto the wharf while the men at the oars made the skiff fast. Ben and Dolph along with Brose Gill came forward and caught the ropes that were tied around the coffins—for now everyone could see they were coffins—plain and unpainted but with the distinctive narrowing at one end. In silence they watched the boxes being eased up over the edge of the wharf, the ropes tossed back to the men in the skiff, watched the men nod to Thomas, then pull away and begin rowing back towards the vessel.

"A person always took care of himself, Thomas Hutchings were—kept his shirts washed and his beard neat—that day, though, he looked like the dog's dinner—glum and red eyed, like he hadn't slept for days. I knowed what it's like being stuck down in the hold of a ship with a baby and might have pitied him, hadn't been for rememberin' how he'd tried to keep me and Fanny from stayin' ashore when I come to the Cape."

Thomas Hutchings stood on the edge of the wharf, staring at the assembled people. He seemed dazed and uncertain. He had no bags or boxes, just a small parcel in one hand and a scrawny boy holding fast to the other. He stood staring at the Cape people for the longest time, then he walked over to Sarah Vincent and kissed her on the cheek. As soon as he kissed her, Sarah began to cry.

"My two," she said and Thomas nodded.

He let go of the child's hand and held onto the sobbing woman, resting his chin on her head so that it looked to those watching as if Sarah was keeping him up.

By the time Thomas turned to them, the Andrews family had gathered around Ben and Meg, who had gotten Lizzie to her feet and were supporting her between them. Mary's three sons stood beside Meg's Willie. Pash, holding one of Lizzie's twins in each arm and with young Toma clinging to her skirt, had moved to her father's side. Jane and her husband Dolph Way, and even Mary, had clustered close as they could get around Lizzie. Only Lavinia was missing.

"I'm sorry. Lizzie it's Joe—your Joe and Peter, both of them. I had to bring them home."

No one said anything. The people on the wharf seemed to draw together, forming a tight circle around the man and the two coffins.

"I had to bring them home," Thomas repeated. He paused, swallowed, looked out over their heads as if hoping someone would come down the path—Ned perhaps or Lavinia.

Then he told them the story he had prepared on the way down. About the night on the ice floes, how Joe twisted his ankle and Peter dropped behind to help him drag the seal carcasses back to the ship. How, in the blinding snow, the brothers had gotten lost, how, holding onto each other through the icy night, they tried to keep walking. How at the end neither of them could move—how they stood, arms around one another, and died.

It was what they would want to hear. Maybe it was even true. When he finished, half the people around him were crying.

"They was brave men, both of them, good men too," Ben Andrews said softly and then there was a long silence.

Not even Meg seemed to know what to do next. Everyone just stood there, stunned. After a long while Mary Bundle asked who the two youngsters were and Thomas gave a start as though he'd forgotten all about the little boy and the baby.

They were Peter's. Peter's and Emma's children, Thomas said. He told them that Peter Vincent and Emma Andrews had been married for two years.

Meg closed her eyes, "Emma's dead too, then," she said.

"No, no Emma's not dead," he assured them. Yet he had no ready explanation for why Meg's daughter had not returned with her children. "She had things to settle up in St. John's," he said lamely.

"You mean to tell me, our Emma let you bring home her two small youngsters and her dead husband—and stayed in St. John's herself!" Ben was incredulous.

"She'll likely be aboard the next vessel—probably with Alex Brennan when he brings the *Tern* down," Thomas told him. Then he pushed the boy forward, said he was Benny Vincent, named after his grandfather, said the baby was a girl but he didn't know what Emma had named her.

By then Meg had the baby in her arms: "Poor innocent little mortal!" She kissed her granddaughter on the forehead and announced the child would be called Comfort.

"And that's how your grandmother got such an outlandish name," Mary tells Rachel.

She finds it hard to explain the strangeness of that long-ago day: "It was all wrong, girl. Unnatural, every minute of it. I kept expectin' someone to call Thomas Hutchings a liar but no one ever did—not ever."

The most terrible thing Mary remembers was that they could smell the bodies. When the first shock had swept over them they were all aware of the smell of putrefaction seeping from the two boxes.

It was Charlie Vincent who took charge. "Maybe," Mary says thoughtfully, "it was then Meg decided to give Char the money she'd been savin' for Willie's education."

The boy did a good job. Stepping forward, he asked them all to bow their heads. "The souls of the righteous are in the hand of God. No torment shall touch them nor death have dominion over them," Charlie recited, his young voice cracking. At the end he added a special prayer for his two brothers. Then the men and older boys lifted the two caskets up, and, under Charlie's direction, carried Joe and Peter back up the hill to where the new church was being built.

"The others followed along, just like always when someone takes the lead. So 'twas Char Vincent, without anyone sayin' a word about it, who shifted the graveyard from down by the sea—what was never a decent place anyway—to up behind the church. And we haven't had a burial on the point from that day to this."

Not quite everyone followed. Thomas Hutchings, Mary and Lavinia, these three were left standing alone on the stagehead. It came to Mary then that no one had asked Thomas anything about himself, where he had been these past years, how he had come to be on the Gosse vessel, not a thing! Nor had anyone but her seemed to think it strange that the man seemed to have forgotten his own son Toma. Thomas hadn't asked if the child he'd left behind was alive or dead, hadn't noticed the wiry little boy holding tight to Pash's skirt.

As Mary watched, Thomas passed Lavinia the brown paper package—which she took without saying one word. "I had me mouth open to ask him a thing or two when Lavinia gives me this spitey look, not like herself at all, and says, saucy as a black: 'Go home now, Mary Bundle, Thomas and me got things to say to each other.' And with that, Vinnie takes his arm and turns him around, same as if they was an old married couple. I tell you, maid, I was that flabbergasted ya coulda knocked me over with a feather!"

Lavinia had resolved in that instant that Mary was not to get Thomas, nor would he leave the Cape again—not if she had anything to do with it. Without any idea how this was to be accomplished, Lavinia Andrews slipped her arm into Thomas's—a gesture of possessiveness she had imagined so often that it seemed familiar.

Thomas hesitated and for a terrible moment Lavinia thought that he would pull away, return to the ship, sail back to wherever he'd come from. She glanced over her shoulder, relieved to see that the ship had gone, was already out of sight. Then Thomas turned and they walked down the beach together, leaving Mary alone on the wharf.

He didn't say a word, and Lavinia did not dare speak, or even look sideways at him. No thought of Joe and Peter dead in their coffins crossed Lavinia's mind—but the shadow of death, of its inevitibility may have added to the reckless exuberance she felt. She was giddy, light-headed with happiness from the solid reality of him standing there, the feel of his arm beneath her hand, from the boldness of what she was doing, from the impossibility of retreating from it.

When they reached the tall rock, the one people called God's Finger, they slid down, just as Lavinia had that first day on the Cape, with their backs against its black surface. She glanced at Thomas's face. He looked ill, bone weary, perplexed.

They sat, shoulders touching, watching the sea advance and retreat. Lavinia was thinking about the time on Turr Island when she and Thomas had hunted for eggs together. How long ago that day now seemed—how many nights since has she lain awake regretting her silence that day, regretting that they had not talked, had not made love!

Today must not be like the day on Turr Island. She has imagined, oh many times, how it would be if they ever met again. Has promised herself she would tell him she loves him. Promised to make him laugh, to beguile him with stories the way Ned had done, to make him love her.

Reality was different, she thought, sitting miserably on the damp sand trying to imagine how one would tell a man such things. It was important to use the right words, words that would not offend him, words he would remember always. She must say the first words. "Say the first words," she urged herself, "just say the first words and the others will come!" But she could not think of the first words and the silence between them went on and on.

Lavinia selected one piece of the driftwood that littered the beach, told herself she would speak before the incoming tide covered it. Her moment of bravado had long passed. She picked nervously at the string on the package Thomas had given her, knowing it contained her journal, wondered if he had read it at all. She tried to remember how much of herself she had given away in the book. If only Thomas would say something—some of the words she had put into his mouth a thousand times in daydreams.

Not a woman in the place wasn't smarter than her! Meg or Sarah or Annie, even Lizzie, and certainly Mary—would know exactly what to say—what to do. But she hadn't wanted that, had not wanted a man you must push and tug at all the time—hadn't want to be like Mary Bundle. Lavinia felt tears burning behind her eyes. Wasn't there anything he had to say to her after all this time?

"Speak! Say something!" Lavinia commanded silently and watched the tide lap against the eel-shaped piece of wood. The next wave would cover it. She had jumped up, walked over, snatched up the driftwood and flung with all her strength.

"I'd rather you was in one of them coffins, Thomas Hutchings, than see you latched onto Mary Bundle!" she screeched as the grey shape hit the water.

From behind her, she heard his indrawn breath—then laughter. Then she felt his arms around her waist. Surprised, she turned inside the circle, leaning back to see his face. She recalled how she used to wish he would laugh, used to imagine how different it would make him look—it did. She began to laugh too, out of pure happiness and relief that the silence had ended. When they stopped laughing they were kneeling in the wet sand, the sea licking in around them. Thomas pulled her toward the rock and they sat with their arms around each other.

"Oh, my love, what patience you're going to need! I'm such a stupid man, only now learning things men like Ned are born knowing," Thomas's voice was so low she could barely hear. But his words seemed like her own and without thinking she began to talk, telling him all the things she wanted him to know.

Lavinia spoke for a long time, ending up telling of the promises she had made to herself about what she would say if he ever returned, "...and just now, when I saw you on the wharf alongside Mary Bundle, I knew if there was a shilling in it for her she'd have you in bed before nightfall..." she stopped.

Thomas took her left hand and lay it beside his, palm upward in her lap, "See those?" he asked, "Those hands tell me there's no fear of my latching onto Mary Bundle—they tell me something quite different."

They did not look at each other but watched his finger trace an imaginary line, first on Lavinia's palm and then on his own. "It's been there all the time, written on our hands but we've been too stupid to read it—written out that I'll marry Lavinia Andrews and live happily forever after—forever after, Lavinia, like in Ned's tales."

Three days before she died, Lavinia, propped up on pillows in the bed she and Thomas had shared for thirty-two years, ended her story there.

"Pure as the driven snow, Vinnie made it sound," Mary tells the girl who is writing in Lavinia's book. "But I knows better—knows more about that day than she give me credit for."

When Thomas and Lavinia turned their backs on her, Mary had watched them for only a few minutes.

"Imagine," she thought, "the likes of Vinnie Andrews orderin' me home like I was a youngster!"

Muttering indignantly, Mary had looked around but there was no one to complain to. So she walked slowly up the hill and back towards the neck, pondering on what Thomas's return might mean to the Cape, and to her.

Beside the half-enclosed church, people stood around watching the men and boys take turns digging into the rocky soil. Mary stood nearby and wondered about the men in the coffins, about what had really happened to them. Perhaps Peter had tried to save his brother—he had, after all, once saved her. She listened to Sarah and Lizzie's sobbing, heard Meg's comforting words, gave her son George a good smack across the head when she saw him sneaking away without taking his turn at the grave digging.

But she had been detached from the sorrow, preoccupied with the knowledge that Thomas Hutchings' return meant she would no longer be in charge of the tally, not be the one to get the few shillings Gosse sent down each fall, would no longer negotiate with Ben about repairs to the store and wharf, nor work with Vinnie making out lists of what would be needed each spring. All her plans for the place would now come to nothing—she would no longer be the one in charge.

Mary had no doubt how it would be. Thomas had left without a by-your-leave and returned the same way. He would be welcomed back as The Skipper—the person Meg, Ben and Sarah have always turned to, the one with the final say about everything.

"I made up me mind then and there I wasn't goin' to just give in to him. It might do me no good, all the same I vowed that next morning I was goin' to face up to Thomas Hutchings, tell him I could be boss well as him, say he was no more than the rest of us now."

For all this resolve Mary had been anxious as she walked towards the store at dawn the next day. Despite her defiance of Thomas she had always been nervous of the man, never easy in his presence. From the day she set foot on the Cape he had treated her like a half-witted, willful child. She tried to fight off her dejection, reminding herself that she had sometimes gotten the better of Thomas Hutchings. Hadn't she made him marry Fanny, made him give her his job when he left. But he had felt guilty then—this time she could think of nothing to bargain with.

As Mary pushed the door of the store open and stepped into its cool, dark silence she had still been searching her mind for something that might give her some leverage with Thomas. She would lose this, too, lose access to the store in the morning, lose that quiet time when she planned out her day, counted the barrels and enjoyed the clean wood smells.

Apart from a few red embers in the grate there was no sign of Thomas. Maybe he had not slept here after all.

Moving silently towards the bunk he had always used as a bed, Mary almost fell onto quilts piled on the floor. She bent forward, staring down at Thomas Hutchings and Lavinia Andrews asleep in each others' arms.

They slept as children might, deep, breathing quietly, their faces innocent. Mary studied them. They looked young, unfamiliar—like the sea creatures in Ned's old yarns, mermaids and gods who lived in caves beneath the ocean. She took several steps back, eased herself down onto the carpenter's bench and sat gazing at the lovers while the room slowly brightened. Ribbons of dust-filtered light picked up the pale blue shadow of lashes on the woman's cheek, the copper gleam of her seaweed hair, cast green reflections on the man's hand cupped under the naked breast, shone vivid as jewels on the scraps of coloured cloth, reds, greens and yellows glowing from the pieced quilt.

"Sittin' there I felt old—old as the hills, older than I feels now—hopeless and bone weary. I got up and left the store, quiet as I could," Mary tells Rachel.

She had walked down the beach, climbed the bank and, skirting the houses, come to the narrow place called the Neck, all without really noticing where she was.

What did it matter if Thomas wanted to take charge of the store and records? What if he did again begin making decisions? She was tired of always pushing and pulling people, sick of the sharp edge of resentment in their voices when they said her name, "...that Mary Bundle," like she was some strange kind of fish—different and unlikeable. In all the years she'd been married to Ned she'd never been accepted by the Andrews crowd, not once in all that time had she ever been called Mary Andrews.

"I'm tired," she told herself, "worn out with keepin' on at them."

It was a marvel to her the way most people lived—how they couldn't see beyond the job they were doing to the job that had to be done. Couldn't see that to grow more vegetables the marsh had to be ditched and drained, that years ahead of when you needed it, wood had to be cut, that larger vegetable cellars had to be dug and stoned in, the river had to be kept from silting up, weeds burnt, barns mucked out, hay made, that roofs, wharves and boats had to be worked on all the time. Oh, they saw the little bits of work all right, but never seemed to recognize that things had to be done in a certain order—a certain way if you were going to fit it all in.

Moving aimlessly through the wet morning grass Mary came to the new graves outside the roofless church and stepped inside. She walked around the rough-framed walls that had weathered to a silver grey. The church, she decided, was a good example of what happened when you didn't have a knack for getting things done. Meg wanted the church, so did Sarah, but they were too nice to make people keep at it, to drive people until no one had a civil word to say about you.

Bits of cut lumber were strewn all around. Inside the empty doorway a partly constructed roof truss lay half covered in dead grass. In one corner warped window frames were propped, in another an iron rod, probably the same one Peter had used to do away with the Indian, rested against some uprights. She recalled Meg's saying the rod should be built into the church, some notion about turning evil to good. It made no sense to Mary, how could you turn evil to good? That was something to be thankful for—at least she'd never cluttered her head with the old religious stuff Meg went on with!

As Mary stood looking at the grey enclosure these thoughts barely skimmed the surface of her mind. Underneath she was still thinking of Lavinia and Thomas, still seeing the sleeping couple, still feeling the wave of weariness, waste and dissatisfaction that pulled at her, threatening to drown everything she was sure of. Could this be what happened to people—what made them take up religion, or become weak and witless like poor Ida Norris?

During the next few days Mary remained disheartened. But she held her peace and watched the pattern of life close over, mesh together as it always did after some upheaval.

Frank Norris came home from the ice with news that there was a big revival going on in Shamblers Cove and that the preacher would be down on the Cape by May or June. Emma's and Peter's little boy Benny became part of Sarah's household, so petted by Sarah, Annie and Charlie, that he went around the place with a great smile of wonder on his face. The Vincents wanted to take Comfort, but Meg would not be parted from the baby. Already two babies, young Toma and Mary's daughter Tessa, spent most of their time in Meg's kitchen. But they were now getting big and both Meg and Pash welcomed the arrival of another infant.

Thomas Hutchings did not say what his plans were, but hove his boat over and began recaulking her as if he'd never been away. Mary marvelled at how quickly things returned to what they had been—like taking a bucket of water out of the sea, she thought. Not one soul asked her advice or noticed the blackness that had dropped down on her.

On the fourth day after his arrival, Thomas let out word he had something to tell them. He asked that they all come up to the store after dinner.

"I don't know why I even went—I promised myself I wasn't going to say one word and I certainly had no interest in hearin' Thomas Hutchings reeve off his great plans for the place."

Mary sat apart from the others, just as she used to do when she first came to the Cape, and occupied herself by counting everyone in the room, even the babies.

"Thirty-one people—only ten more than when I come all them years ago." She remembered Thomas Hutchings saying she and Fanny made twenty-one—"Twenty-one people to feed!" was what he had said. Then, the very night she came, Young Joe had smuggled aboard the *Tern* and the next day Hazel Andrews died—that was how it had been over the years—one coming, another going.

Mary shook herself. If she kept on brooding she'd end up like those old woman who lived on the outskirts of places and got called witches. But how could she be old when she was the same age as Lavinia who sat across from her, looking like a young girl? Looking like butter wouldn't melt in her mouth, Mary thought, marvelling as she often has at the deceitful daytime faces people wear.

Thomas was standing on a box at the front, explaining something, something he had found out on the boat coming down. Mary began to listen to what he was saying.

"...so Timothy Drew owns the Gosse premises now, lock, stock and barrel, in St. John's and here—and in a dozen other little places along the coast. He's a big man in St. John's, this Drew. We talked a good bit on the boat coming down and he told me he's been associated with the Gosse firm for years. As far as I understand, he has it settled that his premises here on the Cape will just be let go."

"Let go?" the men looked at each other, no one understood.

"This new owner, Timothy Drew, he'll just not come here to pick up our fish, or to drop off supplies, nor pay anyone to keep things up here."

Mary could tell from Thomas's tone that he was repeating something he'd said before.

Ben Andrews interrupted: "But Thomas, we been hearin' talk like that time-out-of-mind. Hands on Gosse vessels are forever goin' on about him—one year they tell us he'll be made Governor, the next that his biggest ship's been lost and he's goin' back to England!"

"Mose Skanes told us last fall Gosse'd be leavin' soon—said there's streets and streets filled with mansions in Devon. All built on cod we people catches, on the work of us 'long this coast," Sarah Vincent said and people around her nodded.

"This new man, this Drew who's gone on up the coast, what's he like, then?"

Thomas considered, "Timothy Drew seemed fair enough—his wife was good to the children—helped me with the baby. Drew only planned to come in to the Cape on his way back—but his wife saw how seasick Benny was and she persuaded him to drop us off before sailing up the coast." Thomas paused and studied his pipe, a gesture Mary knew meant he wanted time to think.

"He'll be here tomorrow or next day. Any of you can try to reason with him—I tried—told him this was the place he got his best quality fish from, and a lot of it, too. I have to say I don't think Timothy Drew is one to change his mind. It's only business with him and he's worked out that he'll make more money if he keeps stores only in the bigger places like Pond Island."

"That'll ruin this place altogether—it's hard enough now without havin' to go up to Pond Island for things like salt and rope," Meg said.

"That's not the worst, what about our fish? We'd have to cart all our fish up by water, not knowin' when they'd be picked up! We might even have to pay someone to keep 'em in storage until a vessel come," Mary was surprised to hear such sense from Meg's Willie.

They talked for more than an hour, around and around, but in the end were no wiser. When he saw they had talked themselves out, Thomas jumped down from the box: "We'll make do somehow, like we always have," he said and they nodded, tired of the subject and glad to leave it.

"Now," Thomas said, "we'll make what plans we can. Worse comes to worst we can find some way to get our fish to a bigger place. Let's work out who will be in which boats this summer just the same as if we'd never heard Timothy Drew's name." He took out his tally book and they crowded around like they always had.

That was the way of it—they weren't even going to fight this man Drew! Mary had seen it again and again, the stubbornness, the determination to ignore certain doom—as if by bearing everything, by never hitting back, they proved something. Oh, they would work like dogs and some would pray, everyone would worry and some might curse quietly to wives or husbands—but in the long run nothing would be done. They would just endure—like Sarah said, "What can't be cured must be endured."

Watching them, Mary sank even further into gloom. "Much good your lists'll do, Thomas Hutchings—if we can't get fish picked up we're all goin' to have to leave—that's the long and short of it!"

She wondered bitterly how many times one person could be turfed out to start over again. "No safe place no matter how hard you works," she thought, remembering her mother and Master Potts. "Them's got money owns everything—everything in the earth, everything in the sea— and the likes of us owns nothing."

No one except Ned had ever seen Mary Bundle shed a tear—and they weren't going to now. She bit her lip and listened to her son-in-law Dolph saying, without even a glance in her direction, that he was going to take Ned's boat out and that Henry would be his shareman. Names were called out, Willie Andrews would fish out of Frank's boat, Brose Gill had his own two sons and Annie, who had always gone shares with Joe, said she would take Mary's middle son Alfred, Thomas said he'd take young George who was only twelve, but as good in a boat as any man.

"Char's so good at numbers—I expects he'd best be left with Ben workin' on the barrels," Lavinia, who must have realized that no one had called out Charlie Vincent's name, said.

Thomas gave her a quick smile before turning to Ben: "I saw the staves and rings—what arrangement do you have about the barrels?"

Several people began to answer but Ben finally managed to explain how everyone had helped with barrel making and how all shared in the better price they got for fish and berries packed in their own barrels.

It was just like always, them facing Thomas and him hunkered down on his haunches, talking, nodding, puffing at his pipe, marking down numbers in his little book. Mary noticed that every so often, as if by accident, his eyes met Lavinia's and they grinned, foolish as children. Sometimes Thomas rocked back on his heels—Mary had never seen him look so boyish. A person would hardly credit this was the grey man who had stood on the wharf three days before—she wondered everyone in the room hadn't noticed the change.

"I know something about barrel making," he said, "my father was a cooper." It was the first thing about his past Thomas had ever offered and they all recognized it as a sign that he would be staying. Immediately there was a relaxing of tension in the room. Things could not be all that bad if Thomas Hutchings was going to stay on the Cape.

Mary could almost hear the words they were thinking. She got up and walked through the door. As she left she heard Thomas ask, "Have you tried firing the barrels?"

Bristling with rage, Mary stalked down to the wharf. She pulled off her old sealskin boots and dangled her bare feet out over the water. "Friggers! Not one of 'em give me a bit of credit for all I done—nor said a thing about the barrels bein' my idea. No one asked me a question—not even Dolph, when he and Henry was talkin' about Ned's boat—my boat! And me sittin' right there like I didn't have a tongue in me face. I'd ha' just as well been out on the Funks for all they considers me, now that man's back—acts like he was God going to save 'em all—they'll soon know the difference!"

She stared down at the water that lapped softly around the barnacled piers, counting the connors and jellyfish drifting in and out below the wharf. Then, catching some movement out to sea, she looked up. The vessel that had brought Thomas three days ago was coming in towards the Cape. Again it hove to seaward of the shoals, and again a skiff with two seamen was lowered into the water. As Mary watched, two more men and a woman were helped down into the skiff and the seamen began rowing towards the wharf.

This, she guessed, would be Timothy Drew—the new owner and his wife, the woman Thomas Hutchings had described as kindly. A small woman, wearing a blue bonnet that tied under her chin and a long cloak made of soft brown material. Mary's attention was so focused on the woman that she hardly saw the two male passengers in the boat.

Mary did not stand, nor even move when the skiff bumped the wharf and the three passengers climbed cautiously up the shaky ladder. One man turned and told the seamen to wait, that they would be leaving again within the hour. Mary saw the boatmen exchange looks of resignation as they shipped their oars.

Beneath her cape the woman was wearing a dress the same shade of blue as her hat. Her boots were shiny black leather with a dozen little buttons up the side.

"She were like rich women I seen in St. John's, you could smell her, scented soap and powder, no human smell at all—I used to think about such women, wonder what they worried about. She stood so close I coulda spit on her boots."

Although so many years have passed, Mary is still ashamed of how afraid she felt that day. Afraid of the people standing there beside her, afraid to look up, cowed by their importance, by their shiny footwear, humiliated by her own dirty feet, feeling suddenly stupid and clumsy—feelings anger usually protected her from. She sat very still, seeing nothing above the knees of these strangers who were staring down at the top of her head.

The older man, the one who had given the curt order to the seamen, said, "Hey, you there!" thinking, Mary guessed, that she was an idiot who lolled on the stagehead all day. He even nudged the side of her skirt with his polished boot.

Trying to control her fear, Mary scrambled to her feet, made herself raise her eyes—and found herself staring into the eyes of Tim Toop. There was no doubt of it. The face had changed, puffed out and coarsened, the nose was thicker, redder, but there was no mistaking the sharp, rat-like eyes of the pickpocket.

The two must have stared at each other for a full minute. Then the man pulled himself up to his full height, which, Mary noted, was still not great, and spoke: "Madam, may I introduce myself, I am Timothy Drew and this is my wife, and..." nodding towards the young man hovering at his shoulder, "this is Mr. Matthews, my clerk."

Without pausing for Mary to speak, he ordered Matthews to have a look around the premises. "Make a list of anything of value, and then post the notice—and see if that Hutchings fellow is coming back with us," he ordered, dismissing the man with a snap of his fingers.

Timothy Drew watched his clerk climb the three steps to the stage and disappear into the store before turning back to Mary. Taking his time he looked her up and down, from muddy feet to unkempt hair. "And what might your name be?" he asked.

"It might be almost anything—seems names don't keep—goes rotten—like fish, I s'pose," she said. Her fear had vanished, swept away by rage and astonishment.

He leaned slightly forward and Mary thought she saw a flicker of humour in the eyes peering at her. "So they do, so they do. I, for instance, took my wife's name. It has a nice ring about it, don't you think?"

He turned to his wife who looked mildly surprised at her husband's manner. "My dear, this is Mary, Mary Sprig, the one I told you about. We used to sit on headstones sharing stolen oranges."

"Yes," thought Mary, "shared a jeezely sight more than oranges too." She sized up the woman. Pretty, she was, but not soft, Mary judged, taller than she'd looked in the boat, the narrow plume in her bonnet was several inches higher than the top of her husband's stovepipe hat.

"She had a good face, she'd know a lot more than she'd tell, would Mrs. Timothy Drew," Mary told her great-granddaughter.

Mrs. Drew had smiled and nodded. Mary nodded back politely but turned immediately to the man: "How come you're here, Tim Toop—and what's this news your flunky's goin' to tell us?" she asked although she knew the answer. She needed time to think, to figure what she could get out of Tim.

"I've always been connected with Caleb Gosse's business—you know that, Mary—wasn't I the one got you a job on one of his vessels?"

He ignored her snort and, perhaps because he too needed time to think, took a turn around the salt-crusted wharf, studying the unpainted store, the tiny gardens, the raw houses set down helter-skelter amid the rocks before returning to where Mary stood.

"Now it's your turn to answer questions," he told her briskly. "Two questions: first, where is everyone? And—once again—what are you called?"

"I'm called Mary Bundle, but for your information me name's Mary Andrews—Mrs. Ned Andrews to you. And regards where all hands is, they's inside there," she pointed to the store. "By now I s'pose t'Matthews feller is tellin' 'em whatever news you got for us. How come the crowd in St. John's haven't got you hung yet?"

She looked him in the face as she said this, and saw his eyes change. As if fire had been doused with water, all trace of humour disappeared, replaced by a look of such steely coldness that Mary would have stepped back if she had not held herself in check.

"In St. John's, Mrs. Andrews, I now have some say in who will hang—and as I remember, your name was on the list," he pronounced each word slowly, with great care, as if someone had taught him how to speak.

Mary made herself keep looking into his eyes. She was aware of his wife's reaching out, touching the man's arm. When he turned, breaking the stare, the woman gave a small shake of her head, cautioning or reminding him of something. Mary could feel cold perspiration at the base of her spine.

When he looked back at her he was smiling. "Well Mary, what do you want, what's brewing in that greedy little mind of yours?"

"Don't you even want to know what happened to your daughter?" Mary glanced at the woman but to her disappointment Tim's wife showed no sign of surprise.

"Not particularly," he said, "she's yours, I'm sure you're taking good care of her," he reached into his pocket, pulled out a cigar and lit it. His humour seemed to have returned. Standing there beside his pretty wife Tim looked so rich, so oiled and well fed that Mary would gladly have pushed him off the edge of the wharf and laughed as he sank down among the connors and bits of rotting fish gut.

"She's dead—your daughter died down there—just down on the beach. She died havin' a baby, 'tho she were only a girl herself—not even old as I was when you knocked me up!"

"And your husband, Mrs. Andrews, where is he?" it was the woman who spoke.

"He's dead—he—he were killed, by a, by a..." Mary's voice rasped, "killed by an animal." She took a deep breath, "'Tisn't hard to die in places like this."

"I am sorry to hear that," the woman said.

"We'd best collect that Hutchings man and be off," Tim put his hand under his wife's elbow and turned her towards the store, "it was—interesting seeing you again, Mrs. Andrews."

With clumsy haste Mary moved to stand between them and the store. "Not yet. Not yet, ye don't—last time I saw you, Tim Toop, you said you'd have somethin' for me, said when I come back to St. John's you'd help me get passage to England and give me money to settle down with Fanny."

"That was a long time ago—a lifetime ago. That agreement was made between two people who no longer exist," Tim's smile was fixed but his eyes were cold again.

"Not so long ago, not my lifetime nor yours, not so long I don't remember you ransackin' the Armstrong house—and what's become of that God damned bastard—did me hex work?"

She waited, he didn't speak and she, striking out in the dark, said, "What ever happened to that watch, the one you stole from Armstrong, the one with the letters and leaves on the back?"

The hand that had started to reach instinctively towards his vest pocket stopped. His wife said, "Timothy!"

And Mary, knowing she had him, pressed on, "I got good friends here, people who can read and write, who knows all about you, Tim Toop (this was not true, she had never mentioned his name) friends who'd be glad to write and let the Governor in St. John's know about that watch of yours, know what kind of man took over Caleb Gosse's business."

Leaning towards him, hands on hips, chin pointed, Mary waited, determined that this time he would answer her. Instead he took a step forward, hand raised as if he was about to strike her or push her off the wharf.

"I didn't budge," Mary tells her great-granddaughter proudly, "if he'd laid a hand on me, bejesus I'da killed him!"

But he jerked away at the last minute, stalked over to the edge of the wharf and stood there, staring out to his beautiful ship.

"We should give Mr. Drew a little time to compose himself," his wife said in her soft, well-bred voice. "Now, my dear, what is it you want? A way out of this place? Maybe passage back to England for you and your children—you do have children?"

Such an idea had not occurred to Mary. She thought about it. She probably could get passage back to England out of them, and maybe something more, enough for a little house perhaps? Go back to England? Where in England? With Ned's children? She tried to remember what England was like but could conjure up no picture of the place outside the workhouse, the graveyard and the street skirting it, could not imagine the shape of England's coastline, the colour of its sea or the smell of its air.

"You know, Rachel, I thought in them days I was well along—but I was still not forty. Young! Why me life wasn't even half over!" The old woman's voice is amazed, wistful.

"You sorry you never went, Nan?" the girl stands and stretches, she has been writing for hours.

"I can't say even now, maybe I shoulda. Tim Toop was well able to do it—passage to England woulda been nothin' to him—he'd of tucked we crowd in among salt cod on one of his ships. I'd have gotten money out of him, too. He was rich as God even then and got a lot richer before he died—the old bugger."

But Mary had barely considered the idea. What would she do in England? What would Henry, George and Alfred, half savage and not able to read more than their own names, do? They'd all have to start over again, as what? Gypsies? Pickpockets? Like her father, taking care of some rich man's sheep?

"That's what you two'd like, wouldn't ya? Me stowed safe away on t'other side of the ocean—sure he'd have me hove overboard half way across!" she pointed at Tim's back.

He turned around then, came over to his wife and, as charming as if he'd never thought of murder, told Mary to put her cards on the table. She did, and they bartered just as they had in the space under Gosse's cook rooms, snapping at each other like two crackies, measuring each other's strength, spitting out insults. Tim's careful grammar slipped and his wife wandered off to gaze vacantly down the empty beach.

Mary enjoyed it, was sorry when it ended and they made their sober way up to the store.

As they walked in Mr. Matthews, the clerk, was speaking, coming to the end of his patience it seemed, "...the Cape is known to be dangerous, especially for the larger vessels Mr. Drew plans to purchase from now on. It's not practical to discharge and pick up cargo in every flea-bitten outport along the coast. And that's that!"

When he stopped speaking there was silence. No one objected or asked questions. No one moved, not even to look towards the door where Mary stood beside the new owner and his wife.

"A sheep-like bunch you fell in with," Tim said out of the corner of his mouth. Mary had to agree, wishing that instead of looking down at their boots they would rush up and kick the young dandy's backside.

"They're not half so sheep-like as they looks—someday you might find that out!" she hissed, but did not dare turn to face him for fear he'd see the gleam of victory in her eyes and know she would have settled for less, far less, than he had agreed to.

Leaving his wife and Mary at the back of the room, Timothy Drew walked briskly to the front. Without a word of explanation to Matthews he brushed the young man aside, climbed up on the box and contradicted everything his clerk had said.

"We have decided to continue with Gosse's practice of dropping supplies at Cape Random and, of course, of picking up your fish here. If any of you men want berths to Labrador on Drew vessels you can give Mr. Matthews your name right now, and," he glanced at Mary, "you will get a fair price from my firm for your fish."

The clerk looked dumbfounded, the audience bewildered. There was a low murmur of whispered consultation, people smiled uncertainly. Then, hesitantly, the men went up one by one to Mr. Drew, muttering their thanks: "We appreciates it, sir, that we do," they said, tugging at their caps.

Mrs. Drew walked to the front and whispered something in her husband's ear. He nodded and held up his hand, his stiff authority was all back. "Just remember one thing, you might be hearing the Drew name again—we got sons," he smiled at his wife. "And one day you'll hear of them running for government. When that time comes I expect your loyalty—I expect you and your families to stand behind the Drews same as we stood behind you."

Everyone nodded and smiled and there were even a few half embarrassed cheers as he got down from the box.

Before leaving the store, Mr. Matthews wrote out a paper for Mary. It stated that the Cape Random premises formerly belonging to Caleb Gosse now became hers and her heirs' forever, that Drew vessels would continue to call there for fish.

Down on the wharf the men came forward again to tip their caps and nod before the great man and his wife. "God be with ya, missis," "We appreciates it," and "We'll not forget what ya done, sir," they said. Even Thomas Hutchings thanked them and gave a kind of bow to the woman. Jane and Rose clapped and some of the youngsters cheered. The Drews nodded and smiled.

"It's enough to make a cat laugh," Mary thought, "all of them bein' so meek—and Tim Toop, the little thief, actin' like he was King of England."

Still, she smiled too, smiled and smiled, and stood hugging the stiff paper inside her sweater, saying over and over to herself, "in perpetuity, in perpetuity...." It was a grand word. She had young Matthews read the paper out and explain what each word meant, she liked that one especially.

"In perpetuity," she whispered under her breath, smiling as the skiff carrying Timothy Drew Esq. and his wife moved away from the waving people. "In perpetuity!" She didn't care if she never saw the sky over either of them again.

She never did. But in the years that followed, Timothy Drew's name, the names of his sons and grandsons, as well as the names of Drew vessels—the *Northern Queen*, the *Seahorse*, the *Jubilee* and the *Northern Pathway*—became bywords along the northeast coast. Mary had seen the beginnings of a family empire that would control much of the mercantile and political life of Newfoundland for generations.

Timothy Drew, with the help of his wife's relatives in England, would in twenty years own a huge business. A business based on carrying Newfoundland whale and seal oil and dried salt fish to ports in Spain, Portugal and Great Britain, returning with rope, rum, salt, flour and coal. In a thousand coves and bays, on a hundred tiny islands, thousands of fishermen and their families worked for the Drew empire and depended on Drew vessels for every mouthful of food, every item of clothing. Timothy's descendants became manufacturers, bankers, lawyers and, of course, politicians. In Newfoundland they were considered only a little lower than the angels and a good bit higher than royalty.

But that spring day, standing quietly on the wharf whispering the magic word to herself, Mary Bundle knew nothing of this. Nor, had she known, would she have cared. Never one to brood on what might have been, Mary was overjoyed to know she owned the planks beneath her bare feet, the flakes and the solid wooden store behind her.

thirteen

"I tell ya, girl, that day I watched the Seahorse sail off with Tim Toop I wouldn't ha' called the Queen me aunt! Not one of us wasn't relieved. The grownups looked a bit stunned but the youngsters romped around the wharf like young goats."

They were safe! They had been reprieved!

"I kept thinkin' how it'd be if I had to leave—what it'd be like to get me things together and start off in another place. How it'd be, leavin' with Josh out there on the point and Joe and Peter buried in back," Sarah sobbed as she hugged Meg and Anne.

Each woman had been thinking such things, not only of the graves, either, but of the houses, the solid shelves, the gardens and potato cellars, the half-finished church, of the lilac bushes beside their doors and the sight of sun hitting the water off Turr Island. Never had the Cape seemed so dear, so settled, so filled with friends and fine possessions. In the fading light of a spring evening everything around them took on a golden glow. How could such wonders be abandoned, and, if abandoned, how assembled again in this world or the next?

Willie nudged his father, "We done all right, Pop—we done all right, eh?"

Ben looked at his son and grinned. "I 'lows we did—seems to me Drew be a fair man. That young feller, now, that Matthews, he were all there to turf us out before Mr. Drew come and put his foot down."

The other men nodded, but Meg dried her eyes and frowned at her husband. "I was prayin' the whole time we was up there—prayin' we'd not be left next summer with no one to take the fish we caught—and I allow 'twas the Lord's work we got sove."

Sarah, Anne and Lizzie were quick to agree, it was a miracle, pure and simple. How else to account for that man's change of heart?

Suddenly they were all talking, Meg and Sarah quoting scripture, Lizzie chastising the twins for lack of manners in front of quality, Jane and Rose describing to Pash each button and ribbon on Mrs. Drew's costume. The men, sheepish as children who find when a candle is lit that the monster is only their father's coat, walked in circles, muttering that they must have misunderstood the clerk fellow from the first—and no wonder—he had that strange townish way of saying his words.

No one saw Thomas go over to Lavinia. Only when he cleared his throat did they notice the two of them standing so close together, arms linked.

"We're going to begin living in the store." He looked towards Meg as if seeking approval, "Living together—we'll marry as soon as a preacher comes by."

Meg could hardly believe what she'd heard. What was Thomas saying, right out in front of them all, in front of the children? Mouth agape she looked at him. "What?" she asked.

"Lavinia and me, we're moving into the store to live."

"Thomas! You're not thinkin' of livin' like man and wife without God's blessing—you mustn't do such a thing!" Meg glanced at Willie and Rose who were also waiting, in separate houses, for the arrival of a minister. "'Tisn't decent, besides bein' a bad example."

"Why don't we have Charlie marry us all— just like he done...." Rose's voice came to an abrupt stop, she sputtered and turned crimson, remembering that wedding had been Thomas' and Fanny's.

"Them was special circumstances, Rose Norris— not something we're likely to repeat. There'll be a minister down in a week or so—Reverend Oakley perhaps, when he gets finished in Shamblers Cove," Meg gave her prospective daughter-in-law a black look before pronouncing judgment. "Ye can wait 'till then, all four of ye, 'specially you Vinnie, after all, you're our teacher. I'm pure mortified you'd consider something so sinful—and to talk so in front of children! If need be we'll talk after service on Sabbath."

"We'll not wait, Meg—Thomas and me already waited too long," Lavinia looked around the circle of faces without embarrassment. "This very day Thomas is going to board off part of the store for us to—to sleep in," she did have the grace to lower her eyes on the last words.

"Stiff necked she was, 'tho I do say so." Mary passes her empty cup to Rachel. "Vinnie and me was like sisters in later years but I haves to say, she done what she liked and the devil take the hindmost. Never got held against her somehow, never got bawled out and looked down on, Vinnie didn't."

That day, however, Mary had not cared. Lavinia and Thomas could have rolled around together right there on the stagehead in front of everyone, for all she was concerned. Euphoric from the success of her shouting match with Tim Toop, confidence seeping into her from the paper she clutched against her chest, Mary was interested in nothing but herself. She had clambered up onto the splitting table, stood above them, scowling down until one-by-one, they noticed her.

"A fine bunch ye are—sheep, just like the man said. Sheep! God's sheep or Drew's sheep—or even Thomas Hutchings' sheep—sheep for anyone," Mary yelled down at their upturned faces.

Swivelling around to face Thomas, she shouted: "Who the frig you think you are, Thomas Hutchings? Comin' back here like a lord, takin' over like you owns us! And the rest of ye—actin' like we can't get along without him. What did we do when he was gone, tell me that, what did we do? Didn't we get our boats in the water? Didn't we catch fish and make it? Didn't we cull it and count it and send it off to St. John's?"

They had stared up at her in wonder and bewilderment. What was she carrying on about? Her own boys were shamed by their mother's outburst. Jane whispered to Dolph that he must do something, and pushed her husband towards the table on top of which Mary stood.

"Come on down now, come down, Mamma Mary," Dolph spoke as he would have to a child, or a cat that had climbed up under the wharf.

She slapped his hand away. "Bugger off—and stop callin' me that stunned name—I can't abide it—sounds like some Roman Saint!"

Mary looked around until she found Thomas again, "I minds when I first come here, Alex Brennan asked him over there if I could stay, and he said no. No! This were his place then. Whatever were done, everybody came to he. Them times is gone, Thomas Hutchings! Different times now! Now my man, if you wants to live in the store you gotta come to me—got to ask me—'cause 'tis me owns the store!" Mary screamed the last words waving her paper over their heads. It fluttered out of her hand and she had to make an awkward grab to catch it.

Regaining her balance, she took a deep breath and raved on, pelting years of resentment down on them, reminding them of all she had done to keep the place alive, of every grievance she had ever held, ending with her opinion of their performance in front of Timothy Drew. "...and now ye all stands here like the cats that ate the cream, thinkin' it was yer prayers, or yer kow-towin', the bowin' and scrapin' and tippin' of caps to them buggers that got ye off. Twarn't! 'Twas me—me who made that old crook say his vessels will keep on comin' in to the Cape."

She was like the tide, like the moon, like the great unstoppable icebergs that came down the coast. They stood in silent awe—what she said made no sense but was still a marvel. Even the smallest children knew they were witnessing one of Mary Bundle's famous rages, an event they would some day tell their grandchildren about.

Eventually her fury subsided, her gesturing hands dropped, she looked around. Still standing atop the table she beckoned Lavinia over: "Here, you read this to 'em—and keep ahold of it or we'ums all lost."

Remembering that moment, Mary cackles and closes her eyes to savour it. "Talk about good—my dear 'twas marvellous standin' up like that, watchin' the looks on them faces while Vinnie read the paper out."

Whatever regrets she had felt when she stood over the sleeping lovers were gone, unimaginable as ice is in summer.

Looking down at the people standing below, Mary remembered others, people who had looked down thus at her: Master Potts sitting on his horse telling Una if he didn't get more work out of her, she and her children would be thrown out of the hut; Mrs. Brockwell scowling at the little girls on the workhouse steps, saying they were lousy and must be scrubbed down; Mr. Armstrong leering at her and Tessa, reaching for them with his putty-like hands; Thomas Hutchings telling her she and her child couldn't come ashore on the Cape. And from some great height, all the "thems" who'd killed Tessa and driven Mary Sprig into hiding, the "thems" who'd starved her, kept her poor and overworked all her life. Even Meg's face came to her, looking down at her and Ned, ordering them out of the house, saying they must forget their bodies and care for their souls.

"Tim was right," she thought, "'tis worth anything, worth lyin', stealin', maybe even worth killin' to be the one up here, the one holding onto the whip, not the one feelin' it."

When Mary finishes telling Rachel about the scene on the wharf, she opens her eyes and stares at the girl. No more than a child she seems to the old woman, a child who sits, head bent, still writing in Lavinia's book.

"She's not hard enough," Mary thinks, "not near hard enough for what's comin' to her."

She tries to remember something more she can tell her great-granddaughter, some advice she can give, some spell or hex that will make Rachel stand up for herself when she, Mary, is not there. Something that will keep her safe.

But there is nothing, nothing she can say except what the girl has been copying down for weeks—and maybe Rachel doesn't even believe that—maybe she thinks it's all just a yarn made up by a foolish old woman.

"'Tis all true, ya know, true as the Bible, every word of it!" Mary says sharply.

"I knows Nan, I knows it is—and I got everything you told me writ down," Rachel closes the book. For the first time in weeks Mary seems to be really seeing her great-granddaughter.

"I'm not sayin' they wasn't good people—they was. And hard workers—my maid, you never knowed the like of them people to work! Not like this crowd we got now. Nowhere on this coast is the likes of Meg or Sarah, nor men like Ned and Ben or Josh Vincent or Frank Norris. Times changed, girl—things comes too easy to ye lot."

Rachel expects her great-grandmother to doze off as she has most evenings when the writing is finished. Instead, the old woman sits up, looks towards the window, sniffs, says, "I thinks meself the wind's veered. I doubt there'll be a speck of snow left by morning. We'll have supper now—what about roastin' one of them nice rounders Jack brought over, and we'll toast some of your mother's bread—I must say I'm partial to Jessie's bread."

While the fish is roasting, wafting the smell of sea and woods through the kitchen, Rachel goes down to her parents' house for a jar of jam. It is true, the wind had changed, swung around to the southwest. Winter is almost over.

"Nan's feelin' better. I thinks she's goin' to be alright after all," Rachel tells her mother, partly because it is true and partly to distract Jessie, whose eyes fill with tears every time she sees her daughter's thickening form.

Throughout supper and while Rachel washes up, Mary tells about the years after she became owner of the store.

"Made no difference, really. I can see that now, except for makin' me more content in me mind. Thomas and Vinnie kept on livin' there 'til they built this house. And was true what the clerk feller said, vessels comin' down the coast did get bigger. Then there was them steamers and they stopped comin' in here altogether—still, we made a livin', hung on somehow. The barrels helped. Thomas' idea for burnin' 'em inside done somethin' to 'em. Made our herring and berries taste better—least that's what people come to think—and 'cause they thought it we got a better price."

"What about Thomas and Lavinia, did they get married proper?"

"Not for a good spell—there was a big revival goin' on somewhere along the coast and I s'pose the preacher got stuck in one of them places tryin' to get everyone saved. Anyway, poor Willie and Rose had to wait right through that summer and winter 'til the next summer to marry. Didn't make one bit of difference to Thomas Hutchings and Vinnie. They just acted like they was married. Took young Toma to live with 'em and settled down—never mind Meg and Sarah was havin' fits prayin' over 'em."

Mary talks for a long time that night. Not things she wants the girl to write down, happy things. What she calls old foolishness—banners of memory that float above the changeless cycle of fishing, bearing children, fighting the cold, surviving the winter.

She tells Rachel about the time Alfred hauled in a fifty-foot sea monster longer than his boat, about how Lavinia started telling stories just as Ned had done ("'Twas times I'da almost thought was him, 'steada Vinnie, sittin' across the fire from Thomas Hutchings, yarnin'"), about the winter Ben and Thomas built a big catamaran and all hands went sliding down the hill and out across the frozen reach, about the fall Sarah saw the ghost of the little girl lost in the woods ("But I think meself 'twas Sarah's nerves"), about the summer picnics Thomas and Lavinia used to have on Turr Island ("Course they never asked no one else, but I'd see 'em go off with blankets and baskets—like two youngsters, laughin' and gigglin'. She never growed up Vinnie didn't and after they got together Thomas caught whatever it was and started gettin' younger"). About the Christmas someone left a tin of English biscuits on each doorstep and they never found out who it was, the time every soul on the Cape except Mary got saved, of the day Annie hauled off her oilskins, put on a dress and marched down to propose to Frank Norris, about the time they'd all seen a ship in the sky, plain as day, sailing on clouds with every rat-line in place.

Happy and bizarre stories. Most as familiar to Rachel as they are to Mary, for children on the Cape speak of things that happened long before their births in the same way they talk of yesterday's weather or last season's catch.

Mary is still talking as Rachel helps her undress, settles her on the couch and tucks quilts around her.

"Just like Ned, Vinnie were," she says, her old crony's face cupped in her hand like a child ready for sleep. On impulse, Rachel bends forward and kisses her great-grandmother before blowing out the lamp and going upstairs to the cold bedroom.

Sometime during the night Mary Bundle died. She died alone, which was what she had planned, and she made a good death, which was her most fervent wish. She was lucky. "But then," she thought, just before she slipped into unconsciousness, "I always been lucky."

In the morning Rachel finds her. The girl does not turn hysterical, cry, or go running down the hill to her mother. She walks across the kitchen, which is still warm from the fire she had banked the night before, and stands looking down at her grandmother's face.

The old woman must have gotten up during the night. The knitted afghan has been taken from the rocker and spread neatly over her, her long grey hair is coiled into a bun—Rachel knows that would have been hard for Nan to do with her right shoulder so stiff.

Only one thing is not as Mary had wished. Her eyes, still flinty black as bits of coal, are open. Rachel takes a deep breath, reaches forward and gently presses the lids down. Now the face looks peaceful, more peaceful than Rachel has ever seen it. She wonders where Smut is, has he run off as animals are said to do when their masters die? Then the afghan moves and the cat crawls out from where he had curled against Mary's side.

Rachel goes to the back porch, takes the weighted net from the jug her mother had sent up the day before and pours milk into the cracked saucer behind the stove. Then, seeing Mary's big teacup set down on the fender, she picks it up.

A thick brown residue, like black molasses, has hardened in the bottom of the cup. Rachel studies it a long time, sniffs it but cannot identify the sickly sweet smell. Returning to the pantry, she washes it. As she carefully dries Victoria's face and the chipped curlicues around her crown, the girl remembers how it had delighted Nan to outlive the old queen. She decides she will keep the cup.

Repeating to herself the instructions she and Mary had gone over so many times, Rachel goes upstairs and empties the contents of Lavinia's bag out onto the quilt.("...mind me now, three things to do before ya goes down to call yer mother...take the gold and the book. I wants them hid, no one but you're to have 'em...mind now maid, you might need that money when the child comes....")

Rachel does just as she's been told. First she packs the book away in her own school bag, pushing it under her change of clothing. Next she knots the gold pieces back into the cloth and tucks it, just as Mary had once done, down the front of her flannel shift. The other things—the small roll of merchant's notes, the even smaller roll of bank notes, and the thick parchment—declaring the store and wharf to belong to Mary Bundle and to her heirs in perpetuity—Rachel returns to Lavinia's frayed bag, which she pushes under the feather mattress. Her mother and aunts will find it when they came to lay Nan out.

In the kitchen the blind is still down. Rachel crosses to the window and eases it up ("Gentle, girl, don't pull the guts outta it!"). When the women come they will pull all the blinds down—every blind on Cape Random will be lowered, every curtain drawn until the funeral is over.

For now, though, Rachel watches the pale morning sun move slowly across the scrubbed wooden floor, across the flowered oilcloth on the table, across the old picture of sheep and shepherd coming home along a path lined with trees taller than any Rachel has ever seen. She watches sun fall on the brown and blue squares of the afghan, so neatly tucked under the pointed chin, watches it flicker across the strangely peaceful face of the old pagan who lies waiting for her people to come and take her to the graveyard beside the church she has not entered since the day it was finished.

After studying her great-grandmother's face for a long time, Rachel leaves the house, walks down the path, past the hen house, past the clump of damson and the already green rhubarb that Nan keeps fenced against goats, down to her father's house. Before going in she pauses, gazing for a minute down at the store and the wharf. Smoke is already rising from the chimney of the twine loft where Uncle Willie Andrews will be getting ready for his day's work. Out beyond the wharf the sea is smooth, boats bob on collar, reflected perfectly in the blue water. Out beyond the clean crescent of beach, out beyond the white frills of the Cape, the ice-coloured Atlantic stretches up to what her grandfather calls the Labrador Sea. Rachel takes a great gulping lungful of the cold morning air before going in to tell her mother.

One hundred and twenty-six people stand beside Mary's grave. Half a hundred more lie silently in the graves around. Some graves are old, grass covered and hollow, others are still raw mounds of clay and rock, like upturned boats. The graveyard is bare, jam jars and cups that once held flowers lie cracked by winter frost. Neither rose tree or lilac, nor the Sweet William women plant each year will grow in this high, windy spot.

After the schoolteacher has read the funeral service, after Calvin has prayed, they sing one of the old hymns:

> Unto the hills around do I lift up my longing eyes,
> From whence for me shall my salvation come,
> From whence arise....

The familiar words make Rachel cry. Tears stream down her face as Mary's sons and grandsons slowly lower the coffin into the hole, as the new church bell begins to ring. It keeps on ringing, on and on, rolling across the marshes, down over the hills and the houses, rattling off the great black rock called God's Finger.

The sound, at first doleful, changes, becomes clamorous and fast as the boys pulling the ropes warm to the novelty of their job, it rises to a pandemonium, a great raucous din that crashes out over the sea, rippling the surface of the water, reverberating off the seaweedy tops of sunken rocks, cutting down into the fathomless stillness where millions of cod swim, confused by the dim echoes penetrating their cold, still world.

part three
Lav

fourteen

Turning and turning Lav follows the road up the north side of Bonavista Bay, a route marked on the map spread out on the seat beside her. Under the map is her briefcase, which contains the Ellsworth Journal. She has been on the road since dawn and has so far managed not to think too much about what she has done or is doing.

Almost a week has passed since her melodramatic interruption of the Fishery Minister's press conference. Days of complete silence.

Apart from a visit from Mark Rodway, no one has contacted her. Not one of her accusations, hurled at the Minister and his special assistant, has appeared in the press. No shot of her distributing copies of Mark's report to media people has been shown on television. Mark himself had only heard of it from a friend at CBC.

She had gone to the front door only when the ringing gave way to pounding. Pulling a dressing gown over the disreputable nightdress she'd worn for two days, raking her fingers through her hair, trying to compose herself for God knows what—Wayne Drover come to fire her, Lori Sutton come to reclaim the stolen Ellsworth Journal, a policeman with a warrant for her arrest?

But it was Mark Rodway, jogging in place on her doorstep. "Good for you!" he said, grabbing her hand, shaking it with such vigour that his bouncing feet started her head throbbing.

"Just thought you'd like to know I'm out of jail—'released with a warning' was how they put it." After making this announcement Mark dropped her hand, turned, waved and jumped down the steps. At the gate he stopped, whirled around and bounded back.

"You know, I wondered about you from the first—there was something—something in you I couldn't make out." He peered at her, "Kept reminding myself that any stranger, even one from Ottawa, could turn out to be an angel. Didn't expect the transformation to come so soon, though—or quite that way—'course God's ways are not our ways," he said solemnly before breaking into a smile as if at some private joke.

Blinking into the light she knew must reveal every line and furrow in her morning face, Lav asked sourly what he found so funny.

"Sorry, I'm no longer a civil servant, so everything seems funny," he said and kept on grinning. "Nothin' like a couple days in jail to clear the mind. Bein' locked up with a hard cot and a bucket puts a person in touch with their roots—made me realize I never was cut out for a government job. If Wayne Drover hadn't fired me I'da quit anyway."

"So, he did fire you—what will you do now?"

"Oh he fired me all right, had a snappy official letter waiting at the police desk. Not sure what I'll do—think I might dedicate my life to disruption, start a sabotage movement."

Lav hoped he was joking, but who could tell? "I'm going down to Davisporte for a few days." She told him this not to change the subject—though she certainly wants no more of disruption, no more of sabotage—but because she wanted someone to know where she would be for the next few days and it had suddenly occurred to her that Mark was the only person she could give such information to.

"I've got relatives down there who own a motel—but really I'd like to camp, be outdoors for a day or so." Lav, who has never camped in her life, tried to look healthy and alert, the kind of person for whom camping is as natural as breathing.

Mark had nodded and asked if she wanted to borrow some camping gear. It is he who has provided the lantern, the food cooler, the sleeping bag and the very serviceable light-weight tent now folded into the trunk.

A knapsack, purchased yesterday, lies on the back seat. It contains an unlikely collection of clothing, everything from a skimpy red bathing suit to a set of thermal underwear. Beside the knapsack rests a thermos of coffee and several tape cassettes, covered by a huge khaki parka from Army Surplus.

The inventory of useful things she has brought along reassures Lav. Here is evidence of efficiency, of thought, of planning. She has even phoned Cat Harbour Inn and made a reservation—just in case it rains, or snows—Mark says it often does in May. But, Lav reminds herself, sane means may be used for mad motives. She considers how certain people (not her mother—perfectly sane people like Alice O'Reilly) might view this trip—searching Bonavista North for some old crone, who might or might not be the Rachel who had written the web-like marginalia into the Ellsworth Journal.

Apart from the wispy trail of a jet that must already be halfway to England, the sky is a deep, consistent blue. The almost empty road curves between hills of dark evergreen spattered with light where sunshine picks out the early green of birch and rowan. On the car radio Dvorak's *New World Symphony* is playing. The music reflects Lav's increasingly hopeful mood, matches the spring hills, blends with the bumps where frost has thrown up a series of humped ridges—as if the ice age still lurks just below the black surface of the road.

To Lav the road seems endless. She drives past miles of burnt-over land where fingers of dead trees point skywards: past bleak schools that might have been lifted from any city slum and dropped carelessly in gravel-pits midway between communities—on through half a dozen outports of neat, well-kept houses, of Legion Halls, Beer Halls and Bingo Halls, past wood frame branches of the Bank of Nova Scotia, Sears mail order outlets, Kentucky Fried Chicken outlets, video outlets, car lots and supermarkets, drug marts and beauty marts—and of course churches, any number of churches, Jehovah's Witness, United, Salvation Army, Anglican, Pentecostal.

Each community encircles a deep harbour and is in turn encircled by hills. From a distance each place looks idyllic, remote, beautiful, safe. Then one reaches the outskirts where rusting cars, stoves, refrigerators and rotting furniture lie abandoned in bogs, where broken pop and beer bottles glitter in the grass, where plastic bags flutter, like headless ghosts, from fences, bushes and telephone wires.

Davisporte is larger than most of the other places. It has a bright yellow Society of United Fishermen Hall and a general store which, according to the faded sign, belongs to Alphaeus Hutchings and carries "Rope, Twines and Nettings of all Descriptions." These buildings raise Lav's spirts. She feels quite cheerful as she manoeuvres the car between boys playing hockey and teenagers sauntering three and four abreast down the street.

When she has passed all the stores and is wondering if she could have missed the motel, she pulls over beside the door of a white clapboard restaurant. Against a sign that says, "Kosy Kafe—Drink Pepsi" three young girls lounge, gazing trancelike up the road and eating french fries from paper plates. When Lav rolls down the window the smell of salt and hot vinegar reminds her she has not eaten lunch. The girls stare, first at her then at each other, the smallest girl steps forward.

"Can you please tell me where Cat Harbour Inn is?" Lav asks.

The child's eyes widen, she tilts her head to one side as if assessing Lav's sanity. "No such place I knows of," she turns to the others for confirmation.

"Don't be so stunned, Pam—she's talkin' about the Cat," one of her friends says and shouts towards the car, "Just keep on goin', missis, ya can't miss it."

Not fifty yards down the road, in the middle of a parking lot that has been blasted out of a cliff, Lav finds the barracks-like building, over the door another large Pepsi sign identifies it as Cat Harbour Inn. Half of the motel front is covered with aqua-coloured plastic siding, the rest had once been painted deep purple. Mercifully, most of the paint has peeled away, revealing weathered grey wood.

Pushing open the front door, Lav finds herself in a large room, cold and windowless, empty except for ten arborite tables lined up against one wall. Each table holds a glass vase containing two plastic flowers. On the opposite wall, near the ceiling, a huge television screen has been installed. At the far end of the room is a bar and behind the bar a white refrigerator. A small red lamp on top of the refrigerator provides the room's only light.

Lav lets the front door slam noisily, but no one appears from behind the bar. She coughs and waits. Nothing happens.

She walks around the room inspecting a collection of community relics hung on the walls: a set of oarlocks, a brass plaque inscribed "Davisporte Champs 1986" surrounded by yearly pictures of the Davisporte bowling team, an old-fashioned doorlock and key, many horseshoes. One wall is covered with a fishing net. Caught inside the net are bits of driftwood, a set of a false teeth, shells, two plastic sharks and a long harpoon, used, according to a small square of yellowing paper pinned to the net, to hunt the largest beasts on earth, blue whales that sometimes weigh several tons.

Things have been attached to the walls on each side of the net: a collection of sunsets painted in garish orange on black velvet, a pencilled notice: "Piano Lessons—five dollars per hour, six dollars for advanced students," two calendars, the current one from Hibernia Oil depicts a huge concrete cube rising against a sunrise—"Assurance For Tomorrow!" is written across the sky. The other calendar, dated 1953, is from Pope's Furniture Factory Est. 1860 and has a picture of a ship under canvas. Further along a lovely hooked mat is hung next to a glossy autographed photo of Brigitte Bardot embracing a fluffy white seal and smiling up at a menacing figure holding a club. There are a dozen or so business cards, a varnished lobster and a large framed map of Newfoundland listing ships lost around the coast, beside many of the ships' names, the names of the men who died have been pencilled in.

Lav studies each artifact, reads every name on the map, the same surnames appear over and over again: Gill, Andrews, Davis, Norris, Vincent, Stokes, Hounsell, Blackwood, Hutchings, Barbour.

There is no air in the room, no daylight, no music, no warmth, no sounds, no smells—nothing. The thought brushes across her mind that time has stopped: that outside, no one is left alive—or that everything has changed, gone backward, or forward in time. Lav is becoming accustomed to such fanciful ideas, and for a minute she gives in to them. Afraid, she turns instinctively towards the door, has almost reached it when it opens and a huge box marked Delsey Tissue slides into the room.

Behind the box, manipulating it through the door, comes a thin, fox-faced girl, dressed all in black. The huge dangling earrings and brassy-green spiked hair, the blackest lips and whitest skin Lav has ever seen are astonishing enough, but there is something else about the girl, an intensity, a concentration of energy in the small white face, in the thin arms holding the pile of clean sheets, in the flat, black-clad hip pushing against the cardboard box.

So intent is the girl on getting through the doorway that she does not see Lav. Once in, she lays the sheets on the box and flicks a switch by the door. Twenty or more fluorescent tubes flash on—so suddenly, so glaringly, that Lav gasps.

"Sweet fuck!" the girls green-tipped fingers go to her throat. "I thought you was a ghost." Then, in a more business-like voice, "Can I help you?"

Not waiting for an answer the girl crosses the room, goes behind the bar and begins pulling out drawer after drawer, muttering under her breath.

"My name is Andrews—Lavinia Andrews—I have a reservation. Is Mr. Andrews in?"

"Oh yes," the girl abandons her search, opens a tattered exercise book of the kind Lav had used in school. "I minds your callin'," she licks her thumb and begins flicking through the lined pages. "Well, love, by the look of it you got your choice of rooms—you want to stay in the new rooms up aloft or go out in one of the little cabins? The cabins got stoves and fridges."

"Is Mr. Andrews in?" Lav asks again, as if she must see Alf Andrews before committing herself to a room in his motel.

"I don't allow he'll be in—Grandmother Andrews passed on night before last—the funeral's this afternoon."

"His Grandmother Rachel? She's dead!" Lav feels an immediate and terrible sense of loss. How stupid she had been not to come before.

"Well she was almost a hundred. Nan and Aunt Doss were plannin' a big party for her in July—she'd a got a message from the Queen, even. Aunt Doss says Rachel Andrews were an old woman when she was a girl."

Lav is sure this is true, despite her elaborate makeup the apparition before her can be no more than sixteen. The child's Aunt Doss is probably younger that I am, she thinks, remembering the childhood envy she had felt for the many aunts her friend Audrey had possessed.

"Are you a relative, then?" the green haired girl really looks at Lav for the first time, appraises the linen slacks, the yellow blouse and sweater and is not impressed.

"I think I might be a distant relative." During one of her phone calls Alf's mother, Selina, told Lav that she and Alf were second cousins once removed. While she is pondering what relationship this might be, a door behind the bar opens and a man holding a large glass of whiskey comes into the room.

He knows at once who she is, "I was thinkin' you'd be gettin' in later than this." He reaches into the fridge, drops ice cubes into his drink.

The girl gives him a sharp, appraising look and pushes the exercise book towards him, "Nan said you wasn't comin' in today. Everyone's checked out and I'm finishin' off the back rooms." She glances at Lav, "Dad'll take care of ya now," she says and vanishes.

"Your Grandmother said to get that stuff out of your hair before the funeral!" the man shouts at the swinging door before turning to ask Lav if she would like a drink.

Lav nods. Alf Andrews is older than she had expected—five or so years older than herself. Tall and broad but not fat. He has straight black hair that falls across his face. It is a closed face, hard even, with high cheek bones and a narrow tight mouth. He wears a dark green shirt and a brown suit jacket. When he comes from behind the bar, she sees that the jacket is too tight across the shoulders and a terrible match for the cord trousers. He looks untidy and slightly dusty all over.

Alf Andrews is studying her, too, not bothering to hide it, sipping his drink, taking his time to look her over. There is no more approval in his eyes than there had been in his daughter's.

Lav tries to imagine what he is seeing—a tall woman, just as tall as he, a woman who can no longer be called young. She knows the slacks draw attention to the thickness of her hips and, unfortunately, hide her long, quite attractive, legs. Her hair, which has never returned to its Ottawa condition, hangs shoulder length, speckled with grey but smooth and shiny.

She cannot imagine what he must think of her face. Lav herself has never made up her mind about her face—it is all right, she supposes—not what she would have chosen perhaps, still, nothing to be ashamed of. She has freckles, a sharply pointed nose and a bottom lip far too big for her narrow chin—but in the right light, with the right makeup, she knows it can be a dignified, even attractive face.

She starts to feel uneasy under the long, silent scrutiny. "I'm very sorry—really sorry, to hear about your grandmother," she says.

He leads her to one of the arborite tables. "Yes it's too bad—too bad you had to come all this way," he says when they are seated.

"I didn't mean that. It was a pleasant drive."

"...there was always a trail of people down here in summertime wantin' to see her. Old codgers workin' on their family trees and the university crowd with their tape recorders." Alf Andrews gazes into his glass as if it might contain the secret to mankind's strange behaviour.

"I expect if you wanted to know anything about old times along this coast, the best place to look would be in Memorial's Folklore Department. Lord knows they traipsed back and forth here often enough."

Alf Andrews is right. That is just what she should have done, used the resources of the university. She, of all people, should know that. How crazy she's been—how foolish to imagine some old woman would confide family secrets to her. What would Rachel possibly remember? And if remembered, why would she tell a stranger?

"Could I—could I see her?" to Lav the words sound bizarre but Alf Andrews does not even blink.

"Sure, sure if you want—the funeral's at four. We'll have one more drink, then you can follow me over to the house. She's laid out over at Mother's—didn't want to be taken to the funeral home."

Laid out! Lav thinks, already sorry she has asked to see the old woman. She traces her fingernail over letters someone has scratched into the dull blue tabletop: "Frank A is a cocksucker." Could the A stand for Andrews? And does Frank A know this message is here for all to read?

In the parking lot Alf Andrews climbs into a mud spattered pick-up truck, beckons for her to follow and takes off at what seems a suicidal speed back the way she had come. Past the Kosy Kafe, past the church, the general store. At the post office he swerves suddenly right towards the sea, driving along a steep lane—a path really—between fields of spring grass and recently turned earth. Each bit of land, some no larger than a room, is outlined with a picket fence.

At the end of the lane are two houses, a bright pink bungalow and a square, steep-roofed two-storey. The bungalow faces towards the lane and is built on a high concrete foundation. It has perpendicular steps climbing up to a long veranda on the ocean side. However, it must be impossible to see the ocean from the veranda because directly behind it, separated by a few yards of grass, a wood-pile and a clothesline, is the other house.

Planted on a rock right next to the sea, the second house stands square, white and tall with three small-paned windows under the eaves and two below, one on either side of what must be the front door. It is a beautiful house, much older than the bungalow but freshly painted and tidy, although grass grows right up to the door and there are no curtains at the windows.

"What a lovely old house," Lav says as she goes through the gate.

Alf Andrews glances at the empty house, makes a non-committal noise, says, "Watch out—that bottom step is high," and starts ahead of her up the steps towards the pink bungalow.

"Strange type," Lav thinks. She is feeling slightly light-headed from having downed two drinks on an empty stomach and is as apprehensive as if she were entering an African village to observe some unknown ritual.

At the top of the steps the man holds the door, letting her go before him into what seems to be a large kitchen. Cupboards line the walls but there are no chairs. Men stand around the room, arms crossed, leaning against counters. One woman, young and blonde, wearing tight jeans, is perched on a freezer. Everyone wears outdoor jackets and heavy boots. The woman and several of the men hold beer bottles. A round, comfortable looking man, the only one wearing a tie and suit, is laughing at something the blonde woman has said.

As Lav steps into the room the laughter stops, every face turns towards her. Alf Andrews doesn't even slow down. Edging her past the room's occupants he mutters, "Mother'll be in here," and leads her through to the real kitchen: green and cream paint, pale yellow curtains, gleaming white stove and refrigerator; a table covered with cut glass plates on which cookies, pink, pale green and fluffy white, little sandwiches and neatly sliced fruit cake have been symmetrically arranged. Lav's mouth waters but she is swept past the food, through the kitchen into a third room.

After the dazzling brightness of the kitchen this room seems dark. Curtains are drawn and only one dim lamp, strategically placed at the head of the coffin, is lit. The coffin, set foursquare facing the door, is supported by chairs or benches that have been draped with dark wine-coloured cloth.

The coffin is large. Surely, Lav thinks, much too large for one woman. She studies the shiny brass handles, the open cover padded in gleaming satin. A picture painted on the upper half of the satin, the part that would come down over the face, shows pink and blue angels surrounding the throne of God, long yellow stripes radiate out from the pastel scene. Just below God's feet a nose, a dead putty-like thing the very shape of her own, points upward. It is the only part of Rachel Andrews she can see from the doorway.

Lav becomes aware of a small, perky woman, her hair in tight, peach coloured curls, her head jutting forward between bony shoulders, peering out of the gloom.

"This is Lavinia Andrews, Mother. The one's been callin' about Nan," Alf's voice is as impersonal as his touch. This woman is Selina, then—Lav had expected someone taller, more commanding. The thought is barely formed when Selina's fingers grip her elbow and she is propelled towards the coffin.

"Not another drop for any of that crowd out back—give them all a good cup of tea," Selina calls after Alf who has quickly left the room. Then, sighing dramatically, she turns to stand beside Lav and stare down at the dead woman.

The hesitant, frightened fifteen-year-old, that Rachel who wrote those wispy, web-like lines into Lavinia's journal, is long gone. The head resting on the pink satin pillow could be that of some ancient Egyptian pharaoh, Yuya perhaps who lies in the Cairo Museum, or Una buried in the paupers' field outside Coltsford, it could be Mary Bundle or the Indian, whose graves, though more recent, have already slipped into the sea.

Only the nose is like Lav's. The rest of the face, the dark skin, the protruding cheek bones, the broad high forehead, the mouth, pressed into a narrow brown line, are very like Alf Andrews'. Yet the old woman's face is stronger than her grandson's. Even now with the skin like flaking, transparent pastry, with the eyes closed and the cheeks fallen in, Lav can see the determination.

"She was a determined woman," Lav says aloud—just as if she had known Rachel all her life. She is pleased with the comment, which seems an acceptable thing to say. Perhaps I'll be alright after all, she thinks.

"That she was—right to the end. You know her last night on earth she was still talkin' about havin' the old house out back fixed up before summer. My dear, that woman was so determined she could change the wind around if she put her mind to it!"

Rachel has been dressed tastefully in what looks to be silk, a purple silk dress with a pale lace collar held together with an amethyst pin. Lav wonders if it can possibly be the pin Una had given to her daughter Tessa.

Selina notices her staring at the brooch, "It's a keepsake, Nan got from her great-grandmother. We're supposed to take it off her before the casket's closed. It's to go to Rachel Jane." Selina's sniff indicates disapproval of her mother-in-law's choice of recipient for the brooch.

Lav is surprised to find that she quite enjoys looking at the old woman's face. It has a quality missing from live faces, a kind of calm openness, as if any moment it will reveal some secret. They stand beside the coffin for two or three minutes before Selina, her strong fingers again clamped onto Lav's arm, leads her to a corner. Three sides of the darkened room are lined with women and children seated on straight-backed chairs, watching in such complete silence that Lav has not been aware of their presence. As they approach one woman stands and smiles towards them.

"This is Doris, my daughter-in-law," Selina says.

Lav stares at the attractive, placid face—can this be Alf Andrews' wife?

"It's nice of you to come down," the woman is saying. "I'll be off now—get supper for the boys and be back in time for the service."

Selina gestures Lav into the vacated chair before following Doris out of the room. Lav sits, bows her head and closes her eyes. She is feeling ill from the whiskey and from hunger. No one speaks. The women on either side of her do not move.

They must have thought she was praying because the instant she straightens up the woman on her left turns and whispers, "A good age, she come to a good age," she dabs her eyes with a Kleenex.

Other women murmur agreement: "a good age," "good age," "a good death," "good,"—the words whispering from dim corners of the room.

The woman who had spoken first leans towards Lav, "I'm Mavis Fifield. You be one of the Andrews crowd then? Down from St. John's, I s'pose?"

Lav nods. The woman, eyes bright with expectation, waits. When nothing more is forthcoming she says, "Your father must be Clar Andrews—the one teaches in at the university?"

Thinking her breath must smell of whisky Lav tries to answer the woman without turning her head, "No, no my father's name was David—he's passed on." Lav is astonished at the words "passed on" which rise unbidden—from where? Tribal memory?

Her eyes having grown accustomed to the dark, she sees that most of the women hold teacups. She longs for tea.

"You're David Andrews girl! Well I never!" Eager to be the first with this astonishing news, the woman leans across to pat the knee of the woman seated on Lav's right, "Hear that Ruby? This one's David Andrews' girl!"

"David's girl!" Tilting her head to one side so that her round face folds into chins, Ruby squints at Lav, "Lord bless us! Sure I can see it now—she got the Andrews' mouth."

Once again the echo, louder and more cheerful this time, circles the room: "Yes, I can see," "Well I'll be," "David Andrews' girl."

"He was that handsome when he was young. Didn't you walk out with him one time, Violet?" Lav cannot see the woman addressed or the one asking the question, both sit beyond the coffin in the far, dim corners of the room.

The woman named Violet gives a deep chuckle, "That I did—but 'twarn't me he was interested in—'twas me friend Nina Stokes who played accordian with the Army."

They remember Nina Stokes, she who had died young in the San, talk about her for a time until someone says: "David Andrews was just ahead of me in school—a real torment he was as a boy!"

Lav feels a warm glow seeping through her bones. They all knew her father, or those too young to have known him must have heard of him. They speak as if he had died only yesterday.

They even remember her grandfather—Ki Andrews, the old man her mother had so hated. "You minds me speakin' of Uncle Ki Andrews—how he'd always tell us children stories of a winter's night?" an old woman asks the small child sitting beside her. The children, Lav notes, do not speak but sit very still, their eyes moving from speaker to speaker.

Reminiscences of childhood and young adulthood going back for generations ebb and flow through the dimness. The soft rattle of teacups, the hushed voices—like the voices of adults talking in the next room—enclose Lav. She dozes. She can smell the dust under the stairs in Audrey's house, would not have been surprised to feel her friend's hand clutching hers, to hear Audrey's mother telling Charlotte about the aunts' love lives or some adventure one of the Petrassi uncles has had at work.

Eventually there is a stirring, a rumble of movement that jars Lav into wakefulness. The heavy woman in the next chair struggles to her feet. "My dears, I got to go, Clyde'll wonder what's become of me. Where's Selina? Out there gettin' more food I daresay! I'll see you all at the service." She gives Lav a smile and goes to gaze mournfully down into the coffin for a minute before leaving.

One by one the women stand, collect their purses, their teacups, their children, and move slowly towards the door. Each woman pauses to look at the body before leaving the room. One woman lifts a small girl up to kiss the dry old face.

Before Lav has time to consider what she should do, Alf Andrews comes in. He crosses the room and stands staring gloomily down at her, his expression very like that worn by the women looking at the corpse. As if he is deciding how best to dispose of her with as little fuss as possible.

Feeling rumpled and uncomfortable Lav gets to her feet. "You have nice neighbours," she says to fill the silence.

"Nice neighbours, lovely house, nice sea, lovely sky, nice coffin, lovely corpse," he says in a flat, expressionless voice.

She is speechless with shock at his rudeness.

"Mother says you're to come out to the kitchen and have some tea before we go to the church," he tells her in the same monotone.

"I'd like tea but I'm not going to the church service." She follows him into the empty kitchen, watching as he pours tea from a large flowered teapot.

"Eat up, then, it's a long drive back to town," he gestures for her to sit at the food-laden table but takes his own cup to the window where he stands, watching people leave.

Lav is on her third sandwich when Selina comes into the kitchen. Behind her is the plump man in the suit and tie. "My younger son, Ned—the fisherman in the family," Selina says, "you met his wife, Doris, earlier."

"Ah, Cousin Lavinia—the one who's scrounging through the Vincent and Andrews skeletons," but he is smiling, a real smile. "Welcome aboard," he says and kisses her cheek.

Selina fidgets, rearranging plates, setting out more teacups, "Why isn't Rachel Jane here?" she asks.

"Because she's makin' up beds in the motel."

"Where's Tracy, then?"

"Sittin' out there in the porch entertainin' the troops."

"Well? Why don't you send her back to do her job?" clearly Selina could say more but is biding her time.

Alf ignores his mother's question, which irritates her even more. "I hope the RCMP gets after you, Alf Andrews—lettin' a girl Rachel Jane's age tend bar!

Anyway, you should have closed today. And while I think on it, was it you brought that beer into the house?"

It is Ned who answers, his voice is hopeful, placating, "Now Ma, you knows people got to have a drink or two at a funeral."

"At Roman funerals, perhaps—not at ours! What would she in there say? And I don't know what Reverend Dawe thought of us this afternoon. All hands drinkin' in the back porch and the place smellin' like a brewery."

"They're all gone now, so no harm's done," Ned winks at Lav, the wink includes her in some family joke about his mother and drinking. "I tell you now what happens to people goes lookin' for their roots," he begins a story about some retired couple who had spent years and years tracking the Vincent family back to the Channel Islands.

Grateful that she is not the focus of attention, Lav drinks tea and devours quantities of cookies, all the time watching the two brothers, wondering how long the silent one can go without speaking.

Ned's story ends with the couple having spent their entire nest-egg to discover that the first Vincents were all Catholics and not even Vincents but St. Vincion or some such outlandish name.

"I hope you never told your Grandmother Rachel that one," Selina snaps before turning to Lav, "There's a bathroom just down the hall if you want to freshen up," she says.

In the bathroom Lav splashes cold water on her face, applies makeup, gives Selina time to have a private word with her sons.

She wonders if she will be asked to stay the night. Probably not, Selina is less friendly than she had seemed on the phone—they are different, not what she had expected—not like the people in the journal. Staring absentmindedly into the mirror it occurs to Lav that she now has the opportunity to change her name—in Davisporte she can be Lavinia if she wishes. She tries out the name, "Lavinia, Lavinia"—whispering it at her reflection. But it is too late, her name is Lav—Lavinia belongs to the woman in the journal. She goes back into the kitchen.

"Now Mother, you knows Vicki couldn't get down just for the funeral—after all she was here Christmas," Ned is saying.

Selina leans against the stove sipping tea, she seems weary, near to tears. Alf is still staring out the window.

As if casting around for something to distract his mother from the absent Vicki, Ned begins telling them about a neighbour who's had sonar installed in his boat. When no one comments on this news he turns to Lav, "I'll have to get sonar meself soon. Can't do nothin' inshore anymore. Barely hauled in enough to cover gas last summer."

"Sonar! My son you been listenin' too long to them crowd in St. John's—watch it or your brain'll be soft as theirs!" Alf turns from the window to give his brother a baleful glare. "I worked it out on paper last week, right in Bruce Blackmore's kitchen, worked it out and showed 'em—them crowd with their fibreglass boats, with their Japanese sonar and their American navigation equipment—with their government loans for a million dollars. They'll never be able to pay off that kind of money—never! No bejesus—not if every man jack of 'em hauled full nets day and night 'til they dies!"

"And why should we listen to the likes of you who haven't set foot in a fishin' boat for twenty year?" Lav can see that Ned is gleeful at having jarred his brother into an emotional outburst. "All them experts who been studyin' fish these last thirty year are tellin' us the trap fishery's over. I already talked to the man down at the bank. He says there's a new government loan program, says it's just like when them farmers out West had to get combines, we got to get big boats and sonar—and everything else accordin' to. It's progress, boy—can't stop progress!"

Selina's look of resignation suggests this is a long-standing argument, perhaps the one subject her sons can shout about, discuss safely, can use to hold silence at bay while the women talk in another room.

This time, though, Alf will not be baited. Muttering, "Fuck progress," he sets his cup down and walks to the door. "I'll see Miss Andrews off. Then I'll check on things at the Cat—be back by the time Levi and the Gills get here. It'll take all six of us to get that box down over them steps." He stands, holding the door open while Lav thanks Selina.

As they walk to the car Alf Andrews seems more cheerful. Perhaps the argument with his brother has lifted his spirits, or perhaps he is relieved that her visit is ending. He tells Lav the empty house across the yard belonged to Rachel, "Grandmother had it floated up from the Cape, then dragged here, back when father was a boy. No one's lived in it for years. I expect Mother'll be after us to tear it down, now Grandmother's gone."

Lav would have dearly loved to go inside the old house, which she guesses to be the one Thomas Hutchings had built for Lavinia, the one Mary Bundle had died in. But she cannot bring herself to ask a favour of Alf Andrews.

He watches her climb into the car. "Well I don't expect we'll see you again. We people don't go in to St. John's very often."

"Oh I'm not going back to St. John's yet—I'm going out to the Cape, at least for tonight."

Perversely pleased at the disapproval that floods his face, Lav laughs out loud before telling him not to worry about her, "I'm well prepared. I have a tent, food—even a lantern."

"You can't just drive out there, you know—it'll be dark in two hours and you won't find your way back."

"I'll find my way!" she turns the key in the ignition, "I'm quite capable of walking a mile or so. What's more, I can read a map as well as you." She is sick to death of Alf Andrews.

"Don't be so stupid, woman, it's only May—you'll freeze! Don't you understand, there's no one out there—you'll be alone!" he yells through the open window, his hand is on the car door as if he might physically stop her.

"Do you think I'm afraid of the dark...." Lav starts the car, racing the engine.

He steps back, says, "There's more than dark to be afraid of out there!" Then, as she brings the car around in a tight circle and starts down the lane throwing mud and grass up around him, he shouts, "Stupid mainland bitch!"

She drives through Davisporte in such a rage that when she reaches the highway she has to pull over, roll down the window and take deep breaths of salty air. Finally her face cools and her breathing returns to normal. How childish she's acted! She wishes she had said something dignified, dignified but cutting—something that would have put him right in his place.

Advising herself to forget Alf Andrews, Lav takes a good look at her map and discovers she is headed in the wrong direction, makes a U-turn and starts down the coast towards Cape Random.

fifteen

Lav finds her way easily, as she'd known she would. The last four or five miles are over a brown mud path across marsh and bog. There is not a house in sight. The only sign of civilization, in the general sense—not in the way Philip would have used the word—is a power line strung between poles set down into cages that are filled with rocks. She cannot see the ocean, just sky and bogland.

The road ends in a torn up patch of mud that is littered with beer bottles, Kentucky Fried Chicken packages, condoms and a large roll of filthy carpet. Packing bread, fruit, cheese and the remaining coffee into her knapsack, Lav locks everything else into the trunk of the car and slings the army parka, knapsack and tent bag over her shoulder. She starts down a footpath that is hollowed deep into the bog but a few hundred yards along stops, turns and goes back to the car.

There is something unpleasant about the parking spot. It reeks of mindless vandalism, a kind of casual evil. She cannot leave the journal there. Telling herself that what she is doing is stupid, Lav unlocks the trunk and removes the journal. Wrapping her sweater around the heavy book, she slides it into her knapsack, gathers up her belongings and starts off again.

It is enjoyable walking on the spongy peat path between low marsh plants. Lav fancies she can catch an elusive minty smell—the white winter-shrivelled berries perhaps, or the tiny yellow blossoms growing near the path. Or maybe it's just the brown leaved bushes percolating in the heat. The sun warms her hair and the back of her shoulders. She wonders why she brought the bulky parka.

The path becomes wetter as it meanders towards the sea. It skirts outcroppings of rock and perfectly round ponds of bog water shining like melted chocolate in the sun. She can feel the water, pleasantly warm, seeping into her running shoes, oozing between her toes. Each time she lifts a foot she hears a small plopping sound and when she looks behind sees brown water filling her footprints. Who would have thought that walking through a bog could be a sensual experience? She walks slowly, knowing, despite Alf Andrews' warning, there are still two or three hours of daylight.

She comes to the neck more quickly than she had expected. The strip of land that anchors Cape Random to the shore is today cut by a deeply flowing river. It is not, of course, a river but two arms of the sea. A narrow bridge over the water looks as if it has been deliberately hacked apart and crudely repaired. However, she crosses without difficulty—and is on the Cape.

The expected rush of excitement does not come. According to the journal the church should be nearby—but she sees no building of any kind. The path rises a little, curves around a giant lump of speckled marble, smoothed by wind, snow and ice until it looks like a huge egg resting in a nest of bushes. Lav climbs the gentle curve to the top of the rock—and there is the ocean!

She sees it, hears it, smells it! Around her stretches the long sweep of beach where the sea rolls in and out—its soft swish belied by the ominous roar that rumbles up after each receding wave. Overwhelmed by the combination of sight, sound and smell, Lav drops her belongings, runs toward the wet sand.

Here, along the landwash, the beach is covered in small shells, cream, peach and pale mauve, blue mollusk, purple starfish, amber kelp, long strings of seaweed from which green translucent grapes hang, algae, white corallina and black mermaids' purses, ivory sand dollars and scarlet jollyfish shining like glass bowls. There are broken lobster pots, driftwood carved into abstract sculptures, bits of worn glass that resemble sugared candy and garish plastic containers not even the sea can make beautiful. Lav walks back and forth, gathering things until her pockets are full and her hands smell of kelp and sea weed.

She sits on the sand, watching gulls and seabirds swoop and dive, watching the sea roll up the beach. She tries to imagine a city, but cannot.

Intoxicated by light and air and salt water, she climbs the bank, returns to the speckled rock and tries to orient herself. She picks up her belongings and clambers through thick brush up towards a rock ledge where she guesses the potato garden would have been. But on the brow of the hill there is no sign of cleared land—just alder and wind-stunted evergreens, their bare roots clutching at rocks.

Then, towards the edge of the hill, she sees the mound of stones, grey surfaces half covered with mustard lichen. The stones have been piled in a great heap, carried one by one to this spot to make a kind of rough wind-break for the vanished garden. They are the only sign that anyone has ever lived here. She picks her way over the thistle and dandelion that ring the stones and steps gingerly onto the rock pile. The rocks appear loose but time, weed and lichen have bound them together. It is easy to reach the top where she spreads out the parka and sits down. Scraping back the threadlike tentacles of some subterranean plant, Lav eases a large grey rock out of its place.

She sits, holding the rock, giving herself up to imaginings—wondering which of the women—Jennie, Meg, Sarah or Mary—last touched it? Surely one of them had pried it up out of the ground and carried it, perhaps in her apron, to toss onto this pile. Lav rubs her fingertips over the hard surface. The top of the rock is smooth but its underside has a rough wave-like pattern, incised eons ago by the great ice cap as it retreated, pressing silt and sand down to make the hills, bays and islands along this coast.

Wishing for clairvoyance, Lav closes her eyes, holds the cool rock against her forehead. Nothing happens. No face, no voice, no presence appears before her mind's eye.

"A good thing, too—supposing it worked both ways—suppose they could see me," Lav looks ruefully at her well-manicured hands, her tapered, varnished nails.

Feeling foolish, she puts the rock back in its place, stands, searches for a flat spot to pitch her tent. Down where the houses must have been there is only rock and low bush, no cellar, fence or barn, no lilac tree or wharf. It looks like Tennyson's land, Lav thinks, staring out over a landscape where nothing but the sea moves—a land where no one comes or has come since the making of the world.

The day has grown dull. A haze that is not quite fog hovers over everything. Checking her watch, she sees that it's eight o'clock and climbs quickly down from the lookout. How could people have built anything amid these humps and hollows? She turns left, walking through tall grass and sand towards a shorter curve of beach that cuts out to the tip of the arrow, she sees the high finger of black rock against which Lavinia had sat her first day on the Cape. The tide is in and white foam hisses around the base of the shining monolith.

Lav's first instinct is to set up the tent well back from the sea, in the shadow of the banks that shelter the beach. Then she sees that those mounds, overgrown with wild rose bushes and hanging like porch roofs over the beach, have eroded, have crumbled down in places onto the sand. Having no desire to be buried alive on the Cape, she finally unrolls the red tent right on the beach, midway between the high water mark and the embankment.

She has no trouble driving the eight plastic pegs into the soft sand. In case the wind should rise, she piles stones and driftwood around the posts, wedging each one firmly. The tent has a floor and when she crawls inside, it is like being in a small red box—the size of Rachel's coffin but without God and painted angels staring down inches above her face.

By now Rachel's funeral is over. The relatives from away will be driving towards St. John's or back to Gander to catch the first flight out. Local people will have returned home, will be sitting around their supper tables, talking about the old woman more freely than they had in Selina's front room.

They will track the Andrews family back, remembering Rachel's son who was Selina's husband. A few of them may even know that Stephen Andrews' father had been a Vincent—the handsome, doomed young man who had briefly visited Cape Random. They will recall the years Rachel spent in the States and no doubt speculate on what she had done there that has let her live in comfort for so long. In kitchens all around the shore people are eating late suppers and mulling over the details of the old woman's life. Some of them will mention Lavinia—the woman from town—David Andrews' daughter. It pleases Lav to think of them in their shiny kitchens, saying her name, her father's name.

Still, she is glad to be alone in the little tent. Unpacking the knapsack she sees that she has forgotten the sleeping bag. Will it get cold later? She tries to calculate the distance from here to the car and decides it is much too far to go and be back by dark. Never mind, she will make do with the parka and sweater tonight. If she wants to stay another night she can get the sleeping bag tomorrow.

Sitting cross-legged just inside the tent flap, she eats bread and cheese and drinks the last of the hot coffee, watching the sand and water change colour. She has had a romantic notion of reading the journal out here on the Cape but by the time she opens the book it is far too dark to make out the faded script. She returns the journal to the knapsack, which she is using as a pillow, and lies back, thinking about the day, about Selina and her sons, about Rachel Andrews.

During one phone call Lav had dared to asked Rachel how old she was when she left the Cape.

"Old?" the gravelly voice croaked over the word as if she'd never heard it before. Then she relented a little, "I was thirty-eight, maid. I thought about it for years but it wasn't until my parents were dead and gone and Stephen over twenty and teaching school that I got up nerve to leave."

And that was the only personal information she had gotten out of Rachel, who had been more interested in the present than the past. Wars and rumours of wars, food shortages anywhere in the world, trade and boundaries—all concerned the old woman. But her greatest worry was for the boys and girls, "Gallivanting up and down the road all hours of the night."

It was the danger, she said, that bothered her. "Imagine in this day and age, walking right out on the road without a sidewalk or streetlight!"

But really, Lav thought, it was not the danger of traffic that concerned the old woman. She had other fears. Rachel knew—who better?—about traps nature lay for the young on warm summer evenings.

Nature could be outfoxed only by education Rachel Andrews had not said this, but she had thought it. "What will become of them? What can they do in this world or the next?" she would ask of the teen-agers sauntering up and down in front of her window. She had been delighted to discover that Lav had a Ph.D., "Well now, think of that! That makes four in the Andrews family—five when Vickie's young Stephen gets his finished!" Rachel could, and did, ream off the academic status, not only of her own descendants, but of every descendant of her maternal grandparents. Toma Hutchings and Comfort Vincent, she declared, "were both smart as tacks and would be university teachers if they were alive today!"

Lav falls asleep, smiling, recalling the old woman's litany of degrees.

She sleeps and dreams, not of Rachel, not of the Cape, but of salmon. Of the great rainbow-coloured fish that swims inside a net, circling and circling in a space that grows always smaller. The net closes, the bodies of other fish press more and more tightly. The net is being lifted, water slithers past its scales, it chokes on air, is blinded by light, deafened by the terrible shrieking of winches.

Lav sits up. Her hand is pressed against a raw spot where the knapsack buckle has cut into her cheek. Outside, lights flash. Something roars past, making the tent's sides billow out in a wash of air. The noise is deafening. Something large: motorcycles, jeeps, dune buggies, are racing round and around the tent.

Heart pounding, Lav crawls to the open flap and looks out. At that instant a motorcycle wheel, spitting sand, passes within a foot of her face. She heaves herself backwards, pulls the heavy jacket over her head, covers her ears and crouches at the back of the tiny tent.

The noise is frightful but worse than the noise is a a great empty sense of loss that fills the tent, fills the dark space under the jacket, fills her head. Someone, some child, is sobbing. The sobbing goes on and on. She is drowning in tears, in sweat, she is choking. She untangles herself, lies gasping, eventually the sobbing sound stops but the terrible shriek and grinding continues.

"I am dreaming," Lav tells herself, "just dreaming." She searches in her dream for the salmon, but the fish is gone.

There is only the memory, memory and sound, sound and light circling around and around. And it is real and loud and bright, changing the inside of the tent from fluorescent red to quivering white. Stunning her with light, then plunging her into pitch blackness, over and over as the machines spin around the little tent.

Her instinct is to huddle down again, to hide, to cover her head and hope they will go away. But that will not save her. Now she must block out the memory, block out the noise, must pull on her sweater, her sneakers, haul the knapsack over her head.

And she does. Concentrating on each action, she manages to do each of these things, then to crawl out, to stand upright in front of the tent. The lights blind her, the roar is deafening. She can see nothing but helmeted heads atop a blur of black, red and chrome. Salty sand stings her face as they swerve past.

They are just people, just people riding all-terrain vehicles. Lav tells herself this, makes herself call out, wave her arms. Having had their fun, they will stop, take off their helmets. They will do this, she assures herself, any minute now they will stop, change from giant insects into teenagers looking for a place to build a fire, to drink beer, sing, make love. Any minute they will pull off these plastic bubbles and she will see hair, eyes, human faces. And so she waits, standing in front of the tent, willing herself to be calm.

But they do not stop or even slow down. In fact they whirl faster and faster, blurring like dervishes into a ribbon of light and colour. Something is being shouted at her from the plastic faces. She can understand none of words but the intent is clear. It is the sound of unreasoned hate, uncontrolled savagery, it is the sound prehistoric men, running toward each other with rocks, may have made.

Lav's facade of calm drops. Panic takes over. Where is safety? What can be trusted? Not memory, not dreams, not the evidence of her own eyes. What has happened? What is happening, is going to happen? She stands like an animal caught in headlights, trapped by machines that resemble gods—gods risen from the earth's centre to mete out punishment.

Then one of the machines hits a tent peg—sparks fly, it veers off. There is a break in the circle of light and she races forward toward the sea. She can hear the rasp and cough as the machines are put into reverse, as they turn, gouging new paths into the sand.

Their lights find her again. They circle in loops, playing with her as she races down the beach. She falls against Lavinia's rock, turns and runs madly towards the sand banks—towards the deep shadows where bushes overhang the beach. For a minute they lose her. She stumbles against the high bank and crouches down, shivering, praying they will leave.

She is sobbing now, pressing back against the crumbling hill, holding her hand against her mouth to keep the sounds back. Her trousers are torn. One knee, where she banged into the rock, is bleeding, but the knapsack is still around her shoulder.

They seem to have retreated, returned to race around the tent, whooping and shouting as their machines skid against the rocks she piled around the pegs. Then the formation changes, the lights fan out, they are racing down the beach towards her. In a moment they will see her huddling beneath the overhang. Lav turns and on hands and knees begins to climb. She loses a shoe. The sand slides away from under her so that she must scramble sideways. At the top she inches along, feeling the underside of the overhang until she comes to a spot where the bank has collapsed. Very carefully, she eases herself up, grabbing at weeds, roots, at the thorn-covered branches of rose bushes, expecting every moment that the ground will give way and send her rolling back—down to the beach, down to her tormentors. At last she hoists herself over the top and, just as the lights find her, rolls over the edge into a clump of low bushes.

The motorized beasts converge directly below and begin assaulting the incline. They back off, make a great, roaring dash up the perpendicular hill, roll backwards and start again. Each time they come a little closer. Terrified, she jumps up and heedless of the lights at her back begins to run through the bushes. Slipping on sand, stumbling between patches of grass and overgrown rocks, she runs towards the safe darkness. She is sobbing out loud now, each breath is painful. She runs and falls, runs and falls, until at last she is pitched head-first into blackness. Momentarily stunned she lies there, face pressed into the sand, head throbbing as waves of panic wash over her—as fear fights with anger.

"Goddamned bloody savages! What's the use of a world that can be ruined by barbarians on wheels? I'd like to kill them—could kill them—would kill them if I could! Gladly!"

See her now, Lavinia Andrews, modern woman, art lover, peace-marcher, spa user, scientist, hiding from machines, hiding from monsters, hiding from memory. Here she lies, clothed in linen slacks, silk shirt, sweater, hand-knit—not by her hands but by the hands of some Peruvian peasant—Lavinia Andrews, B.Sc.(Hons.), M.Sc., Ph.D., dazed, bleeding, and eventually sleeping, in the hollow where an Indian once died—murdered by one of her not-too-distant relatives.

sixteen

At dawn Alf Andrews comes walking slowly down the beach carrying a yellow plastic bag. He pauses for a moment beside the flattened tent before climbing the bank and striding noisily through the bushes. Lav is already on her feet, waiting with a large rock ready to throw, when he appears on the rim of the depression.

He jumps down into the hollow, landing neatly at her feet where he squats staring up into her scratched face, studying her shredded sweater, stained slacks, her bare, bleeding foot. "Had a hard night of it, did ya?"

Lav drops the rock, sits down suddenly and with her head on her knees begins to cry.

Alf ignores her. He searches around, collecting sticks and bits of driftwood which he piles inside the circle of blackened stones at the center of the hollow. He takes everything out of the plastic bag, lines up each item in the sand: a loaf of bread, a bottle of water, a brown paper bag, a box of matches, two mugs, a knife, a flat bottomed kettle.

By then Lav has stopped crying. She blows her nose in the sleeve of her sweater and tells him about the night before. As she talks she watches his hands, which are narrow and dark. He lights the fire carefully using twigs and the brown paper bag—its contents, dried caplin, he has already spread on flat rocks around the fire.

"Only our own crowd," he says when she finishes. He pours part of the bottled water into the kettle which he holds on a stick over the flames.

Lav is indignant, "What do you mean—'our own crowd?'"

"Our own crowd—youngsters out for a bit of fun," Alf does not take his eyes from the kettle.

"Fun! You call it fun to terrorize a person? To destroy property? To act like a bunch of vandals?"

"Look, lady! You chose to come out here—this is their place. They were only playin', havin' a little party before bein' shipped off to Ontario where they'll be locked up in factories for the summer. They're the country's great reserve labour pool—Canada's Okies. Why, if wasn't for them we couldn't have free trade, couldn't compete with the third world for cheap labour! So don't begrudge the poor little buggers their last fling!" He pulls her shoe from his jacket pocket and passes it to her, "Here—go get dressed."

She climbs out of the hollow, walks through the cool morning mist down to the sea, pulls off her slacks, wades in a few inches and squats to urinate—a strange sensation. She washes her feet, hands and face, the cuts and bruises stinging with salt and icy cold water. When she returns to the pit Alf is carefully measuring tea into the kettle. They sit in silence, waiting for it to steep.

Lav feels safe and comfortable. She cannot see the ocean but can hear it roaring below the rim of the hill. The fire warms her, the black tea slips down her throat like some wonderful new liquid she has never tasted. She eats quickly, taking huge bites of the crisp caplin—heads, spines, tails, guts and all—rolled in slabs of crusty bread.

"Me and my brothers used to find bits of flint and arrowheads all around this fire—used to build bough houses and play at being cowboys and Indians. We thought it was our very own place, a secret no one else in the world knew about," Alf nods towards the circle of blackened rocks, the bones of burnt trees. "Maybe we were right. It was a long time ago before Al'Vs."

They sit talking in the warm hollow for an hour or more. Lav asks about the geography of the offshore. She knows, but does not say she knows, that the Cape is situated on a huge underwater plateau.

"The sea 'round here is no more than fifty fathom deep—used to swarm with fish—caplin, herring, cod, lobster, anything you'd ever want," Alf tells her.

"In Grandmother's day every bit of ocean was divided up between families who lived along this coast—mostly on the offshore islands. Lots of men went to the Labrador of course—but around home they fished the same grounds year after year. By the time Father was old enough to fish people had motor-boats and were going farther out, to the Funks or up along what they used to call the French Shore. By then the salt fish trade was already in decline. Once refrigeration came, people didn't need salt cod—all had to be fresh or fresh frozen."

"We brought the world's biggest reserve of protein into Confederation and now look at us!" Alf continues, relentlessly pursuing the only subject he displays any emotion about. "Europeans do a great job of protecting their own fishing grounds but no one protects ours. Fact is, Canada signed an agreement in '84 that prevents us from even putting observers on French fishing ships—though we all knew they were taking up to four times their quota. There's fourteen factory freezers out there right now—just out of sight of land. Of course we're doin' the same ourselves—you heard that talk yesterday—nowadays a fish haven't got a chance. It's a wonder any survive—not many do!"

He sounds just like Mark Rodway, Lav thinks. Having no desire to discuss fish she changes the subject, asks how many brothers and sister he has.

"Just Ned and Vicki—she married a U.C. minister, they live in Ontario."

"But you said you and your brothers used to play in this pit."

"I had a twin brother—he died young."

Knowing from his voice that she has trespassed into forbidden territory, Lav quickly asks about Rachel. What kind of woman had she been when she was young?

Amazingly, Alf knows little more about his grandmother than she does. Rachel had left the Cape before he was born and had somehow become a nurse, "Worked for some doctor who had sons. I know that because she used to send us boys their outgrown clothes—in packages from New York, velvet jodhpurs and striped shirts. We hated 'em, made us the laughingstock of the place, Grandmother did."

She asks if Rachel Jane will get Rachel's brooch.

"I dare say," Alf is curt again—not rude, as he had been the day before but clearly setting limits on what questions he will tolerate.

Tired of trying to decipher the protocol of conversation, Lav lapses into silence. She thinks about last night, wonders how long she had slept. How would it have been if Alf Andrews had not come looking for her? What would she have done if she'd waken alone? The memory or dream—whatever it was that had flashed accross her mind during those last moments in the tent—that scene from her childhood, of Audrey, of a motorcycle, hangs on a thread at the back of Lav's mind. Will she have to take it out, examine it, or can she cut the thread, drop the memory back into that unexamined corner it has occupied for thirty years?

"You were right, I shouldn't have come out here by myself," she says.

"Wasn't those young Turks I was thinking about—I was expectin' the great white bear to come out among the graves, or for Mary Bundle to make away with you..." Alf says and when she smiles—though not as confidently as she would have the day before—he does not smile back.

As the sun rises the mist burns off. They walk along the beach gathering up pieces of the ruined tent, the thermos and Lav's parka.

Alf fills his yellow bag with broken glass and plastic containers: "We're the biggest slobs on earth—still dumping anywhere—especially in the sea—we think the sea will take anything. Once or twice a week this time of year I lug home a bag of garbage," he says.

Like the owner of a cherished garden, he leads Lav from place to place pointing out hills and hollows, sheltered places where small purple flowers grow out of sand, the round underwater shadows of flatfish, tiny birds that dart about on thread-like legs, tidal pools shimmering with multi-coloured rocks, breakers cresting over offshore shoals.

They spend the morning making a slow loop of the Cape. But according to Alf it is not the Cape of Thomas and Lavinia, not even the Cape of his childhood—or of yesterday.

"It's never the same twice," Alf says. "Come out here ten days in a row and the shoreline is different each day."

The idea of a place that is forever reshaping itself, or being reshaped by ice and sea, horrifies and delights Lav. She wonders if the Cape will vanish completely some day, but Alf says no, it is the changing that saves it, "One bit of beach crumbles away and another bit appears."

Yet some things remain. He finds vegetable cellars, now caved in and overgrown, shows her the great pointed rock which, he says, is called God's Finger, locates Aunt Jennie's garden, footings of the Union Store, the trenched marshland that had once produced barnfuls of grass, barrels of vegetables. They stand on the granite rock upon which the Vincents' house had been built and look out over the pond that has long ago turned salty.

They visit the graveyards. First the one on the point where many graves have slipped into the sea but where some remain—a few inches of white marble, stone fingers, carved crowns and crosses, the heads of small stone lambs rising from sand drifts. Lav kneels at one of these and with her hands scoops sand away from the white slab.

Feeling the letters with her fingers she reads:

> In loving memory of Ned Andrews
> Born Weymouth, England 1799—Died Cape Random 1838
> Born into the world above,
> They, our happy brother greet,
> Take him to the throne of love,
> Place him at the Saviour's feet.

Other words had been cut below, "Erected by his loving wife Mary," perhaps? But no, Mary would never have chosen such a verse! Maybe Ben and Meg erected the stone, or Lavinia. Lav will never know, sand pressing into the letters has obliterated the lower lines.

Near what Alf calls the new graveyard they stop beside a few feet of crumbling stonework—all that is left of the Cape Random church. Lav asks how such a building could have vanished in just fifty years.

"Years after everyone left the church was pulled down and carted away," he tells her. "Some federal program to keep people from starvin' one winter there wasn't enough stamps to go 'round."

He nods towards the rows of headstones, "Kept them people poor buildin' it, only fair the livin' should make a few dollars tearin' it down. Besides, it was a nuisance. Youngsters used to climb over the rafters and bazz rocks through the windows."

"In civilized countries old churches are protected," Lav says and quotes:

> ...for how can man die better
> Than facing fearful odds
> For the ashes of his fathers,
> And the temples of his gods?

"I can think of a dozen better ways!" Alf snaps. He turns his back on her and walks into the neatly fenced graveyard.

It will be a long time before she learns of Alf's twin brother who hung himself inside the rotting walls of the demolished church. Tossed a rope over a hand-carved cross that had hung above the congregation for fifty years, and jumped. The boy's name was Mark—he had been seventeen.

He and Alf were to have returned to St. John's the next day for their second year of university. He should not have died—by rights would not have died, "I'd stake my life on it—all Mark intended to do was scare Mother—sprain his ankle maybe, so's she'd let him stay home and fish—he had no interest in education," Alf will tell Lav years later.

But the cross had not broken. Boys jigging connors off the Cape found Mark on their way home. He was still hanging from the crossbar that had not, after all, been made of wood but of a long iron rod rusted to the same colour as the wooden beam.

Although Lav knows nothing of this, she knows she has deeply offended Alf. Going to stand beside him at a low stone wall surrounding four identical headstones she apologizes: "When I was a child I use to prove how smart I was by quoting poetry—I still can't resist it," she says. "Besides, I'm still angry about last night."

He will not let her off so easily. "Speaking of the ashes of fathers—why didn't you ever come to see him when he was alive?" he asks, his voice as cold and combative as it had been the day before.

Lav stares, not understanding, "My father died long ago."

He points to one of the marble headstones, reads the words out loud:

In memory of David Albert Andrews
Born Cape Random 1924—died 1975,
For of such is the Kingdom of Heaven.

A cloud seems to have passed across the sun, she shivers, "It can't be the David who was my father—he died before that—before I was born!"

"It's your father, alright—he died less than fourteen years ago. There's his people—Aunt Cass and Uncle Ki beside him—and that's his brother Cle's marker right there."

Lav sits down on the stone wall, "My mother said he was killed in the war. At sea—before I was born."

"He was in the war alright—they both were—but Cle was the one killed," he produces a flask, offers it to Lav but she shakes her head.

Alf takes a long drink, "You mean to tell me, all these years you never knew your father was alive?"

She cannot bother to answer. She is trying to remember everything she knows about her father—very little, only what she was told that night in her mother's apartment. Had Charlotte not known? Had she forgotten? Yesterday Lav would not have entertained such a possibility. Today she knows better.

"Maybe he was reported dead," she says.

"He was reported missing in action. But he turned up in a hospital somewhere in England." Alf speaks in a dull, even tone, "Your father was back in St. John's within six months of the day his ship went down—but by then you and your mother were gone." He turns to look at Lav, "I remember your mother."

"She's still alive—well, why wouldn't she be she's only..." Lav glances at the birth date on the headstone, realizes it does not line up with the age her father was supposed to have been, realizes she probably does not know her mother's real age.

"She's only in her sixties," she ends weakly, adds, "She's recently remarried—living in California." Even as she tells him this Lav wonders if it is true—perhaps everything she knows, or thinks she knows about Charlotte is a lie.

"She would."

"And what does that mean?"

"She was that sort of woman—even then—like a cat. The kind to do whatever made her most comfortable. That kind always ends up somewhere like California."

Lav guesses this bitterness has more to do with some other woman—his missing wife perhaps—than with her mother. "What kind of life did he have—my father?" she asks tentatively.

"Not too good, I'd say," Alf pauses, considers, "But then, who knows? Maybe he was happier than any of us. Come on, let's pick up our stuff and get back to the cars before dark."

As they walk towards the hollow he seems to relent, begins to talk about her father, "We all knew he was missing, of course. There'd be a special church service and prayers whenever that happened—by then there was a good few along this coast missing—defending the ashes of their fathers and the temples of their gods over in England," he gives her a sharp sideways glance.

"Then we heard he was in a hospital in St. John's. He was there for months. Aunt Cass put it around he was in the San—something wrong with his lungs, she said. But wasn't the San."

Alf unscrews his flask, takes another drink before telling the rest of the story. "Late that fall Uncle Ki and Aunt Cass went in to St. John's and got him. I was no more than five or six but I was in school. The teacher marched us all down to meet the boat. All of us—a dozen or so youngster holdin' little Union Jacks lined up on the wharf. We started to sing some song—'There'll Always Be An England'—or some such stunned thing. Then we saw what he was like."

Standing at the top of the gangplank David Andrews had looked the same—a tall red-headed sailor in the tight Navy jacket and flared trousers. But then he started down, falling over himself, shaking with fear, being held up. It had taken forever. When he got ashore everyone could see the simple-mindedness in his face. Flags and song forgotten, the children stood in a silent line watching the young man being led away from the wharf, a parent holding onto each hand.

"Aunt Cass's face was like the rock but Uncle Ki had tears rollin' down his cheeks—the one time I ever saw a grown man cry. It was like the end of the world for them—only had the two sons and by then they knew Cle was gone."

Back in the hollow, Alf says they have plenty of time. He lights the fire and boils the kettle again. They sip whiskey-laced tea and he tells Lav about her father's life.

"Took care of him all their lives, Aunt Cass and Uncle Ki did. When they died he went to live with Maud Stokes and them up in Wesleyville—Maud was a Vincent, Aunt Cass's sister. He got along with youngsters—I can remember skimmin' rocks with him down on the landwash. He would never get into a boat, though—went right crazy it you tried to get him on the water. Still, he was good as the next man in the woods, kept half the place in firewood—used to make wonderful thole pins."

Alf searches for something more to tell her about David Andrews. After some thought he says, "Your father was a good man, never harmed a living soul—and not many can say that."

They walk back down the beach and through the grassy dunes without a word.

"Some of us cut the bridge apart last fall—didn't want the ATV's out here tearin' everything up—but the young crowd got it clobbered back together again," he remarked as they crossed over the little bridge linking Cape Random to the mainland.

Lav does not respond. She is thinking about her father. About David Andrews living here all these years—living like a child—simple-minded, Alf had said. What do those words imply? Had he remembered anything? England? The war? A wife? Could he read? Write? Did he remember having written that letter?

She thinks how strange it is that Charlotte and David—yes and her too—all three should have treacherous memories, memories that deceive, that obliterate, that lie.

They are back in the rubbish-strewn parking space, packing things into the trunk of her car before Alf breaks the prolonged silence.

"Maybe he had as good a life as any. Most of the men who came back from overseas left again—ended up workin' out in Vancouver or up in Toronto diggin' ditches, buildin' ships or houses—or in St. John's sellin' cars or neckties. They'd come back summertimes—you still see some of 'em—yarnin' and drinkin', wonderin' why they ever left the place."

Lav is not ready to accept such a complacent view. "But they had lives—real lives—didn't they!" she climbs into her car and slams the door. Then, "I'm sorry," she says, relenting, for he has been kind, kinder that she would have ever imagined.

"None of the women mentioned anything about that yesterday—about my father being—being," she finds it hard to say the word Alf had used. Her voice drops, "simple-minded."

"No, I s'pose not. I daresay they were trying to remember him for you the way he was before he joined up—the way they think of him now." Alf Andrews leans against his truck and stares back towards the Cape. She has the feeling he is about to tell her something, hopes he will not. But all he says is, "Why don't you come back to the house for supper?"

She tells him no. She does not want to talk to anyone, does not want to ask any more questions, does not want to be told any more secrets. For the first, and perhaps the last time in her life, Lavinia Andrews knows enough—more than enough.

seventeen

Lav will return to the Cape of course, will return and leave, return and leave—plagued by indecision that will become more acute in December when her son is born.

During the first years of the child's life, Lav is still occasionally distressed by her, and now his, lack of history, sometimes tormented by dreams of brooding fish, still sporadically engaged in a battle against sagging breasts, greying hair, against inclinations towards sloth.

Such preoccupations are, however, incidental—mere background to the business of earning a living, of building a life for herself and the boy who, after long deliberation, she has named David Saul. She carefully explains that the boy must be called by both names.

After the day of her outburst at the press conference, Lav never again sees Wayne Drover. Lav's firing, tactfully expedited one bright morning in an expensive Ottawa restaurant, ends all contact with her former colleagues. No one calls except Ian Farman, whose guilt about the Newfoundland fiasco results in a number of good contract jobs coming her way.

During one of her sojourns in Davisporte, Ian even manages to put her in touch with a job funded by the federal government. A bizarre project involving the breeding of certain species of flounder and flatfish to produce a protein similar to antifreeze—one that might preserve body organs longer than anything now available. Ian had phoned to tell her that the hatchery in Valleyfield needed someone to monitor the project. She, being over-qualified, got the job and returned happily to Davisporte.

Lav had enjoyed the winter she spent living with Selina and Rachel Jane. The job was interesting and Selina was glad to take care of the baby. Lav learned how to make bread, ride a snowmobile and play a card game called forty-fives.

Although Alf had a bedroom in his mother's house, a dark gloomy room built below the long veranda, the women hardly saw him. On the day Lav returned with the baby he had nodded, barely acknowledging her, as if they were strangers—as if the day on the Cape had never happened. That winter he seemed to spend most of his time at the Cat, returning late at night and leaving before the women were up. When Lav asked Rachel Jane what Alf did all day, the girl said, "Drink and lecture!"

Rachel Jane had recently bought a second-hand car and said she was sick of working at the motel, wanted to get away. "If Fadder don't stop jawin' people about the fishery we're not goin' to have any customers left, anyway," she told Lav and Selina.

Rachel Jane was forever after Alf to get live music and put a decent dance floor in at the Cat: "That way you won't do so much talkin'. We'd get the young crowd and the place'd be a bit lively. There's lots of groups around—that guy Hounsell I graduated with is a drummer now in Gander—got his own band called 'The Spiked Pig,'" Lav heard the girl tell her father one day.

Alf, leaning against the kitchen window drinking coffee—he never sits at the table—had looked past Rachel Jane and caught Lav's eye.

"Ah, take the cash, and let the credit go,

Nor heed the rumble of a distant Drum!" he said, and actually smiled.

After that acknowledgement that he remembered their day on the Cape, he and Lav often quoted poetry at each other, competing to see who could recall the most lines.

Unfortunately, three months after it opened, the hatchery closed down. A drug company in Massachusetts had challenged the right of the Canadian government to subsidize research on a product that would compete with theirs. The job ended, and in April Lav and David Saul went back to Ottawa.

In Ottawa Lav can always find work. Shamelessly calling in old favours she finds a half-day job at the art gallery where she once volunteered, and contract work in university labs. Sometimes living in the house she and Philip still jointly own, sometimes renting it, she receives financial advice from Philip's lawyer, gratefully accepts the many baby gifts her mother sends and establishes a friendship with Philip's estranged wife Zinnie, who has abandoned the environmental movement for a staid government job.

Her own children having caused her endless anxiety, Zinnie considers Lav mad, but very brave, to bring a child into the world.

"You'd do better with a cat," she had told Lav the night David Saul was born.

According to Zinnie the human race has done itself in. "It's not the world that's in danger—just people. The world will get along just fine without us," she says when Lav tells her the story of what had happened to the Oceans 2000 research.

Despite her grim philosophy Zinnie has a cheerful disposition. She has no patience with Lav's brooding. Introspection, according to Zinnie, is both boring and rude. The two women begin hiking in the Gatineau Hills on Sunday afternoons, taking turns carrying David Saul in a back pack. After a day in the hills they return to talk and eat makeshift meals in Zinnie's decaying house where one or other of her children is constantly in residence, recovering from some financial or emotional crisis. Lav likes Zinnie's children.

"Because you don't have to live with them," Zinnie says, but she is delighted to act as David Saul's honorary aunt—on condition she can disown him when he becomes a teenager.

Lav finds Ottawa noisier, faster, sharper than she remembers. Ottawa air smells of chemicals, its water tastes of detergent. Things are depressingly well-finished—too shiny.

Only Zinnie and the house make the place bearable—but early in 1992 Zinnie leaves Ottawa, moves to Northern Ontario to teach in a small community college, and Lav finds herself thinking more and more of the Cape.

Always on the look-out for mention of Newfoundland in Ontario papers, Lav is aware that cod, or the absence of cod, has become headline news. In one three week period, she sees DFO's estimates of the spawning biomass of northern cod suddenly dropped from well over 100,000 tonnes to zero. Damage control, Lav supposes, someone in the Department trying to cover their ass. Experts will be flown in.

She considers calling Ian Farman, asking about the possibility of a contract job in Newfoundland. Instead, she calls Selina Andrews, who has watched Lav's shuttling back and forth between Ontario and Newfoundland with a jaundiced eye.

"You might just as well come home and 'bide," Selina advises. "There's some, like my Vicki, can walk away from the place and never give it another thought—got no feelings about it. Then there's the other kind—the ones like you and Rachel Jane—never content anywhere else."

For a week Lav agonizes. Ottawa, she thinks, is like a room without a window—safe and secure as a vault. She cannot imagine a future there. But there is a tide in the affairs of men—and of women—and surely moving to Newfoundland now would be going against the tide, going the wrong way. And how will she live in a place so remote as Davisporte? What will she do with her time? How will she make a life for herself and her son in such a place?

In the end she tells Nat Hornsby to sell the Ottawa house. She buys a station wagon into which she packs her four year old son, their cat—a parting gift from Zinnie—and their belongings. Then she drives to Newfoundland.

Lav and David Saul arrive in Davisporte the day before Timothy Drew is slated to make another great announcement. It is almost the first thing Selina speaks of: "Here it is July, and Ned still don't know how much cod him and the boys can take—we're livin' in dread of what that man is goin' to say," she tells Lav.

Then, having kissed David Saul, hugging him until he squirms away and goes racing into the garden, she pours tea.

"Newfoundland is no place to raise children—no future here—I shouldn't have tried to get you to come home," Selina grimly sets a tea pot on the table and settles down opposite Lav.

Watching David Saul jump gleefully up and down in the rain-pool that always collects in the mossy part of Selina's yard, the statement seems so foolish that the women look at each other and laugh.

"It wasn't your doing—I wanted to come," Lav says, knowing this is true.

"I'm worried sick about Ned and them, girl. Remember he got that big loan to have his boat covered with fibreglass? I doubt he's even payin' his interest—last year was worse than the year before and this year they're not gettin' anything."

According to Selina, predictions of doom have been slithering down the coast for months: television commentators, talk show hosts and government experts advising drastic reductions in fish quotas, travellers telling apocalyptic tales about fishermen who caught 675,000 pounds of cod two years ago and have managed to catch only four fish this year.

"For all that, people along the coast are buyin' gear, overhaulin' boats—gettin' ready for the summer's fishery same as always. What else can they do?"

"Nothing," Lav answers, though she knows the question is rhetorical. She taps on the window, but David Saul pays no heed. He is crouched down, hands on knees, eyes closed, ready to leap skyward out of the shallow pool. "He's soaked to the skin—I should make him come in."

Selina nods but neither of the women move. They are held in thrall by the boy's pleasure, by his round, impish face, by the rainbow of spray and light that surrounds him each time his knee-rubbers splash into the luminous green water.

"Still, I'm some glad to have ye two here," Selina reaches across the table to pat Lav's hand. "And who knows—the crowd in St. John's keeps tellin' us everythin's all right. Ned says last week the government gave foreign draggers a quota of 100,000 tonnes of cod inside our 200 mile zone—I can't see them doin' that if they were going to shut us down, can you?"

Knowing that she once had some connection with the Department of Fisheries and Oceans, Selina looks to the younger woman for reassurance Lav cannot give. They lapse into silence, enjoying each other's company, the tea and the sight of David Saul's happiness.

Usually patronized by only a handful of regulars, the Cat is packed full the next night. People who never come near the place are there: Frank Parsons, the school principal; Levi Vincent, the church lay-reader; Cornilie Fifield the social worker and two nurses from the clinic—most of Davisporte—all staring at the big screen, waiting for Timothy Drew's announcement.

Ned's wife, Doris, comes in after the program has started. Looking as if she's been crying, she slips into the chair Alf has vacated, whispering: "I shouldn't have left the house—but misery loves company and the older boys'll keep an eye on Stevie."

Someone says "Hush!" as the obligatory scenes flash across the screen: Newfoundland and Canadian flags flutter over government buildings, nets overflowing with cod are hauled into boats that threaten to swamp under the huge weight. Then comes Timothy Drew—smiling, urbane, nodding at television cameras as he strides through Torbay airport.

Lav catches a glimpse of Wayne Drover in the background, then loses him in a moment of confusion, a protest of some kind outside the airport. The cameras hesitate, swing back to the Minister before Lav can identify the shouting people or read their slogans. She smiles, picturing Wayne trying to drag his mother, or perhaps Mark Rodway, out of camera range.

Doris sees the smile. "Must be hard for someone from away to see why we're all so worked up," she says.

Lav shakes her head. She knows Ned's wife is frantic but can think of nothing that will comfort her.

Selina has told Lav that six years before, when their oldest boy finished school, Ned had built a bigger boat and that he's been improving it ever since. Now Cleary and John both fish with their father but Cleary is talking about getting his own boat. Doris is trying to discourage him, says she and Ned already owe over half a million dollars and that's enough debt for one family.

Ned was one of the men who had started out for St. John's at six that morning, vowing to confront the Minister of Fisheries. To Lav the men had seemed innocent, happy as children as they squashed into the mini-van, holding packets of sandwiches and tins of Pepsi.

"Whatever the old bugger says, he's gonna say it to our faces!" Ned shouted. But Bruce Blackwood, the van owner, had promised the wives there would be no violence.

There is complete silence in the Cat. Women and men lean forward, faces lifted towards the giant screen as Timothy Drew, ensconced behind a row of microphones, declares the cod fishery over—commands them, by midnight tomorrow, to remove all fishing nets and gear from the sea—as enraged fishermen try to pound their way into the Plaza Room—as doors are slammed shut and security guards move into place.

A kind of groan goes through the room as Bruce Blackwood, swinging a chair against the bolted door, fills the screen. A woman begins to cry, a man is saying, "Jesus! Jesus!" but softly. Policemen march down the hotel hallway, surround the fishermen, grab their arms, hammerlocking their necks with billy clubs, prying them away from the door behind which the minister, still unruffled, touches the knot of his tie, tells reporters he does not frighten easily.

"We're ruined," Doris says. "Ned's forty-five—been fishin' near thirty year. Up at four every mornin' from April to November—up and headed out to sea every day of his life—what'll he do if he can't go on the water?" She is crying, gripping the edge of the table, trying to control herself. Alf brings her a drink but she shakes her head, pushes herself to her feet and leaves.

No one else moves or speaks. Even when Alf switches off the television they continue to stare at the white screen as if expecting some message—God perhaps, telling them what to do.

"On the house," Alf walks around the room distributing beer.

Levi Vincent puts the bottle back on the tray: "I don't think so, old man—not tonight," he says. Then he gets up and walks across the room to the big map of Newfoundland.

A tall, lanky man Levi hunches forward, squinting at the map. Everyone is watching him.

Then, just as if he were reading out the lesson in church, he begins to recite a litany of lost men and lost ships: "*Flora May*, foundered off Cape Chidley with Samuel Gill, Charlie Fifield, David Gill and Oram Pond. *Watersprite* burnt at the front, all hands lost. The *Challenge* sunk off Labrador with 300 quintals light salted cod, also crew. The *Seahorse* went to the bottom with Eli Vincent, Alfred Kean, Job Parsons, and three Blackwood men on board. The *Netty Tizzard* broke up in gale-force winds off Cape St. Francis, drowned were Ephraim Green, Stanley Andrews, Matt Gullage and Joshua Burry. The *Florizel* lost north of Cappahayden with 94 men, women and children including Bill Walters, Edward Greening, Clarence Moulton, George Crocker...."

Levi keeps on, reaming off every man and vessel he can remember. Hundreds. Boats lying on the bottom for a hundred years, boats he's only heard of from his father and grandfather. He has no special order, calls out the names of people drowned seven years before when the *Blue Pathway* iced up and rolled over, ahead of those lost on the *Caribou*, the crew of the *Ocean Ranger* before sealers lost in the Newfoundland disaster.

There are so many. Some were fathers, uncles, cousins, brothers or sons of people seated around the room. Even to Lav the names sound familiar. She wonders why no one has ever listed the names on a monument, chiselled them into a wall of black marble, or hacked them into a rock in this land of rocks.

Lav wants to leave, longs to get away from the airless room, from the feeling of doom, but feels she must stay, must sit with these silent, unhappy people listening to this endless roll-call of drowned men. "...Jim Fisher, George Tuff, Mike Holloway, Isaac Norris...."

Finally, though, she can stand it no longer. She rushes out into the drizzling rain, stands in the muddy parking lot taking great breaths of air, wondering where she has left her car.

"A person would be mad to go to such a place!" her mother had said and her mother had been right.

At seven the next morning Alf walks into the house, sober as a judge, for he never can get drunk when he most wants to. Lav is sitting with Selina and David Saul eating breakfast. She has been up all night, has packed, unpacked and packed again. Four suitcases stand in line beside the kitchen couch.

Alf leans with his back against the door and stares first at the suitcases, then at the boy and finally at Lav. "So," he says, "'Tis not too late to seek a newer world. Believe that, I suppose—believe that if you run fast enough and far enough you'll touch the Happy Isles? In Ontario perhaps—or California?"

Lav shakes her head. She knows there are no Happy Isles but cannot bring herself to say so. She would like to take his hand, to lead him to his underground lair, to sleep, to make love, to lie in bed and forget about work, about fish, about striving and seeking.

Time is suspended, nothing in the kitchen moves, the silence seems to go on forever.

Lav tries to think of some quotation but all that comes to mind are the lines: "She is a woman, therefore may be wooed. She is Lavinia, therefore must be lov'd." But that Lavinia was not wooed but raped, not loved but mutilated—her hands had been hacked off and her tongue cut out. Lav shudders, pondering on violence and the bard, wondering who had named the first Lavinia Andrews.

Finally, Alf pushes himself away from the door, "The men are followin' Drew's orders, haulin' in their cod traps. I'm on my way down to watch—you three should come—the boy especially. It's history—somethin' he'll be able to tell his grandchildren—the day the great moratorium started, the day Newfoundlanders had to stop being fishermen."

Although he is not yet four, David Saul understands an invitation. He begins to squirm down out of his chair, but Lav pushes him back.

Selina shakes her head. "No, no thanks—I haven't got the heart for it—neither should you. You'd be better off sittin' down for a cup of coffee and a decent breakfast."

Before his mother has finished speaking, Alf is gone, closing the door softly behind him, not even saying goodbye to Lav and David Saul.

Selina dips a piece of toast into her egg and pops it into the child's mouth. Without looking at Lav, she says "He wasn't always like this, you know."

"What was he like, then?" Lav has the feeling that Selina has somehow read her thoughts, has seen her momentary longing to lie down with Alf.

"He was a good boy—carefree but a good student. First when he and Shirley were married I thought they'd make a go of it."

Probing carefully, Lav learns that Alf's wife, unaccountably, for she had no relatives aboard the oil rig, fell into a kind of black despair when the *Ocean Ranger* went down. That, just a few months after the disaster she left Davisporte, taking Rachel Jane with her. There was never any explanation, not even when the child was sent home a year later.

"Shirley was a Coish, one of the crowd from down Happy Adventure way," Selina says. She has taken David Saul on her lap, is jogging him up and down, "This is the way the poor man goes..." she chants. "I wouldn't say no to another cup of tea," she tells Lav.

Pouring Selina's tea Lav considers how much her relationship with the older woman has changed since they first met. On each trip back she has taken over more and more of the housework, while Selina spends more time visiting or playing games with David Saul.

It's time David Saul and I found a place of our own, Lav thinks. Then, catching herself wondering if the old house in the back yard can be made habitable, she knows that she will not be leaving Davisporte.

Had she ever really intended to? What kind of person is she, anyway? A grown woman, a mother, who doesn't even know her own mind—her mother had never dithered, had always known what she wanted, had gotten it. As always, comparisons with Charlotte depress Lav.

"So Alf's wife was Shirley Coish?" she asks—as much to postpone self-analysis as to hasten Selina's return to the story.

"That's right, she and Alf went to Memorial together—all the Coish family went to university. They're a highstrung crowd. Always were. Good people—lots of educated people in that family—but nervy." Lav is by this time familiar with Selina's narrative style and can see examples of nerviness leap to mind.

After a minute's consideration Selina brushes these distractions aside: "Still and all, I can't see her goin' off like that without a word to anyone—not even her own mother! What I thought then and what I still thinks," the woman lowers her voice, walks across the kitchen and stares down the hallway to make sure Rachel Jane's bedroom door is still shut.

"What I thinks is Shirley was in love with Vern Soper," Selina returns to the table, absently smoothing the flower print cloth with her hands, remembering, arranging life so that it becomes story.

"I used to see them betimes, holidays when Vern was home from trade school and later when he was workin' shifts on the rigs. They'd be walkin' up and down the landwash. I never thought anything about it at the time. Vern played guitar and he was teachin' Rachel Jane to play. The girl'd usually be with them—trailin' along—I used to think it was Rachel Jane had the crush on him—used to tease her about it."

It is the kind of story Lav has always delighted in. She spreads peanut butter on David Saul's toast and listens to the endless threads ravelling out in all directions.

Shirley had relatives here in Davisporte. Her brother had accosted Alf, accused him, unjustly, Selina says, of being hard on Shirley. Vern Soper, too, had relatives—and a girlfriend—a girlfriend he had been going to marry. And the girlfriend later had a baby, a little girl Vern's mother had taken to raise. The baby had been born four months after the *Ocean Ranger* was lost. The same week Shirley and Rachel Jane took off for parts unknown.

"Parts unknown," Selina sighs and repeats the phrase, "must be the permanent address of Newfoundlanders."

Shirley has never returned, but Rachel Jane's been coming and going since she was fourteen.

"Was that when he started drinking, when his wife left?" Lav asks. She knows, wonders if Selina knows that someday soon she and Alf will sleep together. It is just a matter of time, something she has been considering since that day on the Cape.

Selina is non-committal about the origins of her son's drinking, "Worse—I think it got worse after Shirley left," she says. In all her stories, all her explanations of family relationships, she has yet to mention Alf's twin brother, the son who killed himself.

"I s'pose I should be grateful—I got the two boys living here in Davisporte—got to see my grandchildren grow up. Rachel Jane's talkin' about takin' off again. I got Reverend Dawe to speak to the poor foolish creature but she never paid him no mind—wants to be a singer. Wants her own television show! But Rachel Jane'll always come back—Nan knew that, that's why she left the girl her brooch. Rachel Jane's like you, never content away."

Selina pauses, glances from the suitcases to Lav, "Why don't you put them things away? I'm going to wash David Saul, then we'll dodge over to see how Doris is."

Two weeks later, seated behind the wheel of her five-hundred dollar car, across the rusting doors of which she has amateurishly lettered the words Cod Peace, Rachel Jane leaves.

"She'll be back before Christmas—mark my words," Selina says as, surrounded by three disreputable foolish friends, by guitars and luggage, some of which is tied to the car roof with bright bungee cords, Rachel Jane drives off, calling back promises to phone as soon as she reaches Toronto.

As they walk towards the house Selina suggests that Lav might help out up at the motel: "With Rachel Jane gone, they're short handed and busier that they've been in years."

This is true. Amazingly, unexpectedly, the Cat is full every night. As the fish vanish, schools of government officials, hired consultants, social scientists and journalists appear along the coast. Everyone in Davisporte is astonished at this influx of bizarre people—people who ask endless, intrusive questions. People who cannot explain exactly what they do for a living, yet seem to earn vast amounts of money.

At first Lav is reluctant to encounter these people. Suppose former colleagues turn up? Suppose Wayne Drover and his glow boys walk in and find Dr. Andrews tending bar?

Eventually curiosity overcomes. She begins working at the Cat two days a week, eavesdropping on the reporters and academics. Listening as they arrange to rent boats, to take pictures of unemployed fishermen gazing out to sea, to interview teen-agers on their job prospects. Hearing one say he is about to give displaced fish plant workers a series of workshops on managing a small business and another ask Doris if the level of violence has increased in her family—Lav is enraged.

But, "The novelty'll soon wear off—they'll be gone before the first snow," Alf tells her. In the meantime he has installed a fax machine and begun, for the first time in years, to serve breakfast at the Cat.

He is right. Sensing this is a story without resolution, the media people leave first. As the days shorten, officials begin to long for offices, academics for campuses. By October the fax is silent. There is not an expert to be found in Davisporte.

In November banks put attachments on the property of seven fishermen. They claim Ned's house, car and boat. Ned, Doris and their three sons decide they will go to British Columbia where Doris has a cousin fishing. They pile what belongings they have been able to smuggle out before the house was padlocked into Lav's station wagon. The cousin says things are tight in B.C., too, but he can find a place on his boat for Cleary, the oldest boy.

Ned is cheerful to the end, still arguing with Alf that he'd done the only thing he could do. "What choice did I have—keep on hand-linin' and starve? Got to say I was pure dreadin' that meetin' with the bank manager—but he turned out to be decent enough—said he understood, said his own people in P.E.I. went bankrupt in the 30s. So that's it—worst part's behind us."

He kisses Selina, assures her they will be alright, "Look, Mother, I been buildin' boats all me life, built me own house, plumbing, wiring, everything—must be something I can make a livin' at." Refusing the roll of bills Alf tries to push into his pocket, Ned climbs into the wagon, "Keep an eye on things—thanks for lettin' us have the wagon—we'll be back with a Cadillac for ya when our ship comes in," he winks at Lav.

"Anything's better than staying here like beggars," Doris says, she and her mother-in-law cling to each other and weep.

Young Stevie announces that he is not going, he wants to stay and live with Nan and David Saul.

For a few minutes they consider it, Selina says she'd be happy to keep the boy, "At least until the school year's over."

But Ned will not hear of such a thing. "We're a family," he says, "and we're all stickin' together!"

Eventually they drive off, with half of Davisporte waving goodbye as the overloaded wagon passes out of sight.

This leave-taking undoes Selina. She sees it quite differently from Rachel Jane's departure. "They're gone," she says, "they'll never be back—not ever."

"Wasn't for you and David Saul I'd be out of my mind!" she tells Lav and a few days later suggests Lav take ownership of the old house in exchange for the station wagon, "You've been eyein' that house ever since the first time you came. Besides, you got just as much right to it as any living creature."

Later Selina will sign a paper, one Lav is sure has no legal validity, saying the old house is now hers. But she and her son never live there. They stay on in Selina's solid, two storey bungalow, a temporary arrangement which over the years becomes permanent.

At first Lav uses the old house as a retreat, a place where she can be alone to reread the journal, to review her life, to try and decide if she will stay or go. But quickly, more quickly than she would have thought possible, other interests, other occupations take over. She stops dreaming of salmon, forgets to brood and lets her hair go completely grey.

Lav, who had not expected to enjoy motherhood, and indeed had been slightly bored with David Saul as a baby, becomes more and more absorbed in the child as he grows and begins to ask questions. When she discovers he will tell her exactly what he thinks, she is captivated. Not having known enough children to realize that this is an attribute of the young, Lav is sure she has given birth to a perfectly honest creature, the answer to all her dreams. The woman, now clearly middle aged, and the talkative little boy spend hours together every day.

David Saul is a bright, inquisitive child but, unlike Lav, all his questions have to do with nature: Why don't worms have legs? What makes flowers different colours? Would a Chinese dog understand a Newfoundland dog?

During her son's first years in school Lav frequently finds herself waiting at the window, watching for the moment he will turn in to the lane. The instant she sees him she knows what kind of day he's had, knows if he is happy, if he carries a load of homework on his thin shoulders, if he has something special to tell her about. She can even tell if his feet are wet, can actually feel the softness of his flannel-lined jeans or the freezing coldness of his snow-crusted mitts.

This sensitivity is so spontaneous that it does not frighten her. She was sure, is still sure, that her son feels it too. As proof of this she remembers the bright day he brought her home handfuls of tiny blue forget-me-nots, pulled by their roots from someone's garden.

"They're for you," the child said, "because you were sad all day." And she had been! Mourning all day because as they watch him leave for school Selina had said: "They grow up, you know, Lav—grow up and grow away from us. He'll never stay—you got to be ready for that."

During these years Lav learns many things from Selina: how to pickle caplin, to knit, to hook mats, to make jam and make a garden. From Alf she learns how to keep a set of books, two sets in fact, how to brew beer, drive nails. He teaches her to trout, in distant, swift-flowing rivers in summer and through pond ice in winter. With her son she learns to skate, to snow-shoe, to watch Hockey Night in Canada without being bored.

When all around her people feel pressured to leave the coast, Lav is perversely, completely, content to stay. She can see, of course, that roads are deteriorating, that repairs are no longer made to the water and telephone systems, that every year more and more houses are boarded up, that more and more young people leave as soon as they finish school. She knows that Davisporte, like a hundred other small places around the coast, is doomed—for although they dare not utter the word "resettlement," government policy is to relocate everyone, if not to Upper Canada, then to those towns they have designated as "economically advantaged communities."

None of this disturbs Lav's happiness.

Despite the sight of Ned's empty house and the continued absence of Rachel Jane, Alf and Selina also seem content. They get regular letters from Doris—she is taking in babies, Ned has found part-time work in a factory and John is going to university. From Rachel Jane come occasional post cards, scrawled lines that say nothing except she is in a certain city: Toronto, New York, Vancouver, San Francisco.

The idea that Charlotte might sometime go to a night-club and hear Rachel Jane, without ever knowing who the singer is, bemuses Lav. She mentions the possibility to Alf who thinks it unlikely that his daughter will make it into a night-club, "Unless she's got rid of the crowd she left here with," he says.

Yet on one occasion Lav and Selina do see the girl on television. There, in a back-up chorus behind some star, is Rachel Jane Andrews—blue and red lights flashing across her white face, thin hips gyrating inside black leather. Selina sniffs and wonders what has become of the brooch.

Alf rarely speaks of his daughter. Sometimes Lav thinks he has forgotten her. Sometimes she thinks he has forgotten he ever had another family, forgets that David Saul is not his son and she is not his wife.

As Selina points out, anyone seeing them together would think Alf was David Saul's father, but the boy's cheerful disposition, his need to please and placate is like Ned's. Lav can certainly see nothing of Wayne Drover in the boy—and he does look like Alf, the same dark skin, the black hair, the same hawk-like nose.

"Them two are black Andrews," Selina tells Lav. "Now you and your father were red Andrews—the families are all mixed up, of course." Selina avoids saying that Lav and Alf are at least third cousins, that they have several ancestors in common, including, if Lavinia's journal is to be believed, a Red Indian.

In the summer Lav often goes out to the Cape, usually alone. She has set herself to uncover all the old headstones that remain. After carefully digging sand from around them she writes the inscriptions into Lavinia's journal. In the new graveyard she cuts the grass and paints the iron fence surrounding her father's grave and the graves of her grandparents.

One year Lav and Selina dig over and replant Doris's old garden behind the still padlocked house. They have a huge crop of potatoes and cabbage and the next year branch out into lettuce, carrot and brussel sprouts. When David Saul is in grade three, Lav joins a group of women who take turns volunteering at the little library and peddling everything from fudge to gift wrap to raise money for the school. Until the clinic closes she fills in as nurse's aide.

Rarely now does the shadow of a future somewhere else cross Lav's mind. When it does she makes a weak effort to brace herself and David Saul for the inevitable: "Some day we may have to leave Davisporte," she tells him. "Someday you'll have to go anyway—when you're ready for university."

And always, the boy stares at her wordlessly, shakes his head, and Lav gives up. She cannot imagine what his future might be, what he might become. David Saul himself is only interested in going into the woods, in trouting and skating with his friends, in cars and trucks. At the age of nine he is already driving Alf's truck back and forth the lane.

A designer, perhaps, or naturalist, or an engineer? Surely not! Nothing seems right or hopeful enough, nothing wonder-filled enough for her son. She remembers her step-father Saul and how he had encouraged her to be a scientist in that long-ago time when it seemed science could save the world. What can save the world now? The problem is too confusing.

But, Lav tells herself, there is time yet, lots of time—as Selina says, all the time in the world—to consider David Saul's future—the boy is not even ten. She remembers Zinnie, decides that next year she will write to her friend for advice.

epilogue

It is tempting to leave Lav in the still comfortable present. To abandon her here, happily, stubbornly, unconcerned for the future. But wisely or unwisely we are committed to that unknown terrain—are, like her, ruled by curiosity.

Lav has many years yet to live, many things to become—a teacher, goat herder, a midwife, sometimes healer, a hoarder of flour, sugar and tinned goods. She will paint—become an artist. She will save small glass jars in which to collect colour: house paint, marine paint, enamel and fluorescent paint. Whenever she sees someone painting Lav will present herself, holding a bottle which will be filled without question. In time she does not even have to ask for the paint, people bring it to her.

"What a grand colour!" a woman will say, admiring her freshly painted door, "I'll drain off the rest for Vinnie," for by then everyone but Alf has forgotten her other name.

Lav will practice her art on any surface, on cardboard, glass, plywood, on the doors of wrecked cars and refrigerators. She creates garish sea creatures, the like of which no one along the shore has ever seen.

In summertime she embarrasses her son by lining these pictures up for strangers. Arranging them against the fence with a For Sale sign. None are ever sold.

Eventually Alf hangs the paintings along the walls of the bar, nailing them up on top of the fishing net, crowding them in around the varnished lobster, the shipwreck map and bowling plaques. Local wits say that in the Cat it takes fewer drinks to reach that state of inebriation where the walls pulsate and the floor begins to swing.

Lav will find much happiness bringing these weird fish into being. Can fall into a trance stroking points of fluorescent light on long looped tentacles. Can stand, head thrown back, painting, singing gospel hymns, learned from Selina:

> The tumult and the shouting dies:
> The captains and the kings depart:
> Still stands Thine ancient sacrifice,
> An humble and a contrite heart.

So Lavinia Andrews, whose heart becomes less and less humble, less and less contrite each year, sings as she swirls iridescent auroras around strange serpentine bodies. When every inch of the Cat's walls are filled she will begin painting smaller pieces, devising fish-like door stops, fire screens, window shutters and headboards for beds.

When she can no longer give her creations away she stacks them, layer upon layer, filling the rooms of the old house where Thomas and Lavinia had once lived, the kitchen where Rachel died. Sometimes, standing in the cool rooms that still smell of sea and brine, Lav can hear them talking about her work, pondering upon the marvellous creatures that have invaded the space they once occupied.

Eventually David Saul will become a teen-ager. He will stop confiding in his mother. The brightness that had seemed to surround him as a child will grow dim.

As she gets older Lav will spend more and more time outdoors: whole summers roaming the Cape, walking up and down the empty beaches where caplin no longer come, off which a few herring are still sometimes hooked. She will hike for miles through the burnt-over woods behind Davisporte. This area, called "in back," had been ceded years ago to woods companies now moved to the forests of Russia or South America. The living trees are gone, all that remains is a litter of dead limbs, rotting stumps pointing skyward. From time to time these catch fire, burning deep into the earth, smouldering underground for months.

Still, things grow. The earth, as Zinnie said, will survive. Each spring pink mallow with fairy cheese centres, pale purple bell-flowers escaped from old gardens, aspen and alder bushes cover the ground. In autumn the silver-white ghost trees tower over a carpet of colour, red-leaved blueberries, wine-coloured marsh berries, red partridge berries with holly-green leaves.

In winter Lav will paint, read—or brood. Sometimes she will huddle in the Cat with Alf, drinking. Sometimes join Selina and her cronies in a game of forty-fives, in discussions of wars and pestilence, rumours of which sweep down the coast like winter gales.

Like gales, these rumours are always different, always the same. The most persistent is that a multinational company based in New York, in Zurich or Hong Kong has finally agreed upon some monstrous plan: the entire island becoming a launching site for missiles, a place to dump garbage, a place to play war games, a target on which to practice low-level bombing—or just an empty rock establishing America's right to the surrounding ocean.

But Lav will have no time for such talk. By then she will have become a mechanic, an improviser, a scavenger who brings home bits of wood, bricks, wire, sheets of plastic, broken machinery, worn tires and a host of other things abandoned in marshes and old dumps.

Shortages are commonplace, she has learned to mix mashed potatoes with the flour in her bread dough, to pick up faltering television signals by stringing wires around the roof, to grow onion, celery and pale lettuce in the kitchen window, to make a tonic from kelp, wine from dandelion flowers, shoes from seal skin. She can enjoy jam without sugar, clothes without style and months without visitors.

Lav will find that she is not unhappy with any of this, not with the disintegrating highway, the absence of newspapers, the empty Cape to which no ships come. It occurs to her that one should not escape so easily, that her contentment is utterly selfish, that she will pay.

And she will.

The dark age will come, one day her son will leave, one day her lover will die. Wildly, despairingly miserable she will retreat into a small, silent world. During this sad, wasted time she will do nothing but sit on the front steps and stare at the street. She will frighten children—now very few for only the old, the hunted and the maimed live along this coast. The children run from Lav's mad face and fierce eyes.

During these months she will go only once into the lane, to snatch up a rod and chase some official as he steps down from a government helicopter.

Selina will live on and she will force Lav to live. They become old women together. "Don't you dare die on me, Vinnie Andrews!" Selina screams and makes Lav eat.

Then one day, from God knows where, Rachel Jane appears. A skeleton walking up the lane holding a little girl by the hand. Rachel Jane takes immediately to bed. But the child, called Soshiska by her mother but quickly rechristened Sissy by Selina, sits herself down on the step beside Lav and begins to ask questions.

After the little girl's arrival Lav will slowly become sane—or almost sane—she will still hear voices and sometimes forget to eat, will still hold long conversations with Alf, with her mother, with Rachel and Mary Bundle. She begins getting up early again. Taking her cup of tea and one of David Saul's old picture books out front on fine mornings, she will sit and read to the child—to anyone who happens by.

Many years later, standing beside her father's grave, Lav will gaze across the Cape and see caplin roll up on the sand—the first person in decades to witness such a sight. She will call out to Sissy, who is clipping grass on Selina's grave. The two women, the old one hobbling, the young one running, will hurry down the beach towards the line of silver.

Things come back, Lav thinks, things do come back! Caplin first, then cod, then people. Watching Sissy gather up the little fish she will remember what Zinnie had once said about the world being a better place without people—Lav has never felt that way.

One morning shortly after this, the old woman will do something she has been thinking about for a long, long time. She will go into the old house and find Lavinia's journal. Walking all alone she will slowly cross the marsh, carry the book out to the Cape. Sitting in the weak spring sunshine, with her back against the black rock she will open the ledger and begin to write.

She will write, "It is spring and in the great pit at the centre of the sacred hill a fire burns as it has for a thousand springs..."

Lavinia Andrews,
Cape Random, June 2024.

acknowledgements

First I want to thank the readers of *Random Passage*, especially the real Lavinia, whose wish to know more about the Cape people encouraged me to write this book.

Of course I want to thank George, without whose knowledge of computers I would never have finished.

I would like to acknowledge the help of Fran Innes, Gerry Rubia, Jennifer Morgan and other members of The Newfoundland Writers' Guild who read sections of earlier drafts.

I am especially thankful for the critiques of Joan Clark, Helen Porter and Greg Morgan. These greatly improve what I thought was my final manuscript.

I am grateful to people who took time to give me tours of Department of Fisheries and Oceans buildings in St. John's and Ottawa.

The following is a very incomplete list of books by writers, living and dead, to whom I am deeply indebted:

The History of Newfoundland by Prouse;

Dictionary of Newfoundland English by Story, Kirwin and Widdowson;

Politics In Newfoundland by S.J.R. Noel;

The Islands of Bonavista Bay by John Feltham;

Sketches of Labrador Life by Lydia Campbell;

The Decay of Trade by David Alexander;

Newfoundland in the Nineteenth and Twentieth Centuries by Hiller and Neary;

More Than 50% by Hilda Murray;

The Beothucks and Red Indians by James P. Howley;

"Complaints is many and various" by R.G. Moyles;

On Sloping Ground by Aubrey M. Tizzard;

Women of Labrador by Elizabeth Goudie;

The Peopling of Newfoundland edited by John J. Mannion;

A Class Act by Bill Gillespie;

The Story of Methodism In Bonavista by Charles Lench;

No Fish and Our Lives by Cabot Martin;

Industrial Development and the Atlantic Fishery by Donald J. Patton

The Fishery of Newfoundland by Sally Lou LeMessurier

I want to especially thank Paul O'Neill who kindly gave me permission to use the maid's whipping as described in his book *The Oldest City* and Isobel Brown for her stories about women who crossed the Atlantic as war brides.

I must acknowledge quoting from creative efforts of unnamed writers employed by federal and provincial governments to produce press releases, brochures, booklets, Northern Cod Science Program Reports and such publications as *Fish Is Our Future* circulated in 1978 by Premier Frank Moores and *Oceans Policy For Canada* issued in 1987 by Minister of Fisheries Tom Siddon.

PRINTED IN CANADA